I0452558

ELENA RANSOM

AND THE CATALAN ATLAS

by

J.S. WOOD

Illustrations by BRoseDesignz

Small Frye
Publishing

Atlanta, GA

First edition copyright © 2017 J.S. Wood

Second edition copyright © 2018 J.S. Wood

Third edition copyright © 2022 J.S. Wood

Text copyright © 2017 J.S. Wood

Illustrations by BRoseDesignz © 2018 Small Frye Publishing

All rights reserved. Published by Small Frye Publishing

4920 Atlanta Hwy · PMB 436 · Alpharetta, GA 30004

ELENA RANSOM, characters, names, and related indicia are copyrights of Small Frye Publishing.

No part of this publication may be reproduced in whole or in part, or stored in a retrieval system, or transmitted in any form or by any means electronic, mechanical, photocopying, recording or otherwise, without the prior written permission of the publisher. For information regarding permission, write to: Small Frye Publishing, Attention: Permissions Department, 4920 Atlanta Hwy · PMB 436 · Alpharetta, GA 30004

ISBN: 978-0-9978908-4-6

Printed in the U.S.A.

To Jaden, Abigail & Annie

Prologue

1
_____

2
_____

3
_____

4
_____

5
_____

6
_____

¤ Prologue ¤

"Fabius is in the eagle's nest. I'm collecting him now!"

Kenneth shouted into the Broadcaster on his wrist. He broke into a hard run down the Center Hall and into the West Sitting Hall. He removed a translucent, square disk from a pocket on his tactical vest and drew an assault pistol from its holster. As he neared the end of the hallway he knocked enthusiastically on a door and opened it without waiting for a reply. "Kenneth, it's five in the morning," said a man, who was coming out of the washroom wearing expensive slacks and an unbuttoned dress shirt. "The First Lady is still in bed."

"Good morning, Kenneth," said the First Lady, who was propped up against several pillows and drinking from a dainty, flower patterned teacup. "This better be good."

"Mr. President," Kenneth said urgently. "We've had an intrusion."

The President squared his shoulders and looked solemnly at his wife.

"Regina, you know what to do," the President told her.

The First Lady hurried to get up as the President of the United States of America followed Kenneth through another door off the bedroom and into a brightly lit, oval shaped office. He quickly buttoned his shirt and whipped his tie through his fingers. Kenneth had already inserted the translucent disk into a scanner niche. An Optivision screen came to life, hovering in midair above a desk. The screen began blinking furiously, transferring data onto the disk.

As the office door closed, the President could not contain himself. "Tell me what's happening."

"We've received word that Imperator commanded the Droidiers to invade every major U.S. city."

"How could he do that?" the President asked, looking perplexed. "The Droidiers are a peace-keeping army commanded by majority rule in the Oligarki."

"Unbeknownst to us, the army was corrupted during its creation. The soldiers were fitted with a substitution protocol that, if activated, would automatically reset their internal mainframe. Now, they will follow his rule alone. There is nothing we can do." Kenneth paused because the President seemed unable to accept what he'd heard. Then, carefully he added, "The army has begun murdering civilians up and down the east and west coast. They are threatening to attack Washington D.C. as we speak."

"How could they get their gunships inside the electro-magnetic perimeter surrounding the city?"

"Their gunships cannot get through, but they've landed a mile outside the city and are marching on the capitol."

Beads of sweat formed on the President's forehead, but he remained reserved as he straightened his tie and said, "Is that all?"

The desperation of the situation was felt between both men, but this modest statement provided the right amount of tension relief for Kenneth to look up from his work and smile.

"Kenneth, we've been close friends since childhood. I welcome your advice."

"Sir, it is not a matter of advice at this point," replied Kenneth. "We are sequestered to the bunker until further notice. I've already arranged meetings with the other heads of the Oligarki. They will join us there."

The sound of weapons firing came from somewhere outside across the lawn. Kenneth leaned toward the window and noticed a dozen robotic soldiers scaling the fence. From above, he could see rapid fire screaming down across the lawn striking the Droidiers as they advanced. Then, he watched the robots seize, malfunction, and fall to the ground.

"I guess it's a good thing we've always demanded that men stand guard on the roof," Kenneth said. "Our men are shooting the Droidiers, but they can't hold those metallic beasts off forever."

Then, a sudden explosion shook the room, causing the windows and furniture to rattle. The door to the Oval Office burst open and armed guards rushed inside.

"Protect Fabius!" was yelled aloud by several officers at the same time. Kenneth forced the President into a hard run, guiding him by the elbow.

As they tore down the hallway the President shouted, "What about Regina and our son?"

"Anne is bringing them to the bunker," Kenneth reassured him. "We'll be safe."

Armed with this detail, the President turned left down the hall and lunged into an elevator. Despite the rapid descent of the elevator, Kenneth was impatient to get the President to safety. The doors finally opened into a tubular, concrete hallway with metal pipes running along the walls. Teams of people were there to greet them, including the President's family, Kenneth's wife, Anne, and their daughter. The President put his arm around the First Lady and his son and hugged them tightly.

Anne greeted Kenneth with a kiss and said lightly, "All this fuss, I didn't even get a chance to get breakfast."

Kenneth always appreciated how she could stay calm during times of stress, if for no other reason than to keep the children calm. He stared into his daughter's brown, droopy eyes and forced a smile onto his face.

"Breakfast has already been sent down to the family room," he said.

Kenneth turned and hurried the party to a titanium blast door that opened after a quick scan of his retinas. Then, he led them through a chain link gate into a hall with corrugated steel tube walls, while blast doors closed behind them. Together, they moved into a comfortably furnished room with trays of food placed neatly on the table. Kenneth took his two-year-old daughter from Anne's arms. He nuzzled her neck and then placed her in a chair.

"Stay here," Kenneth told Anne and he kissed her forehead. "Try to keep the First Lady and the children calm. Everything will be alright."

A moment later, Kenneth stepped into the Situation Room behind the President. He immediately recognized the Oligarki leaders from Canada, South America, Mexico, Africa, Asia, China, Russia, Australia, and the Middle East sitting around a conference room table. He paused momentarily on the only empty seat, but his brow furrowed at the seat for the diplomat from Europe. A rather young-looking man sat there with his shoulders hunched forward and a look of fear clouded his eyes.

"Who are you?" the President asked the young man.

"My name is P-P-Percival, sir," the man stuttered.

"How is it that you have the Broadcaster that belongs to Prime Minister Darcy?"

"Well, Sir, I was cleaning the loo in the Minister's office when I heard a commotion. Being rather a snoop, I peeked through the door into the office and saw..." Percival's voice failed him.

"Yes, what did you see?" the President demanded impatiently.

"Well, I saw his H-h-humanoid aide sh-shoot him in the head with a Decimator Magnum, I did."

Percival's proclamation was followed by stunned silence and looks of distress were passed around the table.

"After the Humanoid left the room, I went over to the Minister and, realizing he was dead, took his Broadcaster to contact the proper authorities, but I arrived here instead." A curious looked wrinkled Percival's face.

"You arrived here because Darcy was scheduled to meet with us," Kenneth explained.

A sudden chatter of words filled the room in confusing chaos as the other Oligarki representatives began speaking.

"Hold it! Hold it!" the President hollered, and the room was instantly silenced. "One at a time. Representative Liang, how are things in China?"

"The Droidiers have begun executing civilians. I am in hiding, but it's only a matter of time."

"Representative Aleron, what are the reports coming from South America?" the President asked.

"Sir, we received confirmation that the Kearney Virus has been deployed on the southern border," replied a man with dark circles under his eyes. "Once the virus is active, only one in one hundred thousand will be immune."

"The virus has been deployed in Russia as well," said another person at the table.

Kenneth noticed the looks of despair and the uneasy glances.

"Mr. President," said Percival in a squeaky voice. "What should we do?"

The President stood from his chair and proclaimed, "We will call every able man, woman, and teenager into action."

"But how, Sir?" asked Representative Mason from Canada. "We don't have any weapons."

Kenneth knew that to be true. Years ago, Imperator had convinced the Oligarki members and the entire world that Droidiers were the best answer to maintaining law and order so that young men and women wouldn't have to die should conflict arise between the provinces. The system had worked well for twenty years, but that didn't matter any longer.

The President hung his head. "We gave away our right to take action and defend our people a long time ago."

Kenneth had never heard him sound so defeated.

"Are you saying there is literally nothing we can do?" Representative Mason shrieked.

The President shook his head and cleared his throat loudly. "Each member of the Oligarki must now do what's best for his or her own territory. Good luck to you and Godspeed."

The room flickered with lights as the holographic representations of each Oligarki member disappeared. When the other seats in the room were vacant, Kenneth stared in silence at the empty seat where Imperator once sat for their meetings.

The President sat down heavily and put his face in his hands. "We were so desperate for peace and in our desperation we became foolish. We gave away too much power. Now, we will perish."

"Not necessarily," Kenneth said slowly.

"What do you mean?"

Kenneth was somber. "Imperator means to destroy the entire human race except for a select few so that he can create one master race of people."

The President said slowly, "What do you mean a *master race of people?*"

Kenneth sighed heavily. "I couldn't tell you before. No one from the Oligarki was to be informed, but it seems I don't have a choice now. Shortly after Imperator was elected to be the representative for the World's People, he encountered an Oracle who gave him an unsolicited premonition. She said that one day a person would come to rule over the entire earth and that people would recognize this one person as their ruler.

"Of course, Imperator demanded to know the identity of this person, but when the Oracle refused to tell him, he murdered her and set out to find someone that could refute her premonition.

"Imperator elicited help from twelve Prophets, Oracles, and Seers, but none of them could give him the name of the coming sovereign. He decided that the only way to change the future was to design a world where he could manage humans. However, with ten billion people on the planet, he knew that he would never be able to control such a number.

"He had the Kearney Virus developed to exterminate off most of us and that's what is happening out there right now, Mr. President. The virus has been deployed. Soon, the majority of the world's population will perish."

"But, what about our army?" the President asked.

"The Droidiers were commissioned to create mayhem and to kill every person that isn't on the *master list.*"

"*Master list,*" the President repeated.

"Imperator selected a number of people based on ethnicity, power, wealth, and intelligence. They are to be branded with what he calls *Trademarks* and sent to live in domed cities so that he can monitor everyday life. Then, if it happens that a person could arise in power against him, Imperator will know immediately and be able kill him or her," Kenneth explained.

"How do you know this information?"

"I have a close friend who works for Imperator and can verify that what I say is true." Kenneth noticed the look of confusion on the President's face, but he pressed on. "My friend created an organization called the *Renegades* to help fight against Imperator's growing power."

"The Renegades!" the President blurted. "But they're the enemy."

"No, Sir, they have been protecting us. If you'll allow it, I can have them here in a moment to explain."

The President had barely nodded when the entire table was filled once more with men and women.

Kenneth wasted no time. "Welcome, Renegades, to the meeting of the minds. Roster, you first."

A man, slightly balding, stood from his chair and said, "Droidiers are moving up and down the western seaboard from Canada to Mexico. New York City is preparing for an invasion. Best we can guess, Imperator will land there within two hours."

"Why is he targeting Charles first?" Kenneth asked.

"Because Charles has the Cryptext," said Roster.

"What on earth is going on?" the President blurted.

"Oh, excuse me," Kenneth said sincerely. "My dear Renegades, let me introduce you to the President of the United States. Mr. President," Kenneth turned toward his friend, "These are the men and women fighting against Imperator. They will take us to safety."

The space between the President's eyes was wrinkled in anger and confusion but he calmly asked, "What is a *Cryptext*?"

Kenneth laid a hand on the President's shoulder. "Remember when I told you about the Oracle's precognition? The original words were hidden inside a device called the Cryptext and it's with one of our representatives in New York."

"If Imperator is going there first, it means the Renegades have been betrayed!" Roster said loudly.

"We can't worry about that at this moment," Kenneth said calmly. "We've got to follow our evacuation procedure."

"Where is the Atlas? Is it safe?" asked Roster.

Kenneth looked at the President. "We have an artifact called the *Catalan Atlas* that holds some keys to removing Imperator from power. We've been working on it for many years." Then, Kenneth turned back to the Renegades. "The Atlas is safely hidden where they could never imagine looking for it.

"Now, onto more pressing details. We are obligated to follow the evacuation procedure that was set up to protect our way of life. Area 47 is secure and ready to receive the Renegades and the President. We'll board the evac shuttle momentarily. Then, we will reconvene after we're in safety."

The room flickered with lights again until all the seats around the table were empty. Kenneth looked at the President sympathetically.

"I know this is a lot to process in such a short amount of time, but it's imperative that we strive to protect our way of life. Being Trademarked and forced to go to a domed city is a lifetime sentence of slavery."

The President reacted to this statement so quickly that Kenneth didn't have even a moment to respond before he was lying on the floor with the President's legs pinning his arms down by his sides.

"You've been working with the Renegades all this time!" the President said fiercely. "I was going to bring you on the inside after all this messy business was over. I was going to give you a seat at the high table. You would have reported directly to Imperator."

Kenneth's eyes widened in disbelief. He never dreamed his friend had been working for Imperator. As surprised as he felt, it only strengthened the nature of his resolve.

"You're a traitor to humanity!"

"No!" the President said. "Imperator is the future. All who follow him will be saved."

"Don't do this," Kenneth pleaded. "You don't have to sell your soul for a seat at his table. Help me and we can save the future of mankind from his tyranny."

"I was going to save you and keep your family safe. But now, you will have to die."

As the President tried to take Kenneth's assault pistol from his tactical vest, Kenneth arched his back and rolled his hips, sending the President tumbling across Kenneth's right shoulder. Then, Kenneth wrapped his left arm around the President's head, pressing his forearm against the President's throat. The President buried his elbow into Kenneth's side, and he let out a gasp of air.

Kenneth was a skilled fighter, but unfortunately, the President was, too. They had trained together during school and were familiar with each other's strengths and weaknesses. Punches were thrown, legs were kicked, and fingers were broken as the two men struggled for their lives. The assault pistol was tossed, kicked, and thrown around the room.

Finally, the President maneuvered into the perfect position. Kenneth grabbed the pistol and slammed it against his friend's temple. The President fell heavily to the floor, unmoving. Kenneth hurried to make sure his friend still had a strong pulse. Then, he pulled some wire from his tactical vest and bound the President by hand and foot.

"Truman!" Kenneth hollered into his Broadcaster. In a moment, a man with a pencil thin, black beard appeared holographically on Kenneth's wrist. "Where are you?"

"On my way to New York," replied the man named Truman. "What's happened?"

"The President is a traitor!" Kenneth said wildly. "What should I do?"

Without hesitation, Truman replied, "Take the President and his family and follow your evacuation procedure as scheduled."

Before Kenneth could respond, a sudden explosion sent him spinning across the room. His eyes were filled with smoke and his lungs with dust. Then, he felt something heavy smack his chest and he was suddenly gasping for breath. Kenneth could hear his name being called but it took him a moment to understand that it was coming from the Broadcaster on his wrist.

"Kenneth! What's happened?" Truman shouted.

Kenneth groaned and rolled over. He looked at Truman's holographic face on the Broadcaster and coughed out, "There was an explosion."

"What about the President?"

Kenneth tried to see through the cloud of ash and wreckage in the room. His eyes finally landed on the President's face. His body was crushed to the floor by part of the ceiling. He closed his eyes, feeling grieved.

"The President is dead."

But as the words came out of his mouth, his eyes flew open.

"My family!"

Kenneth struggled to his feet and groped his way through the damaged room, over chairs and under fallen ceiling, and through the mangled hallway until he reached the breakfast room. The room was filled with debris, but he couldn't see any bodies. Then, along the wall he noticed the First Lady, the President's son, Anne, and his daughter twisted together on the floor.

"Truman!" Kenneth called out erratically. "Dead! They're all dead!" He reached for his daughter and scooped her lifeless body into his arms. He sat on the floor, rocking her and weeping. "My daughter...she's dead!"

Then, Kenneth heard an unmistakable cough.

"Hello?" Kenneth called. "Is someone alive?"

"Kenneth..." The sweet voice of his wife carried across the wreckage. Kenneth set his daughter down gently and pulled the First Lady's body away from his wife.

"Anne, are you hurt?"

"I don't think so," Anne replied. "Where is she?"

Kenneth looked into Anne's eyes, his own eyes spilling over with tears. Anne closed her eyes and sighed deeply.

"Kenneth!" Truman called from the Broadcaster.

"Truman, it's Anne," Kenneth said, sounding somewhat relieved. "She's alive!"

"Initiating Secondary Protocol," said Truman's holograph.

Kenneth felt a sudden rumbling coming from somewhere near him. Then, a wall inexplicably opened and the hololights from a hovercraft lit up the entire bunker. Kenneth shielded his eyes from the light, but saw a Humanoid exit the hovercraft and, without a word, it lifted Anne and put her safely inside the hovercraft.

"Kenneth," Truman said. "Tiny is going to take your family to safety."

Kenneth was still numb from shock, his eyes blurry with tears, but he lifted his daughter's body into his arms and proceeded toward the hovercraft. He laid her on one of the seats and sat beside her, examining her lifeless face.

"Kenneth, Kenneth," Truman spoke sharply. "I need you to focus now."

Kenneth slowly turned his head toward the holographic Truman. "What should I do?"

"I'm sending you to the Galilee Province. Your new last name is *Foreman*."

Twelve Years Later

◻ | ◻

1600 Pennsylvania Avenue

Elena Ransom bolted straight up in bed.

She'd been sleeping so deeply that her sudden consciousness caused a dull ache behind her eyes. She leaned back on her elbows. The room was mostly dark, but the light from the timepiece on the wall let her know that she'd been asleep over an hour, though to her it felt like several days. After some effort, Elena was finally able to make herself sit forward and swing her legs over the side of the bunk bed she was lying on.

Tenderly, her toes touched the floor, and she felt a tingling through her feet. She slowly made her way across the titanium cabin to the wash station where a hololight flickered awake automatically. Her ragged, mirrored reflection stared back at her. Elena's fiery red curls were a tangled mess and the brown freckles under her eyes were barely visible because of the dark patches that encircled them.

Her almond-shaped green eyes filled with tears as the past several months surfaced to the forefront of her thoughts. Her parents had recently died. In fact, a ruler named Imperator had murdered them. This act alone had been enough to elicit vengeful thoughts from Elena, but since their death she'd also discovered that her parents were part of an underground organization called the Renegades. They'd been fighting against Imperator to help free the thousands of people that he kept enslaved inside the three domed cities.

Being a slave herself, Elena now felt it was her duty to remove Imperator from power. Fortunately, she wasn't on her own. Her best friend, Austin Haddock, had worked relentlessly with her during the end of their first year at Grimsby School of the Republic to find out everything they could about their parents' secret organization.

Elena stood in the mirror reflecting on the tremendous conspiracy that Hopper, her Resident Advisor, disclosed only days after her parents' death.

"Imperator infected people with the Kearney Virus so that people would suffer and die. Then, with the world's population reduced to half a million people, Imperator declared himself supreme ruler over the earth. He had everyone Trademarked and sent to live in one of three cities that were built to hold humans."

Elena pulled her right sleeve back and scrutinized the Trademark implant that confirmed her identity. She obsessively scratched the barcode number 03111980 hoping that it might somehow come off. She didn't enjoy thinking about how Imperator used it to track her every move at home in Atlanson.

Elena grabbed at the chain around her neck and looked at her Kairos, the necklace her dad had given her for her thirteenth birthday. It was an elaborate crystal shaped like the North Star, not that Elena had ever seen the North Star, except in a book. The stone was multidimensional with several nooks and corners.

She wished her parents were with her now, especially since Elena and her friends were illegally headed toward Washington D.C. to look for an artifact called the *Catalan Atlas*. She had no idea what it was nor why they needed it, but Austin was determined to find it and she didn't want to let him down.

After Elena spent a fair amount of time feeling despair over the hopelessness of her situation, she splashed her face with water. Then, she changed into a fresh shirt and combed her fingers through her hair, knotting it into a bun.

She followed the hallway outside her cabin. As she walked, lights turned on and off below her feet and above her head. Eventually, she arrived in the galley where she found Gribbin Pigg cooking breakfast and Austin sitting at a nearby table with Declan Bowen and his cousin, Abria.

"We saved you some breakfast," said Declan, his blue eyes radiating warmth and kindness. He pulled out a chair at the table for her to sit beside Austin and squeezed her shoulder as she sat down.

"Did you sleep?" Austin asked with a wrinkle of concern on his brow.

"Not well," Elena said gloomily.

Pigg hurried over with a plate. He normally had a nervous look in his brown eyes, which was only subdued while he was in the presence of food. He set something that looked like a pancake down in front of Elena and she noticed that the words "Happy Birthday" had been spelled out with sliced almonds.

"Thank you, Pigg."

Pigg had also transformed some powdered eggs and melba toast into an extraordinary cuisine. Elena took a large bite. This was better than the wilderness cooking that she'd learned during the few basic food prep lessons during Survival Training at Grimsby.

"Pigg, where did you learn to cook so, like, well?" asked Abria Bowen. She looked ravishing, with her shiny blonde hair pulled back and fresh gloss on her lips.

"I started to teach myself when I was about five-years-old after Mom found me in the cupboard where I'd eaten all the cereal and pastries. I was always so hungry, and she isn't much of a cook so I experimented a lot."

Abria made an attempt to smile at Pigg's story but was quickly distracted by Elena's frizzy red curls that were sticking out over her head.

"Elena, would you let me do your hair today? I could braid it back really nice."

In a world where everyone had brown or blue eyes and perfectly manicured black or blonde hair, Elena knew that she stood out as an oddity. But with everything that had happened in the past few days, having a makeover was the lowest priority in her life.

"Where's Fergie?" Elena asked, ignoring Abria's question completely.

"She's been in the research lab hoping to learn more about the Cryptext and the Amulet," said Austin.

"Do you really think that Amulet is going to help remove Imperator from power?" Declan asked. "I mean, it's such an insignificant little thing."

"Well, we almost died in New York trying to get it so I hope it's worth something," Elena said bitterly.

"We can't know for sure until Fergie is finished with her assessment," Austin admitted. "But I am hopeful."

"I'll go see Fergie now," Elena said. "How long until we're in D.C.?"

"Don't you think you ought to eat more and then rest?" Declan asked abruptly. "It doesn't look like you slept at all."

"I'm alright. Really!" Elena said shortly after receiving some skeptical looks from her friends.

"I'll walk down with you," said Austin. "I want to see how far she's gotten."

Elena got the feeling that Austin only offered to come so he could keep an eye on her, but she didn't stop him as he followed her out of the galley. As they walked through the halls, doors opened automatically and lights flickered on and off as they left rooms. To Elena, the Independence felt more like a moving city than a hovercraft with its dozens of cabins, command bridge, research lab, and cargo bay. The hovercraft was also beginning to feel like home to her.

"Are you sure you don't want to rest more? You still have some time before we get there," Austin said.

"Austin, I can't sleep anymore," Elena said. "Not when we're about to do what we've got to do."

Austin put his arm around her as they reached a wall of glass. Elena peered through the window into the research lab where Fergie Foreman was bent rigidly over a table. Her short, raven black hair was pulled away from her face, but she was leaning so close to the Amulet that it was almost touching her nose.

The Cryptext that had been entrusted to Declan Bowen's dad, the Ransom Dossier written by Elena's dad, and the Alpha Manuscript from Austin's father were placed carefully around the Amulet as well.

As Elena and Austin entered the room, Fergie sat up straight, resuming her typical, seamless posture and inspected Elena with cheerless eyes.

"It appears that sleep did not agree with you."

"Is that a nice way of saying that I look terrible?" Elena asked. Fergie gave her a wry smile as she dropped into a chair at the table. "Are you making any progress with all this stuff?"

"Unfortunately, no," Fergie said in a formal tone.

She held up the shiny, multi-layered object with a golden ring at the base and a triangular medallion set on top so that Elena and Austin could see it better.

"I dare not open the Amulet until we return to school where we have superior equipment for testing liquid."

She pointed the Amulet to the light so Elena could see the green fluid that was kept safe inside. Then, Fergie looked at the other items on the table, shaking her head slowly.

"The Cryptext is a curious puzzle made even more curious by the fact that Declan's dad left it in the wall so that someone could retrieve it at a later date."

Elena picked up the black cylinder with numbered keys encircling the entire outside.

"Let me ask you again about when you found the Amulet in a secret library under the Statue of Liberty," Fergie said, and Elena nodded. "The Kairos rose in the air and opened. Then, the Cryptext operated on its own accord?"

"That's right," Austin confirmed. "The Cryptext sort of rose in the air. Then, the letters and symbols around it started spinning and twisting. Suddenly, the Amulet appeared out of nowhere."

"It is not likely that the Amulet appeared out of *nowhere*," Fergie corrected him. "However, it is likely that the Amulet was kept was hidden from the human eye until it encountered the Cryptext or Kairos, at which point it was revealed. The Alpha Manuscript doesn't mention the Cryptext or the Amulet directly. However, as I have stated previously, some of the pages are blank."

"What about the Ransom Dossier?" Elena asked. "Have you checked that for clues about these items?"

Fergie shook her head. "I confess I was hoping you might be able to enlighten me on it since you have already spent time reading through it."

Elena gazed at the Ransom Dossier feeling hopeless. She ran her fingers along the cover.

"Most of it is a jumble of symbols and numbers that I don't understand. Dad had some oratory files, but I don't know how to access them." She felt a sudden longing to hear his voice.

"It is unfortunate that we are unable to open the Kairos voluntarily. Though, in time we may add that to our discovery," said Fergie.

"We're nearing the city," said a voice that filled up the room and outer hallway. "All hands to the con."

Elena had almost forgotten that Kidd Wheeler, the one person that she loathed most in the world beside Imperator and her Drill Instructor at school, was on board the Independence. Several days had passed since he'd helped the Firebirds leave Grimsby School of the Republic. He'd flown the Independence to New York City and had helped them. Yet, in her opinion, Kidd was a miscreant and she detested taking any orders from him.

Elena had foolishly expected that their time together would change his attitude and bring them closer as a team, but in fact, it seemed that Kidd was more distant and, if possible, ruder. Elena seriously considered ignoring the summons, but her curiosity about exploring the ruins of Washington D.C. got the better of her.

"What took you so long?" Kidd Wheeler barked as Elena, Fergie, and Austin came through the door onto the command bridge. He had a scowl set on his face. "Big Ears, Blondie, and Blonder came right away."

Elena looked over at Pigg, Declan, and Abria. She hated it when Kidd used nicknames to degrade them.

"Nicknames are super fun this early in the morning," Elena said hotly.

Austin stepped in between her line of sight and said, "So, Fergie, this is your city. What's the plan?"

"I have already told Wheeler to navigate the Independence down Constitution Avenue and that will lead us to Pennsylvania Avenue. After that, the White House should not be far."

Elena peered out the window. A heavy mist was settled on the city of Washington D.C. so it was impossible to see very far in front of them, but buildings began to rise on the right and left, overgrown with shrubs and weeds.

Then, quite suddenly, the United States Capitol building came into view. Elena thought that the building was architecturally impressive and reminded her of pictures she'd seen of buildings in ancient Greece and Rome with its columned porticos and hundreds of crumbling steps. However, the white-washed walls looked dull, a portion of the rotund roof was caved, dozens of the windows were broken, and ivy was crawling up five levels high.

Elena felt the hovercraft shift slightly as they moved steadily down Pennsylvania Avenue. The capital city was as ruined and vandalized as New York had been except that this city was dangerously overgrown with greenery. It was eerily silent, even more so than New York City because there were no flashing advertisements to distract them.

As the Independence pushed through the thick mist, Elena saw a metal fence appear, part of it lay broken as though it had been pulled down. Beyond that, a white-washed house emerged from the fog with dozens of pillars supporting a neoclassical portico. A large hole had been blown out of the south portico wall.

"Look!" Pigg yelled, causing Elena to jump a mile in her skin. "There are people!"

"Wheeler, stop the Independence," Austin said seriously.

Elena peered out the window. Hundreds of men and women were milling around the lawns and porches.

"How can they be living out here?" she asked.

Elena watched Fergie access a couple Optivision screens from the dashboard. Full scale versions of the people appeared on the command bridge, but something was very different about them. Elena could see from the hologram that they had mechanical insides.

"These are not humans. They are Humanoids," Fergie said formally.

The Humanoids looked identical to humans except that they were wandering around with vacant expressions, with no emotions, and with no particular purpose.

"Should we try to, like, help them?" Abria asked nervously.

"Oh, sure!" Kidd said sarcastically. "Let's take them home with us."

"I just meant..." Abria started, but Kidd interrupted her.

"They don't need help. They don't have brains, or feelings, or requirements. They're just here until their batteries run dry."

"Excuse me!" Fergie said sharply. "It is possible for them to have feelings if they were given intelligent design."

It was the first time in a year of knowing Fergie that Elena had heard her raise her voice above a steady calm.

"But they are not hostile, so I believe it will be safe for us to disembark and approach the building," said Fergie.

"Wheeler, land the hovercraft on the lawn toward the center of the portico," Austin said authoritatively.

A moment later, Elena and her friends pulled on their tactical packs, preparing to exit the Independence. However, she noticed instantly that Kidd made no effort to move.

"Are you coming?" Austin asked Kidd.

"After what happened in New York you'll understand why I'm just gonna sit right here."

"What are you going to do while you, like, wait?" Abria asked.

"My nails, Blondie."

Elena rolled her eyes.

"Fergie will go first with the Touchdot as a guide and Declan as her lookout," Austin said. "Elena and Pigg will follow with Abria and me bringing up the rear. Let's go."

Fergie set the Touchdot in front of her where it hovered in midair. Then, it began to move forward, and she followed it with Declan close at her side. Elena ascended a staircase to a colonnaded loggia and stepped through a shattered window into an oval shaped office. *Disheveled* was the word that came to Elena's mind as she tried to make sense of the room that was littered with glass and broken furniture.

The Touchdot led them to the right and through a door into a hallway that had been blasted apart. Elena could tell from the Optivision screen that they were headed toward the southeast corner of the second floor of the White House.

Finally, Elena followed Fergie and Declan into a solitary room with a rosewood bed, slipper chairs, and ornate rugs that were covered in a thick layer of dust.

"Are we in the Lincoln Bedroom?" Elena asked.

"Do you know it?" Fergie asked.

"My dad has a book about the White House in his library." Elena leaned forward and examined a holograph copy of the Gettysburg Address, which was displayed on the desk.

"Fergie," Austin said. "Where is the Catalan Atlas?"

Fergie left the Touchdot floating in midair and stepped over to the rosewood bed, pulling a small knife from her tactical vest as she went.

"The Catalan Atlas had to be concealed very carefully because Imperator would have certainly scanned the room. The Renegades prepared a casing to make the map appear as though it was merely part of the mattress."

Elena watched Fergie slit the mattress in a thin line. Then, she pushed her hands into the mattress and yanked. A large object, squarely shaped, was pulled from the bed. The object had a series of numbers and symbols encircling it, which looked like constantly revolving bands of ribbon.

"Wow!" Pigg breathed. "Would you look at that technology? Brilliant!"

"How did you know to do this?" Austin asked.

"My parents explained it to me," Fergie said.

Elena thought it strange that Fergie's parents were so honest with her about the Renegades' plans to remove Imperator from power when her parents had tried so hard to keep it a secret.

Instead of saying anything about how she was feeling, she watched Fergie access several Optivision screens that eventually encased her in a multidimensional workstation. Fergie laid the object in the center of the Optivision display and began to touch different sections of the screens.

"No, wait!" Austin shouted, causing everyone to jump. "You put in the wrong sequence."

Fergie eyed him suspiciously. "What do you mean?"

"I can't explain it," Austin said. "But the code looks similar to the kind I saw when Elena and I broke into the Vault and then again when we found the Amulet. The code that you used is not correct. I can see the real code on the ribbon."

Elena stepped forward. "Are you sure?"

"I'm positive," Austin said.

Fergie took a step back from the Optivision display and said, "I trust you."

Austin entered a different code into the Optivision display and then Elena watched in awe as the ribbons of symbols around the Atlas melted away to reveal an oblong piece of weathered leather that was closed with a red clasp.

Fergie grabbed the Catalan Atlas and closed the Optivision screen but left the Touchdot hovering in midair. Then, she set the Atlas on the floor, pushed on the clasp, and Elena watched as the object opened and spread itself across a large portion of the floor. She saw flags and shields bearing different crests, illustrations, text, continents, and seas.

"What does this mean?" Declan asked.

"I am not entirely certain," said Fergie. But then she pointed at certain objects on the Atlas. "These symbols represent cosmography, astronomy, and astrology. This other indicates information given to sailors of old about the changing of the tides. But I do not know what the rest means."

Once Fergie stopped talking, Elena noticed a strange humming sound which, after thinking about it more, sounded like the energy that comes from the metrorail moving along the tracks. Her friends seemed to notice the noise as well and began to look around for the source.

Fergie jumped up rigidly and accessed an Optivision screen with her Touchdot while Elena followed her ears slowly toward the window. She peered out onto the front lawn and saw that the hundreds of Humanoids were suddenly looking alert and walking directly toward the White House.

"Fergie," Elena said nervously. "What's happening?"

Fergie's normally calm demeanor was replaced with frantic hand movements as she labored and surveyed the many blue screens that encased her. Then, Elena saw a full-scale version of one of the Humanoids appear on an Optivision and a separate schematic of what appeared to be their generic, internal framework.

"These Humanoids were not placed here inadvertently. They are engineered to protect the White House from foreign invaders," Fergie said calmly. "In this case, we are the foreign invader."

"What are they programmed to do?" Austin said.

"Exterminate any and all evidence."

"Are *we evidence*?" Pigg screeched.

"We're about to be!" Austin exclaimed, as there came a tapping at the nearest window.

"This started after you opened that map," Elena hollered over the ever-growing humming sound. "They're not programmed to protect the house. They're protecting the Atlas."

"Fair point," Fergie agreed. "However, it appears this is no longer a place we can afford to discuss this matter."

Windows were now shattering through the rooms and hallways and a terrible noise arose like a wave of moaning.

"Get back here now!" Kidd screamed from Elena's Broadcaster. "Or I'm going to leave you here."

Elena and Pigg bumped into each other as they hurried out the Lincoln bedroom after Austin, Declan, Abria, and Fergie. They crashed down the hallway, sending dust and debris flying in every direction. Elena could hear that she was being chased, but she didn't dare look behind her. She skidded through the door to the Oval Office and ran for the window, but she could see that a Humanoid was already climbing through it. Declan, Austin, and Abria wasted no time fighting the Humanoids that were already in the room.

Elena closed her eyes and ran full force into an approaching robot, sending it off balance and affording her enough room to jump through the smashed window. She ran down the steps from the balcony and then noticed dozens of

Humanoids hurtling themselves against the side of the Independence. She took little comfort in knowing the Humanoids didn't have weapons because they were very strong.

"Austin!" Elena yelled. She turned around to see that her other friends were coming down the stairs. They were being pursued on every side by angry-looking Humanoids. "What do we do now?"

Before Austin could answer, Elena heard the roar of the hovercraft engines. The Independence rose clumsily off the ground with Humanoids hanging off in every direction. Elena had a fleeting thought that Kidd was going to fly off and leave them, but then the hovercraft rolled and shook in the air, sending Humanoids flying over the grounds.

Then, the Independence came barreling across the grounds, pushing Humanoids away from Elena and her friends.

The side door popped open, and Elena could hear Kidd scream, "Get on!"

In a jumble of arms, legs, and bodies, Elena and the other Firebirds flung themselves into the Independence and collapsed together in a heap on the floor. Elena felt the hovercraft rise and gather speed quickly.

"Do you realize," Pigg squeaked in a slightly whiny voice, "we've nearly been killed twice this week?"

"Yeah, and it's only, like, the second day," Abria said.

2

A Carefully Constructed Lie

The Independence was speeding away from Washington D.C. and away from danger, but Elena felt her skin crawling with Humanoid fingers. She and her friends were still lying in a pile at the door to the hovercraft and she was happy to stay there. After Austin and Declan had caught their breath, they jumped up and helped the others to their feet.

"What was that about?" asked Kidd as they entered the command bridge.

"We think Humanoids were programmed to attack once the Atlas had been moved, or opened, or something," Austin said. "Anyone want to guess who set that up?"

"It is likely that my dad set that response," Fergie said.

Elena's mouth fell open in disbelief. "If you knew your dad set it up, why didn't you warn us that the Humanoids would attack?"

"I knew my dad designed protective measures. However, he never indicated that the Humanoids were programmed to respond aggressively."

"But it's also possible your dad didn't put them there at all." Austin sat down in one of the command chairs and rubbed a finger over the scar on his chin, which Elena knew meant he was trying to decide something important. "What if he only designed the casing around the map?"

"Who else could have set the Humanoids to attack?" asked Declan.

"We may never know. It's not like we can ask anyone," Austin replied.

"I suppose I could ask my dad about the Humanoids," said Fergie. "Though I am not certain how I could ask without disclosing that we have been here."

"I'm starving," Pigg blurted. "Anyone want a snack?" But he didn't wait for a response before he took off down the hall toward the galley.

Elena suddenly felt wrecked. "I think I'll go lie down."

She stumbled down the hall, her eyes blurry with tears, and collapsed onto her bed feeling bewildered. The Catalan Atlas had essentially been a trap that someone had set to kill anyone who was searching for it. If it hadn't been for Kidd and the Independence, she was sure that they would have been crushed to death. In addition, Liberty Island had sunk underground, and they were only saved because they were inside the Independence. Someone had set these traps. Someone wanted any person that hunted artifacts to perish in the attempt to retrieve them.

"How are you doing?" Austin asked, entering the room. He sat beside her on the bunk bed. "You know, with everything that's happened since…"

"My parents were murdered?" Elena supplied.

Austin nodded, looking concerned.

"I'm so confused about what's happening now. The whole of Liberty Island sunk and those Humanoids back there were on attack mode." She chewed her thumbnail. "I didn't expect that finding artifacts would be so life threatening."

"I don't think those traps were meant for us or for the Renegades. I think they were left for Imperator. If we'd known the correct coding or steps to take maybe the Humanoids wouldn't have attacked us or Liberty Island wouldn't have gone into the ground that way," Austin said. "But we're alive."

Elena looked at him, feeling skeptical. "What if we get into a situation where we can't luck our way out of it? What if someone gets really hurt or dies?"

Austin made a face that Elena had never seen him make before. Did he look concerned? Or contemplative? She couldn't tell.

"How do we go back, Austin? How do we go back to our regular lives?"

"We don't have a choice, Lena. We've got to stay in school to keep up the charade that we're students so that no one catches on. Plus, we need Grimsby's mainframe and the Firebird Station to research what our parents were doing. And we need our friends to continue helping us. We're all connected to this somehow. Now, we need to figure it all out."

Doing something as normal as school was a bizarre thought to Elena. Since her parents had been murdered, she had one singular focus, bringing justice to their death. This desire had consumed her to the point that she'd forgotten that she was supposed to be a fourteen-year-old starting her second year of boarding school.

"So, you want me to *pretend* to be happy and suffer through it?"

"Nah, if you act happy then everyone'll know that something's wrong." Austin smiled playfully while Elena made a face at him. "I'm saying that you need to accept this life that you have now and move forward in it as your normal, charming self."

"I'm not charming," said Elena defensively.

"I beg to differ," said Declan as he entered Elena's cabin. "Come on, Abria wants to talk."

"Oh, that's a surprise," Elena replied sarcastically.

Elena followed Declan back to the command bridge where Abria was speaking quickly and passionately.

When she saw Elena and Austin, she stopped mid-sentence and said, "Oh, I'm so glad you're here. I was asking Fergie how we are gonna, like, get back home?"

"What do you mean?" Elena asked. "We're going back in the way we came out, right?"

"But how can we? We left from school. We went out through the Atlanson sewers. If we go back through the sewer, we'll be in Atlanson. How are Declan, Fergie, and I going to get back to the Galilee Province without anyone knowing?"

"I have been devising a plan for re-entry since before we left," Fergie said stiffly. "If you allow me, I will explain it to you."

"This better be good," Kidd said curtly.

Fergie lifted her arm and Elena watched the Touchdot shoot from the Broadcaster on her wrist. A green screen materialized along with a schematic of the Firebird Station. Then, what looked like a dozen little red veins appeared, each one connecting to the Station.

"These red lines are access tunnels, leading to the Firebird Station. I believe that we can use these tunnels to get in and out of the Station without being detected" — she traced her finger along one of the lines — "This is the line we took to the Atlanson sewers. This line, here, leads from the station to the Galilee Province."

Austin looked over the map and pointed. "That other line leading toward Atlanson, where does that start from?"

Fergie pulled up another Optivision holographic screen. An image of a massive series of crushing waterfalls appeared. "This is called Niagra Falls. It is not far from our present location. If we use the tunnel from this waterfall, it will take us straight into Atlanson."

"That still doesn't solve how we're to get home," Declan pointed out.

"Yeah, school starts in three days," Abria added. "I think someone will notice if we're on the train coming from Atlanson."

"Why can't you take the train with us?" Elena asked.

"Elena, you really need to watch the, like, Grimsby Initiation Memorandum," Abria said.

"Section twelve of module twelve states that each child is required to submit identification from their city of origin to confirm their identity," Fergie said formally.

"I can take them to the Galilee Province using that tunnel there," Kidd said, pointing at the map. "Then, I'll leave the Independence in the Firebird Station before coming back to Atlanson."

"How will you get back in time to catch the Grimsby Channel for school?" Austin looked concerned.

"Don't worry about it," Kidd replied shortly.

—

"Plus, won't someone from home be looking for you?" Elena added.

"No one at home will miss me," Kidd said shortly. "Do you want me to take them or not?"

"Yes," Austin said kindly. "Thank you."

With that, Kidd turned in his chair and set a course for the place called Niagra Falls. To Elena, it seemed that only minutes later the Independence was cruising up a hill adjacent to a river. Except, Niagra Falls wasn't the powerful, raging waterfall from the images Fergie showed them. The face of the mountain was dotted with merely a few trickling streams.

Fergie's fingers played across the green Optivision screen. For several breathless moments nothing happened, but then the rock face opened. An arm extended out through the trickling falls and a door opened wide like the mouth of a whale. Kidd directed the hovercraft toward the opening into the tunnel. Then, the mouth closed, swallowing them whole. They were in darkness except for the lights at the front of the Independence bouncing off the tunnel walls.

For several uneventful hours, the Independence moved through the tunnel. Elena moseyed around the ship, eating in the galley with Pigg, and listening to Abria talk about shopping for shoes. Then, she packed clothes in her carrier bag and stopped by the research lab to add the Ransom Dossier to the items she was taking home.

As she began to put it in her bag, Fergie arrived at the door. "What are you doing?"

"I'm taking my dad's dossier home."

"That is not the best course of action," Fergie said.

"What's not?" Austin asked as he walked into the room.

"I was about to point out to Elena that it is unwise to take the Ransom Dossier to Atlanson. The safest place will be on the Independence in the Firebird Station."

"Thanks for sharing your opinion, but I'm taking it with me," Elena said stubbornly.

"Fergie's right," Austin said. "We should keep the artifacts and dossiers in the safest place possible and that's in the Station."

"You can't be serious!" Elena said, holding up the diary. "I'm not parting with this now."

She watched Austin and Fergie share a look.

"We know your house is under surveillance," Austin said. "What if someone comes in to steal the diary? Then, we will have lost the info that's gonna help us find the other artifacts."

Austin made a good point that she couldn't argue with. Even though Elena didn't want to part with her dad's writings, she begrudgingly opened her carrier bag and left dossier in the research lab with the Cryptext, Amulet, and Catalan Atlas.

Hours later, Kidd said, "This is as far as I can take you. If you follow that tunnel you will arrive at Terminal West, Level Two. Can you find your way home from here?"

"Yes," Austin said, throwing his rucksack onto his shoulder.

Elena stood beside Declan, Abria, and Fergie looking at each of them. They'd journeyed so far together; she was finding it hard to see them go.

"We'll see you at school in a few, like, days." Abria embraced Elena first and then Austin and Pigg.

"Stay out of trouble," Declan warned, a smile on his lips.

"Fergie, thank you," Elena said, giving her an awkward hug that was returned by a stiff pat on the back. "We couldn't have found the artifacts without you."

"You about done?" Kidd said coldly, not even bothering to look at any of them. "We've still got quite a trip ahead and I'm getting tired."

Elena rolled her eyes and then disembarked with Austin and Pigg. They watched the Independence reverse back down the tunnel where they came. Then, Elena, Austin, and Pigg hiked along the maintenance tunnels.

"Pigg, remember to look through your house to see if your parents have a dossier," Elena said.

"Oh, do I really have to do that?" Pigg groaned. "When we were talking about that before I didn't think you were being serious. I can't go snooping through the house. My mom would certainly know because I'm so clumsy and I never put things back in the right spot. Plus, remember the time I tore up her entire closet looking for my birthday presents. She went ballistic and said I couldn't have a piece of *my own* birthday cake. I still wake up in a cold sweat remembering that birthday."

"Pigg!" Elena said abrasively, cutting him off. "We've got to find out if your parents were assigned an artifact. If they have a dossier, then we'll know that we need more research. Everyone else is looking through their parents' things."

"Not Wheeler," Pigg reminded her. "Remember, he flat out refused."

"We can deal with him later," Austin said. "Just try, okay? It's important."

Pigg gave an uncommitted grunt as they reached the access door and stepped out onto Terminal West. Dozens of pedestrians were walking the street, hurrying here and there to the various monorails, but no one seemed to notice them. Elena heaved a sigh of relief. Pigg hopped onto a train headed uptown while Elena and Austin climbed onto the elevator that was headed up to their resident tower.

As the elevator broke the surface of the street level, Elena could see a spectacular view of the tree park, miles of trails, a myriad of fountains, and the three other resident towers that outlined the city like points on a compass.

Not long ago, this elevator ride was one of Elena's most favorite things about Atlanson. But now, as she looked over the city and observed the dome above it, she felt like she was living in a prison.

"Dad would always say that ignorance is bliss," Elena told Austin. "I never understood what that meant until this moment."

Austin put his arm around her. "We have a plan now. One day, we'll be free from this place."

"Not soon enough," Elena replied glumly.

Finally, Elena and Austin stepped off the elevator onto their resident hall. Elena could see her front door but couldn't tolerate being inside the place without her parents. Even their Humanoid, Tiny, was no longer there. She felt lonely thinking about it.

"Could I come home with you for a while?"

"Sure." Austin smiled.

Even before Austin could swipe his Trademark against the scanner on his front door, it slid open, and Grandma Haddock stood there with a mixture of anger and relief etched through her slightly wrinkled face.

"Where have you been?" Grandma Haddock demanded in a stern voice. But then, she pulled them both into a deep hug and Elena heard a tremendous sigh of relief.

"We told you we were staying with our friends Declan and Abria Bowen," said Austin.

"I think everyone knows you didn't go there!" Grandpa Haddock had joined them in the entryway, but he didn't look relieved to see them. He only looked angry.

"Why would you say that?" Austin asked, pulling away from his grandmother's grip.

Grandpa Haddock grabbed Austin by the arm and held it up so that they could see the barcode that was tattooed on his wrist.

"Your Trademarks were not picked up by any scanners in the Galilee Province. The authorities have been here three times in the past seven days asking questions about your whereabouts."

Elena looked at Austin and he gave her a blank stare. Austin had many amiable gifts, lying was not one of them. She realized that she was going to need to come up with a suitable excuse to cover them both. However, before she could speak again, there was a knock at the front door.

From the surveillance monitor that was inset in the wall, Elena saw a very familiar person displayed on the other side of the door. General Hannibal, the commander of the four Units that formed Aves Company at school, stood there in his perfectly tailored military uniform with his salt and pepper hair combed neatly.

Elena felt a strange mix of hope and terror. The last time she'd sat alone with Hannibal it was because she'd struck Major Marshall. The General had been wise, calm, and merciful, but now his enormous, kindhearted eyes were dull, and his brow creased.

Without a word to the others, Grandma Haddock scanned her Trademark to open the door.

"Hannibal, thank goodness you're here. Please come inside."

"Nice to see you, June," Hannibal said pleasantly enough. "Although I wish it were under better circumstances."

As his eyes turned on Elena and Austin, his brow furrowed again. Then, he turned toward the door and Elena saw that Pigg was standing behind him looking sick to his stomach. Pigg's parents, Norman and Emelie Pigg, were with him. Emelie had such a sour expression on her face that Elena felt in fear for Pigg's life.

"Long time, no see," Pigg said nervously to Elena and Austin.

"Please sit," Hannibal said to them, gesturing to the chairs in the living room like it was his house they were being invited into.

Elena, Austin, and Pigg squeezed shoulder to shoulder together on the couch. She felt very childlike sitting there. She remembered back to a time when she was ten-years-old and had come home with a black eye. Her parents sat her down to ask her what happened, and she'd confessed that she'd tried to defend Austin against a group of bullies. Her dad sent for Austin and his grandparents. She and Austin sat side by side on the couch as the adults coaxed the entire story from them.

She hadn't lied to them and if her parents were here, she might not feel it necessary to fabricate a story. But under the current circumstances, deceit felt like their only option. Elena needed to carefully construct a dishonest tale, though she wondered how convincing it would be with Austin and Pigg sitting beside her. One thing she'd learned in the time between ten and fourteen was that she didn't have to tell the entire truth, her story needed to be partly true with the appropriate amounts of lies that would cause confusion and doubt.

"I hope you can appreciate the seriousness of your absence from Atlanson and the Galilee Province," Hannibal began. "Where have you been for the past seven days?"

"We were in New York," Elena said flatly.

Elena was proud that Austin didn't react, but Pigg let out an audible gasp that sounded like he was trying to suck all the oxygen out of the room. Emelie Pigg also gasped at the same time, so it was impossible to tell which was louder. Grandma Haddock clutched her husband's arm. Hannibal stood expressionless with his eyes fixed on her. Elena couldn't decide what he must be thinking.

"You were in New York City? In the former United States of America?" Hannibal asked.

"That's the one," she replied lightly, as if it weren't a big deal, but she began to feel tightness in her chest.

"What could you possibly be doing there?" Grandma Haddock exclaimed.

"We were looking for a friend of my dad's," Elena said.

"A friend?" Hannibal said, sounding skeptical. "Of Truman Ransom?"

"My dad left something for him, you know, in the event of his death," Elena invented. "A sort of last will and testament thing. I found it when I was clearing out dad's things, so I decided I would take it to him."

"You took something to your dad's friend," Hannibal said slowly. "A friend who lives in New York City. In the United States of America."

"You're sort of slowly repeating everything I say," Elena said coolly. "Are you having trouble understanding or are you in shock?"

"Lena!" Austin hissed under his breath.

"This is no laughing matter, young lady," Grandpa Haddock said sternly.

"Stephen," Grandma Haddock said in a kind voice. She laid a hand on his forearm and Elena noticed Grandpa Haddock relax.

"What was it?" he asked in a measured tone.

"What was what?" Elena asked, trying her best to look innocent.

"The thing you took your dad's friend," Grandpa Haddock said impatiently.

"I don't know," Elena said, sounding thoughtful. "It looked like a bracelet."

"How did you get to New York?" asked Hannibal.

Elena hadn't thought she'd get asked this. It was one thing to admit that she and her friends had done something illegal, but it was quite another to implicate Hopper as an accessory to their little adventure. She also wasn't ready to expose that they had access to an unregistered hovercraft that had enough gadgets and gizmos on board to rival a small nation.

Amazingly, Austin piped up. "We stole from Hopper's motor bike collection. One for each of us."

Elena realized that the lie was getting bigger, but at least that would help explain how they got to New York without giving away the Independence. "Where are the bikes now?" Hannibal asked.

"We had to ditch them when we climbed back in through the sewer," Elena said.

Hannibal looked at her quizzically. "How did you manage to get in and out through the sewer? The doors are locked and can only be accessed by authorized personnel."

"Well...um..." Elena hung her head because she didn't want to say the next sentence out loud. "Pigg opened the door using a program he designed on his PocketUnit."

Hannibal shot Pigg a look and he let out a groan and a squeak of terror.

"Did you find your dad's friend?" asked Grandpa Haddock.

"Yes," Elena said truthfully, but then she added, "Poor man is living like a hermit. He scrounges around for food and shelter" — which wasn't true at all because she'd eaten quite well when she stayed in the underground of New York City with Fallon and the other refugees — "We offered to bring him back here, but he's a little, you know, *crazy*. Been alone too long. I read a story once about a guy who'd been kept in solitary confinement, and he was like that."

"Elena," Grandma Haddock said kindly. "You can tell us the truth."

Elena didn't believe that for a second. The only thing she knew for sure was that people directly involved with challenging Imperator's power ended up dead. She couldn't risk involving the only adults she had left in her life.

"I just have."

"Are you aware that it's illegal to venture into the United States?" Hannibal asked.

"No," Elena lied. In fact, she'd known since she could talk that it was illegal to leave Atlanson, much less go into the United States.

Hannibal surveyed her face for a moment and then looked at Austin and Pigg. "Elena has done most of the talking. Do either of you have anything to say?"

Pigg's chin quivered, but he managed to squeak out, "I was taken against my will."

Elena was relieved to hear him say that. "That's true!" She jumped in quickly. "It's not Austin or Pigg's fault. They didn't want to go, but Austin refused to let me go alone. We thought it would be helpful to have three of us."

"The three of you?" Hannibal asked. Elena did not like his tone of voice. "Did you not have others with you?"

Elena felt her chest tighten more. She wondered if everyone in the room could hear her heart pounding against her ribs, in her throat, and in her ears.

"I don't know what you mean."

"The scanners did not register several other students from the Firebird Unit during the same days that you were absent," said Hannibal.

Elena sat very still and silent.

"Declan and Abria Bowen, Fergie Foreman, and Kidd Wheeler have been missing as well. In fact, Hopper is in the Galilee Province right now questioning Declan, Abria, and Fergie. When I leave here, I will be visiting the home of Kidd Wheeler."

Elena suddenly realized how foolish they'd been. They hadn't even discussed a proper cover story with the others. Hopper was her Resident Advisor and though he sort of sanctioned their trip, he by no means gave them permission to go. Also, she knew that Hopper couldn't be questioning her friends because they weren't even home yet.

"First off, Kidd Wheeler is *not* our friend," Elena said forcefully. "So, I have no idea what he does in his spare time from school. Furthermore, we've never been to the Galilee Province so how would we possibly know what other students from our Unit do with their time off? Plus, we've been out of touch with everyone for days and days."

Hannibal's eyebrows rose but he said nothing in response.

"How much trouble are they in, Hannibal?" It was the first time Norman Pigg had spoken. His voice was strained, and he had tears in his eyes.

"It is impossible to say at this point," Hannibal said. "There is no precedent set for this offense. To be honest, it has never been done before. As illegal as it is to travel outside the domed cities, it is even more illegal to go into the United States."

Hannibal paced the length of the room seven full times. Elena felt herself growing impatient, but she remained quiet.

"I will explain to the authorities that the Firebirds were on a mission that I designed for extra credit but that they got carried away and misunderstood my instruction. That will buy us some time. Then, I will have my crew fabricate directives and paperwork that will hopefully have the case closed quickly."

Elena felt suspicious about the effort Hannibal was taking to try and lie for them, especially when he had so much to lose.

"Why would you do that for us?"

"Because, otherwise, you will be imprisoned at the detention center indefinitely." Hannibal spoke with such a commanding voice that Elena felt a prickle of fear. "There would be no trial or committee hearing and you would never see anyone you love again."

Elena looked sadly at Austin and Pigg.

Hannibal sat down across from the three of them, looking extremely serious. "I must *demand* that you never leave the confines of the dome cities again. Is that understood?"

"Sir, yes, Sir," Elena, Austin, and Pigg said together.

Moments later, Hannibal excused himself, shaking Grandpa's hand as he left the apartment. Then, Grandpa and Grandma Haddock escorted Norman and Emelie Pigg to another room so they could talk privately, leaving Elena, Austin, and Pigg still sitting on the couch.

Elena's forehead dropped into her hands, feeling exhausted after Hannibal's interrogation.

"I want to go home and get some sleep."

"Oh, you can't do that!" Pigg said urgently. Then, an intense look appeared on his face, and he whispered, "Remember about the bug?"

Several weeks ago, Pigg had discovered that Elena's apartment was under surveillance. He had called it *bugging*, though he still hadn't figured out how to trick the "bug" into thinking that Elena was there when she wasn't.

"Oh yeah," Elena grumbled.

"Pigg, can you see if my house is bugged, too?" asked Austin.

Without a word, Pigg unzipped a pocket on his sleeve and pulled out a diamond shaped object. He opened a holographic screen from his PocketUnit. Elena knew that he had a Sensory Skulk program that could detect any electronic transmission.

"We're safe," sighed Pigg.

"What are we going to do now?" Austin asked. "I mean about our friends?" "Do you think Hopper will tell on us?" Pigg asked.

"Nah, he practically suggested that we go," Elena whispered. "But I wonder what Hopper will ask them or what they'll say to him about what we did."

Somewhere down the hall, Elena heard shouting. Then, she heard heavy footsteps as Pigg's mom arrived in the living room.

"Gribbin, come along," Emelie said shortly, giving Elena a nasty look. "We're leaving."

Pigg looked pitiful as his mom marched him out of the apartment with Norman following closely behind.

"Austin, would you please come in here," Grandpa Haddock said. He was standing in the hallway leading toward the back bedrooms. Austin left the room abruptly, leaving Elena alone with Grandma Haddock.

Grandma Haddock made herself busy in the kitchen, pulling red fruit and white cheese out of the refrigerator. Elena could tell that she was trying her best not to say anything.

"I guess Grandpa Haddock wanted to scold Austin privately." Elena sat down in a chair at the table, she saw no point in denying the obvious tension. "I suppose you're going to scold me, too."

Grandma Haddock looked up and said gently, "Elena, losing a parent is painful. Losing a child is also painful. You know, we lost Austin's mother unexpectedly during his birth. Then, we lost Austin's father on that expedition. I think about them every day. I know you're grieving, child. I hope you know that you are loved and that we want what's best for you and for Austin. It would break my heart if anything bad happened to either of you."

Truth and love. Elena hadn't expected that. Her throat constricted and she found it hard to swallow.

"If it's okay with you, I'd like to stay here tonight."

Grandma Haddock nodded.

"I need to go get some things from my house. Elena jumped up and hurried to her apartment.

Bugged or not, Elena had to get out of Austin's house for a while. She placed her Trademark against the scanner niche and the door to her apartment slid open. Her house appeared in perfect condition and didn't look different from the last time she'd been there.

The walls of the spacious living room were made of glass and aligned with marbled columns. Patches of carpet were tastefully laid between the marbled floors and were adorned with contemporary furniture. She wandered aimlessly into the spacious, modern kitchen and straight to the refrigerator. She accessed the message center and read the last note her mom had ever left her; "Clean Your Room!"

Eventually, Elena walked into her dad's office and toward the elaborate bookcase that stretched the entire wall. The shelves were oaken and embroidered with rounded emblems. She shifted the third emblem from the left side of the cabinet and slid her finger into the hole behind it. A door opened into a secret room, filled with books from floor to ceiling on shelves, and even some stacked in piles on the floor.

Elena knew that it was illegal to own books, but she suddenly found herself wondering if her dad had told her the truth when he'd said he had special permission through his job to have the books there.

Elena sat on the floor in the middle of the room absorbing the bindings with her eyes and wishing that the Kairos would open again and tell her what to do. When the necklace was still silent after a few moments, she lay down on the lavish carpet and examined the ceiling. She'd never given much thought to the complicated fresco before, but she'd always thought it was beautiful.

In the stillness of the space, Elena's mind began to race as she remembered everything that Hannibal had told them and about how nervous the parents had been. Hannibal was planning to lie for them. He was going to take full responsibility for their actions. But why would he do that? Elena rubbed her eyes forcefully, as if trying to make her brain think harder to come up with an answer.

Elena's vision was a little blurry when she opened her eyes but that's when she noticed the ceiling again. The way it sloped and arched with constellations and symbols was rather strange. Suddenly, it was beginning to look familiar and like something she'd seen very recently. Elena's eyes zipped back and forth across the ceiling as if daring herself to arrive at a different conclusion because, honestly, she'd only seen the Catalan Atlas spread out once and only for a moment. However, the ceiling was beginning to look more and more like the Atlas.

Then, she saw it. Her mouth dropped open and her eyes blinked rapidly. She tried to remember back to first semester Phonology when they'd studied the ancient Akkadian language. Learning language skills had been extremely difficult for Elena so she wasn't able to retain much of the pictographs after the exams were over, but she did remember one word specifically because Instructor Niva had required it on every single assignment she submitted. Technically, it wasn't even a word. It was a *name*. She was quite sure that she could read *her name* spelled out in ancient Akkadian letters in the ceiling.

▭ 3 ▭

Theories at Sector 7

Elena ran across the hall and knocked on the Haddock's apartment door.

"I suppose it's time to add your Trademark to the scanner niche since you'll be living here now," Grandma Haddock said after it slid open silently. "Sorry I didn't think of that before."

"Is Austin able to talk now?" Elena asked.

"Yes, Grandpa Haddock is finished speaking with him. Austin is in his room."

Elena hurried down the hallway, trying not to run so that Grandma Haddock wouldn't be suspicious and found Austin lying on his bed staring up at the ceiling.

"Austin," Elena whispered. "I was just in Dad's library and I found my name written in the ceiling."

"Why are you whispering?" Austin was smiling at her like she was crazy.

"My name was written in ancient Akkadian."

Austin sat up. "Are you sure?"

"Yes. It's the only Akkadian I can remember," Elena said earnestly. "Fergie tried so hard to help me remember the ridiculous language, but I can still only read a couple words, including my name. What if my dad left me a message in the ceiling or somewhere in the library?"

"Let's go check it out," said Austin.

"We can't go look at it." Elena shook her head. "We don't know anything about the surveillance in my apartment."

Austin looked deep in thought. Then, he reached for his carrier bag and withdrew his Broadcaster. "If we set up the Touchdot correctly, it will scan images of anywhere we are. It's so small I'd doubt anyone would notice it, even if your apartment has surveillance. We'll sit in your dad's library and talk about school. That seems normal, right?"

"It's so crazy it might work," Elena said.

Elena watched the Touchdot shoot from Austin's Broadcaster and hover in midair. He opened an Optivision screen, selected the scanning function, and gave it some directions. Then, the screen closed, and Austin began to walk forward with Elena behind him hoping that the device was scanning.

"We're going to Elena's to pick up some of her things," Austin told Grandma Haddock as they stepped out of the apartment.

Elena and Austin sat in the middle of Truman's library and talked extensively about the fourth quarter exams they'd finished at Grimsby School of the Republic. Periodically, Elena would get distracted by the Touchdot zooming around overhead and found herself wondering how they would tell when it was finished scanning everything in the room.

At length, the Touchdot hovered down from the ceiling and silently reattached itself to Austin's Broadcaster.

"Well, I'll go get that shirt from my room and then we can go," Elena said to Austin.

They stood up together, but he said, "I'll wait for you here. There are some books I'd like to look at if you don't mind."

Elena shrugged and started for her bedroom, feeling desperate to look at the Touchdot scans, but accepting that she'd have to wait until she and Austin could be alone in the Sector 7 clubhouse away from any prying eyes.

The next morning, Elena arrived at the breakfast table and her jaw dropped open. Grandma Haddock had set out a smorgasbord of banana graham nut pancakes with bacon syrup, tiramisu biscuits with coffee syrup, spinach mushroom omelets, berry brioche french toast, and bacon, breakfast ham, and sausage links. Four different coffee roasts were brewing, there were carafes of orange and pink colored juice, and there was also a jug of chocolate milk.

"What's all this? A carbohydrate overload?" Elena whispered to Austin, who was already sitting at the table.

"Cooking relieves her anxiety," Austin whispered back as he nodded toward Grandma Haddock. "After my mom died, Grandpa said that she baked thousands of cookies in dozens of flavors trying to find her favorite."

As Elena sat, she watched Grandma Haddock bring a plate of cubed fruit to the table. Then, she sat and wrapped her wrinkled hands around a coffee mug.

"Good morning, Dear," Grandma Haddock said to Elena.

"Thanks for the great breakfast," Elena replied.

"It was nothing," she replied, but Elena could feel Grandma Haddock's eyes on her as she filled her plate with food.

Grandma Haddock made loud sipping noises as Austin spoke animatedly to Elena about the Grimsby Initiation Memorandum they'd received. He'd stayed up late to watch the holographic recording that detailed their new class schedule, rules and requirements, uniform specifications, and info about the new modules in Basic Training.

Elena recently decided that anything coming from Grimsby was propaganda sent by Imperator and had refused to watch it.

"Grandma, can we go see Pigg?" Austin asked.

Elena was absentmindedly cutting a piece of red velvet pancake with cream cheese syrup into a million pieces, but Austin's question caused her to jerk suddenly.

"He said he was going to be down on Meeting Street today trying out the new Simulabs before we have to go back to school."

Grandma Haddock looked at him with a concerned grimace. After a short pause, she said, "You both have always been allowed to walk the streets freely but given the recent events I would feel more comfortable escorting you."

"Grandma, I know we messed up by going to New York…" Austin said steadily.

"And for lying about it," Grandma Haddock added.

"But we're not going to do that again. Plus, we can't physically leave anyway now that we know our Trademarks are tracked so thoroughly."

"Well, thank goodness for technology," she said dryly.

"I promise we won't get into any trouble," Austin said.

Grandma Haddock considered both of them. "Fine, if you promise to return home promptly at six for dinner. I want you to call me at least once while you're out."

Elena gave Austin a wry smile and then slowly rose from the table. "I'll grab my shoes."

In Austin's room, Elena didn't get her shoes. She wandered over to the desk and picked up the Smartslate that had been automatically updated with the new orientation hologram. She pulled up several Optivision screens and selected a module of the orientation that dealt with her new agenda. She was familiar with her class schedule because it had been the same in her first year. The only difference that she noticed was that she'd be downloading Level 2 assignments on her Smartslate after she returned to school.

With a bittersweet pang in her chest, Elena remembered that it was only a year ago that her parents packed her up and sent her off to Grimsby. At first, she thought she'd hate boarding school. However, she'd soon found a rhythm for her class work and had made some good friends, so she began to view Grimsby as her home.

Elena's favorite class the previous year had been Advanced Historical Analysis, taught by Instructor Booker, a very strict man. She was brilliant at history, which she attributed to her dad's love for history and reading, yet now she had mixed feelings about the subject.

Her Resident Advisor, Hopper, had informed her several weeks ago that the history she'd learned throughout her life had not been a complete depiction of reality. She realized that some of the key beliefs she held were, in fact, complete lies. For instance, she'd grown up believing that she lived in the domed city of Atlanson to protect her from the harmful effects of the Great Drought.

However, Hopper had explained how the story of the drought was fabricated to conceal the fact that Imperator wanted to keep humans enclosed so that he could monitor them. This new information made Elena feel that history was not going to be her favorite subject this time around.

Elena's first year of Grimsby classes had been a progression of information, taking the students through a couple thousand years of recorded history. Each class built on the previous class, providing a full-orbed education. But now that Elena knew that there was more going on than classwork, she felt curious about where her education would take her next. Still, she knew she could count on a few things to keep her spirits up at school.

First, Hopper was her favorite teacher. She smiled as she remembered the first time she saw him. He'd driven into their Firebird orientation on a motorbike with a wild mess of hair dyed every color of the rainbow. She remembered how she'd hated his scraggly, long goatee and the repulsive silver ring through his nose, but it had turned out that he had been a close friend of her parents. Also, there was the Firebird Station. Hopper had given Elena, Austin, and their friends access to a private place on campus where they could get away from everything else.

"Well, I guess there is something that can be said for consistency and tradition," Elena said aloud after she sensed that Austin had joined her.

"To help us achieve the optimum level of retaining what we learn," Austin said in a mocking of Fergie's voice, which made Elena smile. "We should get going though, the streets will be crowded today."

Austin told Grandma Haddock that he wanted to see Pigg on Meeting Street, but Elena knew that he had no such intention. Elena and Austin hopped off the resident elevator and joined the crowd of people hurrying in every direction of Underground One. This vast, strategically mapped infrastructure of restaurants, beauty salons, clothing shops, and grocers was adorned with ornate marbled columns and mosaic tile floors. The arched ceiling was a sophisticated hologram, sometimes displaying a crystal blue sky and at other times a Renaissance fresco.

Elena and Austin walked closely together down King Street, trying to avoid the holographic figures that patrolled the walkways, the three dimensional advertisements, the Android clerks, the helpful Humanoids, and the vending carts with organic products. As the street curved around, they cut down an alley between the Rising Loafer Bakery and the Murphy's Paw Kennel.

When they were well out of earshot from any passersby, Elena asked, "So, what did Grandpa Haddock say to you last night when he took you to the other room?"

Austin sighed heavily. "He said that he expected more from me. That I was foolish not to consider your safety."

They stopped in front of a metal hatch door where Elena entered the code to unlock it. Austin held the door as she walked through the access tunnel to a strange world of machinery, electric modems, and power grids that powered the city of Atlanson. Then, they walked on toward Sector 7 where a crude clubhouse stood between stack pipes and silver ducts.

"Well, what did you expect him to say? It's not like your grandparents could understand what we're trying to do." But Elena noticed a look of concern on Austin's face, and she knew that he was thinking Grandpa Haddock was right.

"Austin." She wanted to sound strong and determined, but her voice was beginning to tremble. "I do feel afraid. I mean, we almost died, twice. But I'm going to keep looking for the artifacts until I find them all. I'm going to do this whether you help me or not."

"I know you want to and you know I want to," Austin said. "But I shouldn't be willing to put your life at risk."

"This is my choice," Elena said as they entered the clubhouse, and she took a chair. "Besides, my life is already at risk. Imperator made that clear when he targeted my parents. He knows where I am now and that I'm a Renegade child. I can't figure out why he hasn't tried it yet."

"Tried what?"

"You know…" Elena said and then she paused because Austin shrugged. "To kill me too. Why hasn't he come in here with the whole Droidier army to take me? Or why haven't I had my *accident* yet? The fact that he's keeping me alive makes me nervous."

"Me, too." Austin pulled out the Broadcaster and a dozen Optivision screens filled the walls of the clubhouse as the Touchdot came to life.

Elena could see different scenes from her dad's library. After studying them in silence for a while she realized that they would probably need Fergie's help if they were ever going to be able to interpret it. The ceiling was extremely complex, and the details were beginning to give her a headache.

"What do you think it means?" Austin implored.

"I don't know," Elena said, feeling frustrated. "It's not like my dad was clear on his instructions except that we're not supposed to do anything about all this. Maybe it's a map to an unknown galaxy far, far away."

"Maybe it somehow correlates to the Catalan Atlas," Austin said, thumbing the scar on his chin. "I feel like I've seen this grouping of stars before and I think I saw it on the Atlas."

"Or it could be a key that opens a magical wardrobe to the land of dwarves," Elena continued sarcastically. "Or it could be absolutely nothing and we're looking for something because we think that it has something to do with the mystery about stupid artifacts."

"Wow! Someone's in a mood."

Elena rolled her eyes. "I'm tired of getting my hopes up that somehow I'll learn to read this."

"So, you're not going to try anymore?" Austin asked.

"Fergie is the only one who might be able to help with these scans." Elena dropped to her knees, pulled up some planks from the floor and said, "I'm gonna skate for a while."

She retrieved her skateboard from the hiding spot under the floorboards and walked out the back of the clubhouse to a series of ramps that made up their skate park. Stale air whipped her curls around her face as she kicked off from the platform.

The skateboard glided easily down the ramp and onto the path. She became engrossed with each twist and turn, not thinking, concentrating on her footwork and tricks. It was the first time since her parents died that she felt completely happy.

After a while, Austin came out and asked her to come with him to get lunch. They made their way back out of Sector 7 and to Meeting Street where they stopped in at the Dante Down the Hatch tavern. Elena scanned her Trademark to pay for a sandwich and her favorite fizzy beverage infusion and then she and Austin found seats under an umbrella table outside.

"I haven't seen Pigg," Elena said. "I wonder if his mom has punished him into oblivion."

"It's too bad she has to be so..." Austin started, but then a girl with black hair appeared at their table and he turned his attention to her. "Oh, hi there, Vivienne. How are you?"

"Not too bad," replied Vivienne Castellow, one of the girls in their Unit at school. "I can't believe how fast our holiday has gone by. We'll be back in school in a blink and back to life as the Firebirds. How was your time off?"

Elena eyed Austin and then quickly stuffed some sandwich in her mouth and nodded.

"Really great and relaxing," Austin replied. "Did you get to do anything fun?"

As Vivienne began to tell them about shopping trips and Simulabs, Elena began to think about the Ransom Dossier and parachuting out of the Bowen's apartment in New York City and about Humanoids chasing her from the White House in Washington D.C. She and her friends had been on such a fantastically bizarre adventure that it was hard to believe people still did normal things, like buying new shoes.

Elena was swallowing another bite of sandwich when Kate Bagley, another one of their fellow Firebirds, also joined them. Elena remembered how this petite, short blonde-haired girl with striking blue eyes had been a strong leader and good Lieutenant during their Level 1 studies in Basic.

"Hey, you two!" Kate greeted Elena and Austin with a warm smile. "Had a good holiday?"

"Yes," Austin replied at once. "Vivienne was telling us about the new hang-gliding Simulab you did today."

"Yeah, you should give it a try before we have to get back to school." Kate turned toward Vivienne and linked an arm through hers. "Come on, my chocolate-sprinkle friend. Your mom said to hurry up."

As Kate Bagley and Vivienne Castellow turned to leave, they both shouted, "See you back at school."

Austin rubbed his belly. "Well, I'm full. I need to call home."

Elena followed Austin to the nearest window dimensional, a pane of glass used for holographic messaging. He scanned his Trademark against the translucent faceplate and a moment later Grandma Haddock's face appeared.

"Are you staying out of trouble?" she asked.

"Yes," Austin said. "We're being very good today, though we haven't seen Pigg at all."

"I guess we shouldn't be surprised. Emelie Pigg was quite upset when she left here yesterday. Be good and home by six."

"You got it," Austin said and then the screen faded to black.

Elena looked down at her Trademark and frowned. "I feel sorry for Grandpa and Grandma Haddock. I feel bad for everyone that doesn't know they're being tracked every day of their life."

"I think it's actually a good thing they don't know," Austin said. "Imagine how devastating it would be to learn that you've been a slave your whole life."

"I don't have to imagine it. I already know how that feels."

Austin was quiet for a few minutes as they walked back through the crowded street. Finally, he asked, "Are you glad to be going back to school?"

Elena had to think about it for a moment.

"It's hard to know that I'm living under Imperator's control. But, then again, now that I know that Hannibal and Hopper are defying Imperator right under his nose it makes me feel happy that I can do the same."

Austin smiled. "I know what you mean."

"Except now I have this panicky feeling like everyone I love is going to die." Elena sighed heavily. "I know it's a short list, but it's still mine."

"Lena, everyone you love will die one day."

"I know," Elena grumbled. "I meant die suddenly when I'm not ready to deal with it."

"Well, we're not going to die today. So, let's get back to Sector 7. We've got work to do."

"Don't you mean skateboards to ride?" Elena said.

¤ 4 ¤

A New Firebird

The next morning, Grandpa and Grandma Haddock escorted Elena and Austin to terminal west where they hopped onto the metrorail transport. After a few minutes, the train pulled into the Grimsby Channel station. Elena looked down an elaborate marble staircase to the cavernous room below that was filled with a bustling crowd.

Dozens of piled brick columns lined the room supporting a vaulted arch ceiling. Elena gazed up into the green, celestial patterned ceiling and noticed for the first time how similar it looked to the ceiling in her dad's library. Before she had a chance to point it out to Austin, Grandma Haddock was hurrying them down the staircase into the busy school-based activity.

At the center of the room, a four-faced, brass clock stood atop a booth with the word "Information" scrawled along it. Below, several students stood along a row of window dimensionals, scanning their Trademarks to access Optivision screens. A few students were choosing Grimsby insignia flags or armorwear shirts embossed with Grimsby logos from a cart.

Elena caught the familiar scent from the bakery, which offered pastries that were marked with the different school Unit logos. She could see the Firebird symbol iced across several different colored pastries and breads. The deli, coffee shop, and gourmet market were busy with people getting a quick breakfast.

To Elena's right, she could see another silver bullet-nosed metrorail, but this one flashed the words *GRIMSBY CHANNEL* spectacularly down its side. However, unlike the previous year, Elena noticed something new. A rather large Optivision display had been set up near the entrance to the Grimsby Channel and a holographic figure was repeating a message about the recent changes to the security protocol.

The last time, Elena had scanned her Trademark before she stepped onto the train. This year, a barrier had been put up. Boys and girls stood in a line, submitting their carrier bags for inspection, and scanning their Trademarks for verification before they were allowed to board the train.

Elena noticed that Grandpa and Grandma Haddock eyed one another significantly, but then Grandpa turned to her and said, quite steadily, "Let's get you checked in."

Elena entered the line for baggage check right after Austin and they stood quietly until it was their turn to be inspected. Then, a robot checked her bag quickly with a handheld laser scanner. After this, they returned to Austin's grandparents.

"Remember," Grandma Haddock pulled Elena and Austin into a hug, "we want you to be safe."

"So, no leaving school except for authorized areas," Grandpa Haddock added.

"Love you," Austin said to them.

"Have a good year," Grandma Haddock said.

"You too," Elena said.

She smiled and waved at them as her Trademark identity was verified by a Humanoid. Then, Elena was permitted through the barrier to the loading platform where she and Austin began to wind their way through the other students to the metrorail.

"That was weird for Grandpa to say," Elena said. "It's not like we could leave again."

"I'm sure he only wanted us to know that he expects us to behave," Austin said. "Look! There's Wheeler."

Elena followed Austin's finger down the platform and locked eyes with Kidd. She gave him a half-hearted smile that she was sure probably looked more like a grimace. He gave her a look of complete disgust and turned away.

"I guess friendship is off the table," Austin said.

"What's his problem?" Elena asked, feeling angry.

"Maybe he got into trouble when Hannibal went to see his parents. Come on," Austin said. "Let's get seats."

Elena noticed that the train's interior had changed a bit since she was last on it. The boxcar was modern and comfortable but there were more Optivision screens playing security warnings and safety messages. Austin scanned his Trademark and a storage compartment opened beneath their feet. He dropped his and Elena's bags into the bin as she slumped into a seat and glanced out the window.

She could see over the barrier and noticed that Vivienne Castellow was crying on Olivia Nelson's shoulder. Students were kissing their parents good-bye. Another student from her Unit, Crosby Gamble, appeared to be arguing with his dad, while Frankie Smiley was walking arm in arm down the platform with his mom. Elena pulled the Kairos into her fingers and fiddled with it, feeling lonely.

"You know," Elena sighed. "One year ago, my parents dropped us off at the station for school."

"Your parents would be really proud of you," Austin said.

"I'm not ready to do this without them," Elena said. "They were my lifeline last year when I was having trouble at school."

"I know it's not the same, but you have me," Austin said.

Elena smiled at him. "It's not the same, but it's more than enough for me."

At that moment, Pigg stumbled into the seat beside Elena looking thoroughly disgruntled.

"Mom said I couldn't be friends with you anymore because you cause too much trouble."

Elena's mouth fell open in disbelief.

"But I reminded her that given my unusual mannerisms, propensity to eat everything I see, and my lack of masculine characteristics that it was unlikely that I would make any new friends. And then, I would be bait for bullies," Pigg finished.

Elena couldn't help but laugh. "What did she say?"

"That she'd have me transferred to another Unit." Pigg tossed a Rock Popper into his mouth. "But she can't really do that. Can she, Austin?"

"Nah, the placement of students is established before Level 1 begins and you can't move to a different Unit once you've been classified. It might even be nonnegotiable. Hannibal can't put you in another Unit, no matter how much your mom complains."

Pigg sighed and said, "I thought so. I tried to tell her that, but she started screaming something about parents having rights or some such nonsense. I couldn't even understand what she was saying because the squealing was so high pitched. So, did anyone else see Wheeler on the platform?"

Elena and Austin nodded.

"I said *hello* to him and he said if I didn't get out of his face that he'd pull my underwear over my head. I tried to say that I didn't think it was physically possible while I was wearing it, but he was already walking away."

"He's a dimwit," Elena said. "We should ignore him."

"That'll be hard now that he owns the Independence and can come to the Firebird Station anytime that he wants to," Pigg said.

Elena hadn't even considered that fact before. She slumped further into her seat and said, "Of course he'd have to ruin my favorite place at school."

"You know, I thought for a moment that he might be on our side, but then something seemed to happen to him after we stayed with Fallon," Pigg said. "Do you think he regrets going with us?"

"Oh, I'm sure he does," Elena said. "But at least we won't have to ever do that again."

"Do what?" asked Pigg.

"Leave school with him, dimwit," Elena said. "Now that we can't leave the domes, we won't need him to take us anywhere."

A bell tone sounded, and several copies of the same holographic woman appeared in the aisle along the length of the train.

"Welcome to Grimsby School of the Republic," said the hologram in a calming, yet clinical tone. "Level 1 students, your first year of school is sure to be informative, educational, edifying, formative, and enlightening.

"For your safety, please remain seated until the signal for lunch to be served in the dining car."

The window morphed into a familiar display of images from the Grimsby campus. Elena had watched it the previous year, so she tuned out as the hologram gave the Level 1 students directions. She began to chew her nails, trying to think up a way they could get the Independence back from Kidd until she felt a jab in her ribs and heard Austin encourage her to pay attention.

"Level 2 students are not required to visit the medical registration table or the room assignment registration booth," the hologram said. "You may proceed at your own pace to the same resident tower as your Level 1 studies but remember to stop by the Uniform Locker to be fitted for your new uniforms.

"For added safety this year, more Trademark scanners have been added around the campus as well as additional surveillance to the resident towers and grounds. We hope you have an excellent year at Grimsby School of the Republic."

As the hologram faded into nothing, Elena turned to Austin and said, "I guess the new scanning requirements and safety precautions are because of us."

"Do you think the forest will have surveillance?" Austin asked, looking concerned.

"I hope not," Elena said gloomily. "I guess we'll need Hopper to tell us where the gaps are in the system."

An hour later, the train pulled into the station. Elena could see the golden gates with the words "Grimsby School of the Republic" engraved into the entire crest of the entrance. Beyond the gates, the shining complex was awe-inspiring. The campus simulated clear blue sky with a bright sun.

Austin opened the compartment under their feet and handed Elena her rucksack. Then, she stepped from the train into bitterly cold weather.

"Ugh!" Pigg exclaimed. "Maybe one day I'll remember that the first months at Grimsby are cold. Although I still don't see why they can't make it warm all the time."

As Elena pulled on her coat, she looked at the four resident towers that were rising in the sky. The towers were distinctly postmodern with a triangular and rounded façade outlining the different floors. Glass elevators on the outside of the building hurried up and down, delivering new students to their dormitories.

"Look at those little refreshment carts," said Pigg excitedly. "I don't remember that from last year."

"That's because they weren't there," Austin said. "Since we don't have to go to medical registration, we're free to do whatever we like."

"I like the sound of that," said Pigg excitedly. "Ohhh, that cart there has those little cream puff things. Can we eat?"

Elena rolled her eyes at Austin but stopped with Pigg so he could get some food. Then, they chose a table in the shade of a beech tree. Elena opened a bag of cucumber dill wafers and a bottle of sparkling grapefruit juice and leaned back in a chair feeling relaxed for the first time all day.

"This is so much better than last year," Pigg said, sounding relieved as he stuffed a piece of puffed pastry in his mouth. "I was so nervous when we got here last time. And then we got stuck with a needle. Remember?"

Elena looked around, suddenly feeling uneasy. It was literally a perfect day, which made it hard to accept that they were living under Imperator's strict control. She gazed far into the sky and noticed the familiar glass dome that covered the entire campus. As she suddenly remembered talking to her mom about the domed cities, she became suspicious of everything.

In her first year, she never considered how they didn't interact with the older grade levels. They had eaten separately from everyone and had their own resident building for classes and living.

"What do you think goes on in those other resident towers?" Elena asked.

Austin looked around and said, "What do you mean? One of them is for the Animalia students, the other is for Maritime students, and that one is for Levels 4 through 6."

"But don't you think it's weird that we never see older students?" Elena pressed.

"We're being conditioned," Austin said plainly, lifting his shoulders into a shrug. "In our fourth year we'll get transferred to that building for Special Ops, but until then we're here."

"But aren't you curious why they keep us separated?" Elena asked.

"I guess we're too young to be around them." Pigg had cream smeared in the corners of his mouth. "I don't mind. I don't want to be bullied by upperclassmen. I get enough of that already."

"But what about the Vault. If our building has one, do you think the other ones do, too?" Elena said. "What if the Headmaster has one in each building and artifacts in each Vault? How would we even go about trying to find out what's in there?"

"Elena!" Pigg sounded exasperated. "We've been at school maybe seven minutes. Could you give the whole *grand conspiracy* thing a rest until tomorrow?"

Before Elena had a chance to snap back at him, Declan ran toward them, looking anxious.

"So glad you are okay. When Hopper showed up…"

"Declan!" Fergie interrupted as she caught up to him. "This is not the optimum place for a discussion about fourth quarter break."

Declan's demeanor changed instantly, and he sat smoothly at the table, picking up Elena's bag of wafers. "So, how was your break?"

"Fine." Elena, Austin, and Pigg answered at the same time. They shared an uncomfortable laugh and then Elena asked, "Where's Abria?"

"Off somewhere gabbing away," Declan said after tossing a chip in his mouth. "She acts like we've been away from here for a year."

"Have you been to the Uniform Locker?" Fergie asked and Elena shook her head. "May we join you?"

"Of course," Austin said. "Let's go."

A minute later, Elena stepped inside the stunningly beautiful foyer of their resident tower. As always, the floors were sparklingly clean and there were dozens of areas for relaxation. The center of the building was hollow up to a glassed ceiling several stories above. Hundreds of windows looked out and down.

Elena followed her friends into a Grimvator with translucent doors. As the box climbed, descended, and slanted, she caught glimpses of some of the other floors. Frankie Smiley was already in the exercise ward using the weights. Several girls from the Maritime Company occupied the lap pool. Olivia Nelson was sitting in the tavern, sipping a fruity looking beverage and chatting with some girls that Elena didn't recognize. She also saw a series of Simulabs with students competing in boxing, karate, and tennis.

At length, Elena and her friends stepped onto the Uniform Locker floor. She hurried into the nearest available stall and scanned her Trademark. After the door locked behind her, a drawer popped open from the wall and she began to remove several clothing items, including a violently orange one-piece suit with half-length sleeves and pant legs.

Elena attempted several times to get into the stretchy material, but it was extremely complex. Finally, she had the thing zipped and turned toward the mirror.

"This. Is. Awful!"

She burst through the changing room door. Austin and Declan were standing in the hall mirrors examining their new wetsuits.

"Wetsuits! Remember last year when we picked up a rain poncho and then it rained through our first Gauntlet run? That was miserable. I wonder what we'll be doing this year?" Elena said.

"Maybe there's a pool hidden under the Gauntlet that we didn't know about," Declan said, acting pensive in a sarcastic way. "Maybe instead of running laps for Marshall this year you'll be swimming laps."

Austin and Declan started laughing, but Elena felt annoyed.

"I look like a caution cone," she said grumpily. "Do they think we'll get *lost* in this magic pool underneath the Gauntlet?"

"What does it matter what you look like? As long as you don't drown," Declan chuckled.

Rolling her eyes, Elena stepped back into the changing room. After her new measurements were recorded, Elena and her friends moved on to the Media Room where rows of long tables were affixed with eye level glass window-dimensionals separating each side of the table. She selected a mostly empty table and slid her Smartslate across the table to the bottom of the window. The device connected and uploaded the Level 2 assignments automatically.

"I guess we'll see you at dinner," Austin said to Elena and Fergie after they were finished.

Elena and Fergie hopped onto a Grimvator across from the boys.

"I expect a Simulab later, Ransom," Declan hollered as the Grimvator doors slid shut.

Elena and Fergie scanned their Trademarks and the elevator headed slantways until it arrived at a circular vestibule. Red, orange, and yellow patterned cozy couches were placed around the room and a row of charcoal-colored worktables sat in front of a picture window that looked out over the lake.

The Firebird, a bright orange bird of prey, was etched into everything and it was even carved into the bedroom door where Elena scanned her Trademark. After the door slid open silently, she attempted to cross the threshold, but almost fell over.

"Oh, I'm so glad you're here!" Abria flung herself into Elena's arms. "So, Fergie says we can't talk about...well...*you know what* until this weekend when we can get to...well...*you know where*. But that's okay because I'm so excited to be back at, like, school."

Elena dislodged herself from Abria's clutches and moved into the comfortably furnished room that was lined with a half dozen beds. She tossed her rucksack on her bed and noticed that it was already stacked with poly bags containing her new uniforms. She scanned her Trademark to open one of the doors to her wardrobe. Then, she grabbed one of the poly bags from her bed and tore it open, removing the armorwear combat shirt that was packaged inside.

"Being a Level 2 student comes with certain perks," Abria said as Elena began to hang her uniforms in the closet. "For instance, did you know that we are allowed leave campus on weekends and during break? I can't wait to go visit Harleston Village, can you? I mean, I've always heard the most amazing things about that place.

"We're also allowed to wear makeup and nail polish, not that it stopped me last year, but it's nice that I don't have to pretend. Another perk is boys! They've gotten so much better looking in the past few weeks. Did you notice that Frankie Smiley got a little taller? I mean, he was cute before, but now that he's taller than me it improved everything. I think I'll ask him to have lunch with me tomorrow.

"Oh, and did you see the orange wetsuits? I just love them, don't you? Swimming modules are going to be so fun. I can't wait to be in the, like, water. It's been so long." Abria paused for a moment and gave Elena a funny look. "Elena, are you, like, okay?"

"Of course, I'm okay," Elena said defensively. "Why?"

"Well, you haven't said two words since you got here."

Elena dropped onto her bed causing the Firebird monogrammed pillow to pop out of place.

"That's because you've been talking non-stop since I got here."

Abria laughed, her voice tinkling like crystal.

"We should leave now to meet Hopper so we are not late for orientation," Fergie said suddenly.

"We just got here. Why are we meeting him so early?" Elena asked. "Last year we didn't see him until after dinner."

"The new schedule from the Grimsby Initiation Memorandum informed of the change. Did you not watch it?" Fergie said.

"The *Manual of Manipulation*? Nah, I make it a point not to watch that thing."

Fergie attempted a smile. "Hopper will be meeting with the new Firebirds after dinner."

"What do you mean *new* Firebirds?" Elena asked.

"Hopper is the Resident Advisor to all Firebirds, silly," said Abria. "So, he'll meet the Level 1 Firebirds after dinner at their resident tower. Since we're Level 2, we're scheduled for 0500."

Elena followed Abria and Fergie onto a Grimvator and selected the Firebird common area from the Optivision screen. When the doors slid open, they entered a courtyard that was lined with modern furniture, pupil stations, and lounging chairs. A rich red and warm golden banner, which bore the Firebird logo, was stretched across the wall.

Hopper, their Resident Advisor, was already waiting for them. He was the picture of controversy with his wildly curly hair that was dyed every color of the rainbow. He was not built muscularly lean like the other men but was thick skinned and heavy set. He was covered over with baggy style clothing instead of the proper uniform that the other Instructors wore.

Elena hurried over to him and blurted, "What happened with Hannibal?"

"We can't talk here," Hopper whispered, "but I'll meet you at the Station on day six this week."

Elena had the distinct feeling that it was going to be a long week.

"Okay, rugrats, welcome back," Hopper said loudly. "Everyone come around here and get close." He waved his arms around until everyone was gathered. "So, I have some sad news to start us off. Kate Bagley and her parents were killed in an accident."

A sharp intake of breath sounded from several students. Elena felt her face grow hot. In typical consoling fashion, Abria crossed the room at once to throw her arms around Vivienne Castellow's neck. Vivienne's eyes were red with tears and now Elena knew why her classmate had been crying on the Grimsby Channel platform. Elena couldn't even imagine how she'd feel if Austin died.

"I know this comes as a shock, so let's take a moment of silence to remember her."

As Hopper bowed his head, Elena's heart seared with anger. She didn't know Kate's family, but she was sure they hadn't died in an accident. They'd been murdered by Imperator, as her parents had.

Elena's anger turned to sadness as she remembered Kate's kindness. She'd been a strong teammate during Basic Training and had helped the rest of the Firebirds when they were having trouble with Phonology. She felt Austin's hand close on hers, but she couldn't look at him. Instead, she looked over at Vivienne again, who now had her face buried in her hands.

Elena wasn't even close to being finished mourning their fallen comrade when Hopper said, "So, Firebirds, now that Kate is gone we have an opening in our Unit. Let me introduce you to Pamela Linus."

A petite and pretty girl stepped forward. Her long blonde hair was braided down her back and bangs swept her forehead. She had expressive eyes, high cheekbones, and a smile that was captivating.

"Oh, please, Instructor Hopper," she said sweetly. "Call me *Melly*."

Hopper smiled and said, "Very well, Melly. I am confident that the Firebirds will help you settle in properly. Now, I've got to go, but you rugrats keep out of trouble. And Melly, please let me know if you need anything."

As Hopper left, Austin and Declan walked straight over to Melly and introduced themselves, but Elena turned to Fergie and whispered, "I wonder who Imperator thinks they were. I mean, Kate Bagley's parents must have been important if *he* killed them."

Fergie looked worried and shook her head slowly. "I am interested to know how we are ever going to locate the artifact that her family was responsible to protect."

Elena hadn't even thought of that. Now that Kate's parents were gone, no one would ever know what their artifact was or where it was hidden.

"We're free to go to Simulab," Declan said. "Care to try me at Judo again? I know you're still disappointed that I destroyed you last time. Or we could try something else."

Elena looked at him with her mouth open in astonishment.

"Hopper said that Kate died. Don't you even care?" And then, lowering her voice again she added, "I saw her yesterday and now Imperator has killed her family."

Declan looked stunned for a moment. "I didn't even put that together. I'm sorry, Ransom."

"Just forget it," Elena said shortly as she walked away.

She climbed on the nearest Grimvator and headed back to her room feeling desperate to find a quiet place where she could be alone to mourn her parents once more.

▢ 5 ▢

Oscar Hunter

"Good morning, girls."

Elena heard the sound of birds chirping and water trickling. She opened a
sleepy eye and could see the outline of the morning Telecaster hologram,
though it was quite blurry. Elena groaned and rolled over, wiping sweat from
her brow. She'd been having a horrible dream with people running and
screaming between skyscrapers. Then, she'd seen her parents, but they ran so
fast she couldn't catch them.

"This is your first warning for breakfast service at 0600 in the Mess Hall."

The hologram faded on the spot, but Elena didn't have any intention of
moving, until Abria pounced on her bed.

"Geez, Abria!" Elena grumbled. "Can't you give me five more minutes?"

"What's the point of taking five more minutes?" Abria asked. "You have to
get up anyway so get up right now."

Elena kicked her feet like a child having a tantrum, but Abria only
laughed. Slowly, but surely, Elena grabbed some clothes from the wardrobe and
made her way to the washroom where she found Fergie applying some lip-gloss.

"Oh, no..." Elena sighed. "Did Abria make you do that to yourself? She bribed you to wear that, didn't she?"

Fergie gave her a quirky little smile and said, "She did not bribe me. I am attempting an experiment to see if this change in my appearance effects how I am perceived by other people."

"That's a lot of words when you're really trying to say that she bribed you."

"Com' on, girls! Everyone else has gone down." Melly Linus' face appeared from the other side of the washroom door. She looked as awake and put together as Abria. Elena wanted to clobber her.

It was bad enough that she already had one roommate that was too much of a morning person but adding a second had Elena on sensory overload. She noticed Vivienne look over at Melly's bed with red, blurry eyes. All last year, that bed had belonged to Kate Bagley.

"Hey, Vivienne," Elena called. "Want me to hold Melly down so you can mess up her hair and makeup?"

Vivienne half smiled. "Maybe not today, but I'll let you know."

When Elena finally arrived at the breakfast table, the boys had almost finished eating. Her plate was filled with an egg scrambled with smoked salmon, asparagus, and goat cheese.

"Aw, the morning egg scramble," Declan said after eyeing her plate. "It was superb."

"Really?" Pigg said. "You thought so? Mine needed more salt and the salmon was a bit dry."

Elena could sense that Austin was watching her.

"Did you sleep okay last night?" he asked.

She nodded without looking at him and then shoveled some eggs into her mouth. Elena had no desire to tell everyone at the table that she'd had a horribly awful dream about her parents running away from her.

"Melly asked Frankie Smiley to lunch before I got a chance," Abria complained to everyone at the table as she buttered toast.

"Abria, I haven't even eaten breakfast. Could you give the boy talk a rest until I get the morning stimulant in my system?" Elena grumbled.

"You and Melly stayed up late talking about boys, did you not?" Fergie said and Abria nodded. "Did you tell her that you wanted to ask Frankie to lunch?"

"Of course I did," Abria said.

Elena wasn't sure why, but the thought of Melly asking Frankie to lunch when she knew that Abria was planning to infuriated her. "Aren't you mad at her?"

"For what?" Abria asked, giving Elena a blank stare.

"Stealing your idea, sneaking behind your back and being a..." Elena started, but Abria interrupted her.

"How can I be upset when Frankie is so cute?" Abria said, shrugging her shoulders in a quizzical way. "Melly has every right to go after him. Plus, it doesn't really matter when I know I'll win him in the end."

Elena smiled at Abria's ability to have such confidence, especially when it came to the topic of boys.

"Girls talk about the weirdest stuff in the morning," Declan said sleepily. He yawned loudly. "All I'm thinking is that I'm glad we don't have to do placement tests this morning."

Elena was thankful for that, too. She knew that the Level 1 students would begin a week of placement tests, physical exams, and vaccinations, but the Level 2 students would go straight to classes.

Therefore, not long after breakfast, Elena and her friends entered the Advanced Historical Analysis classroom, which was modeled similar to an amphitheater with a stage and stadium seating around the room. She noticed right away that the room began to fill quickly with students from the entire Aves Company.

"What's going on?" Elena asked Austin. "Why is everyone coming in here?"

"We're going to take classes with our whole Company this year," Austin replied. "Didn't you watch that in the orientation memorandum?"

"You know I never watch that dimwit thing," Elena said, feeling slightly uncomfortable with the sheer amount of people that had filled Booker's classroom.

"Welcome to your Level 2 studies," Instructor Booker said, quieting the voices in the room instantly. His bushy black eyebrows seemed to have grown while they were away from school and were sticking out all over the place. "Take out your Smartslates and access the chapter one assignment."

While the students readied their Smartslates, Booker opened a huge Optivision screen that filled the entire space in front of him.

"Our Level 2 studies in this first quarter will begin with the five hundred years of history between 1000 to 500 BC. During this time, Europe and Asia developed elaborate trade routes, which subsequently began to eliminate the geographical gaps between them. This change helped enhance cultural exchanges. Global development and infrastructure were achieved throughout the expansion of commerce, transmission of ideas, and the sharing of technology. Can anyone name three of the major civilizations that thrived during this time of expansion?"

As Elena expected, Fergie raised her hand before anyone else, but Booker called on a student from the Harrier Unit.

Elena looked around at the room full of trainees. The students in Aves looked the same as everyone else with either black hair and brown eyes or blonde hair with blue eyes. In fact, the only way she was even able to tell them apart was by their uniforms. Each Unit had its own logo and color palette.

She was glad to see that the Raptor Unit had chosen seats on the opposite side of the room, the farthest away from the Firebirds. Though, for some reason she felt that she was fielding a lot of nasty looks from Oscar Hunter, an arrogant looking boy with black hair that Elena only recognized because Austin and Declan had studied his Basic Training habits the year before. She was also annoyed that Instructor Booker allowed the Raptors to whisper throughout his entire lecture.

Elena was completely distracted in her thoughts until she vaguely heard Booker say, "The advancement of writing is exceptionally important because it is through written word that we gain facts and data about many cultures. As the written word progressed, we began to see patterns of stories that developed. One such story is an account about a worldwide flood."

At the words *worldwide flood*, Elena sat up a little straighter in her chair.

"The Akkadian version of this flood was compiled sometime between 1300 and 1000 BC. The Hebrew text and the Quran Islamic text record a similar story about a man named Noah. Furthermore, this story can be found in Native American Quiche writings, in the Sumerian Epic of Gilgamesh, and in Greek mythology through a man named Deucalion."

Elena couldn't explain it, but for some reason this story felt familiar to her. She thought about her dad's library for a few minutes. She'd memorized where each of the books were placed on the shelves. Did he have a book about this story? Had Truman Ransom read it to her before?

"Now, for the remainder of class we will break into groups of four," Booker said, interrupting Elena's thoughts again. "Your goal is to begin to build a profile on these three ancient cultures based on the written word that was available during their time. The information you need is in chapter one. Let's get to work."

Elena immediately grouped with Austin, but then she noticed that both Abria and Declan moved toward Melly. So, Elena and Austin were able to join Fergie and Pigg without anybody feeling left out. As they began to work on the written text from the Persian Empire, the cluster of students to their left distracted Elena unexpectedly. She was becoming aware that Kidd was talking, and she turned so she could hear him better.

"…Who knows if she'll be better at Basic, but Melly is certainly a visual upgrade from Kate Bagley." The boys that were sitting with Kidd laughed. "And Phonology is next, so I guess we'll see if her tongue is as talented."

Elena hurried to get out of her seat. Her desire to pummel Kidd consumed her every thought. However, she felt a hand grasp her forearm.

"Don't, Lena." Austin had been watching her. She gave him her best set of angry eyes, but he didn't release his grip on her arm. "Let it go for now, okay?"

Elena wrenched her arm from Austin's grip and stomped out of the classroom. She hurried to the nearest washroom and splashed water on her face. She was irritated that everyone was already acting as though Kate Bagley and her family had never existed.

Elena didn't dare go back to class, so she waited outside the room, hiding in the hallway until class was over. As students began to file out of the room, she noticed Kidd and several of the other boys were walking Melly to their next class.

"What's wrong?" Austin asked, coming up beside her.

"I think it's weird that we're carrying on as though Kate was never here," Elena said. "She was a part of our Unit for a year, but everyone is fine that she's gone. And *how* she's gone."

"*How* would anyone know that Imperator killed her?" asked Austin. "And it's not like we can tell them what really happened to her."

Elena sighed and put her head on his shoulder. "I had a terrible dream about my parents last night."

"Want to talk about it?"

Elena shook her head.

Austin put his arm around her. "Come on, let's get to class."

Elena was moody for the rest of the day. She barely listened as Instructor Niva told them how the Arameans were mostly defined by their use of the West Semitic Old Aramaic language and how their language was first written using the Phoenician alphabet, but that over time it was modified to a specifically Aramaic alphabet.

At lunch, she pushed the food around her plate instead of eating. Then, AstroPhysics and Social Science went by in a blur. By the time she crawled into bed that evening Elena couldn't help but think that pretending to be normal was going to make this school year a long one.

On the second day of the week, Elena entered the Survival Training classroom. This room was similar to Booker's classroom with its high, white walls crafted specifically for holographic learning. However, instead of tables and chairs the seats pulled down from the walls and desktops folded out from the seats. Again, the room filled with the entire Aves Company.

Hopper entered, his wildly curly hair bouncing around as he walked.

"Glad to see you rugrats back for my class. So!" He clapped his hands loudly. "This year, during the mornings we'll study the development of military advancements and historical warriors. Then, right before lunch we'll learn how to survive in the wild."

A holographic map of the world appeared, and Hopper looked almost supernatural in the ethereal blue-green light of the hologram.

"Now, the Assyrians were one of the most ferocious dudes in the ancient world." The Optivision screen magnified to a specific part of the earth. "Their home was here, in Mesopotamia" — Hopper pointed with a laser light — "And, during the best years, their empire stretched from the Persian Gulf to Egypt. Can anyone tell me how many warriors an Assyrian king would take into battle?"

"Fifty thousand," said the arrogant looking boy with black hair.

"That's right, Hunter. But next time, raise your hand first, Dude," Hopper said. "So, they divided their Companies similar to what we do here at Grimsby. Soldiers were divided into squads of ten and then it took twenty squads to make a Company."

An Optivision screen filled with warriors and their weapons.

"These dudes were awesomely skilled at fighting. They used two-wheeled chariots to travel, iron-headed battering rams to bring down walls, and mobile wooden towers so that archers with iron tipped arrows could fire into walled cities. Their capital was Nineveh."

The image of a city appeared on the Optivision as Hopper moved around the room.

"Obviously, trade was very important and one of the ways that they moved goods and people was on boats.

"Last year we covered basics of human survival. We studied patterns for survival, natural reactions to stress and how to prepare for it, using survival kits, basic survival medicine, medicinal plant life, water procurement, and food procurement as the different cultures in the world would have used in their civilizations.

"This year, we're going to focus on navigation, water safety techniques, and open sea survival techniques that were used by the ancient Greeks, Romans, Persians, and Chinese. So, Abria Bowen," said Hopper. "What do you do if you find yourself hopelessly lost at sea with no supplies?"

"Die a slow, painful death from either starvation or dehydration," Abria answered flippantly.

A few people around the room laughed and even Elena smiled.

Hopper smiled, too. "I suppose that's one option, but let's say for argument's sake that you need to survive…"

"Oh, Instructor Hopper, I am certain I couldn't survive lost in the wild," Abria interrupted him. "I'm too addicted to cosmetics and comfortable living." Hopper let out a deep laugh from his belly and there were a few more giggles around the room.

"Well, for this class we'll learn the importance of navigation and locating proper food, water, and shelter for those of you that have a fighting spirit. So, why would building boats and sailing be instrumental in the continued growth and development of the world?"

Fergie raised her hand and said, "Seafaring gave humans greater mobility than land travel. It also enhanced trade between cultures and increased the capacity for food cultivation through fishing."

"Aw, someone was listening to Instructor Booker's lecture yesterday," Hopper said. "The first boats we see in history were dugout canoes, but the Assyrians had carvings of these style boats." The Optivision screen lit up with a long boat with a curved prow and dozens of rowing oars. "Eventually we'll discuss the different seafaring vessels from popular cultures, like the Viking longship and the Chinese oceangoing combat junks.

"Last year, we briefly discussed the Age of Sail originating from ancient seafaring exploration in the Mesopotamian region, the Far East, and the Arabian Sea. But now we'll discuss this in more detail, including some early inventions like the astrolabe, which was the chief tool of celestial navigation in early maritime history. It was invented in ancient Greece and developed by Arab astronomers.

"Let's, uh, break into groups and see how celestial navigation was used for military advancements during this time period. I want you in groups of four, but I want you to meet some new people. So, you can pair off with one person from your own Unit and then with a pair from another Unit. Off you go."

Elena turned toward Austin but noticed that he was already headed across the room. She followed him closely until he came to stand in front of Oscar Hunter. Austin extended his hand in a friendly way.

"My name is Austin Haddock. We've never formally been introduced."

"I know your name," the Raptor boy said rudely. "We've been here for over a year now. Didn't you memorize the class list?"

"Apparently, not well enough," Elena said from behind Austin's shoulder.

The Raptor boy sighed and rolled his eyes. "My name is Oscar Hunter. I was born and bred in…"

"Captivity?" Elena supplied.

"Galilee Province," Oscar continued without pausing to even make a face at her comment. "I have black hair, brown eyes, my favorite Simulab is Stratego, and I'm best at tactical analysis. Now, do you want to know my favorite flavor of ice cream or can you leave me alone so I can get to work?"

"I came over to see if you'd like to pair up with us for the assignment," Austin said politely.

Elena felt her face grow warm. She definitely did not want to join Oscar Hunter for group work. She looked around quickly to see if the other groups had been formed yet so she could pair with someone else, but then turned sharply as the Raptor boy replied.

"Let's get one thing straight, Haddock. I'll only do group work with you if it's assigned by an Instructor. You get me?"

Austin smiled and replied, "Why's that?"

"Bowen says that you're," Oscar poked him hard in the chest, "the best leader in the Aves Company."

"I'm certainly the most intelligent," Austin replied.

"Oh, really?" Oscar declared. "How do you figure that one?"

"Two reasons." Austin held up a finger like he was counting. "One, I don't let a simple brag dictate my emotions, especially when I'm aware of the correct information. And two, I would never pick a fight with someone in such close proximity to an Instructor."

Oscar looked around and saw Hopper coming toward them. He looked back at Austin and smiled.

"The Firebird Unit couldn't even get through the first quarter exam in Basic, whereas *I* was able to lead the Raptor's to a successful completion of the course in record time."

"Austin wasn't even the Lieutenant during that exam," Elena spat. "So, how about you keep your little dimwit thoughts to yourself."

Oscar cut his eyes at Elena and grimaced.

"Everything okay here?" Hopper asked as he approached them.

"Fine, fine, Instructor Hopper." Oscar ran a hand through his hair. "We were about to agree that pairing off for this assignment might not be the best idea. I think I'll go see if I can find someone more clever at astronomy."

Elena wanted to lunge forward and grab Oscar by his neck, but Hopper said, "Hey Ransom, stay after for a moment, will ya?"

The blood that had rushed into her face after Oscar walked away drained as quickly when she looked into Hopper's face.

"It will only take a minute," Hopper assured her.

When class ended, Elena hung back and approached Hopper's desk timidly.

"Haddock told me what Wheeler said yesterday about Kate Bagley during Booker's class," Hopper said. "I took it straight to Hannibal and he disciplined Wheeler."

Elena felt a little comforted as she imagined Kidd running laps in the freezing cold with Marshall standing over him.

"And," Hopper added, "Hannibal wanted me to thank you for not overreacting to Wheeler's comment and causing a scene."

Elena rolled her eyes, but Hopper didn't scold her for it.

"I know that Hunter was disrespectful during class," Hopper continued. "Thanks for not punching him."

After a hearty helping of soybean succotash in the Mess Hall, Elena and her friends pulled on their heavy coats and tromped through the frosty campus to the quad for roll call. In fact, it was so cold that Elena could see Marshall's breath in the bitter air as he barked at them.

"Your performance last year was adequate for first year training," Marshall hollered. "However, make no mistake that this year the physical training will be strenuous. I expect optimum performances from each of you. Today, we begin a dryland swim training program. Let's get started."

Similar to her first year, a hologram appeared and started yelling commands and modeling the different stretches they were expected to do. But the exercises they did were very different from the hamstring routine and metabolism boosters she was familiar with. Her elbows and shoulders were stretched and squeezed, she was forced to sit on the tops of her feet with her knees suspended off the ground and then she had to stretch from a plank position.

Elena noticed right away that Melly seemed to be keeping up well with their exercises.

She leaned a little toward Abria's exercise mat and asked, "How is Linus keeping up so well? I could barely manage last year and that's with the training my mom had given me."

Abria looked sideways at Melly and then back to Elena.

"I don't know." She let out a hefty breath as they moved from a lunge position to resting. "Maybe her mom trained her, too."

Elena didn't have time to think on it further because her attention was drawn in Marshall's direction where he could be seen barking at the Raptor Unit. She knew that she had no right to feel smug about this because the Firebirds had been criticized enough, too, but something about seeing Oscar Hunter's face burn red with anger made Elena feel happy.

Once they'd finished this routine, Elena was sure it had been two hours and that class would be over. However, the torture continued into a base low position where she had to alternate toe points every five seconds. Then, she was forced into push-ups with shoulder touches and hip touches. Finally, there were scissor kicks, situp-getups, pike alternates, rainbow twists, and flutter kicks.

After this, the Company was expected to practice on climbing nets and rope ladders suspended over shallow pools of water. Climbing up and down towers hanging with twine ropes and swinging back and forth on iron rods were also part of their workout. Elena hadn't exactly been lazy while they were away from school during fourth quarter break, but her muscles were protesting every move she made.

By the end of class, Elena's lungs were aching with cold, her hands were chapped on one side and bleeding on the other, and her head hurt so badly it felt like a nail was being driven through her temple.

"That was truly pathetic," barked Marshall. "It was like watching a room full of babies learning how to walk. Apparently, none of you retained a shred of physical stamina from Level 1 training. Expect next class to be more of a workout to compensate for your laziness."

As the Firebirds walked back to the resident tower, Pigg whined, "That was really awful!"

"Yeah. Did you hear Marshall say that our performance last year was *adequate*? How can he pretend like it wasn't hard?" Elena said. "Half the Company almost died from heat exhaustion during first quarter basic training. He makes me want to spit fire!"

"Really? No one could tell," Declan said playfully. "How about you go get changed and we can go try the jousting Simulab? I bet that'll take your mind off Marshall."

"I can't," Elena said tiredly. "I feel like an ice cube that's been shattered into a million pieces. In fact, the only thing that keeps me walking for the resident tower instead of screaming for the Grimsby Channel to take me home is knowing that I can relax at the Firebird Station this weekend."

❑ 6 ❑

Water Torture

Elena awoke to the sixth day of the first week of school feeling excited about being able to go to the Firebird Station. During breakfast, Austin gave Elena and their friends a plan for leaving the school, which included entering the forest at different places so that no one would see them leaving together.

"What if the forest has surveillance now?" asked Declan. "Did you hear those extra safety messages on the way to school?"

"We have to take a chance," Austin said. "Even if we're caught and can't ever use the place again we've got to get back there to get the artifacts. How about we bring our Smartslates? That way, if anyone catches you and asks what you're doing, explain that you came out to the woods to do homework in quiet.

When it was Elena's turn, she hurried beyond the schoolyard, through the orchard to the edge of the school boundaries, and down a steep hill. At length, she stopped at the base of the foothill where a myriad of trees was covered with creeping plants. She grabbed a fistful of foliage and pulled it back to reveal a steel plated door.

On the front of the door, etched directly in the center, was the Firebird emblem. Elena smiled as she pulled down a steel lever and there came a loud scraping sound of metal on metal. She marched straight inside, leaving the door slightly open, and down the main hallway that led into a wide, circular room. Elena and her friends had spent a lot of hours during their first year of school in this room.

On one side, there was a stainless-steel kitchenette, an island cooking station with a half dozen high-rise stools, and a six-top table with chairs. Metal bunk beds lined another wall and to the left was a set of shelves stacked with illegal books.

Before long, Austin and Pigg arrived and took seats around the table. Eventually, Declan and Abria joined them, with Fergie appearing last.

"It's great to be back!" Declan said, easing into one of the cushiony chairs that surrounded the main Optivision pupil station in a circular fashion. "So, we've been dying to hear what you did when you got home from our little trip."

"Hannibal came to visit us," Austin said.

Abria's mouth dropped open and she gasped. "Hopper didn't tell us that! What did he, like, say?"

"He said that the authorities were trying to figure out where we'd been for two weeks because our Trademarks hadn't registered anywhere," Elena said.

"Then, Elena invented some story about how we went to New York to drop off a bracelet to one of her dad's friends," Austin added. "Hannibal didn't seem convinced, but he offered to speak to the authorities on our behalf."

"Then, he asked us about you three being gone," Elena said. "And Wheeler, too. So, we lied and said we didn't know what you were doing. But Hannibal said that Hopper came to see you. What did he say?"

"Hopper said nothing serious was going to happen and that we shouldn't say anything because Hannibal would know what to do," Declan said.

"Yeah, he wouldn't even, like, let us tell him what actually happened," Abria added.

"Plausible deniability," Fergie said and then after she noticed the confused looks on their faces, added, "It simply means that if Hopper does not know what happened he can say that honestly if questioned."

"You forgot the part about Hannibal lying for us," Pigg squeaked.

"Oh yeah, that's the craziest part," Elena said. "Hannibal said he'd lie and tell the authorities that he'd asked us to do some kind of schoolwork, but that we'd misunderstood and that's why we ended up in New York. We assume he means that he's going to lie to Imperator for us, but we don't understand why he'd do that."

"That is, of course, obvious," Fergie said.

"Really?" Austin said. "It wasn't to us. Hannibal said it was to keep us out of indefinite detainment."

"Hannibal and Hopper seem to be protecting secrets for the Renegades," Fergie said. "If Hannibal suspects that we left the domes to do work for the Renegades, or if he knows we left because Hopper informed him of thus, then he will attempt to disguise his participation using any means at his disposal."

"But why would he risk his career for us?" Elena asked. "It doesn't make any sense."

"We need to talk to Hopper," Austin said. "When's he supposed to be here anyway? We have so many questions."

"I don't know," Elena replied. "He said he would meet me here sometime today."

"Fergie," said Austin. "Elena found something unusual about the ceiling in her dad's library. We were wondering if you could look at it to see if you can decode it."

Fergie nodded and Austin opened several Optivisions around the pupil station in the center of the room. Then, his Touchdot automatically inserted into the scanner niche and opened the scans from the library. Using his fingers, he pieced the images together so that a perfect replica of Truman's ceiling was hovering above them. In absolute silence, Elena and her friends scrutinized the image.

After a short while, Fergie said, "Unfortunately, this does not make sense to me. However, it may be that we need a key to interpret the ceiling. In which case, we may find the answer in the Ransom Dossier. I left the dossiers and artifacts in the research lab on the Independence. We can go there now to retrieve the items while we wait for Hopper. Furthermore, I will need to set up an analysis operation in the Research & Development room so that we can catalogue our findings."

The Firebirds followed Fergie down a tunnel that looked like it had been carved out of solid rock. At the end of the tunnel, they arrived at a vast limestone cave that had been converted into a hangar and there on the hand paved landing pad was the Independence.

"Well, at least Wheeler returned it. I had serious doubts that he would," Elena said as she started down the forty-foot staircase to the hangar floor. "But how did he get home from here?"

"He used one of those Speedsters from the cargo bay," said Declan. "You know, those motorbike looking things. Wonder where he stashed it, though? It's not like he could ride it in the city."

They each took an armful of items from the Independence, except Elena who clutched the Ransom Dossier close to her chest. Then, they went into the Research & Development room. Pupil stations lined the walls and center aisle, but it was Fergie who directed them as to which artifact belonged in each workspace.

Fergie set the Catalan Atlas down on the longest pupil station and opened the clasp. The Atlas unfolded again and again until it covered the entire desktop. Then, she sat at a separate workstation and set down the Amulet, a shiny, multi-layered object with a golden ring at the base and a triangular medallion set on top.

"Isn't the fancy script etched into the sides of the Amulet, like, fascinating?" asked Abria. "It's so beautiful."

"I hope, somehow miraculously we'll be able to understand why we even need this artifact," Elena said matter-of-factly.

Fergie opened a leather case full of strange looking utensils that were lined neatly in a row. Then, she placed a pair of magnifying spectacles on her face.

"Where'd you get all that?" Elena asked.

"I found them in one of the cabinets," Fergie replied. "I think this is exactly what I need."

Elena and her friends bent as close as they could toward Fergie to watch as she prodded the Amulet with one of the tools from the leather case.

After several failed attempts using a switchblade, a ratchet, and something that looked like a plastic tube, Fergie finally selected a silver penknife and some tweezers. She careful manipulated the outside of the Amulet until, quite unexpectedly, it opened with a *POP* causing everyone to jump back.

Using tweezers, Fergie pulled the ampoule of emerald shaded liquid from the center of the triangular medallion.

"If you're looking for someone to taste-test that, don't ask me," Pigg said nervously.

"It would be unwise to taste any form of matter before testing the chemical elements," Fergie said prudently. "Therefore, we will not attempt an explanation for this today. However, we do have enough work between us with the dossiers and the Atlas, so let us carry on."

Elena dropped into the chair at the nearest pupil station and opened the front cover of the Ransom Dossier. "What exactly are we looking for?"

"Our next clue or something that explains why we need the Catalan Atlas," said Fergie.

"You don't know why we need it?" Elena asked incredulously.

"I was never given details about the purpose of the Atlas, only that I was intended to retrieve it," Fergie replied.

Elena felt irritated that Fergie's parents had essentially sent her into a dangerous situation without even explaining why she was sent there, which seemed reckless and un-parent-like. She bent over the Ransom Dossier with a frown on her face and began to read.

The diary was filled with stories of betrayal, murder, adultery, blackmail, and mass executions. She also saw many images of the effects of the Kearney Virus and details about branding people with Trademarks. Elena found it hard to believe that these horrible things had been done so that Imperator could gain power over mankind.

"Anybody hungry?" Pigg asked after a while.

Elena looked up from the Ransom Dossier. Pigg was sitting with Fergie in front of an Optivision screen that was taking meticulous scans of the Catalan Atlas. Abria was sitting at another pupil station with her stuffed horse, Chocolate Charlie, propped in her lap while she reviewed analytic data. Austin was at yet another station reviewing the scans from the Alpha Manuscript, and Declan was reviewing the Touchdot ceiling scans from Truman Ransom's office.

"I'll make us some lunch," Pigg insisted as he hopped up and ducked out of the room quickly.

After he left, Fergie began to go back and forth between Elena and her friends trying to make notes of specific details she noticed from each of the artifacts. Pigg interrupted them occasionally to bring in trays of snacks and drinks. He only stayed in the room for long periods of time if there was a specific equation that Fergie needed help with.

At long last, Fergie said, "The Ransom Dossier and the Alpha Manuscript each contain several logs of symbols and numbers that I do not recognize. And, of course, there are still the blank pages throughout the dossiers that we will need to contend with at some point."

"Remind me again, what does it matter if there are, like, blank pages?" Abria asked.

"Historically, in chronicling, a blank page between pages of text was intentional, which means that the pages have a premeditated function. We need to discover the value for each page in order to have a comprehensive understanding of the dossiers and these other artifacts," said Fergie. "It is similar to translating an unknown language. We need to know the key to unlock the details of the language so that we may read it."

"What about the Catalan Atlas?" Austin asked.

"The Atlas presents its own mysteries. Most of the sentences and symbols are encrypted," Fergie replied.

"Is there anything we do know?" Elena asked impatiently.

"You're very grumpy today." Hopper had arrived, looking happy to see them.

"Where have you been, Hopper?" Elena asked hotly. "We've been waiting here all day."

"Easy with the tone, Rugrat," Hopper said steadily. "I'm an Instructor and have responsibilities that have nothing to do with trips to the Firebird Station. Now, let me pull up a chair and then you can ask your questions."

Elena waited impatiently, but she let Austin speak first.

"Hopper, what happened after we left with the Independence?" asked Austin.

"Headmaster Bentley started asking questions about where you were. He said that the authorities had been asking him questions. You were about to be in heaps of trouble because leaving the dome is illegal," Hopper said.

"But you practically told us to go," Austin said.

"Okay, I'll admit that was bad judgment on my part."

"Bad judgment!" Elena screeched. "Why didn't you tell us that the scanners wouldn't pick up our Trademarks and then alert the authorities?"

"I didn't know that would happen," Hopper said. "No one has gotten out before. But anyway, I told Hannibal what I'd done."

"Wait a minute!" Austin said. "Hannibal knew that we'd left for New York in the Independence?" Hopper nodded his head. "Then, why didn't he say anything when he came to my grandparent's apartment?"

"How could he admit, especially to your grandparents, that you'd gone outside to find an artifact that the Renegades left behind?" Hopper asked. "So, he and I designed a lie to explain where you'd been. A tribunal has been called to assess your whereabouts and determine the reason for your being outside the dome. So, we'll have to wait now and see what happens."

"Will we be required to testify in open court?" Fergie asked formally.

"Nah, since you're underage you won't be held accountable. But Hannibal will," Hopper said.

"Why is he risking his career for us?" Elena asked warily.

"His *life*," Hopper said sharply. "He's risking his *life*. And he's not doing it for you. He's doing it for everyone. Hannibal can't admit that he knows anything about the Renegades or about what you were doing because Imperator would kill him for sure."

Austin stood and walked the length of the pupil station, saying, "These are the items we've found so far. Can you help us decipher these things?"

"Nah, nope," Hopper said, shaking his head. "You rugrats aren't supposed to have anything to do with this anymore. Hannibal made me swear."

"We're going to keep researching," Elena said. "Even if you don't help us."

Hopper looked around the room and Elena noticed that he seemed a little defeated by their stubborn faces.

He sighed heavily and said, "If you promise not to leave the domes again, I'll help you work through this stuff, if for no other reason than to help Hannibal."

Fergie began to lead Hopper around the room.

"This is the Cryptext that we recovered in the Bowen apartment in New York. Do you know how it works?"

Hopper held it in his hands but shook his head. "Sorry, dudes. No idea."

"We also found this Amulet," Fergie said, holding it up for him to see, "which I believe you already knew about?"

"Yes," Hopper said. "It was mentioned in the Alpha Manuscript, but I don't know what it's for. Some of the pages are blank."

"We know," Austin said. "We have it right here."

Hopper walked slowly to the scans of the Alpha Manuscript that were hovering in midair above one of the pupil stations.

"How did you get this?" Hopper exclaimed.

"Elena and I broke into the Vault a few months ago and we scanned it," Austin said.

"Do I want to know how you knew about the Vault?" Hopper asked and Austin shook his head. "This one manuscript alone contains thousands of lines of code that must be logged, cataloged, and decoded. It takes a lot of time and it's incomplete with the blank pages."

"Perhaps we could try and help you with that," Fergie said. "Would you attempt to retrieve the Alpha Manuscript from the Vault and bring it here."

"I can't remove it without Headmaster Bentley noticing," Hopper said. "He's consumed with trying to figure out what's on the blank pages."

Elena took the Ransom Dossier from the table, handed it to Hopper, and said, "And there's this. My dad's dossier."

Elena watched Hopper's mouth drop open.

"I can't believe you have this. Your apartment was searched extensively after your parents...you know. But Imperator couldn't find it."

"So, he was in my apartment!" Elena exclaimed as she felt her face grow warm with anger. "How did you know my apartment was searched?"

"The Headmaster told me," Hopper said.

"Imperator stole my dad's things! Stuff from his office that was important to me," Elena said sternly.

"I'm not advocating what happened," Hopper said, as he thumbed through the pages of the dossier, seemingly unaware of the turmoil he'd caused her. "I'm saying that's what happened."

"Why didn't you tell me before they sent me home for the funeral?" asked Elena.

"This is amazing!" Hopper exclaimed, turning the book toward them and ignoring Elena's question entirely. "It's an ancient form of Akkadian writing. Truman Ransom is such a smart dude."

"Why? What does it mean?" Austin eagerly asked.

"Imperator wouldn't have any knowledge of this language, so even if he found the diary and was able to reveal the writing on the page, he wouldn't know how to read it. There're very few people on the earth who could read it properly."

"Do you know how to read it?" Austin asked.

"Of course I do, Dude," Hopper said. "This isn't just a pretty face. I'm one of the leading experts in crypt analysis and code breaking. I can't start today, but I'll make time in my schedule so I can come down here and start translating this stuff for you rugrats this semester."

"But what about the new security measures?" asked Declan. "Is it still safe for us to come out here?"

"Yep, set it up myself," Hopper said.

"Set what up?" Austin asked.

"The new surveillance system." Hopper was smiling in a way that Elena had never seen before. "There're certain areas of the forest that aren't being surveyed."

Hopper went to a pupil station and accessed an Optivision screen with a holographic map of the school and the surrounding areas.

"There's surveillance here, here, and here," he indicated with his finger, "But there's nothing anywhere near the Firebird Station and nobody knows any different. Headmaster Bentley trusts me, so I'm sure no one will ask questions."

Hopper turned and walked toward the door. "It's really good to have you dudes back. Place was boring without you."

A few days later, Elena and the Aves Company stood over a huge Optivision screen that was somehow immersed in the floor of Hopper's classroom.

"Last year we learned how dugouts were the oldest boats used in recorded history," said Hopper as the Optivision displayed a long wooden structure that had been carved out through the center. "During your Level 2 studies we'll learn the advancements that were made in the architecture of boats and how they became essential for trade between 1000 and 500 BC."

Then, Hopper went on to lecture about the ancient Greek, Roman, and Persian use of boats and their systems of navigation and trade. He asked the students about the psychology of survival and varying environmental conditions that these ancient civilizations would have endured.

Finally, Hopper said, "I've set up different workstations around the room where you can learn techniques for boat building, weaving various kinds of rope, and tying specific styles of knots. Off you go."

Elena started around the room with Austin by her side. The different pupil stations played holographic recordings of Hopper explaining about dock lines and rigging lines on boats. From another Optivision they learned about the different sails for the mast.

Then, they learned how to make rope out of several different objects, including twine, yarn, and hanging vine. At yet another station, they learned about whipping frayed ropes, fusing frayed rope, and using a knife to cut rigging quickly.

"Is anyone else worried that Hopper's teaching us how to make rope?" Pigg asked as they were leaving Hopper's class for the day. "It's like we're being warned that we'll actually have to use this skill."

"Yeah, like I was worried when they gave me a wetsuit as part of our uniform," Elena said. "Like I worried when we were told we'd have to wear it to Basic Training today."

After lunch, Elena, Fergie, and Abria went back to their room to get changed for Basic Training. Elena put on the bright orange aquatic suit with the word Firebird etched across the chest and winced as she looked in the mirror. They couldn't have picked a more unflattering orange color for a redhead.

"This is such a disaster," Elena grumbled.

"Really?" Abria had arrived looking beautiful, her hair braided down her back. "I think the suits are, like, totally cute."

"That's because you look good in everything." Elena gathered up her hair and pulled it into a frizzy bun.

"I think the suites are totally cute, too," Melly commented from across the room.

"Do you think Marshall will be able to tell which Unit is which in these suits?" Elena added sarcastically, as if Melly hadn't even spoken.

Abria laughed sweetly and said, "You're so silly. Do you see the word Firebird on the front of this suit? Well, each Unit has their name imprinted across the chest so that Marshall can tell the difference."

"I've never been around a pool before," Elena said nervously.

"I have," Melly chimed in an almost boastful way. "We swim all the time in Crowfield Plantation. There's really nothing to be worried about."

"Except for Marshall," Elena grumbled. "Who knows what he'll do when he gets us near water."

She didn't have to wait long to find out because minutes later she, Abria, and Fergie entered a large room equipped with four, fifty-meter pools. Elena stood at the edge of water where the Firebird Unit would swim and stared across the placid surface.

"For class today, we'll learn water safety and sea survival techniques," Marshall barked. "By the end of this class, if you cannot tread water for five minutes, then you will attend a remedial swim class until you can perform to my standards. Let's get started."

A Telecaster hologram stood before the Firebird Unit and began to give them instructions about water survival and safety. They practiced a dryland swimming routine and learned basic kicking techniques. Then, the Telecaster described the fundamentals of being on the water, the technique of pushing air through the mouth and holding one's breath, and the importance of using their survival training to keep from panicking in the water.

When this was finished, Elena barely had a chance to catch her breath before Marshall called, "On my whistle, everyone will jump into the pool."

His whistle sounded, but hardly anyone jumped. In fact, Elena was still watching the water and hadn't really registered the whistle. Then, she was shocked to see that Marshall had begun to walk the length of the pool and push students in along the way.

Elena decided quickly that she didn't want to be pushed in, so she jumped voluntarily. Her entire body completely revolted as the nearly freezing water pierced through her skin like a thousand stinging needles. She'd never been in real water before and the swimming Simulab in Atlanson certainly didn't qualify as experience for this situation. However, her survival instincts activated, and she struggled for the surface, gasping for breath. Then, she somehow managed to kick to the wall where she clung on for her life.

She turned back and noticed that Declan and Abria were hauling some of the students from their Unit to the side of the pool, including Pigg and Kidd. Austin was also above water, swimming alongside Melly who seemed to be fine. But Elena suddenly had a strange sensation. As she looked down into the water, she noticed that Fergie was at the bottom staring up at her.

"Bowen!" Elena hollered at Declan, feeling panicked. "Fergie's at the bottom."

Elena grabbed Pigg from Declan and drew him toward her. Then, Declan dove quickly down to the bottom of the pool and hauled Fergie to the surface. After that, the hard work began.

The Aves Company learned to push air out of their nose and mouth underwater. They learned how to paddle, float, and hold their breath under the water. Elena quickly decided that swimming was challenging work, a lot harder than running because at least when she ran, she could take an extra gulp of air whenever she needed one.

When they were finished with this round of instruction they were told to get out of the water and stand at the edge of the pool.

Elena's teeth were chattering uncontrollably as Marshall barked, "On my whistle you will jump into the pool and tread water for five minutes. This is our last routine for the day. I demand that you finish strong."

When the whistle sounded, Elena jumped in and kicked for the surface. She checked to make sure that the Firebirds were in the water safely and then she noticed a clock on the wall counting down from five minutes.

"I h-h-hate being in water," Pigg stuttered.

"It's not totally awful," Abria said, her head bobbing up and down slightly.

"The water is f-f-freezing!" Pigg exclaimed. "It's like the time that we were in Dante Down the Hatch and the waitress was taking too long bringing dessert, so I went into the kitchen and got locked in the freezer."

"How did you manage to get locked in the freezer?" Elena asked, feeling dumbfounded.

"Firebirds!" Austin said sharply. "We still have to tread water for four minutes. Best not to talk. Conserve some energy."

Elena tried not to watch the clock, but it was impossible not to stare at it because she felt so desperate. Each second felt like an hour. Her arms and legs felt heavy. Then, she noticed some boys and girls getting out of the other pools, dripping wet and shaking uncontrollably. She began to shout encouragement to the other Firebirds so that she didn't have to concentrate on how weak she was feeling.

After the last second ended, Elena watched Declan and Abria get out of the pool and then begin to help the others out as well. Declan gave Elena an arm up and smiled at her.

"You made it," he said. "I was a little worried at minute three, but you pulled through."

—

Elena felt strain in her chest and lungs as she replied, "I barely made it. I don't think I could have held on for another second."

Fortunately, everyone from the Firebird Unit had survived the full five minutes, even Fergie and Pigg who had looked the weakest during the session. Then, Marshall barked at them to get in formation and the Firebirds stood at attention with the other members of the Aves Company.

"That was truly disgraceful! For those of you that got out of the pool early you will be required to take remedial swim lessons until you improve. Dismissed!"

As Elena watched Marshall march toward the exit, she saw Pigg walk toward him. She wanted to stop him, but her brain was still fuzzy from the lesson.

"Sir, is the water heater broken?" Pigg managed to ask through chattering teeth.

"Excuse me?" Marshall had stopped walking and looked at Pigg as though he were a pest.

"Well, the pool water is f-f-freezing so I was wondering if the heater that warms the water is broken because I'd be happy to take a look and fix it...you know if..."

"Pigg, take ten laps around the pool for wasting my time." Marshall sighed and turned to leave as Pigg began to run.

Elena felt angry at Pigg for thinking that it would be fine for him to speak to Marshall about anything and she was angry that Marshall was so cruel all the time.

"Where did you learn to swim so well?" Austin asked, looking at Declan and Abria.

"Oh, swimming is a part of life back home," Declan said.

"If that's true, why are you afraid of the water, Fergie?" asked Austin.

"I had an unfortunate experience in the water when I was younger," Fergie replied, but she did not elaborate, and Elena was too tired to care.

"Should we wait for Pigg?" Abria asked.

Elena noticed that he'd barely started his second lap around the pool.

"I'll wait for him," Declan offered. "You can get changed for dinner."

As Elena and her friends turned toward the shower rooms, she noticed that Kidd was talking rather loudly to some of the students from the Raptor Unit.

"...That's because Pigg only has two speeds, slow and off," he said, and a few people laughed.

Elena looked at Pigg struggling to do laps. He looked similar enough to other boys with his black hair, brown eyes, and genetically altered physique, but it was true that Pigg didn't often act like other boys. He certainly wasn't as strong or as confident as he was designed to be. Still, Elena didn't see that gave Kidd any right to be mean to her friend.

She marched straight up to Kidd and demanded, "Why do you always have to be such a bully?"

"Always coming to his rescue," Kidd said menacingly. "Mind your own business, Freckles!"

"Pigg is my friend so that makes him my business. But I guess I shouldn't expect you to understand since *you* don't have *any* friends."

Kidd's face changed in an instant from a mocking smirk to solemn fury. "You know, *Freckles*, out of all the letters on that suit, those two stick out the most."

Elena followed his fingers and noticed that he was pointing to her chest where the Firebird block letters were monogramed across her suit.

Twelve minutes later, Elena watched herself punch Kidd in the face from the Optivision screen that was floating above Hannibal's desk.

"The Humanoid on duty in Medical said that you broke his nose," Hannibal said calmly.

"Oh, well that's something," Elena said without thinking. But then she noticed Hannibal raise his eyebrows in apparent disapproval. "I mean," she added quickly, "I feel really bad about that. Sorry."

"You do not need to apologize to me. However, there is a boy in the Medical Station that you might want to apologize to."

Elena thought his suggestion was borderline insane.

"You will be serving detention with Instructor Marshall for three weeks."

"That seems a high price to pay for defending myself against Wheeler's immature attempt to humiliate me," Elena replied. And then, hoping to embarrass Hannibal in some way, she added, "Where's the outrage over the fact that he was mocking my breasts?"

However, Hannibal didn't seem the least bit uncomfortable as he replied, "Miss Ransom, one day I hope you will learn that problems between Instructors and fellow students shouldn't be solved with violence."

▢ 7 ▢

Damsel in Distress

By the end of the following week, the Aves Company had only completed three swimming lessons, yet Marshall expected them to be experts. He barked orders and blew a whistle between giving directions. He complained often about their progress, even though Elena found it difficult to even comprehend everything he asked them to do.

Marshall had the students performing relay races way before Elena thought they were ready. He made them complete a two-hundred-meter kick, with and without a buoy. Then, they had to do another two hundred meters with paddles and swim fins.

In addition to this, they started partner pulls where the first swimmer pulls the second swimmer across the pool, but they also had to switch positions every twenty-five meters. And they had to rotate with every student in their Unit, so there were times that Elena had to partner with Kidd, which she found extremely annoying.

Eventually, the Company moved into multi-stroke swim training where they learned the sidestroke, breaststroke, and butterfly. They also began a strength training routine that required them to pull a twenty-pound weight up and down the length of the pool, and they had to repeat this for seven rounds.

The long hours in the water caused Elena uncontrollable skin irritants. She developed patches of raw skin in several places on her stomach and back where the wetsuit rubbed her the wrong way, her scalp had become dry, and she was sure that the feeling of nausea in her stomach was from ingesting too much pool water.

By the end of the second week in the pool, Elena wanted nothing more than to go to the Firebird Station to study in peace and quiet, but Austin was determined to help Pigg and Fergie get better and more relaxed in the water.

"You two are the best swimmers," he said one afternoon to Declan and Abria. "Would you give Pigg and Fergie extra lessons each evening after homework?"

After they agreed, Austin talked the rest of the Firebirds into nightly swim practice. Everyone in the Harrier Unit and a couple students from Falcon also started to attend the extra lessons because Declan and Abria were so good at teaching.

Unfortunately, Pigg and Fergie were making extremely slow progress. Elena had never seen anyone more scared of the water than Fergie. And while Pigg was in the pool he was like a fish out of water, constantly flapping his arms too wide and making large splashes instead of easy arm strokes.

After their seventh practice, Fergie still looked tense while diving for weights and every time Elena tried to help Pigg she felt like she wanted to pull all the hair out of her head.

"Pigg! You've got to stop splashing so much," Elena hollered, pulling him out of the water by the scruff of his neck. "If you would slow down and concentrate it wouldn't be so hard."

"I used to think swimming would be fun. You know, there's a big pool and lots of girls in bathing suits. But now, I hate it with a passion," Declan said, coming alongside Elena. "Here, I'll help Pigg. You go help Melly. She's been trying to ask me to sit with her at dinner tonight and it's getting annoying."

Elena smiled and swam off to the other side of the pool where Melly was standing in the shallow end with Austin, who was trying to teach her the best way to exchange places during partner pulls.

"We've been in the pool so much that my fingers are permanently pruned," Elena said as she approached them. "See?"

She held her fingers up and Austin smiled, but Melly did not.

"Haddock," Melly said girlishly. "You were about to show me that arm hold that you use for partner pulls."

"I thought you said you swim all the time in Crowfield Plantation," Elena grumbled.

"I do," she giggled sweetly, though Elena thought she saw irritation in her eyes. "But I am always eager to learn new skills."

Elena turned so that no one would see her eyes rolling and that's when she noticed Oscar Hunter arrive with some of the other students from the Raptor Unit.

From the beginning of their practices, Oscar had been coming, not to participate, but to tease the students from the other Units for being poor swimmers. The first couple times Elena had ignored him because Austin asked her specifically to leave Oscar alone, but the last time she pushed Oscar in the pool as they were leaving. Unfortunately, this action seemed to make Oscar more determined than ever to bother their practices.

Since Austin was busy with Melly, Elena immediately got out of the pool and made her way over to Oscar.

"Clearly you have nothing better to do than torment people, Hunter. Is it because you only hang out with Raptors and are you bored spending time with them?" she taunted.

"You know, you talk so much it's amazing you don't have better scores in Phonology," Oscar said earnestly.

"Yeah, I'm really better with my hands," Elena said coldly. "Care to try the mortal combat Simulab? Or are you too afraid that a girl might beat you?"

"I would be except you don't qualify as a girl."

"Wow, Hunter, that might be the most impressive retort I've ever heard," Elena said sarcastically. "How about you do everyone a favor and think up some creative insults and practice a bit before you start using them?"

"Ransom, I know you think you're better than everyone else because you spend time with all the losers in the Company and somehow that makes you a saint or something," Oscar said. "But you're not a saint so get over yourself."

"Hunter." Austin had arrived and stood deliberately between Elena and Oscar. "We're doing the swim lessons because our goal is to make Aves Company the best in Basic out of the three Companies. I would hope that *you* would appreciate the effort we're making, especially considering what a perfectionist you are about marks for the Raptor Unit. So, you and the rest of the Raptors are welcome to join us, but don't distract us."

If looks could kill Austin might have been dead on the spot. But instead of responding, Oscar Hunter and the rest of the Raptors simply turned and walked away.

"That guy is such a dimwit!" Elena shouted. "How can you stand being so polite to him?"

"I wasn't trying to be polite," said Austin. "I was trying to keep you out of detention."

◻

During the first day of the last week of the second month, Booker began to explain the ancient records from the Hebrew Bible and how that compared with writings from other cultures around the world during that same time in history.

"In the few hundred years during and after King Solomon had built the Holy Temple in Jerusalem there were other civilizations across the globe that were beginning to thrive, were at war, or had already established culture.

"For instance, in North America, the Woodland period was taking form as the Adena culture. The Assyrians, from ancient Mesopotamia, were at war and in 722 BC they destroyed the city of Samaria. The Greek city of Corinth became a unified state and began to construct large scale public buildings and monuments. The Zhou Dynasty was thriving in their established culture with intensive agriculture, which was directed by the government."

In Advanced Phonology, Niva expanded on Booker's class by making the Aves Company compare and contrast the different symbols and pictographs that represented the different civilizations' way of writing and speaking.

During class with Copernicus, Elena's head began to ache as the Instructor explained the use of mathematics during the Zhou Dynasty and how they'd used hydraulic engineering to aid in agricultural irrigation. And finally, Emerald expanded on the lesson from AstroPhysics by requiring the students to create their own version of the irrigation canal system, first using their Optivision screen to create a simulation of it, and then practically from materials he'd brought into the classroom.

Throughout the day, Elena noticed that Melly sat with a different group of boys in each class. She found herself wondering if Melly ever planned on being friends with girls. However, this reminded her of a time not too long ago that her dad was encouraging her to be friends with girls instead of only boys. Elena smiled a little at the thought, because now Abria and Fergie were two of her most treasured friends. Would Truman Ransom have been proud? She wanted to think so.

"Remember how Hopper said that each of the students in the Firebird Unit had been chosen specifically to be together?" Elena whispered as she leaned over the spot where Austin was creating an irrigation canal for Emerald.

"That's a random thought, but yeah," Austin replied, looking curious.

"What do you think it means that Kate Bagley died and has been replaced with Melly Linus? Do you think that Melly's family has an artifact? Or do you think that her family is now in charge of the artifact that the Bagley's were supposed to keep safe?"

"Those are good questions," Austin said. "I don't see how we'll ever know the answers unless we ask Mellly if she knows anything. But, if we ask her, that puts her in unnecessary danger. Let's keep it to ourselves for now."

However, as the evening ended and a new day dawned, Elena began to get more and more curious about why Melly was at school.

During Survival Strategy and Tactical Analysis, she noticed that Melly sat with Oscar Hunter and the other Raptors. Paying attention to Hopper as he explained how the kingdoms of Israel and Judah emerged and came into the Assyrian sphere of influence over a period of three hundred years was difficult as she watched Melly and Oscar whispering back and forth.

But then, Hopper captured Elena's attention with a riveting tale about how the ancient city of Rome was founded. She was interested to learn about the early years of the culture, which included the merging of local cities.

"The Etruscan civilization was a predecessor to the republic of Rome. Italian tribes like these would raid neighbouring areas in an attempt to gain territory and acquire valuable resources."

As Hopper spoke, the Optivision screen morphed into a boot-shaped land mass and filled in with colours that represented conquered territories.

"If they took prisoners, those people could be sacrificed on tombs as an honour to fallen leaders of the Etruscan society. Now, for the rest of class, we'll break into groups and rebuild their culture."

As Elena moved off with Austin and her other friends to the nearest available pupil station, she couldn't help but wonder which group Melly would choose. As Fergie opened an Optivision screen and the group began to trace the development of the Etruscan League, Elena saw Melly lean over to whisper in Oscar's ear.

"Lena," Austin whispered in her ear. "Stop thinking about Melly and pay attention to what we're doing."

Elena stuck her tongue out at him as Fergie began to read the lecture notes about how the government changed from a monarchy to an oligarchic republic. Then, Declan summarized the details of the military traditions in the Etruscan society.

After lunch, Elena likened Marshall's relentlessly cruel behaviour to that of the raiding Etruscan people. Swimming had already become a burden to Elena each week. But after Hopper's class, Marshall stretched the Aves Company to the limit with a new swimming drill.

"For class today we are doing a relay race," barked Marshall, after he'd made each Unit line up in swimming lanes along the edge of the pool. "You will swim fifty meters with your head above water. Then, you will swim back under water. When you've reached the edge, the next member of your Unit will dive into the water, swim fifty meters with head above water, and swim back under the water. You will continue to do this until each member of your Unit is finished.

"Then, as a Unit, you will move a twenty-pound weight down the length of the pool. You are each required to carry it at some point during this exercise, but there are no rules as to how far. You will be timed. You may have one minute to choose swimming order and make a plan for moving the weight."

As the Firebirds came together, Declan looked at Austin and asked, "What's the plan?"

"I think we should rotate a strong swimmer with a weak one," Austin replied. "Bowen, you go first, then Pigg will follow. After that Abria, Fergie, Ransom, Smiley, and Wheeler. Nelson and Castellow are fairly matched so you can go one after the other. Finally, Gamble and Linus, and I'll finish."

"But what about the twenty-pound weight?" Elena said. "How are we supposed to get it across the pool?"

"We'll set up a relay to carry it in short distances. Marshall said we each have to carry it, but he didn't specify how long. We'll stay partnered, one strong swimmer with a weaker one. After each pair has carried the weight as far as they can manage the next pair will dive in and follow up. We'll keep going that way until we reach the other side."

"I don't think I can do this," Pigg whined.

"Yes you can, Pigg," Austin said, laying a hand on his shoulder. "Besides, you don't have a choice. You have to go in voluntarily or Marshall will push you."

All the color drained from Pigg's face, but he squeaked out the word, "Okay."

A horn suddenly blasted. Elena looked up to see that the clock had started. Declan dove in immediately. He was the strongest swimmer on their team, so he made it down and back in no time. Pigg was not graceful in the water in the least. It was painfully slow for Elena to watch him struggle down the lane. He couldn't hold his breath long enough, so he kept surfacing for air the entire length back.

After Abria and Fergie, Elena dove into the pool and instantly felt the water press against her face and engulf her body. Her head broke the water and she started strong, throwing one arm over the other, cutting through the water and kicking her legs to help propel her forward as fast as she could. She knew that Frankie would be following her and that would slow the Firebirds down again, so she pushed faster.

Coming back down the lane was fairly easy. She'd practiced so much that Elena had become the best in their Unit for holding her breath under water.

As she neared the wall, Elena noticed a colossal round ball with handle grips sitting at the bottom of the pool. When she reached the edge, she watched Frankie dive over her head. She came up out of the water dripping wet and arms burning.

"Did you see the ball of doom at the bottom of our lane?" Elena asked Austin.

"It's huge!" Austin said. "I hadn't expected that."

"We may need to relay in teams of four," said Elena.

"Great idea!" Austin replied as they both turned back to see Frankie struggle to get down the lane.

Elena managed to chew off three fingernails before all the Firebirds finished the swimming relay.

"Okay," said Austin. "Time to try and get that ball across the pool. Bowen, Pigg, Abria, and Foreman are up first. Get it as far as you can, then we'll reassess."

Declan, Pigg, Abria, and Fergie dove in and Elena watched them kick to the bottom of the pool. For a moment, it looked like they couldn't move the weight, but then Elena saw them inching forward very slowly. Moments later, they each surfaced, sputtering and gasping for breath.

"It's a lot harder than it looks," said Declan. "I think it would be faster if we set up three teams of four at different points down the lane. It means some of us would have to tread water, but at least we wouldn't have to get in and out of the pool and swim back and forth."

"You heard him," said Austin to the Firebirds. "Everyone get in."

Elena watched Austin, Melly, Crosby, and Vivienne dive in and swim to the farthest side of their lane. Then, she dove with Olivia, Frankie, and Kidd and swam toward the center where they began to tread water and wait for the others to bring the ball down.

After a short time, Kidd grumbled, "This is taking too long. I'm going to try and help them come down the lane."

"What if you get too tired to help us later?" Elena said.

"Then Haddock or Gamble can swim over to let me and Bowen have a break," Kidd said, but he didn't wait for Elena's reply before he kicked off for the bottom of the pool.

Elena was irritated that he left without even asking if the others cared, but she was even more annoyed when the iron ball arrived suddenly below their treading position. Kidd had been right to help them because it made the whole process faster.

"I guess my plan worked," Kidd said nastily to Elena.

She couldn't think of anything to say back so she made a face at him.

"I think I can go again," said Declan.

"Me too," Kidd said.

Elena dove under the water with the rest of her team and kicked to the bottom of the pool. She closed her hand on one of the weight grip handles. Even with the five of them, it was a struggle to move the ball. Besides simply trying to lift the thing, Elena kept floating around uncontrollably.

At long last, Elena could see the last team treading above them. She kicked hard for the surface and gulped a huge breath.

"That thing is so hard to move!" Elena blurted.

"All of you are finished. Go relax!" Austin ordered.

Elena and the others obeyed. She climbed out of the pool and stood, watching and waiting for the last team to go. She didn't have much confidence that Austin would be able to move the weight the last part of the lane with only Melly, Crosby, and Vivienne helping him. And, after a few short minutes it appeared that Kidd didn't either.

"I'm going to help them!" he exclaimed. "There's no way that they'll ever get here."

Elena couldn't argue with him and since she noticed that the Raptor Unit already finished the exercise, she was anxious for the Firebirds to complete the task more quickly. Kidd dove headlong into the water while the others waited on the edge of the pool.

"I can't even, like, see them," Abria said. "Can you?"

"No," Elena said. "Either the ball is too deep or the ripples from the movement in the pool is making it too hard to tell what's going on."

"At least were not in last place," Declan said after taking a look around the room. "It looks like the Harriers and the Falcons are also having trouble. Too bad we didn't beat out the Raptors. Hunter looks smug."

Elena didn't want to look. She wanted the exercise to be over.

Soon enough, Austin's head broke the surface of the water. The Firebirds helped their friends out of the pool. Then, they scanned their Trademarks against the Optivision screen to stop the time, except that the clock didn't stop.

"Who didn't scan their Trademark?" Austin asked.

Elena looked around at each of them, feeling confused.

"Where's Melly?" Pigg asked.

Austin walked straight back to the edge of the pool.

"Do you think she's still in the water?" Declan asked Austin.

Austin looked at Declan and, without a word, they both jumped back into the pool. Elena waited with her toes dangling on the edge of the wall. She wished she could see farther into the water, but it was impossible to tell what was happening. Finally, Austin and Declan's heads appeared with Melly seemingly unconscious between them.

"Her foot was caught in one of the handles on the ball," Austin sputtered.

The Firebirds reached forward, pulling Melly's body out of the pool to the floor. Then, Marshall's booming voice sent prickles up and down Elena's spine as it echoed around the room.

"Stand back! Away from her!"

The Aves Company had only taken two classes about cardiopulmonary resuscitation, but that was at the beginning of the quarter, so Elena could barely remember the steps. However, Marshall knew exactly what he was doing. As he turned her head to the side, Elena saw water pour from Melly's mouth. Then, Marshall began to pump Melly's chest with his hands.

Seconds passed. Elena realized that she was holding her own breath in anticipation. She heard a small sniffle from Pigg, and Abria reached out and grabbed his hand. Then, Melly gave an explicit cough and sucked in a deep breath.

"Good!" Marshall said. "That's good. Deep breaths in through your nose and out through your mouth."

Elena had never seen Marshall look so calm and sincere. But then, the Drill Instructor turned toward them and shouted, "Firebirds, get cleaned up!"

As everyone turned to leave, Elena watched Marshall help Melly sit forward. Then, for one second, she saw a distinct glint in Melly's eye and a smirk on her lips.

But the moment was over as soon as Marshall began to ask Melly some questions about how she was feeling. She put on a frown and whimpered her answers. Elena turned, feeling a sick knot twist in her stomach as she wondered if Melly had faked a drowning to get attention.

◻

Melly's near drowning caused quite a riot of sympathy to be thrown at her during the week. First, there was the overly annoying retelling of the story in the Firebird girl's bedroom each evening, accompanied with words of concern from Abria, Olivia, and Vivienne. Elena learned quickly that her pillow couldn't block out Melly's voice. Also, several boys from the other Units started walking Melly to classes and began to help her carry meal trays. She even saw one boy filling in the answers of Melly's AstroPhysics homework one afternoon in the Media Lab.

Elena was tired of the extra attention that Melly was getting. In fact, it was making her downright angry, especially since she believed that Melly had faked the whole scene.

"I thought she was supposed to be an expert at swimming," Elena said to Austin one morning over breakfast. "She certainly bragged enough about it."

"Just because a person is a good swimmer doesn't mean they can't make a mistake that could cost them their life," Austin pointed out.

Elena didn't want to hear excuses.

By the end of the week, Elena was completely worn out from classes and swimming and Melly's sob story about drowning that she felt like she might explode.

She was in the Media Lab doing homework with Austin and Pigg but was having an extremely hard time concentrating on the history lab for Booker because Melly was off in the corner with a group of boys that were eager to talk to her. Finally, she pushed away from the pupil station and rubbed her eyes tiredly.

"I can't do this anymore. I'm going to the Station to see how the scans are coming from the ceiling in dad's library," Elena said.

"Elena, Fergie said it will take weeks before the program can compare and categorized the entries in the dossiers with what's in your dad's ceiling," Pigg said. "Can't you give it a rest for a little while longer?"

"My parents are dead, Pigg!" Elena snapped irrationally. "So, I can't give it a rest. Besides, I haven't been down to the Station in forever because I've been trying to help you learn to swim. We all know how much time that's been taking."

Pigg's face turned pink as Austin put a hand on Elena's shoulder and said, "I could use a break too. Let's go see if we can get on one of the new Simulabs."

Elena let Austin steer her toward a Grimvator, leaving Pigg behind in the Media Room.

"Pigg doesn't understand how important the info is to me," Elena blurted after the Grimvator doors slid shut.

"You shouldn't expect him to," Austin interrupted.

"What?" Elena demanded.

"His parents are alive and well at home," Austin said. "He's never felt loss like you, so why should you expect him to have the same passion about your dad's ceiling?"

"Because he's my friend," Elena said. "He should try to be empathetic or sympathetic or something like that. Just like I always defend him when Wheeler picks on him."

"He's not strong like you," Austin pointed out. "Plus, I seem to remember a certain brainiack who came with us to New York and Washington because he wanted to help."

"He didn't want to come," Elena grumbled. "I threatened him with torture."

"What else is bothering you?"

Elena wanted to talk about the odd feelings she was beginning to have about Melly, but instead she replied, "Nothing."

As the Grimvator doors slid open on the Simulab floor, Elena pulled her red curls back into a clasp. Abria was off to one side of the room in the kickboxing Simulab with a boy from the Harrier Unit and Declan was on the opposite side of the room in a fencing simulation with a boy from the Falcon Unit.

"How about water polo?" Austin suggested.

"Water polo is stupid," Elena grumbled.

"Oh, I know," Austin said. "Stratego is supposed to be intellectually stimulating. Plus, its Hunter's favorite. Whadd'ya say we beat his top score?"

Elena shrugged and said, "Sure."

Austin led her over to a simulation floor where they each pulled on a Transmitter suit. A moment later, Elena arrived on a grid of squares with Austin beside her.

He pulled up an Optivision and said, "Our object is to capture the opposing team's flag by strategically moving our game pieces across the board and defeat their pieces."

"What game pieces?" Elena asked, but it was as if the game understood her because the pieces suddenly appeared on the board.

The characters were as tall as grown men and were equipped with weapons of every kind, so they were a little intimidating.

"We've got battering rams, trebuchets, fortified towers, an army of three thousand men on horseback with swords and seven thousand on foot with spears. There's one king, one queen, a commanding general, and a flagged tower," Austin said. "So, do you want to play together or against one another?"

"Let's go together," Elena said. "How do we play?"

"On our turn we move our pieces up and down the board, though we won't be able to see what the enemy is doing. When we land on a square that's occupied by the enemy we'll compare the values of the pieces. The higher ranked piece wins the square." Austin turned toward her. "Ready to get started?"

"Yep."

Elena and Austin worked together selecting the best position for each of their pieces on the board. When they were finished, Austin selected the start button from the Optivision screen and it disappeared.

Then, Elena watched the enemy line move one space forward.

"Our turn," Austin said.

Elena and Austin started with their battering ram, moving it forward across the board. And so began an hour-long game in which they advanced their pieces, lost some but gained some from the enemy.

They rarely disagreed about when to move their pieces and only once did it take them longer than a minute to decide. In the end, they won the enemy flag and qualified for the top score over any of the other students that had played the game before them, including Oscar Hunter.

When Elena and Austin came out of the simulation, Declan said, "Wow! Really good match. I bet Hunter will want a rematch with one or both of you later. That's his favorite Simulab and you beat his high score."

"I think that might be *my* new favorite Simulab," Elena said. "I guess Hunter will have to pick a new one."

"Care for a refreshment?" asked Austin

"Yes, please," Elena said as she walked with him and Declan over to the refreshment bar. "Anything but that one that tastes like pineapple."

Elena turned and looked around the room and that's when she noticed Melly for the first time. She had a crowd of boys around her waiting for turns at the shooting gallery. Elena thought it was embarrassing the way she kept missing the targets so the boys could teach her how to aim and shoot.

"Linus seems nice," Declan said after he caught Elena staring.

"Compared to what?" Elena asked, accepting a bottle of green color fluid from Austin.

"Give it a rest," Austin said, but he was laughing. "Remember how long it took you to like having Declan, Abria, and Fergie around last year? And now, they're good friends of ours."

"Yeah, but she's extra annoying. I already told you that I think she faked the whole drowning thing."

"She didn't fake the drowning," Austin said. "Why would anyone do such a thing?"

"She did it because she's silly about boys and she wanted the extra attention," she grumbled.

"Abria is silly about boys, but you are friends with her," Declan pointed out.

"You say that like *I* had a choice," Elena said, while Austin and Declan chuckled.

❑ 8 ❑

Ransom Secrets

During the first week of the third month, after Instructor Booker's class, Elena sat in Phonology feeling frustrated with the new symbols that Niva expected them to learn. They'd already studied the transition of the Aramean language into Aramaic and the development of a new Greek alphabet. But today, they were expected to review how the Sanskrit and Chinese literature thrived during the Iron Age.

Elena had hoped that they would study something that would help them interpret the symbols in the Ransom Dossier and on the Catalan Atlas, but nothing she'd seen so far looked like anything on the artifacts they'd collected.

"The use of alphabetic characters is the principal feature that distinguishes the Iron Age from the preceding ages," Instructor Niva told the class. "The development of this type of written language enabled literature to flourish and historical record to evolve into a similar pattern of data that we use today."

After her lecture, Instructor Niva broke them into groups and Elena got stuck with Melly Linus, Olivia Nelson, and Vivienne Castellow.

Then, Niva explained that each group would need to read the key and interpret a story that had been written in ancient Chinese.

"I've already learned Chinese," Melly said haughtily after Niva gave them permission to begin. "One of the benefits of living in Crowfield Plantation is the option for home school, which provides a better quality education."

"Is that why you weren't at Grimsby last year?" Olivia asked.

"Yes. If your parents are important enough, they can have a tutor brought in," Melly said in a singsong voice. "Both my parents are government officials and everyone loves them."

Elena wanted to point out that her parents were blindly working for Imperator and that was nothing to be proud of, but she held her tongue.

"Then, why are you at Grimsby?" asked Olivia.

"My parents thought it would be good for me to socialize with my peers and there was an open spot, so here I am."

"It's too bad they couldn't keep you home," Elena said, and she saw Olivia stifle a smile behind her hands as Melly glowered at her.

"Ladies, please," Vivienne said seriously. "We've got to interpret these symbols. I barely understood half of what Niva said, so I'd like to get as much done as possible while we're together because we have swim lessons again tonight."

Vivienne made a good point, so Elena bent over her work feeling lost and confused. Melly did not prove to be a good tutor because, though she understood the text perfectly, she could not explain clearly how to interpret the symbols. Therefore, after class, Elena gobbled down her lunch and then hurried to the Media Lab with Fergie to get some help on their Phonology homework before their next class with Instructor Copernicus.

After AstroPhysics, Elena gathered with the other Firebirds and the Harrier Unit for their Social Science lesson in an area of campus that she'd never seen before. Instead of the hydroponic farm, Elena arrived at an outdoor paddock that also had a red barn attached to it. She stood along the fence with her other classmates.

Instructor Emerald's greasy black hair looked even more slick than usual as he said, "During the Iron Age, advances were made in agriculture, horticulture, and husbandry, which incidentally created a framework for supply and demand in a semi-modern culture. The Mediterranean suddenly desired exotic goods like furs, amber, slaves…"

At the word *slaves*, Elena felt a prickle run up her spine. As Emerald chattered on about fortified settlements in the 800's, farming communities, manufactured goods for trade, and domesticating animals, Elena's thoughts drifted to the fact that she was living in captivity.

She examined the Trademark that had been a part of her body for as long as she could remember. The code that was branded into her wrist by Imperator ensured that he knew where she was during every moment of her life. But not only her. Every student in her class, every man, every woman, every Humanoid was marked to serve at Imperator's will.

"So, to prove that we have as much skill as the ancient Europeans, we're going to raise domesticated sheep and goats this quarter," Instructor Emerald said, interrupting her thoughts.

Elena heard a few people groan, but Abria squealed with delight as the barn doors opened behind Emerald and a herd of goats and sheep trotted out into the fenced yard.

"Come inside the fence," Emerald beckoned the class. "Each of you can choose one animal and they will be your responsibility for the remainder of the quarter."

Abria and a few of the other girls and boys ran forward at once, but most of the class moved slowly into the paddock, looking at the animals as though they may bite.

"Aren't they cute?" Abria laughed as one of the sheep began to lick her knees.

Elena held her nose. "You'd think with all our technology they'd have found a way to make them smell better."

"Look at Pigg," Declan said, and Elena saw that he'd already chosen a small, gray goat. "What are the chances that Pigg will kill and eat that goat by the end of the week?"

Elena laughed. "I'm gonna say pretty high."

◻

At the end of the week, Elena sat with Fergie in the Research & Development room at the Firebird Station. It was absolutely silent, and Elena was glad. They'd been so busy lately that she was thankful for some time to get her bearings.

While Elena tried to catch up on her Phonology homework, Fergie was using a dropper to take samples of the fluid from the Amulet. Then, she deposited each of the samples into one of the three clear, plastic dishes that were sitting on the table.

Elena was beginning to write out her last line of Chinese characters when she heard the Station door open.

"Ugh," Elena grumbled. "I hope that's not Pigg or Abria. They're both so loud that I..." But she stopped suddenly because she heard a thumping of feet through the main room and down the hall.

Then, Pigg appeared in the doorway, but he was running so quickly that he slid on the floor and lost his balance. He fell face first into the pupil station where Fergie was working. The stand that the Amulet was resting on tipped over and some of the fluid spilled messily onto one of the blank pages inside the Ransom Dossier.

"Geez, Pigg!" Elena screamed. "You spilled the Amulet fluid! It's not like we can get more of that."

She begrudgingly got up from her chair to help him up off the floor. He already had a small bruise coming in on his cheek from where he hit the table.

"Why were you running so fast, anyway?"

"Austin said I needed to come get you right away."

"Look!" Fergie breathed.

Elena noticed that she was pointing to the Ransom Dossier. She looked down and saw that the spilled ink was beginning to fill the pages, making lines and curves that were forming letters and symbols. Her mouth fell open in complete astonishment.

Fergie pulled the book toward her and, taking a small brush from her assessment kit, began to rub more of the Amulet fluid on the diary page. Eventually, the entire page was moist and filled in with writing.

"Listen to this entry," said Fergie. *"After the President of the United States joined the Oligarki he helped the efforts being made to reduce the world's population. He used the United States treasury to finance the creation of the Kearney Virus. Two years after his election, he levied charges and had false documents created for every person elected to Congress and Senate. He branded everyone that held in a place of authority as a traitor and executed them."*

"Filthy traitor!" Elena said. "What happened to him?"

"He was killed in an explosion at the White House," Fergie responded.

"Where does it say that?" questioned Elena, leaning over the book.

"The book does not mention that specifically. However, I know because my dad was with him when he died."

"Your dad was with him?" Elena said quizzically. "How? Why?"

"My dad worked for him directly," Fergie replied. "They were very good friends, though my dad did not know that the President was working for Imperator."

Elena sat down, feeling heavy hearted. The President had killed the citizens of the country he'd sworn to protect. "It's a good thing he died."

"It is regrettable that he died. The Renegades could have used him for information," Fergie flipped to another blank page in the diary and began to paint the Amulet fluid on it.

"Pigg, I need you to go back and get Austin and the others," Elena said.

"But Austin said I should come get you…" Pigg started, but Elena interrupted him.

"This is really important, Pigg. I need you to go get everyone right away, including Hopper."

Pigg looked like he wanted to say something else, but instead he turned obediently and left the room.

As the next blank page of the diary began to fill in, Fergie began to stare at the Kairos around Elena's neck.

"You said your dad gave you that necklace before he died and that it once belonged to your grandmother, I believe."

Elena nodded. "Yeah, that's right. Why?"

"Not to impugn your dad, but I do not believe the Kairos could have belonged to your grandmother."

"Why's that?"

"Because a schematic of the Kairos is on this page in your dad's dossier."

Fergie turned the book so Elena could see. "It details how the necklace was manufactured. From this entry we can logically deduce that the Renegades formed the Kairos, perhaps in order to reveal the Amulet in the book room in New York. I believe it is safe to also assume that the Kairos will reveal a multitude of secrets in due time."

"Dudes, I was in the middle of my afternoon siesta." Hopper arrived looking irritated. Pigg, Austin, Declan and Abria were also with him. "So, this better be important."

"We have discovered that the fluid from the Amulet reveals the writing on the blank pages of the Ransom Dossier," Fergie stated formally.

Everyone crowded around the dossier, hoping to get a look.

"Hopper, at this point, we require the physical Alpha Manuscript. We need to determine if this fluid will also work on those blank pages," Fergie said.

"I told you already that I can't remove it from the room without Headmaster Bentley noticing."

"But, if I could get a replica, would you replace it with the real one?"

Hopper looked as stunned as Elena felt. She and the Firebirds shared some confused looks as he said, "Where would you possibly get a replica?"

"My parents would create one, of course," Fergie said. "But I believe you knew that already."

Hopper looked frustrated. "I could get in so much trouble for helping you, dudes. The Headmaster already busted me when I told him that I didn't know that you were going outside the dome. The work I do is secret for a reason and helping you complicates things."

"You owe me and Austin for telling us to go to New York," Elena said. "And you owe my dad."

Hopper paced up and down the room a few times and then turned to Fergie and said, "Fine. Have your parents create a replica and I'll make the switch for you. Now, I've got to get back. Stay out of trouble, dudes."

After Hopper left, Declan said, "I really hope we don't get him in too much trouble. He's been good to us."

"I need to go visit my parents," said Fergie.

"To get the replica dossier?" Austin asked.

"Yes, but also because of this." Fergie handed the Ransom Dossier to him, and they listened as he read the page about the President's betrayal aloud.

"My parents were inside the White House when it was bombed by Imperator twelve years ago," Fergie said.

"That sounds terrifying," squeaked Pigg.

"I believe that they will be able to give us more information about this event and possibly about the artifacts that are on the list," Fergie said.

"When do you want to go?" Austin asked.

"During first quarter break."

"Oh-wa," Abria said suddenly. She'd been silent up to this point, but this idea obviously struck a nerve. "I wanted to go to Harleston Village."

"By all means, go to the village," Fergie said. "But I do feel that I need to go home."

"I'm going with her," Elena declared.

"Me too," said Austin.

"Fine, I'll go with you too," Abria sighed. "But only if you promise that you'll come with me to Harleston Village during our next break."

▭

Near the end of the third month, Grimsby's campus simulated skyline was bright blue with patches of fluffy white clouds. However, this beauty wasn't enjoyed by any of the Level 2 students because they were standing outside for Basic, waiting for Marshall to give them orders.

After roll call, the Drill Instructor stepped to the front of the class and barked, "Today we're running the Gauntlet. A Lieutenant for each Unit will be chosen at random."

Marshall turned toward the Optivision screen that was hovering in midair beside him, and Elena watched several student faces flashing across the hologram until it landed on her face.

"Elena Ransom will be the Lieutenant for the Firebird Unit."

A few of her friends smiled, including Austin, but Kidd looked miserable. Elena felt confident leading her Unit through the Gauntlet because she'd been through it at least a dozen times in her first year. Granted, she'd never led the Firebirds through it, but by now they were familiar enough with the course that she was sure they could finish in record time. And, since they hadn't been instructed to wear their aquatic suits to class, she felt relieved that she wouldn't have to try and get Pigg or Fergie through any kind of water challenge.

When the time came, each member of the Firebird Unit was given a tactical vest and began the one-mile trek across the grounds to the obstacle course. They'd walked this road so often during their Level 1 studies that Elena knew they'd get there in twelve minutes flat and that they'd be on the other side of the Gauntlet forty minutes after that.

However, when they arrived at the course, Elena peered over the ramparts and her breath caught in her chest. The Gauntlet looked nothing like it had in her first year of school. The rappelling towers, rope swing, and mud pit were gone and an entirely new set of obstacles covered the training floor in a confusing mess of chrome.

In addition, the entire course was soaking in pools of water, water slides, and waterfalls, which meant they would be swimming. Elena thought for a moment about puking, but then remembered that she was in charge and had to prove herself.

Elena wished there was time for Abria to braid back her hair, but she gathered it into a messy bun as she called the Firebirds into a group.

"You think they could have told us to wear aquatic suits instead of combat uniforms," Declan said. "The boots are going to make swimming tough."

"Not to mention these tactical vests," Elena said, pulling hers off. "Everyone check your vests to see what you have."

As the Firebirds opened their packs, Elena began to give out instructions.

"We should pair up again, so keep your same partner as you've had in other swim lessons."

"Look, swimming slippers," Austin said, pulling two mesh-toned shoes from the side pocket of his vest.

Elena felt relief wash over her. "Does everyone have slippers?"

Everyone nodded and murmured.

"Great. Leave your boots here and put on the slippers."

Elena also pulled a bottle of sun protection cream, a swim mask, tweezers, paramedic scissors, a cold compress, vinyl gloves, a bottle of refresh tear eye drops, a rescue breathing mask, a whistle, and a life hook from her waterproof pack.

"Let's try to condense some of our supplies. For instance, I don't think we'll need twelve bottles of sunscreen, so let one person carry a bottle and we'll leave the others here. Got it?"

"Can we get a move on?" Kidd asked rudely. "We're wasting time."

"We've been standing here maybe two minutes," Elena replied.

"One minute and forty-seven seconds to be precise," Fergie added.

"We need to take some extra time given our surroundings. We have some weakness in the swimming area," Elena said.

Kidd made a noise between a snort and a sigh.

"It's hard for you to take instructions from a girl, isn't it?" Elena said.

"Of course it's hard," Kidd replied, giving her a nasty look.

"Well, the good news is that I'm allowed to order you to sit this one out. Then, you can take a fail for the day," said Elena confidently.

"How's that good news?"

Elena laughed sarcastically. "Oh, I meant to say that it was good news for me."

She turned from him and said, "Firebirds, remember to try and conserve energy where possible. There's no point to get tired in the first pool because there are five others."

Elena felt a little nudge in her back and turned to see Austin looking concerned.

"Look at Fergie," he whispered.

Elena's eyes wandered through her classmates to Fergie's face. She was standing at the edge of the platform staring at the slide that dropped straight into a pool of water. Elena had never seen her look so terrified.

She approached Fergie quickly and asked, "Are you okay?"

It seemed to take Fergie a moment, but finally she tore her gaze from the course and locked Elena's eyes.

"When the time comes, you will have to push me."

"No, I'm sure you'll do fine," Elena said, trying to sound more confident than she felt.

"Seriously, Elena," Fergie said forcefully. "Declan will need to push me."

Elena wrapped an arm around Fergie's shoulder and directed her back to their group.

"Okay, no problem."

Elena quickly explained Fergie's issue to Declan as the Firebirds came to three metal tube slides that appeared to drop thirty feet to a pool of water.

"Four per slide," Elena shouted at her comrades.

Then, she climbed into the first tube and let go. The fall through the almost vertical black tunnel was frightening. Elena hit the water hard on her left side, but then was immediately tilted back off balance. She barely had a moment to recover when Melly dropped into the water beside her. Then, Pigg came out of the slide flailing his arms and legs and splashed into the water beside her.

As Pigg's head broke the water, he screamed, "Elena!"

"It's alright, Pigg," she said loudly. "The vest has a floatation device."

As Austin splashed down, Elena noticed that Melly's nose was bleeding and she cried, "Pigg kicked me in the nose!"

Elena resisted the urge to laugh as Austin helped Melly. Then, she escorted Pigg across the water to the far side of the pool where a rope ladder net was growing out of the water like a tree. Two at a time, they helped each other climb the ladder to a platform where they fell to their knees gasping for breath.

"Your nose is fine," Austin told Melly as he examined it. He pulled the cold compress out of his waterproof pack and handed it to her. "Apply some pressure."

While Melly nursed her wound, Elena made sure that the Firebirds had arrived safely. Then, she turned to Fergie and whispered, "Are you okay to keep going?"

Although Fergie looked a little queasy, she said, "Yes, I am perfectly fine."

Elena squeezed her on the shoulder and then turned her attention to their next challenge; three, one-foot-wide beams above a deep pool below.

"It looks like we need to cross on the beams," Elena told the others. "At least it will be quicker than us trying to swim. Come on, let's see if we can make up some time."

Elena started off on the beam in the middle while Austin and Declan took the right and left sides. She felt her beam shake a little as Pigg followed behind her.

"You doing okay, Pigg?" Elena called over her shoulder.

"I'm fine," Pigg said, though he sounded terrified.

Then, suddenly, Elena felt pressure around her waist as Pigg crashed into her, sending them both falling to the beam. She held on as tight as she could, but she could feel that she was being pulled down as Pigg began to slip from the beam. A moment later, she was barely hanging on with both arms while Pigg gripped her around the waist screaming for help.

"Geez, Pigg! You're so thin that I never realized how heavy you are!"

Elena could feel her grip beginning to slip and screamed, "I can't hold him!"

She felt the beam shake again and then noticed that Declan was there, pulling at her arms. A moment later, Austin grabbed her other arm and also Pigg's and she began to feel the weight subside from her waist. Somehow, they managed to get across the rest of the beam without falling in the water. But the course was far from over.

Next, Elena saw three metal tubes suspended in midair above another pool of water. The tubes were not connected in any way and appeared quite far apart.

"Bowen, you go first," Elena ordered Declan.

As soon as Declan climbed into the first barrel it began to swivel uncontrollably. Austin lunged forward and caught the barrel, trying to hold it in place.

"Great idea!" Elena praised. "Bowen, see if you can climb through to the third barrel and hold it steady."

Elena watched Declan move as quickly as he could.

"Austin, you go next and try to hold the second and third barrel together the best you can," said Elena. "Wheeler, hold one and two together. Smiley, you stay here and hold this barrel so we can send everyone else through."

Long, hard work lingered before them. Getting everyone into position and then helping each Firebird get up into the first barrel was not a simple task. Elena decided to go last this time and it was painful for her to watch the slow progression of students through the barrels.

When it was finally her turn, she was thankful they'd taken things slow, for even though the barrels were being held steady, they shook violently anytime a person climbed through them. When she reached the end, she watched Frankie, Kidd, and Austin stumble out of the barrels feeling happy that no one had fallen through to the water below.

Elena didn't think she had the strength to go on, but she had a Unit to lead so she took a deep breath and gawked at the twenty-foot wall standing before them.

"Anyone else totally exhausted?" Elena asked.

Everyone except Kidd raised hands.

"Thank you, Wheeler, for volunteering to go up the rope first," Elena said. "When you reach the top, I'd like you to support each person as they climb the rope after you."

Kidd scowled at her, but he obeyed her orders and hurried up the twenty-foot wall. Then, the Firebirds took turns climbing the rope and helping to support the weight of the next person that needed to climb. Elena had hoped this climbing meant the end of their exam, but once she reached the top and peered over the side, she realized they were going to rappel down a waterfall and swim through yet another pool before they could get to yet another wall of three-foot-high steps.

Rappelling through the waterfall was dangerously slick. Elena's hands were rubbed almost raw. In fact, she was so uncomfortable on the rope that she let go and dove headlong into the water. She and the Firebirds swam one hundred meters across the pool and helped each other onto the platform on the other side.

Elena was gasping for breath again as she started up the three-foot high stepping walls, but she wasn't willing to give up. She pressed forward, pursuing the dozen steps on her hands and knees, feeling desperate in every move that she made. She could hear the groans of the students on every side of her, but still they ascended the obstacle.

As Elena groped her way to the very top of the stepping-stones, she saw an Optivision clock in the distance counting down the Firebirds' last forty-seven seconds. She took off running for it, scared to breath or even think. With her last few steps, Elena pulled her arm from her sleeve and skidded into the Optivision screen, scanning her Trademark as she went. Then, she fell to the ground, gasping for breath.

"That. Was. Terrible."

"But at least we finished under the, like, time limit," said Abria, after sinking to the ground beside her.

"You did great!" Austin praised as he pulled off his tactical vest.

"So, do you think they sit down in a room and decide what's the most awful thing they can do to us and then make it happen?" Declan asked.

"With Marshall in charge, I wouldn't doubt it," Elena said bitterly.

The Galilee Province

The day after the first quarter exam ended, Elena stood in silence with Austin in the Firebird courtyard as they waited for their friends. She tried to focus on how well she'd done in the exam so that she wouldn't worry about the journey she'd take later that day.

The exam had taken place inside a classroom she'd never been in before. The room had been filled with hundreds of Optivision screens hovering in the air. Elena had found the screen that displayed her face and was startled after she'd scanned her trademark and Instructor Booker's face appeared suddenly.

"During the exam, you will be given a certain point of time in history," Booker had said. "This will be different from the other students in this exam. You will need to ascertain the time period, answer the historical analysis questions and use the appropriate social science, whether that is agriculture, husbandry, or manufacturing. You will be required to give your answers in the native language of the time. The test is not time sensitive, so make sure to move at your own pace through the simulation."

Then, the lights around her station dimmed and the sound from the other students in the room faded away. Elena felt that she'd been completely encased in a cocoon of technology. Then, the screen filled with the first section of her questioning, written in Akkadian. Through the maze of strange letters, she was finally able to decipher one name, Nebuchadnezzar. Once she'd translated it into English she was required to go back and translate his name into Hebrew, Greek, and Aramaic.

After this was finished, the rest of the test began to come into focus. Elena recognized the dates of Nebuchadnezzar's rule from 604 to 562 B.C. She answered questions about his lineage and how he was the oldest son of Nabopolassar who destroyed Nineveh and delivered Babylon from three centuries of reliance on Assyria.

She eased through the section about Nebuchadnezzar's marriage to Amytis of Media, which he arranged to ensure peace with the king of Median. And Elena answered questions about the significance of him capturing Jerusalem.

Then, the test morphed into a screen featuring the ancient planetary theory and she answered questions about astrologers, arithmetical predictions, cosmology, and astronomy. After that she wrote paragraphs describing land cultivation and trade. Finally, she plotted Nebuchadnezzar's advance against Zedekiah, the last King of Judah.

After an eternity of giving answers, reviewing her selections, and making any final changes or additions, Elena submitted her test and the cocoon of technology melted away. She couldn't remember a more bizarre testing system in her life.

However, as much as she wanted to escape school, she wasn't emotionally prepared for what they were doing over first quarter break. Fergie had arranged for them to stay with her parents in the Galilee Province for the weekend.

Elena was now spending the last few moments before they left digging through her carrier bag to make sure she'd packed deodorant and toothpaste, trying to ignore the fact that Austin was staring at her. She didn't want him to ask the questions that she knew he would ask.

"Are you nervous?"

"About going to meet Fergie's parents?" Elena tried to say innocently. "Why should that make me nervous?"

"I mean are you nervous about asking them the questions we need to ask?"

Elena was nervous. For her, it was going to be very hard to look an adult in the face and ask how they were involved with the President of the United States, what they knew about Imperator, and if they knew the truth about her parents' death, but she didn't see any point in admitting it.

"No," Elena lied. "I'm not nervous."

"I am," Austin earnestly stated. "What if they tell us it's none of our business?"

"Ok. Fine!" Elena sighed and shrugged. "I'm nervous. Can we not talk about it? Talking makes it worse."

Fortunately for Elena, the door opened, and Fergie and Abria appeared.

"Sorry it took so long," Abria said cheerfully. "I insisted that Fergie let me do her hair."

Abria had somehow managed to twist Fergie's short black hair into a fancy braid.

"It looks really nice," Elena said.

Fergie opened her mouth to speak, but Abria said airily, "Thank you, I have a gift. Where are Pigg and Declan?"

"Oh, Pigg said he was grabbing something to eat from the commissary and Declan said he had something to do really quick," Austin said. "Oh look, here they are..."

Declan and Pigg arrived with carrier bags slung over their shoulders.

"We ready to go?" Declan asked.

Elena and her friends tromped across the yard toward the Grimsby Channel and joined a group of other students that were also headed off campus to their homes.

"I still can't believe how intense that exam was," Abria said, though she'd already talked about it at length while Elena was trying to fall asleep the previous night. "All those questions about the Arameans almost killed me. I saw Melly coming out of the test and she said she had 776 BC in Greece and

I'm totally, like, jealous. I would have loved to answer questions about the beginning of the Olympic games. Well, whatever," she flipped her blonde hair out of her blue eyes, "At least we're going home today!"

As Elena dropped into a window seat on the train, she noticed that it simulated miles of white sand beaches. Abria and Declan chatted merrily about the things they couldn't wait to show Elena and her fellow Firebirds. Fergie listened quietly while Pigg asked questions about customary ways to prepare food in the Galilee Province.

An hour later the Grimsby Channel rose out of the ground and over an extravagantly lush and vibrant city. Instead of docking at a station, the train continued along a rail line that was built on the outskirts of the town. Tree topped mountains encircled the city, which did not have a single skyscraper, but tall buildings that were adorned with rotund roofs that were painted different colors of the rainbow. The streets and buildings were embellished with greenery and vibrant florals. In the distance, Elena could see aerocrafts flying through the sky on the opposite side of the city in the same direction the train was headed.

"Is all the transportation above ground?" Elena asked Abria.

"Yep. People live in the surrounding mountains and fly to work, but everyone docks their hovercrafts in the terminal. Look, there it is."

Elena looked out the window and saw a landing strip surrounded by granite cliffs that were growing with foliage and flowing with waterfalls. In the distance, she could see a row of aerocrafts easing through the skyway. Then, she watched several of them land on a slow-moving sidewalk. Men, women, and children stepped from their vehicles and into one of the many glass elevators that were riding up and down the side of the cliffs.

The Grimsby Channel finally eased into a docking station and came to a stop. As she stepped from the train, Elena could hear the subtle hum of aerocrafts landing nearby. Abria and Declan led them through the terminal to a glass elevator and it carried them up the side of the cliff with cascades of water falling around them.

As they stepped onto street level, Pigg breathed, "Ohhhh." He stopped walking and closed his eyes in reverence. "Rosemary. Grape. Olive oil. Basil. This must be the yummiest smelling place on earth!"

Elena rolled her eyes and then followed Declan and Abria down a long boulevard that led to a vast stone courtyard with a moat of sparkling water and an orchard of olive trees. Another avenue contained an expansive columned courtyard with bubbling fountains, vibrant gardens with multicolored flowers, and stone gazebos.

The clothes people wore were simple and light, flowing and vibrant. Elena began to feel that people in Atlanson would look too stiff and formal if they wore their fashions in the Galilee Province. Also, everyone here moved slowly, taking time to enjoy the day; there was no rushing from place to place as there was in Atlanson.

Fergie led them to a beautiful, expensive-looking building with a forest green rotund roof. The *Destro Electron System* logo was featured on the front. They entered a lobby that was filled with Humanoids, their hair cropped short and the letters D.E.S. tattooed on the backs of their necks.

Elena had an immediate flashback to their trip to Washington D.C. Walking through a room filled with Humanoids was certainly intimidating now that she knew they would attack humans. She quickly wiped a little sweat that had formed on the edge of her brow.

"Fergie, I thought you were taking us to your house," said Austin.

"My home is located within the building," Fergie replied. "My parents live here full time."

"They live and work in the same place? That's interesting..." Elena said, though she thought a more appropriate word to use would have been *odd*.

Elena followed Fergie onto an elevator and the Firebirds rode it to the top floor. They stepped off into a circular vestibule that reminded her a lot of Grimsby and she watched Fergie scan her Trademark into a front door. Elena felt astonished as she walked into the house and saw a woman that looked almost identical to Fergie with raven black hair and a steady build. However, unlike Fergie, this woman had very cheerful eyes.

"Fergie, your hair looks fantastic!" the woman said genially. She embraced Fergie, who returned the hug stiffly.

"I did it!" chimed Abria.

"Abria, darling, how are you?" the woman then enveloped Abria in a motherly hug.

"Fine, Mrs. Foreman."

Mrs. Foreman smoothed her fingers through Abria's hair in a way that made Elena long for her mom.

"Declan, how's school treating you?" she went on.

"Like a slave driver," Declan replied casually. "Especially Marshall. He's determined to kill us."

Mrs. Foreman laughed freely.

"Mother, these are our friends Austin Haddock, Gribbin Pigg, and Elena Ransom."

"Pleased to meet you. My name is Anne Foreman."

Anne shook hands with each of them, but she stopped at Elena and said, "Nice to finally meet you. Fergie has told me so much about you, of course."

"Mother, where is Daddy?" Fergie asked formally.

"This way." Anne turned and led them through the apartment, which was large, simple, and modern. Humanoids were standing everywhere, constantly asking if their services were required.

"I guess Fergie has told you that we manufacture Humanoids. We train each one before they go into retail."

They soon arrived at a door with a window set in it. On the other side of the glass, Elena could see a man hunched over a table in a Fergie-ish sort of way. He appeared to be tinkering with something, though she couldn't tell what.

"Kenneth is always very in his head," Anne said, twirling her fingers in an obscure way around her own head. "He'll sit in there for hours to manipulate microchips, electrodes, pieces of metal, and wires until he feels like he has created something truly extraordinary. And then, he tosses the invention in the trash and begins again. Only one thing in the world can take his mind off his work."

Anne leaned toward the door and opened it.

"Kenneth, dear," she said robustly, but he did not look up. "Fergie is home for a visit."

At the mention of Fergie's name, Kenneth's head jerked toward the door. When he saw her, his face lit into a warm smile. He ran toward her and picked her up in a swinging hug.

"Monkey!" he exclaimed. "Oh, how I've missed you."

It was the only time Elena had heard Fergie laugh or appear somewhat relaxed.

"How is school?" Kenneth asked his daughter. He was so wrapped up in her that he hadn't even noticed that anyone else was standing there.

"It has been academically adequate this quarter."

"I hope you're saving some time to have fun."

"The notion of *fun* is relative and based on..."

"What each individual determines is enjoyable," Kenneth supplied. "I know. We've discussed that many times. I suppose I should have said that I hope you are finding things to do that you deem enjoyable."

"Kenneth," Anne interrupted them. "Some of Fergie's friends are visiting from school.

Kenneth looked around and said "Declan! Abria! Good to have you home."

"This is Austin Haddock and Gribbin Pigg," Anne Foreman said. "And this is Truman Ransom's daughter, Elena."

Elena noticed a cloud pass over Kenneth's face as he looked at her.

"Nice to meet you," Kenneth said solemnly and shook her hand clumsily. "I was sorry to hear about your parents."

Elena swallowed hard. "Yeah, thanks."

"Well, it's really so nice that you could come home for a visit," Kenneth said to them. "But I've got to get back to work now. Fergie, come by later and I'll show you my latest invention."

Fergie smiled as Kenneth Foreman closed the door to his office.

"Anyone hungry?" Anne asked.

"Yes!" Pigg blurted and Anne smiled.

"Come have some lunch," Anne continued as she led them into the kitchen.

She instructed two of the Humanoids to bring them food, but the rest of the robots stood and stared as if longing to receive a command.

Elena and her friends sat at a table that was long enough to seat twenty people and she watched in awe as the table quickly filled with plates of flatbreads smothered with garlic olive oil, different colored tomato relishes, deep red grapes, brick oven melts, and fresh tomato mozzarella salad.

"Tell me everything about school," Anne said after sliding into her chair.

Elena wanted to ask her right away about the Humanoids in D.C. and about the artifacts and about her parent's death, but she felt it wasn't the right moment. So, instead, Elena and her friends took turns talking about school and how she had done a great job leading them through the last Gauntlet.

"But Fergie was so terrified of the water, even though we had tons of water safety and swimming lessons," Elena laughed.

Anne looked pointedly at her and said, "That's because Fergie is a Humanoid, dear."

Elena's mouth fell open in disbelief. This pronouncement was so shocking that she didn't know how to respond. Did Anne Foreman really say that Fergie was a robot? Elena looked at Austin and noticed the same look of confusion on his face.

"It's counterintuitive for her to be in water," Anne Foreman continued. "Even though we've assured her many times that water repellent skin is laced to her entire frame and could never leak."

"I'm s-sorry," Austin stuttered. "Did you say that Fergie is a Humanoid?"

"Fergie." Anne started in a kind, but reproachful way. "You haven't told your friends yet?"

Somehow, Fergie managed to look embarrassed. Elena felt completely confused. How could a Humanoid register such an emotion in the face?

"I guess I should have explained my condition by this point in our relationship, certainly before we arrived here. Mother, perhaps you should assess the judgment center of my mainframe."

Her mother gave Fergie a wry smile and a wink. Then, she said, "Our biological daughter was killed in an explosion at the White House. So, we created a new daughter."

"But...but..." Elena was now the one stuttering. "Fergie eats food."

"We inserted a customized stomach that converts food into reusable energy," Anne explained as she looked fondly at Fergie. "Because of our work it was easy to give Fergie this uncommon upgrade. Also, every year we give her a new skin graft to make her appear older. She's a perfect specimen."

"Abria, did you and Bowen know about this?" Elena asked.

"Well, sure." Abria shrugged. "Kenneth and Anne raised us after our parents went into long term care at the hospital."

"You never said you lived here," Austin said, looking at Abria in astonishment.

"I guess we've never actually talked about our lives outside of school," Declan said. "There isn't really much to tell."

Elena thought that Fergie being a Humanoid was actually a lot to tell.

"The fact that Fergie is a Humanoid is a family secret." Kenneth Foreman had entered the room and had spoken with a specific authority. "So, you will understand when we ask that you keep it."

"Isn't that dishonest?" Pigg asked. "I mean, no wonder she gets such good grades. She already knows everything."

"Pigg!" Elena exclaimed. She felt like popping him in the head for asking, yet she was curious to know the answer to his question.

"No, that's quite alright," Anne said. "We don't mind explaining the technology. Fergie is programmed to know basic information for her age. However, once she learns something it is then stored forever on her mainframe. She would be able to recall anything she learned during the course of her life, instead of misplacing the information as human minds tend to do. Her retention and recollection is similar to having a photographic memory. We don't consider it cheating because having a photographic memory is a gift that even some humans possess."

"So, you live and work inside this building?" asked Austin. Elena could tell that he wanted to change the subject from Fergie, who continued to look embarrassed. "And you build Humanoids."

"Yes, for the domed cities in the United Republic. Although, the Crowfield Plantation province doesn't seem to use many Humanoids. They don't even have one per house like the other provinces do. They are a little behind the rest of us in technology, but they like it that way," Anne said. "The most unfortunate part of our work is that we're required to build Droidiers."

"You build Droidiers?" Elena said sharply. "For what?"

"Aw, Imperator requires that the army be updated and enforced," said Kenneth. "The Droidiers aren't technically on active duty. Each of the provinces has their own army to provide basic protection to the city, but it's for show, truthfully. People don't commit crimes in public view."

"So, you work for him? Imperator, I mean?" Elena asked.

Anne looked at her kindly and said, "That's the trick, isn't it? Because technically, we all work for him."

Elena wasn't expecting her to admit it so freely, especially in the presence of the Humanoids. She wanted to ask more questions, but Anne turned toward Fergie and said, "Your dad and I have to work late tonight. Feel free to explore the city and take your friends out for a nice dinner."

"What if we're still hungry now?" Pigg asked.

"Don't worry, Gribbin, dear," Anne said. "I don't think the entire province will run out of food."

After Pigg had eaten his fill, Abria and Declan led the way down the marbled Galilee walkways, along rows of manicured hedges and through fields of honeysuckle. Marbled statues and white-washed columns graced buildings and entryways. Vines of hanging yellow flowers covered entire lanes and there was archway after archway of painted fresco.

As Elena and her friends stepped on the other side of a butterfly garden, they came to a vast body of water with dozens of fishing boats. Men were pulling in nets of fresh fish, crab, and shrimp.

Food carts lined the harbor with vendors selling fragrant rosemary, dill and cucumber, watermelon, and every color berry Elena could have imagined.

"We have a year-round growing season," Abria said. "And the lake is actually a seafood farm, so we always have fresh catch. The local farmers raise grass-fed sheep. We always have fresh pecorino cheese, which is my personal fav."

And that's when the eating began. Fergie scanned her Trademark again and again, bringing them delicacy after delicacy to try. Elena laughed at Pigg as he declared every new food his favorite.

While they ate, Abria gossiped nonstop about someone named Moriah Kirkley from Falcon and how she liked some boy from the Raptor Unit. And she talked about how she and Melly were starting to get to know Stacia Bassi from the Harrier Unit.

When Abria finally drew breath, Declan told them about a fight Oscar Hunter had been in with Frankie Smiley.

"Oh, I hate that guy," Elena said, thinking about how rude he'd been the first time they met.

"Why? What'd he do to you?" Abria asked.

"Nothing really," Elena admitted. "I just find him offensive."

"Well, we can't have that," Declan said, laughing.

"You should not let Oscar Hunter register for you on an emotional level," Fergie said formally.

"It's too late for that," Elena replied.

"Remember how we talked about you not overreacting to every little thing that other people do?" Austin asked.

"You say that like I have control over my own feelings," Elena said. "Sometimes I react. I can't help it."

As Elena's friends laughed at her, she couldn't help but feel that it wasn't a laughing matter. But Abria had already moved on to telling them a story about Adrien Segers from the Raptor Unit, so she decided to keep quiet.

After they finished eating, Abria and Declan toured the others around the city for several hours. By the time they returned to Fergie's apartment it was dark. Elena noticed right away that Fergie's parents were nowhere in sight.

"It's late," Elena said. "Are your parents still working?"

"They do their best to work in the evenings," Fergie said. "They enjoy sleeping late in the morning."

The entire houseful of Humanoids converged on them, and Elena began to feel nervous and claustrophobic again. The robots began asking Fergie all sorts of questions to make sure that she and her friends didn't need anything before they went to bed.

"Have the rooms been made up?" Fergie asked formally.

"Yes, ma'am," one of the Humanoids replied. "And the carrier bags have been deposited."

Elena thought it was strange that the robots were speaking with Fergie so respectfully. First, because Tiny (the Humanoid that Elena had grown up with) had always treated her like a child. But also, Humanoids were usually indifferent to one another, only addressing their owners.

Elena said goodnight to the boys and then followed Abria and Fergie to their room. When the door opened, she looked to the right and saw a plain bed and dresser with a few trinkets on its top. To the left, it was as if a container full of pink ribbon and sprinkles had exploded. She watched Abria flop down on her pink bed.

Meanwhile, Fergie had moved toward the opposite wall. She scanned her Trademark and an extra bed slid out like a drawer.

"You have the whole building and you share a room?" Elena said quizzically.

"We like sharing. It makes us feel like sisters. And," Abria added quietly, "we don't feel as alone."

Elena said nothing because she knew exactly what Abria meant. She sat down on the pop-out bed and removed her shoes.

"I'm so tired but thank you so much for showing us your town. I think it's the most beautiful place I've ever seen."

Abria smiled. "That's what I like to hear."

She moved toward a pink, sparkled vanity and took a seat, looking at herself in the mirror.

"Elena, does knowing I am a robot change your opinion of me?" Fergie asked suddenly. "Or alter our friendship in any manner?"

Elena could see feeling in Fergie's eyes. It was quite strange that she acted, looked, and seemed to have human feelings and, yet she was a robot.

"Who says we're friends?" Elena caught Fergie's eye and laughed. "It doesn't matter to me what you're made of as long you're someone I can trust. And you've certainly proven that you're worthy of that title."

Fergie smile genuinely.

"Your parents are really nice," Elena told Fergie as they settled into their beds.

"Yes, I could not have asked for better parental units," Fergie said.

"Your dad really loves you a lot. Seeing you together makes me miss my dad." Elena didn't want to cry so she bit her lip.

"Do you really believe he loves me?" Fergie sounded uncertain.

"Of course. Why?"

"I have often wondered if he loves *me* or if he loves the image of his biological daughter."

Elena felt a dull ache in the back of her throat. She tried to imagine how hard it would be to go through life not knowing if your parents really loved you. Even though Elena's parents died too early, she knew she'd been loved for who she was.

"Maybe you should ask him," Elena suggested.

"I could not, even if I wished to," Fergie stated. "Our relationship is not a true one between a father and daughter. In a true relationship, one would be free to ask what one likes in order to seek truth for the purpose of building trust. Our relationship was designed to ease Kenneth's grief over losing his daughter. I am duty bound to be silent on this matter and accept his love without the condition of a true relationship."

"Well, I love you just for you," Abria said. "And I know your mom does, too."

Elena yawned loudly and deliberately. "I'm sorry, but I'm so tired. I've got to sleep. Night."

She rolled over quickly so that Fergie and Abria couldn't see the tears that were beginning to leak from her eyes.

▭ 10 ▭

Katatonia

In the morning, Elena didn't see Kenneth or Anne, but a plethora of Humanoids waited on them hand and foot, bringing platter after platter to the breakfast table. Pigg kept asking the robots to fill and refill his plate.

"Why are there so many Humanoids here?" Elena asked, marveling at the speed at which the robots were able to clean one plate away and set down a new plate of food. "I know your parents build them, but it's a little creepy that they're around all the time."

"The Humanoids are in training," Fergie said. "Before they are able to be sold to families they are required to go through conditioning."

"Sounds like us at Grimsby," Declan said moodily.

As Elena was opening her mouth to ask why Declan was so grumpy, Abria said brightly, "Declan and I are planning to visit his parents today. I can't wait to tell Aunt Sarah about our year so far."

Elena thought her mood was strange considering that Aunt Sarah wasn't able to speak. She had expected sad tears from Abria, not smiling.

"Do you mind if I join you?" asked Austin. "I'd like to see the hospital."

Elena knew that Austin had been curious about Charles and Sarah Bowen's condition since he'd heard they had Katatonia, a state of comatose. But, as far as Elena knew, the disease no longer existed.

"We'd love for you to come," Abria said happily. "Anyone else want to come?"

Elena noticed that Austin gave her an unambiguous look.

"I'd love to come," Elena said slowly.

"Hospital. Sick people?" Pigg began to whine. "I think I'll pass on that. Can I hang here? I want to ask Kenneth about the schematic for the Droidier mainframe."

Fergie nodded.

"Fergie, do you think we'll be able to speak with your parents about Washington D.C. today?" Austin asked.

"I am not certain," Fergie admitted. "I sense that Mom knows we have come for that reason, but she seems reluctant to discuss it at the present time."

"On our way to the hospital we'll take you around to the wine presses," Abria said, changing the subject abruptly. "Our mountains grow grapes year-round. The ladies get into large barrels and stomp barefoot through the fruit, pressing it into juice that will later be made into wine. It's so delightfully fun. Don't you think so, Declan?"

Elena watched Declan shrug his shoulders in a non-committal way and noticed the downcast look on his face as he stuffed honey toast into his mouth. She'd never seen him look so serious.

"Well, it's Charles Bowen's favorite thing," Abria continued cheerfully.

After breakfast, Abria and Fergie led Austin and Elena back through the D.E.S. facility. Declan followed behind them slowly. The serenely quiet manufacturing building that was filled with Humanoids felt ominous. Elena wondered if there were other robots walking around the earth that were disguised as humans, like Fergie.

Once they were on the street, Abria slowed her pace, taking in the shops with her eyes. It was a glorious morning! The sun warmed Elena's cheeks as she walked with her friends down the brick lined streets. A scent of rosemary and olive flowed through the vending carts and breezed through open shop doors.

"Elena, we should totally get you a manicure while you're here," Abria said as they passed a vending cart that was stocked with fingernail polish of every color one could imagine.

"No, thanks," Elena replied, as she peered into a restaurant that was selling wine, cheese, and baguettes to people sitting at umbrella topped tables.

"I bet you'd like it," Abria said imploringly in a singsong voice.

Elena rolled her eyes. "Fergie, has she ever talked you into a manicure?"

"I am ashamed to admit it," Fergie said. "But yes, one time."

Elena and Austin smiled at one another. She also expected a hearty laugh from Declan because this was usually the sort of conversation that he thrived on, but he only diverted his eyes away and pushed by them down the street. They followed behind Declan to an avenue that was vibrant with colorful fabrics and flowers that morphed in color every few seconds.

"This is the flower market," Abria said cheerily. "They sell lots of normal flowers, but they also have a section of exotic flowers that have been enhanced. Some of them change colors, some snap at fingers, and some lick your toes when you walk by!"

"Are there some that can keep a person from speaking?" Elena mumbled under her breath to Fergie who returned a smirk.

"Oh, there's my favorite spot to sit!" Abria squealed, pointing to a purple umbrella topped table that overlooked a tranquil river and the mountains in the distance.

Elena and her friends wove through the other umbrella-topped tables to the one that Abria indicated. She didn't even look at the menu as she ordered focaccia topped with prosciutto and cheese, basil bruschetta, and fruit cocktail from a waitress wearing a flowing white dress and a dazzling smile.

Then, a parade of women in free-flowing skirts filed out along the deck to a series of stout, wooden barrels. While the women sat in chairs, the men came to wash their feet. Then, one by one, each woman was lifted into a barrel and dozens of crates of multicolored grapes were dumped at their feet. The crowd around them cheered and whooped and hollered as the women moved around the barrel, stomping grapes, and clapping their hands. Elena couldn't help but smile at the merriment.

Abria laughed and clapped along.

"Okay," she looked at Elena pointedly, "You ready to try it?"

"No way," Elena said, shaking her head. "The idea of that stuff squeezing between my toes grosses me out."

"I can see why your dad would like it, though," Austin said genially to Declan. "It looks like a lot of fun."

"Can we get going?" Declan asked suddenly. Elena saw a strained look on his face again. "Abria, you know that I like to visit early."

Abria gave him a slightly disappointed look, but she responded with, "Of course. Let's go."

She led the others down several side streets, through a park with benches sitting under shady trees, and down sidewalks that were covered by tunnels of hanging flowers, all the while telling them tidbits about the town.

At last, they came around a corner to a grand basilica with columned porticos. Rows of sand-colored buildings rounded out a courtyard and a mote of glistening emerald water ran around it with an island in the middle that flourished with hummingbirds.

"This is the hospital," Abria said. "Isn't it magnificent? I think it's the most beautiful building in the city."

To Elena, the hospital in Atlanson had always felt sterile and impersonal. This hospital was the complete opposite. The foyer was richly decorated with lush carpets, hanging tapestries, and plush furniture.

An official looking Humanoid immediately greeted Abria and Declan by name and then invited them into a registration room where they each scanned their Trademarks. Then, the robot led them through a door and down a long hallway that was lined with unique paintings and priceless antiques that Elena had never even seen in a book. Everything was beautifully kept and extremely clean. However, Elena began to feel confused as they passed room after room of adults that were in varying stages of illness. In Atlanson, there was no sickness that couldn't be cured immediately.

As they walked by what felt like the hundredth room, Elena felt a tug on her hand. She turned and saw a man in a gown with a slightly manic look in his eyes. Elena turned back only to watch Austin and her friends vanish down the hallway; no one had noticed that she'd been stopped.

She tried to pull away from the man, but he gripped tighter. His hair was scraggly, his fingernails were unusually long, and he had drool hanging around the corners of his mouth.

At first, Elena had a feeling of pure revulsion. But then, as she looked deeper into the man's eyes, he seemed familiar to her. She realized that he reminded her of the simple-minded folk that she'd met in New York City only a few months ago. As Fallon had led them around the underground city, he'd explained that their minds were like children.

Elena's heart flooded with compassion for the man standing there. He was trying to hand her something that was round in shape, but then a Humanoid appeared, as if from thin air, and pulled the man's hand off Elena's arm.

"Poor, Mr. Horace. He has multi-infarct dementia and will never recover," the robot said in a very human-like tone.

Elena felt her body convulse. "But, in Atlanson, we've developed procedures to help enhance the patient's brain function."

"Don't be silly, child," the robot snapped. "There is no help for him."

Elena didn't dare stay a moment longer. She hurried down the hall and turned the corner, looking longingly into each door she passed to see where her friends had gone. Finally, she noticed Austin and Fergie standing on the inside of one of the rooms. She stood close to Austin, still feeling anxious about her interaction with Mr. Horace. The Humanoid that had first greeted them was reviewing an Optivision screen in the corner of the room.

Abria was sitting on the edge of her aunt's bed, but Sarah Bowen's eyes were covered with some kind of tape that kept her eyelids from opening. Abria stroked her hair and talked in her ear with a bubbly voice.

"We started our swimming modules in Basic Training and Declan and I are doing swimmingly. And we just finished our first quarter exams and I think I really did a good job."

Elena's eyes shifted to Declan. He sat silently beside his dad, staring into his face, even though his eyes were also taped shut. Elena stood with Austin trying not to be intrusive, but she couldn't be quiet for long.

"Austin, these people," Elena started in a barely audible whisper. "Does it seem strange to you?"

"Lena," Austin whispered back. "We can't talk about it here."

Elena looked at him and noticed that he wasn't watching Abria or Declan, but he was stalking the Humanoid's movements with his eyes.

"Austin, what are you doing?"

"Tell you later," he replied.

A few minutes later, Abria stood and switched places with Declan. If it was possible, Declan looked even more upset sitting with his mom than he had with his dad. Elena took a few moments to observe some holophotos, the fresh bouquet of flowers that Abria purchased from the market, and handmade cards that covered every nook of the room.

"We went to the grape festival today," Abria told Charles Bowen. "The women pressed the grapes and it was so fun. Do you remember the first time you put me in the barrel? I was seven and I fell over and got my dress stained, but you picked me up and told me that getting messy was part of the fun of stomping grapes."

Elena saw tears welled in Abria's eyes and she felt a lump of grief grow in her own throat.

"It's such a beautiful day today," Abria continued. "I wish you could have been there."

Suddenly, several short blasts of a horn sounded through the halls and the robot that had escorted them looked up nervously.

"Please excuse me," the Humanoid said formally. "You may stay as long as you wish. Find one of the nurses to help you checkout when you've finished your visit."

The robot left promptly, and Elena turned back toward Abria.

"The doctors say Charles and Sarah don't know when we visit," Abria said, her voice calm and steady. "But I don't believe it for a second."

She smiled so genuinely that Elena could feel her heart ache with pity.

"Aunt Sarah knows my voice and Uncle Charles always squeezes my hand when I talk to him about the grape harvest. Crushing grapes to make wine was one of his favorite things to do."

"My parents have the Humanoids bring flowers every day," Fergie explained, pointing at the various bouquets around the room.

Austin removed the Suturand from his pocket and twisted the wand to activate the scanner. Elena remembered him doing this when Abria had fallen during their first time running the Gauntlet for Basic Training. He walked directly toward Sarah Bowen and held it near her face, but Declan grabbed Austin's arm and pulled it away from his mom.

"What are you doing?" He sounded extremely stern and so unlike himself.

"I'm sorry," Austin said. "I should have asked first. I would like to check the brain activity for each of your parents. Katatonia is curable, so I'm wondering what's really going on here."

"Can that hurt them?" Abria asked.

"No, it's perfectly safe," said Austin. "I can show you the inside of Elena's head if you'd like."

Abria eyed Declan and they shared a look that Elena didn't recognize; perhaps it was something only cousins understood. Then she saw beyond their concerned faces and began to feel it creeping up her own spine, the feeling of helplessness when you want to protect your loved ones and are not able. The weariness of watching, worrying, and wondering about Charles and Sarah Bowen had been worn throughout the years like a tactical vest and, though it was damaged and frayed, it was as heavy as it had ever been.

Elena reached forward before she could stop herself and grabbed Declan's free hand. He turned toward her, looking surprised at first, but then he focused on her eyes.

"Let Austin check them," Elena said with such desperation that a tear escaped from Declan's eye before he could turn his face away.

Declan released Austin's arm and nodded his head. Austin moved the Suturand back toward Mrs. Bowen's head and Elena watched an Optivision appear. The inside of her skull appeared with a clear view of her brain.

For several breathless moments, no one spoke or moved while Mrs. Bowen was examined and then Austin moved toward Mr. Bowen.

After a long time, Austin finally said, "Bowen, your parents don't have Katatonia."

Tears spilled down Abria's cheeks. "What do you mean?"

"They're in some kind of neural interactive simulation," said Austin.

"What does that mean?" Declan demanded.

Austin looked at him steadily. "Your parents are dreaming."

"I'm s-s-sorry," Abria sputtered. "I don't understand this. Declan, are you getting this?"

Elena looked at Declan, but he simply gazed at Austin, unmoving and unblinking.

"These machines are keeping their brains in a simulation," Austin said carefully. "It's like our Simulabs at school except instead of experiencing an alternate reality in the physical space around us, your parents are experiencing an alternate reality in their minds. They appear in this sleep state, but with the correct stimuli we could wake them up."

Abria stood abruptly and looked around the room frantically, like she was searching for a door to run through or a window to jump from. Then, her eyes settled on Fergie, and she shouted, "Why didn't your parents tell us?"

▭ 11 ▭

The Twins

Abria was walking down the street so quickly it was nearly impossible for Elena and the rest of the friends to keep up. So, Austin and Elena slowed down to let Declan and Fergie chase after her.

"At least we know where she's going," Elena said. "And I'm not in a hurry to hear her screaming at Fergie's mom."

"Me neither," Austin said. "But this might be our chance to ask about our own parents. For some reason, Abria thinks that Fergie's parents have known about Mr. and Mrs. Bowen's condition this whole time. We need to know if that's true."

Elena walked beside Austin quietly for a while and then asked, "Austin, why do you think they're keeping people sick here?"

"I don't know," Austin said, thumbing his finger over the scar on his chin. "They're big on agriculture here and holistic, organic living so maybe they don't have the medical advancements available. Of course, that doesn't explain why they don't *try* to find help for these people. You know, bring professionals from Atlanson. I'd hate to think that they're doing this on purpose."

"But that's what it looks like, right?" Elena asked. "Because that's what it looks like to me."

Austin nodded but didn't say anything else.

When they arrived at the D.E.S. building, the front door slid open silently. Elena could immediately see that Abria was at the far corner of the building demanding that each one of the Humanoids tell her where Kenneth and Anne Foreman were working that day. Declan was trying to talk to her, but she kept on yelling at the different Humanoids.

"Abria!" Anne Foreman's voice filled the entire lobby, and everyone turned to see her standing on the second floor landing.

Abria stomped to the nearest elevator with Declan and Fergie hard on her heels. As the elevator doors were closing, Elena and Austin managed to jump on, too. Elena could feel the tension in the air as the elevator climbed. When the door opened, Anne Foreman was waiting.

"Did you know Declan's parents didn't really have Katatonia?" Abria shouted at Anne. This was the first time Elena had seen Abria really upset.

"Yes," Anne Foreman replied simply.

Abria gasped, looking angry. But then, tears began to leak from her eyes as she sobbed, "Why didn't you tell us?"

Anne put an arm around her and said, "Come up to the apartment and we'll talk."

The elevator ride up to the top floor felt like it took an eternity. Elena felt irritated with Fergie's mom and hoped that she had a good explanation for lying to Declan and Abria all these years. They entered the Foreman apartment and took seats in the living room, except for Anne who called one of the Humanoids.

"Please tell Mr. Foreman that we need him in the living room right away."

When the Humanoid left, Elena couldn't tear her eyes away from Abria who was sitting on the couch, weeping into Declan's shoulder. Anne Foreman began to order hot drinks and snacks from various Humanoids and Elena assumed this was to pass the time.

At long last, Kenneth entered the room with Pigg by his side. They were both grinning from ear to ear.

"Anne, this boy is amazing," Kenneth said. "Pigg was able to solve this one problem that I've been working on for five months now…" But he stopped speaking as he noticed the faces in the room and a look of concern crossed his eyes. "What's happened?"

"Kenneth, please take a seat," Anne said. "You too, Gribbin."

When they had both settled, she continued to her husband, "They went to the hospital today. They know that Charles and Sarah do not have Katatonia."

Elena watched the color drain from Kenneth's face. He stood immediately and took a seat beside Abria, who moved from sobbing on Declan's shoulder to sobbing on his shoulder.

"Why didn't you tell us?" cried Abria.

"When they first got sent to hospital, you were so young," Kenneth said soothingly. "We weren't sure we'd be able to explain it to you."

"Also, what difference would it have made for you to be hurt by the knowledge that they were fine, but couldn't be home with you?" Anne asked. "They're in that facility because Imperator wants it so. And, in some ways, I envy them. Sometimes I'd rather be asleep than do the work we do."

Declan stood and stalked across the room with his back toward them. "We had a right to know!"

"I agree, which is why we should tell you the rest of the story." Anne looked at Kenneth, who nodded. "Abria, Charles and Sarah are not only Declan's biological parents. They are yours as well."

After a sharp intake of breath, Declan spun around wildly.

"It was Truman Ransom who gave you new identities during the exodus twelve years ago," Kenneth added. "As he gave new identities to all the Renegades to protect our lives. No one was to know that you are twins."

Abria and Declan gazed at one another for a long moment. Then, she stood up, stepped toward him slowly, and buried her forehead on his chest. His arms wrapped around her so tightly that Elena was certain her friend couldn't breathe.

Elena tried to imagine what it must feel like to find out that she'd been lied to about having a twin. But then she realized that she'd already experienced those feelings of betrayal when she learned from Hopper that her entire life had been a lie. So many lies.

"Even now, no one can know that you're twins," Kenneth said seriously.

"No one can know?" Elena blurted angrily. "You keep this secret from them their entire lives and now you want them to go on lying."

"Lena..." Austin said in a calming tone.

"No, it's fine that she's upset," Anne said. "She has every right to express her anger."

"Imperator is always hunting us," Kenneth said. "It is our secrets that allow us another day to work toward our freedom."

"Yet, we need to ask your forgiveness," Anne said to Declan and Abria. "We made a judgment call and we're very sorry that it has caused you grief."

Declan released Abria. Then, they both hugged Anne Foreman tightly.

"We need to ask you about the incident at the White House," Fergie said changing the subject abruptly before Declan or Abria had a chance to break apart.

Anne sighed and dropped her head, "Kenneth, I told you that was why they came here."

Kenneth Foreman stood up and walked toward Fergie with an unflinching stare. "That was a nasty business. I'd grown up with the President, but had no idea how involved he'd become with the destruction of mankind. He used the US treasury to fund the Kearney Virus. He also worked at the highest levels of the Oligarki to ensure that people could be Trademarked and moved into the domed cities in the most efficient way possible."

"How did you find out he was working for Imperator?" Austin asked.

"He told me," Kenneth said. "Right before he died in the explosion that also killed our daughter." He cupped Fergie's cheek in his hand. "But I am so thankful that you are here."

"After Imperator assumed command, he said he gave authority back to the people. He created the United Republic under the false pretense that citizens would be able to vote candidates into positions of authority. However, when officials are elected they're told that they work for Imperator. If they refuse, their families are executed and the official is sent to *Oubliette*, a prison that was built to ensure that the person forgets everything about his or her former life."

"Why doesn't he execute the official?" Elena asked.

Kenneth Foreman let out a strange laugh that sounded more like an angry snarl. "Imperator wants to make sure that anyone who defies him suffers before they die. The mind can suffer years before the body dies."

Elena was having a hard time staying focused now. Blood was boiling in her ears, and she could feel her heart pounding aggressively.

"I suppose you know that we have resumed the work the Renegades were doing," Austin stated. "And that we intend to continue."

"Yes, we do," Kenneth said.

"Then, you know how important it is that we find the artifacts so we can defeat Imperator?" Austin asked.

"Hang on just a minute," Pigg squeaked. "Did you hear what they said about that Oubliette thingy? I mean, what if that was one of us? I don't think I could survive in prison. Not to mention the fact that no one knows what Imperator looks like. How can you possibly expect to find him without knowing what face you're looking for?"

"Actually, I do have one photograph of him," Anne said and Pigg groaned.

She walked to the wall where a piece of holographic art hung and swiped her finger over its surface. The hologram melted away. She took a small, square object from its frame.

"I am one of the last people on earth that probably has this. It was taken as Imperator arrived in New York City and it was published by the news media that second. But the person who published it had an *accident* shortly thereafter and copies of this image were destroyed."

Anne handed the image to Austin and Elena hurried over to get a look. A single person appeared in the image. The imposing figure was shrouded in a black cloak and wore a silver-studded mask that made him appear fierce and indestructible. Imperator was standing atop a pile of rubble with the familiar looking New York City skyscrapers. In the background, an army of Droidiers were standing around him.

"He looks really scary," said Pigg, wrapping his hands around his own throat. "Like he could choke me using only his mind. Do you think he can do that?"

"Do you know what he was looking for in New York?" Austin asked.

"No," Kenneth said. "Our job for the Renegades was to create and dispense codes to the different members. Each member was responsible to imprint the portion of his or her code on an artifact. Then, they were required to hide it. We were never told, nor were we ever supposed to know, what the objects were or where they were hidden."

"What are the codes for?" Elena asked.

"When the codes were input in the correct order it will give us the information, we need to defeat Imperator forever," Kenneth said.

"Elena, your dad worked with Imperator and knew his plans to destroy the people of earth," Anne said. "Truman Ransom also knew that Imperator had been given a prophecy about a ruler that would rise more powerful than any other ruler in history. Imperator could not tolerate the idea that there would be someone more powerful than he and that's why the domes were created and why everyone was Trademarked. He wants to keep track of every man, woman, and child so he will know instantly if an individual was gaining too much power."

Austin stood and crossed to the other side of the room. As the others continued to speak, Elena watched Austin carefully until his eyes finally locked on hers. She knew instantly what troubled him. The knowledge that Imperator was searching for one unique person was worse than what they'd already learned about their situation. If he was that obsessed about one soul, then Elena knew he'd stop at nothing to maintain dominance, greatly decreasing their hope for freedom.

"Can you give us the codes you gave to the Renegades?" Austin asked.

"Unfortunately, no," Anne said. "We'd finished creating the last code when the White House was destroyed. Kenneth destroyed the records during our evacuation."

"Can't you create a new one?" Elena asked impatiently.

"It doesn't work that way," Kenneth said. "The code was written once and then divided into pieces. It is impossible to duplicate, which was the goal in the first place."

"E-e-excuse me," Pigg sputtered. "Let me see if I'm following. Are you saying that a code was created to defeat Imperator? But, then the code was broken into pieces and given to Renegade members. Then, those pieces were imprinted on artifacts and hidden in different spots in the entire world? Because that's what it sounds like you're saying. And if that is what you're saying I need to lie down."

"That assessment is correct," Anne confirmed.

"Why was the code broken in the first place?" Declan blurted in anger. "Why didn't you eliminate Imperator when you had the chance?"

"We were missing one key piece of the code," said Kenneth. "Truman called it the *Firebird Disc*, but he was the only one that knew what or where it was located. He said that when the time was right, the pieces of the code would be joined together, and the *Firebird Disc* would unite them."

Austin looked at Anne directly in the face. "Do you have a dossier? Because my parents had one and Elena's did, too."

"Fergie is our dossier," Anne replied.

Elena looked at Fergie and suddenly it was if her eyes were opened, and she was seeing clearly for the first time. She realized why Fergie's parents had told her more about the Renegades than the other parents had, why she'd known about the Catalan Atlas, and why she'd been able to understand parts of the dossiers that no one else could. She was programmed to know.

"Can you help us interpret the dossiers we have?" Austin asked. "They are very complex."

"Kenneth and I are not allowed to leave the building," said Anne. "Imperator has us on complete lock down, a condition of our contract. Furthermore, we won't be able to research anything from the building without being discovered. The safest place for research is the Firebird Station and it's also the safest place to keep those dossiers."

"If you are willing, we urge you to continue the work you're doing. We'll try to help you the best we can from here," Kenneth said.

"But we can't leave the domes again," Elena said. "Everyone knew that we didn't go home on break because our Trademarks didn't register."

"A very good point, Elena," Anne said. "Come with us. We have something to show you."

Feeling curious, Elena followed quickly behind Kenneth and Anne as they led them through their expansive apartment to a very ordinary looking wall. Anne slid her left index finger across it at eye level and, a moment later, it miraculously melted away to reveal a rather large room filled with odd electric trinkets, glass jars of strange flesh-colored objects, and a wall of glass cabinet doors.

Elena walked forward, unblinking and mouth open, toward one of the glass doors where she saw a perfect replica of her face. Then, the door slid open automatically and she stepped closer to get a better look at herself.

"You obviously can't leave your homes again without being detected," Kenneth said. "So, we created these Humanoids for you. These *Decoys* will stay in your homes while you're on breaks from school. They walk like you, talk like you, and act like you. You simply need to scan your Trademark against the one on its wrist and the robot will wake up to become...well...you."

Elena reached forward timidly and scanned her Trademark into the Decoy. Its eyes opened.

"What do you want?" the robot asked shortly.

Beside her, Abria's Decoy said in a bubbly voice, "Hi! I'm Abria Bowen."

The Humanoid Elena responded with, "Yeah, whatever" while Declan's Humanoid said, "Dudes, this is awesome."

"Actually, this is bizarre," said Declan.

Elena gawked for a moment and then said, "Yeah, I'm flippin' out."

"What do you mean?" Abria squealed, eyeing her Humanoid with admiration. "She's perfect. Fergie, what do you think?"

"Since I am already a Humanoid this aberration is neither overwhelming nor welcoming."

"It is, however, inconsiderate to be postponed in receiving instructions," the Humanoid Fergie remarked.

"My apologies," Fergie said to her Decoy. "You have been programmed to return home from school and carry on a normal existence."

"This is brilliant!" Austin said to Anne and Kenneth. "How can we ever thank you?"

"It was nothing," Anne said with a wave of her hand.

"Though we must warn you," Kenneth said. "It would be unethical for you to use these Decoys in your place for educational purposes."

Elena thought it was a little strange for Kenneth to be giving them a lesson in ethics when they had a daughter that was already a Humanoid and also since he and Anne were essentially giving them a way to lie about leaving the domes.

"I'm assuming that Wheeler's Humanoid wasn't hard to program," Elena scoffed. "It can't be too complicated to design a surly teenage boy with no good personality traits."

Pigg, who hadn't even tried to turn on his Decoy, said, "Can we keep Wheeler's Humanoid to operate the Independence so the real Wheeler won't have to?"

Elena thought this was a fantastic suggestion, but Anne was already shaking her head.

"Sorry, the Decoy wasn't programmed to operate heavy machinery. So, the real Kidd Wheeler will still need to be with you."

"They couldn't give us a break on that one," Pigg whispered to Elena, and she smiled.

Later that night, Elena lay awake for a long time after everyone had gone to sleep. She thought about Fergie being a Humanoid and wondered if anyone from school knew. Kenneth and Anne Foreman had purposely created her, purposely equipped her with the knowledge about the codes and artifacts. Fergie was a walking, talking dossier with a multitude of unknown secrets.

The story about the code that would defeat Imperator seemed insane. And it was overwhelming to know that the Renegades had hidden artifacts around the world. Elena looked at the Trademark on her arm and rubbed it like an itch she couldn't satisfy. She'd been traced, tracked, and watched her entire life for a specific purpose, so that Imperator would feel better about his place of power.

Feeling bitter and extreme sorrow, Elena left Fergie and Abria's room, feeling sure that somewhere there was a Humanoid awake to fix her a warm drink and possibly a snack. When she arrived in the kitchen, she found Anne sitting expectantly at the countertop.

"I had a feeling I would see you tonight," Anne said. "I'm surprised that Abria didn't join you."

"Why?" Elena asked suspiciously.

"Girls process everything differently from boys. I figured that you girls would need to talk a bit more about what happened today so you could get it straight in your mind."

Elena sat on the bar stool beside Anne and asked, "Do you approve of what we're trying to do?"

"Of course I approve. It is my life's work as well."

"But why are you okay with sending a group of teenagers out into the world without protection or proper resources?" asked Elena angrily.

Anne Foreman gave her a quirky little smile. "Because I believe it's your destiny."

"What's destiny?" Elena asked, feeling confused.

"Oh, my dear child," Fergie's mom said, stroking Elena's hair. "Destiny is like the Kairos hanging around your neck."

Elena intuitively grabbed her necklace and held it in her hand.

"Did you know that the ancient Greeks had two words for *time*? The first was Chronos, which referred to sequential time. But the other word, Kairos, referred to the supreme moment in time. And *that* is destiny, the perfect moment in time."

"Do you believe my parents were *destined* to be murdered?" She wanted to continue being angry, but her voice broke at the end of her question.

Anne looked thoughtful for a moment and then said, "I believe it was their supreme moment in this realm for their physical bodies to pass from this earth. Their death inspired your journey, giving your life a new purpose and a determination for justice."

"But aren't you afraid we'll get hurt?" Elena said. "Or that we'll die?"

"Perhaps I would be afraid if I believed this world was the end of all time. However, I happen to believe that we live beyond this world into eternity. I believe that the death of our physical body is merely the means by which our souls move to their final resting place," Anne said. "I have already lost one daughter, a genuine tragedy. But life goes on and hope lives on in me. My daughter's life was destroyed in vain if we do not succeed in removing Imperator from power and establishing freedom to mankind on earth."

"Maybe that's true," Elena said, tearing up a bit. "But I wish my parents hadn't died. I miss them."

"Elena, we can't change the past." Anne was looking at Elena so intently it made her blush. "But we can change the future of where that past was going to take us."

"How?"

"By our choices, dear one." Anne cupped Elena's face in her hands. "We can choose to fight for freedom from the bondage of slavery. Through freedom we can find truth, peace, and a hopeful future."

Anne reached into a nearby drawer and withdrew a large, square object that was wrapped in brown paper.

She handed it to Elena and said, "Fergie asked us to make a replica of the Alpha Manuscript. When you retrieve the real one, I hope you will find the answers you seek within its pages."

Elena walked back to Fergie's room holding the fake manuscript tightly to her chest. After she was back in bed, she thumbed the Kairos between her fingers. Anne had mentioned her necklace. Did she know that it opened or how it worked?

Elena wasn't sure how she felt about destiny. Her parents had never really spoken about such things with her. Her mom had worked in the medical field and had dealt with practical, concrete facts. Her dad had taught Elena history. They'd rarely talked about the future. In fact, the only time Elena remembered discussing anything having to do with upcoming events was when she was getting ready to attend Grimsby for the first time.

Then, suddenly she recalled the night her dad gifted the Kairos to her. He had said she was destined to accomplish greatness in the world. What had he meant?

Elena rolled over in her bed feeling confused and full of questions. Questions that she feared would never be answered.

◻ 12 ◻

An Epiphany

Elena wished she could go to the Telepost Office to see her mom and to ask her dad what she was supposed to do because the trip to the Galilee Province had been confusing. She wasn't exactly sure how she felt about seeing Charles and Sarah Bowen in that hospital or about everything Kenneth and Anne Foreman had told them, but she didn't have time to process any of it because second quarter classes began on the first day of the fourth month with the entire Aves Company in Instructor Booker's classroom.

As Elena took her seat, she noticed that all her teachers were present. Before she could even begin to wonder why, Booker said, "A great number of significant events took place from 500 BC to 1 AD. Some of the more significant events include the development of Greek culture, the Peloponnesian Wars, the escapades of Alexander the Great, the growth of the Persian Empire, the expansion of the Roman Republic, and most notably the creation of a few major world religions following the life of Buddha and the birth of the Hebrew prophet Jesus.

"During this second quarter, your Instructors and I will be teaching you these events in preparation for a unique second quarter exam. In a moment, you will be divided into groups. Your groups will be assigned a period of time and the historical civilization that existed during that time period.

"Your group will be required to develop a simulation based on the civilization you've been given. A culmination of what is learned in every class will help you design the simulation, but some standard modules for the project must include social achievements, standards of government, agriculture practices, development of military, and advancements in technology. You will present your second quarter exam to the entire class. The quality of the simulation will count as fifty percent of your grade."

Before Elena had a chance to process everything he'd said or begin to panic about the group she'd be put with, Booker stepped in front of an Optivision and the Firebird logo appeared. Then, it shuffled through a series of student faces until Austin, Declan, and Crosby Gamble's faces appeared.

"Team 1 includes the following students: Declan Bowen, Austin Haddock, and Crosby Gamble," Booker said as the Optivision began to blink again. Then, the words "Alexander the Great" appeared. "Team 1 is assigned the time period for Alexander the Great."

As the Optivision selected the next team, Elena leaned toward Abria and Fergie and said, "I hope that we get teamed together. The thought of working with anyone else…"

But Instructor Booker called Fergie's name, so Elena turned back toward him.

"Fergie Foreman, Pamela Linus, and Elena Ransom are Team 4 and you will study" — the Optivision blinked — "the Byzantine Empire."

After Instructor Booker finished giving the Firebirds their assignments, he moved on to the Raptor Unit, but Elena tuned him out.

She turned back toward Fergie and whispered, "I can't believe we have to work with Melly! It's bad enough that we share a room with her."

"I am positive that it will work out fine," Fergie replied.

"Or not," Elena said moodily.

At long last, Booker was finished giving out their assignments and said, "For the rest of this week, your Basic Training classes have been suspended so that you will have adequate time to familiarize yourself with the procedure that is required to design the intricate details of your simulations. Once you're dismissed you will find your team syllabus in the Media Room, but you'll need to scan your Trademarks together this first time in order to access your assignment.

"The rest of your classes are cancelled today. Instructors will be present in the Media Room in case you have questions about the syllabus or the time period in history that you were assigned.

"You will each be required to write to an individual portion of the simulation, and you will also complete a group module that must be present in the simulation. We expect perfection on the group work and the individual work, so I must stress the importance of starting work on this project today. You are dismissed."

The forty-eight students in the Aves Company rose from their chairs at the same time and hurried to the Media Room to try and find a pupil station. Fortunately, Elena and Fergie found a good spot right away with ample tabletop space for multiple Optivision screens. But, when Elena looked around, she couldn't see Melly anywhere.

"Did you see Melly come in with anyone," Elena asked Fergie. She was standing on tiptoes, trying to see over the tops of heads. "I can't believe this! Look, everyone else has already started."

"Be patient," Fergie said. "She cannot be far behind us."

Three minutes of waiting turned into ten and that turned into twenty, but Melly had still not found them.

"Okay, maybe I'll go look for her. It's crowded. Maybe she couldn't find us," Elena said.

Elena immediately began to walk determinedly around the pupil stations and worktables through the entire Media Room. Finally, she noticed Melly sitting in a far corner of the room with Oscar Hunter and some of the other Raptor boys.

Elena stomped over to her and said, "Melly! What are you doing? Didn't you hear Booker say that we can't begin unless all our Trademarks are scanned together?"

"Sorry, Ransom," Melly said, almost laughing as Oscar and the other boys snickered. "These boys offered to walk me and I guess I got distracted."

"Fergie and I are over here," Elena said shortly. "Come on, let's go. I want to get started sometime before dinner."

Elena turned on her heels and stomped back through the room with Melly following behind her, chatting with everyone she passed. When Melly was finally settled and their Trademarks were scanned, half the students had already left for lunch.

The Optivision screen lit up with the words Pax Romana and Elena read, "Pax Romana is Latin for *Roman peace*. Approximately 207 years of relative peace existed in the Roman Empire between 27BC to 180 AD."

Then, Elena began to read a complicated series of dates, historical facts, names of magistrates and patricians, laws in the Republic, specifics of daily life, architecture achievements, and notable Roman inventions from the syllabus. After this, she began to read the technical details of building the simulation, which were also complicated and varied.

Feeling overwhelmed, Elena stopped mid-sentence and said, "Fergie, what do you think we should do first?"

"Instructor Booker directed us to create individual segments and design a group module. Therefore, I propose that we analyze each topic and assign segments based on our individual strengths."

"I'm fascinated with the entertainment that was offered, the working life, and family culture of the time period," Melly said. "I'll do that part."

"You're fascinated with the fact that they fed humans to the lions for entertainment?" Elena questioned.

"Oh, you know what I mean," Melly laughed and though she smiled, Elena felt that her eyes looked a little agitated. Then, Melly's eyes shifted, and Elena turned to see Oscar Hunter leave the Media Room with his friends. Melly jumped up suddenly and grabbed her Smartslate.

"Where are you going?" Elena said. "We're getting started."

"We have ages to design our simulation," Melly said. "I have things I want to do today."

Elena watched her walk quickly after Oscar, calling out, "Hey, boys, wait for me."

She turned back to Fergie as Austin and Declan dropped into the vacant seats at their table.

"That girl is gonna be trouble for us."

"I think a more appropriate term might be *inadequate*," Fergie replied formally.

"What's going on?" Declan asked.

"Oh, Melly is more concerned with what Oscar Hunter is doing than the exam that counts for half our grade," Elena said bitterly.

"Talk to Booker about it," Austin suggested.

"Not everything has to be handled by our Instructors, Austin," Elena said. "I know I can handle Melly if I find the right thing. Ugh! I wish we didn't have to share a room with her. She's getting on my nerves! Maybe if I got Oscar's group to sit near ours while they're designing their simulation..."

"And you thought I was silly about boys," Abria said, appearing at their table.

"You *are* silly about boys," Elena said. "She's worse."

"Oh, speaking of boys, Vivienne Castellow likes Crosby, but he has a thing for one of the Raptor girls. And then, Frankie Smiley totally likes Stella Grooms from Harrier, but she thinks that Austin is *to die for*. Her words, not mine." Abria looked at Austin pointedly. "Not that I don't think you're cute, Austin, but *dying* is pretty serious business."

Austin laughed loudly.

Elena rolled her eyes. "Who do you have a thing for, Abria?"

"Oh, there are too many cute guys here to settle for one," Abria said flippantly. "But, if I had to pick one now, I'd still go with Frankie Smiley. I love those dimples."

"Is anyone else concerned this project counts for so much of our grade?" Fergie asked suddenly.

"I am," said Abria. "I mean, the Chou Dynasty had absolutely fabulous clothes, but I'm not sure I want my whole grade to be based on it."

Elena felt that she was perfectly justified in feeling worried about Melly's participation in their project. If today was any indication, she was sure that she and Fergie would end up doing most, if not all, of the work.

During the hours that should have been Physics, she tried to speak with Melly again about their project but was basically dismissed because Melly was "too busy talking" to her friends to discuss their group work.

As the day finally came to an end, Elena sat against the pillow on her bed and pulled her knees to her chest feeling frustrated and restless. She wished she could bring the Ransom Dossier into her room and sleep with it under her pillow so she could feel close to her parents. However, since Anne Foreman told them that the dossiers would be safest in the Firebird Station, she knew she'd have to keep it there. She removed the Kairos from around her neck.

Abria sat down on the foot of Elena's bed and said, "What's wrong, Elena? You look sad."

Elena looked around quickly. Melly seemed to be looking for something in her closet while Vivienne and Olivia were giggling across the room. Still, she didn't want anyone else to hear her.

"I don't know," Elena whispered. "Being in the Galilee Province was strange. Seeing Fergie with her parents and you with yours made me miss mine."

Fergie sat on her own bed and looked at Elena kindheartedly. "You can borrow my parents anytime."

Elena gave her a half-hearted smile. "Thanks, but I wish I could see my parents, you know?"

Abria and Fergie nodded, looking solemn.

Elena suddenly wished that she could be alone somewhere so she could grieve in silence, but the next morning at breakfast it was clear that being alone was not going to be possible because three different people stopped by the table to ask Elena how she was feeling.

"That was weird," Elena said to Austin as they walked to their first class.

"What was weird?"

"Those trainees asking me how I was feeling while we were eating breakfast," Elena replied. "I wonder what's going on."

"Nothing's going on. People are just being nice."

Elena wasn't sure she agreed with him but decided to dismiss the strange sensation in her stomach because they were starting the day in Booker's class again, instead of with Hopper.

When she arrived in the classroom, Frankie Smiley was sitting in Elena's favorite seat, but he got up when he saw her and said he'd sit somewhere else. She felt her face grow warm in confusion, so she took the seat quickly and put her eyes down on her Smartslate.

Then, Booker arrived at her seat suddenly and asked, "Ransom, how are you feeling today?"

"Fine, Sir," Elena replied.

"The code writing for the exam might be strenuous today, so please let me know if you need a rest," Booker said, before turning on his heels and calling the class to order.

Later on, after Niva's seminar, the Instructor broke the class into groups to work on symbol writing for their individual modules of the simulation they were writing for second quarter exams, but she stopped by Elena's group before they'd even had a chance to start.

"Ransom, you're welcome to skip this part of group work today. I'm fine if you'd like to leave class a little early."

Elena felt puzzled and replied, "No, thanks. I'll work with my group."

Instructor Niva gave her a sympathetic look and said, "That's fine. But feel free to leave whenever you wish."

By lunchtime, Elena was annoyed by the extra attention she'd been given, but when Olivia Nelson came up and asked if she wanted an extra slice of pie, she almost lost her mind.

"Okay," said Elena, putting her fork down on the table firmly. "What's going on with everyone today?"

Austin looked perplexed and said, "What do you mean?"

"Everyone is treating me *weird* today."

"People are being nice, Elena," said Abria as she cut the lamb tagine on her plate.

"Too nice," Elena said, looking at her friends. "Booker excused me from homework and Niva said I didn't have to do the group work. I wouldn't have minded that except that Fergie would have been alone with Melly. Still, what's going on with everyone?"

Everyone at the table shrugged, but Elena continued to feel uneasy as they started their AstroPhysics lesson. Although Instructor Copernicus didn't give Elena any extra attention, she got the sense that a few of the other students were giving her covert glances.

"In the year 236 BC, Ptolemy III appointed a man named Eratosthenes as the librarian of the Alexandrian library," Copernicus said to begin his lecture. "This man was a mathematician, an astronomer, and he was also the first person to use the term *world geography*."

Instructor Copernicus accessed an Optivision screen that filled nearly the entire room with a globe of the earth.

"Ptolemy was able to calculate the circumference of the earth and the distance from the earth to the sun. But, for this class, his most notable achievement was that he created the first map of the known world, inventing a system of longitude and latitude."

Gridlines suddenly appeared, crossing this way and that, along the simulated projection.

"The red vertical lines on this map are called *longitude* and are also known as *Meridians*. The blue lines are called *latitude*," Copernicus continued. "They are equidistant from each other and are known as parallels.

"To precisely locate points on the earth's surface, longitude and latitude are divided into minutes and seconds. There are 60 minutes in each degree. Each minute is divided into 60 seconds. Seconds can be further divided into tenths, hundredths, or even thousandths..."

Elena's eyes darted across the room. She watched Oscar Hunter whisper something behind his hand to the girl with dark hair sitting to his left. Then, they both looked directly at her. Elena's face grew uncomfortably warm. She looked in the opposite direction and fielded a sweet simper from Melly Linus.

"Longitude and latitude!"

Fergie had shouted so loudly that Elena lurched sideways off her chair. She wasn't the only one. Ferige's sudden outburst caused the entire class to startle in their seats.

Elena's gaze slowly focused on her friend. Fergie was on her feet beside her pupil station with a far off look on her face.

"I am so ignorant!" Fergie blurted.

"There is evidence that contradicts that statement, Miss Foreman," Instructor Copernicus said kindly. "Although, a psychological evaluation may be needed to determine why you have so energetically interrupted this class..."

But Copernicus didn't finish his sentence because Fergie gathered up her Smartslate and sprinted out of the classroom.

Instructor Copernicus looked dumbfounded for a moment, but then said, "The use of longitude and latitude will be a requirement in the simulation you're creating for the second quarter exam."

As his lecture continued, Elena became more and more distracted by Fergie's absence. She looked for Fergie on the way to Social Science but couldn't find her friend anywhere. Fergie also never showed to Instructor Emerald's class, but he didn't even notice as he began to explain how the social, religious, and government practices in the Roman Empire developed over the decades.

Before Elena's eyes, the land of Italy appeared on Emerald's Optivision screen and a schematic of the original town. As the Instructor continued speaking, layer upon layer of the city was built and demolished and built up again, forming a perfect holographic model.

Elena almost forgot about the morning when Emerald broke the class into groups for their lab work.

Since Fergie wasn't present, she and Melly got placed with Vivienne Castellow, who said, "Ransom, if you want to, you can skip our lab today for Emerald and I'll catch you up later."

"Why would I skip it?" asked Elena, feeling confused.

"Because of your parents."

"Huh?"

"Melly said you were crying all last night about your parents...you know..." Vivienne dropped her voice to a whisper and said, "dying."

Elena looked over at Melly with a bubble of rage rising from her stomach. The fact that anyone would talk about her parents infuriated her, much less a person that she barely knew or could tolerate.

"Did you tell everyone that I was crying about my parents last night?" Elena said forcefully and in such a way that Vivienne made an excuse about needing to use the restroom so she could leave the table.

"Yes," Melly said simply.

"First of all, I wasn't even talking to you," Elena continued, the edges of her words pointed with irritation. "Second, you had no right to go tell anyone, much less the entire school, what I said because I said it in the privacy of our room."

"I was only trying to apologize for being late to our first meeting about the second quarter exam simulation. I don't know why you're making such a big deal about it," Melly said flippantly. "You got out of some homework today and everyone is treating you like a queen."

"I don't want to be treated like a queen. And I certainly don't want you exploiting my parents' death! And telling people I was *crying* when I wasn't!" Elena knew that her voice was beginning to rise, but she no longer cared about disrupting class. "How would you like it if I told lies about you or gossiped about the things you share in the privacy of our room?"

"What do I care?" Melly shrugged. "I don't have any secrets."

"Keep your mouth closed and your nose out of my business!" Elena hollered and then she stomped out of Emerald's class.

"Well, at least you didn't punch her in the, like, face," said Abria.

Elena hadn't even noticed that Abria was following her. "Though I can't say I wouldn't mind watching her fly across the room and hit the wall."

"Slow down," Austin said, grabbing Elena by the hand and pulling her to a stop. Declan and Pigg also gathered around her. "What Melly did was wrong, but you've got to calm down."

Elena didn't want to calm down. She was embarrassed and wanted to hit someone.

Instead, she asked gruffly, "Has anyone seen Fergie?"

"Not since she flipped out during Physics and ran out of the classroom," said Declan.

"Maybe she had a system malfunction." Pigg laughed and snorted, but Elena didn't find his comment funny.

"Shut your mouth, Pigg!" Elena rebuked him.

"What?" Pigg said and then he added quietly, "I was making a little joke about her being a robot."

Elena stiffened. "Since when did you get so arrogant?"

"Why does it matter if I make a little joke?" Pigg said defensively. "It's not like she has feelings."

"Her parents gave her feelings when they created her. She's no different than you and me in that respect, except I'm sure that she has more compassion than you!" Elena spat. "Fergie is our friend, so act like one."

A look of guilt filled Pigg's face, and he blushed with embarrassment.

"Lena, calm down," Austin said soothingly.

"I'm going to look for her," Elena said, brushing him off.

However, she didn't have to look far. Fergie came hurrying toward them, though she did this in such a stiff way that she looked like she was in pain.

"Glad to see you, Fergie," Elena said, shooting Pigg a dirty look. "We were worried about you."

"I have deciphered a portion of the Alpha Manuscript and the Ransom Dossier using longitude and latitude," Fergie said with as much excitement as her robotic system would allow.

☐ 13 ☐

Longitude and Latitude

Elena ran through the forest behind Fergie, noticing for the first time how incredibly fast her friend could run. She heard Pigg fall behind her, but she didn't slow down or stop to check on him. She kept on until they were inside the Firebird Station.

Elena gathered around the pupil station in the main living area with Austin, Declan, and Abria while Fergie pulled up several Optivision screens. The Ransom Dossier lay open on the pupil station surface while Fergie accessed numerous pages from the Alpha Manuscript on the screens above the table.

"You could have waited for me!"

Elena heard Pigg shout from the Firebird Station doorway. He arrived at the pupil station with smudges of dirt on his cheeks and a torn shirt.

"Sorry, Dude," Declan said, clapping Pigg on the back hard enough to make him stumble over a bit. "We're excited."

"As you will remember," Fergie began. "The diaries contained a series of numbers, but we did not understand what they represented until today. As we were having our lesson about longitude and latitude, I realized that this might be the key to unlocking some of the secrets in the dossiers."

Fergie's face looked eerily green in the lights from the Optivision screen as the globe of earth came forward. She made it expand in midair. Then, the sea came into better focus and, finally, the continents. "Observe what happens as I input some of the numbers from the Alpha Manuscript."

Fergie grabbed a holographic page from the Alpha Manuscript and dropped it onto the map of the earth. Then, Elena saw a red dot appear over the area of New York City.

"You see, when I input the numbers from the dossier using longitude and latitude logic, the destination of the Amulet was revealed. In truth, this is quite brilliant logic because the system is no longer in active use. Now, observe..." Fergie said rather excitedly as she pulled two additional Optivision screens toward her.

Elena recognized one as the ceiling in her dad's library and the other as the Catalan Atlas. Fergie dropped the two holographs onto the map of the earth and Elena watched the map light up with little red dots in many directions across the globe. She noticed one in Washington D.C. but there were other, more intriguing dots, some on mountains and in river basins, and there was even one that appeared to be in the middle of the ocean.

"Elena, the ceiling in your dad's library is an ingenious composition that actually coordinates with the book titles on the shelves and with the Catalan Atlas," said Fergie.

"Do you think each of these dots represent artifacts?" Austin asked.

"It is certainly possible," replied Fergie.

"Or they could be a misleading trap," said Pigg. "We've almost been killed twice this year! Am I the only one who remembers that?"

"But, we did find artifacts at both those locations," Declan said, pointing at the dots over New York City and Washington D.C. "So, maybe there are artifacts at those other dots."

"I believe that Truman Ransom may have known what each artifact was and where each was placed," Fergie said. "Hopper told Elena and Austin that the Firebird Unit was not chosen at random. We assumed that we would need the other members from our Unit to help with this quest, but if Truman already knew the locations of each of the artifacts then we will not need to put the others in danger. Nevertheless, it is a complicated puzzle, so we cannot expect to be able to locate everything instantly. We will have to take the map apart piece by piece and use reason to determine the relevance of the sites listed here."

"But how are we going to, like, research each dot?" said Abria. "There're so many of them."

"Plus, wouldn't we need to know what artifact goes with each coordinate and how are we supposed to find that out?" Elena asked. "We only have two dossiers. We only have one diary and scans of another since we're still waiting for Hopper to get the real Alpha Manuscript from the Vault."

"Also, hasn't anyone noticed that some of these dots are across the ocean?" Pigg said. "Hovercrafts can't go over water."

"That is indeed accurate," confirmed Fergie. "Unless they have aviation capabilities."

To Elena, needing the Independence to fly introduced a wide range of unexplored problems, but Austin said, "Okay, so we give the Independence an aero-upgrade. It's not that hard, right Pigg?"

"It's actually incredibly hard," said Pigg, shaking his head slightly. "Above and beyond needing the parts to make it fly, we'd have to completely reformat the command module, control panel, navigation systems, and fuel cells. And that's just the beginning."

"Okay, okay!" Austin held his hand up for silence. "We don't have to find all the artifacts or know what they are today. Maybe the Independence can't fly, but there are plenty of dots on this side of the ocean. We'll work it all out when the right time comes. Meanwhile, we'll wait for Hopper to bring the Alpha Manuscript and we'll keep deciphering the Ransom Dossier. We have plenty to of work and we don't need to waste time worrying about things we can't control."

Fergie accessed a new Optivision that displayed a schematic of the Independence and said, "A way may exist."

"A way for what?" asked Austin.

"To give the Independence an aero-upgrade," Fergie said. "I could ask my parents to send the supplies we need directly to the Firebird Station. They could not bring the parts by their own hand, but they have plenty of Humanoids ready for instruction. However, we would require Wheeler's services to give us the list of supplies and then help complete the upgrade to the hovercraft."

Elena laughed out loud. "Oh, come on! Wheeler got the Independence as payment when he agreed to help us go on our first trip. What makes you think he'd help us do anything again?"

"I have no doubt he'll do whatever it takes to make the Independence fly because he'll be interested in the technology," Austin said. "In fact, I bet that he'll exchange flying capability for helping us get to our next destination."

"Oh, there's a happy thought," Elena said sarcastically. "All of us back on the Independence having to deal with Wheeler again."

As the days stretched on, Elena and Fergie committed every spare minute to designing the simulation for their second quarter exam even though it was still weeks away. Elena was almost finished writing her individual portion of the exam, which included a replica of the Roman Senate, the Forum Magnum, government offices, tribunals, temples, memorials, and statues. She also had an exquisite timeline of the names of rulers and senators from 27 BC to 1 AD that included family lineage charts. She and Fergie spent time watching their simulations together and making suggestions for improvements.

The only problem was that they could never get a study session with Melly. Every time Elena asked her about the group portion of their project, Melly would say something snotty about how she was busy working on other things or doing homework with other people.

Finally, one afternoon after Melly had put Elena off for the third time, she said, "Fergie, I think we're going to need to design the group simulation without Melly. I don't think she'll work on it with us and I'm not failing because of her."

Fergie pulled up an Optivision screen from a pupil station in the Media Room and accessed their modules.

"I wonder if she plans to complete her portion of the individual section of our project. It says here that she has not started."

Elena dropped her head into her hands. "What do you think happens during the exam if she doesn't write any code in there?"

"I believe that after our modules are complete, her module will be blank for the entire three minutes of her portion and then the group simulation would begin," Fergie said, but she didn't sound positive that would happen.

"Do you think we'll get points off for her not doing her module?" Elena asked nervously.

"That is difficult to say," Fergie admitted. "However, it is not as though we could design the individual portion for her. Her module can only be accessed with her Trademark."

"Maybe we could knock her out and then drag her in here. We could scan her Trademark and finish it for her," Elena suggested.

Fergie smiled a little. "Yes, that would not appear suspicious in the least."

"Sarcasm?" Elena laughed. "Really? From you?"

"I have been known to offer a quip a time or two."

Elena and Fergie decided that they would stay after Booker's class to discuss Melly's lack of cooperation, but when they arrived at class the following day, the students were lined up in the hallway outside the door.

"What's going on?" Elena asked Olivia as she, Austin, and Fergie arrived. "Why is everyone standing out here?"

"Booker is giving us a surprise inspection," Olivia replied.

"Huh?" Elena could feel her face growing red.

"He's going to get a progress report from each group to make sure that we're doing a good job putting our simulations together," said Declan.

Elena swallowed hard, hoping that they wouldn't be asked to show what they'd done so far because she and Fergie had only started on the group work the night before. Plus, they knew that Melly hadn't even tried to start on her individual simulation.

Elena wanted to corner Melly to speak with her about what they were going to say about their group work, but Instructor Booker poked his head out of the classroom door and said, "Can I please have Team 4?"

Elena looked at Fergie meaningfully as they followed Melly into the room. Booker's classroom felt humongous without the other students present. They were told to take seats in chairs that had been brought near his desk.

Then, the Instructor said, "Ladies, this is your mid-quarter progress report on the group work you were assigned for the Roman Empire. So, tell me how it's going."

Before Elena could even think about how to communicate Melly's lack of participation in the nicest way possible, Melly said, "Sir, I have to be honest and say that these girls have left me out of almost every decision. It's always Elena and Fergie doing all the work and when I ask to be involved, they tell me not to worry about it."

Elena knew her mouth was hanging open, but she didn't care. The only part of Melly's statement that was completely true was that she and Fergie were doing all the work, but that was primarily because Melly hadn't attended any of the scheduled study groups. Elena was thankful that Fergie was sitting in between her and Melly because she had a sudden urge to spit in her face.

"Is this true?" Booker asked, surveying Elena and Fergie's faces.

"Um…let me think about it…" Elena said sarcastically. "No!"

"Are you saying that Miss Linus has given a false report?" asked Booker.

"Oh, I'm sorry, I'll try that again without the sarcastic slang," Elena said bluntly. "I'm calling her a *liar!*"

"I have *never* told a lie in my life," Melly said in a sickly-sweet voice. "And I can't even believe you'd suggest that."

Elena opened her mouth to yell, but Fergie said, "Instructor Booker, it is true that our group has displayed some different opinions about how to accomplish the tasks you have assigned, but we are working hard to complete them."

This seemed to satisfy the Instructor because he replied, "Very well. I will leave you to it."

When they were dismissed, Elena felt stunned as she entered the hallway outside the classroom. She rounded on Melly immediately.

"What was that about?"

"What do you mean?" Melly said innocently.

"You lied to Booker!" Elena hollered, beyond caring who overheard their conversation.

Melly flipped her hair over her shoulder and turned to march down the hallway.

"I don't know what you're talking about," she called over her shoulder. Then, after noticing a group of students at the other end of the hall, Melly called, "Oscar, wait for me!"

Acid was boiling in Elena's stomach as she watched the back of Melly's head disappear into the crowd.

She looked frantically up and down the hallway and, after seeing Declan, shouted, "Bowen! I need to Simulab. Wanna go?"

Declan approached her steadily and said, "Um…you seem a little crazy."

"Does that mean you're not up for a little kickboxing?" Elena asked, her eyebrows rising.

Minutes later, Elena stepped onto the simulation floor and pulled on the Transmitter suit. Once Declan's suit was securely fastened to his body, a holographic gaming projection of Elena and Declan appeared inside the matted ring in front of them. The timer counted down ten seconds during which Elena and Declan's holographic projections stared at one another. When the buzzer sounded, she wasted no time moving in on him, throwing punches and blocking when necessary. She was being particularly aggressive, and she knew it.

"Easy, Ransom," Declan said after a couple minutes. "You're throwing punches too hard. You're gonna hurt yourself."

Elena was already so angry and didn't appreciate being told she was doing something wrong, so she threw an extra hard punch. Declan's simulation flew off his feet, twisted through the air, and landed hard on his back.

"Nice one," Declan managed to cough out.

The simulation Declan staggered to his feet. Elena was working up a sweat and their fight was gathering quite a crowd of screaming and cheering students.

After the twelfth round, Declan and Elena were tied, but in the thirteenth round she managed to get one last hit in for the win. She should have felt great about her victory, but she didn't feel any satisfaction in winning because her thoughts were consumed with Melly's lies to Instructor Booker.

And that's precisely why Elena found it shocking when she saw Pigg sitting with Melly at a pupil station in the Media Room after classes the following afternoon. Unable to control herself, Elena marched straight over to their table and reached for Pigg's arm.

"What are you doing?" she asked, the edges of her words filled with disbelief.

"Gribbin is helping me with my homework," Melly answered for him.

"Don't call him Gribbin," Elena replied through gritted teeth.

Melly's smile engulfed her entire face.

"Perhaps he likes to be called Gribbin." She turned to Pigg and asked, "Don't you like it?"

Pigg looked from Melly to Elena and back to Melly.

"Confrontation makes me uncomfortable," he managed to squeak.

"Pigg, we're over there." Elena pointed to the pupil station where Austin and Declan were sitting. "You can come with me. Don't feel like you have to stay here with *her*."

"Elena, why is it so incomprehensible for you to believe that Gribbin wants to help me with my homework?" Melly asked.

"Have you ever met you before?" Elena asked dryly.

Melly looked back at Pigg until their eyes locked. "Elena, we're busy doing homework. Perhaps you can ask Gribbin to help you with your homework another time."

Elena waited to see if Pigg would look at her, but when he didn't, she turned and walked away from the table with confusion spreading through her body like wildfire.

Over the next few days, Pigg started spending more time with Melly and Elena's mood changed from bad to worse. She was terse when responding to everyone that spoke to her, she was temperamental during class toward Instructors, she wouldn't answer any of Booker's questions during his class (even when he called on her), she skipped her Phonology tutoring with Fergie, and she was so irritated with the sheep she was supposed to be caring for during Social Science that she tried to sell it to Declan.

Elena wanted to do something malicious to Melly in retaliation. She'd seriously considered cutting off her blonde hair while she was asleep in their room. She'd also thought about throwing Melly's clothes off the balcony, but everything she considered came with serious consequences.

She let thoughts of revenge consume her until one afternoon when she arrived in the Media Room and found that Pigg was studying with Austin, Declan, and Abria. Elena walked over silently. She took a chair at their table, made eye contact with Austin, and smiled at him. She liked having her friend back.

Elena took out her Smartslate and began to work on her homework. She and her friends studied in silence for a long while, until finally she dropped her Smartslate on the table.

"I hate homework!" she blurted.

"Does anyone actually like homework?" Declan asked.

"I only like the Social Science lab module because I get to stand close to Frankie Smiley for an extra, like, hour after class," said Abria.

Pigg groaned out a loud yawn.

"So sorry to bore you with my story," Abria said to him.

"Oh, it's not that," Pigg said. "I was up late helping Melly with her homework."

"You mean *doing* her homework," Elena said unkindly.

Pigg's face turned red. "I think she really likes me."

"She doesn't like you," Elena scoffed. "You're the twelfth guy she's done this to."

"Done what?" asked Pigg.

"Oh, at first she gives you complete attention. Then, she flirts with you so much that you feel like you like her. After that, she starts getting you to carry her Smartslate to class and sit with her at meals. Then, she asks if you can start studying with her after school. Eventually, you're doing her homework while she starts chatting it up with the new guy sitting next to her. Sound familiar?"

Pigg shrugged and said, "You're just jealous that she's giving me attention."

"I'm *not* jealous," Elena said forcefully. "She *lied* to Instructor Booker. She said that Fergie and I were doing everything and leaving her out. I was so stunned I couldn't even speak."

"*You* couldn't speak to defend yourself?" Declan asked, sounding shocked. Elena could see the corners of his mouth twitching with a smile. "I can't even imagine it."

"Oh, sure, laugh at me." Elena made a face at Declan. "Melly is the most evil partner ever. I wish she'd get sick so she can't come to class. No, I wish she'd get that disease where you can't speak ever again," Elena paused to think and then said, "Wait, I got it. I wish she would get lost in her own simulation and never return."

"That can't really happen, can it?" Pigg whined.

"Why? Would you be devastated to lose your lying, cheating girlfriend?" Elena asked.

"She's not m-my g-girlfriend," Pigg sputtered.

"You spend enough time together *studying*!" Elena hollered.

"Wow, you really don't like her," Abria said thoughtfully.

"Nah, we're besties," Elena said sarcastically. "Haven't you been listening? Melly's a nightmare. The next time I see her I think I'll spit in her perfect, blonde hair."

Everyone at the table was silent for a moment. Elena realized they were looking at her with concerned faces. Austin appeared almost disappointed. Maybe she'd gone too far, but she was too frustrated to care. She stood suddenly and grabbed her Smartslate.

"I'll see you later."

Elena hurried out into the hallway and to the nearest Grimvator, but before the doors slid shut, Austin hopped on with her. She looked at the floor, at her nail bitten fingers, and at the Optivision screen that was rotating through the floors, anything to keep her from looking at Austin.

Finally, Austin said, "Lena, don't let Melly control you like this."

"I'm not!" snapped Elena.

"Really?" Austin said, his eyebrows rising high on his forehead. "You've been in a bad mood for three days now."

"She shouldn't have lied to Booker," said Elena. "Unless she was lying to make us look good. I mean, where was her team loyalty?"

"You can't expect to get along with everyone."

"I don't," Elena said. "The fact that I can tolerate Wheeler is proof of that. But she made us look bad. Now, she's using Pigg. I can't stand it!"

"You and Fergie are going to do fine on the exam without Melly's help. So, let it go," said Austin. "Also, you have to let Pigg make his own mistakes, as painful as it is to watch."

Elena ripped her pinky fingernail off with her teeth and said, "I think some act of payback might be a better solution."

¤ 14 ¤

The Riddle

"You want to cross the ocean? Are you crazy?" Kidd Wheeler asked in disbelief.

Yesterday, Elena had been plotting revenge on Melly, but now she was sitting at the Firebird Station with her friends accepting that she was going to do something else that would risk her life.

Austin and Fergie spent twenty minutes describing their theory about the longitude and latitude concept to Kidd. He seemed flabbergasted and irritated.

"You can't cross that much water in a hovercraft," Kidd said forcefully.

"You are quite right," Fergie said stiffly. "We cannot cross the ocean as the Independence is currently constructed. Which is why we are relying on you to rebuild the hovercraft with the necessary aircraft propelled engines that will enable it to fly."

"You got one of those engines stuffed up your skirt, do ya?" Kidd asked rudely.

"He can't do it," Elena said.

"You're all crazy!" Kidd blurted. "I don't know why I'm sitting here listening to this."

"My parents have already begun to send the necessary materials to give the Independence an aero-upgrade," Fergie continued steadily.

"They've sent machine parts to the school?" Kidd said skeptically.

"Not to the school," Fergie replied. "To the Firebird Station. Remember when I showed you the schematic of the tunneling system in and out of the Firebird Station? One of the tunnels opens directly under the building where my parents work. They have been sending Humanoids with machine parts for several days now."

"At least have a look at it, Wheeler," Austin urged. "If you can get it to work then you have an enhanced hovercraft that can do more than you could have ever imagined."

Kidd looked at Austin in silence for a moment and it appeared to Elena that he was at least considering the option.

"Why do you want to do this?" asked Kidd. "We can't leave the domes again anyway."

Elena looked around at her friends as Fergie said, "I suppose it is time to show him."

Fergie and Austin led the way down the hall to the Research & Development room with Kidd following closely behind them. Fergie walked to the opposite side of the room and opened the cabinets on the far wall to reveal the Decoy Firebirds that her parents created.

Kidd stared in awe at his Decoy. He walked the length of the room slowly, never taking his eyes off his Humanoid.

"My parents built these Decoys. They are equipped with replicas of our Trademarks and a basic program of our daily lives and personalities."

"How did your parents get my Trademark?" Kidd asked.

Fergie looked at him steadily and replied, "My parents have access to many types of pertinent data."

Austin stepped forward and said sensibly, "It's possible that we'll have to cross the ocean at some point. We want to be ready for that sooner than later."

Kidd turned around slowly, shaking his head.

"Show me what you have, and I'll see what I think. But I make no promises about being able to help."

As Fergie led Kidd from the room, Austin immediately opened an Optivision screen.

"What are you doing?" asked Elena.

"I'm going to make a schedule so that we can each be on a rotation to come help Kidd with the aero-upgrade. If we come in shifts, hopefully no one gets suspicious about how much time we're away from the school during second quarter break."

"I thought you said that we could go to Harleston Village during break?" said Abria, her words laced with protest.

"Sorry, Abria," Austin said, looking at her apologetically. "I don't think I'll have time to do that. But you should go with some of the other girls and have fun."

Abria pouted her lip out. "But we could go for, like, a short little time?"

"Maybe next quarter," Austin said vaguely, but Elena noticed that he'd already finished making a shift schedule and started reviewing the plans for the aero-upgrade. Hopper said that he'll try to get the Alpha Manuscript out of the Vault for us. Who knows how long we'll have to wait for that, but I want to be as prepared as we can be for whatever comes next."

"How can we be prepared when we don't even know what we're preparing for?" Abria asked impatiently.

"That's why we're studying all this," Austin said. "In case something new is revealed to us. We'll never know unless we've read every single entry and interpret every single code."

Abria sighed heavily. "I just wanted to get some of that lip gloss that tastes like sour apples. You'd think we could spare a few, like, minutes?"

"I'll go with you," Declan offered and then he looked expectanty at Elena.

"Don't look at me like that!" Elena replied. "I'm not interested in sour apple anything."

Abria smiled happily and looped her hand through Declan's arm.

"Come along, brother. Good-bye to all of you." She waved her hand at Austin and Elena in a dismissive way. "And don't expect me to bring you back anything yummy."

❑

As the fourth and fifth month slipped away, the Grimsby campus began to simulate warm summer weather. Instead of lazy weeknights spent walking the grounds or squandering the evenings in Simulabs, Elena was beginning to feel that sleeping in the Media Room would be a better use of her time so she wouldn't have to walk to and from her bedroom each morning and evening.

The simulation she'd been writing for her second quarter exam was near perfect, but the group module had been slow and complicated because only she and Fergie were working on it.

Fortunately, Fergie's simulation flowed into hers and into the group simulation as well. However, Melly hadn't offered to help nor mentioned anything about her contribution to the project. And, since Elena had refused to speak to her after the lying incident with Instructor Booker, their time together in the Firebird girls' dormitory and in classes was rather uncomfortable.

In addition to this, Elena's attitude toward Melly seemed to get worse when they were under a lot of pressure during Basic Training. And even though the next Basic with the Aves Company was held outside on a fine afternoon, she tensed when she saw Melly and Pigg walking together down toward the lake.

"What do you think those are for?" Abria exclaimed.

Elena tore her gaze away from Pigg and Melly to see where Abria was pointing. Her stomach dropped. Four shipping vessels rose spectacularly out of the lake, each one hanging with a different set of Unit colors. As she got closer to the water, she noticed that Hopper was handing out supplies to each student.

"Where's our tactical vest?" asked Elena as Hopper handed over a pair of aquatic slippers that had webbing laced between the toes.

"No vests today, Ransom," Hopper said.

After roll call, Marshall stood before the Aves Company and barked, "As you see, there are four ships on the lake, one for each Unit. As a Unit, you will swim two hundred meters out to your vessel. Using the human ladder system, you will board the ship. The rest of the exam directions are on board. You will have only one hour to complete the exercise."

Marshall opened an Optivision screen and Elena watched the logo for the Aves Company appear.

The screen began to flash through student faces until Marshall said, "The Lieutenant for the Firebird Unit is Declan Bowen. The Lieutenant for the Raptor Unit is…"

Elena didn't hear the rest of what Marshall said because she shook her head, wondering how Pigg would ever manage to get across the lake without a floatation device. In fact, going that distance as a Unit seemed impossible. How could Declan get everyone across the lake in one piece?

When Marshall was finished speaking, Declan was quick to call the Firebirds together to pair each of the strong swimmers with a weaker trainee. As Elena guessed, Declan chose Pigg to be with her.

"Don't you want to ask Melly to swim with you?" Elena asked Pigg scathingly.

"And suffer the embarrassment of having her help me," Pigg said. "No way!"

"Yet, she's not embarrassed that you do her homework for her," she pointed out.

"That's completely irrelevant given this situation. Besides, you know I only like to swim with you." Pigg punched her lightly in the arm and for a moment he felt like the friend she remembered.

"You're a dimwit," Elena said, rolling her eyes.

A moment later, Declan was calling the Firebirds into a huddle.

"The first, most important thing is to make it to the boat. Everybody ready? Okay, let's go."

Elena watched Austin dive head long into the water and start for the ship using a long arm stride. When it was her turn, Elena and Pigg dove together from the platform. Compared to the pool, the water felt grainy and slimy. She found it hard to move her arms and legs properly. She watched Pigg carefully as they made their way across and was thankful that they both reached the docking platform in one piece.

As Elena pulled herself from the water, she noticed that a human ladder of boys was already in progress, with Crosby Gamble standing at the bottom and Austin standing on his shoulders. Kidd was climbing up Austin's shoulders as the last few Firebirds made it to the docking platform.

"Elena," Pigg said weakly. "Did you see Vivienne get in the boat? She had to *step* on everyone to get up there."

"Yeah, I saw," Elena said. "What did you think Marshall meant when he said *human ladder?*"

"Well, I certainly didn't think he meant that we'd be using our own bodies," Pigg said. "I don't think I can climb up someone's shoulders and arms that way. Also, what if I fall? There won't be anyone to catch me."

"I'll stay down here to catch you, okay?" Elena replied. "You go now after Abria. I'll tell her to stay at the top and wait to help you up and over the side. Then, I'll be right behind you, okay?"

As Pigg stepped on Crosby's thigh to start up the ladder, Elena shouted encouragement at him. Then, she began to hear the other human ladder boys shouting encouragement at Pigg, too. Once he was near enough to the top, Elena began her ascent.

The human ladder was a physically challenging exercise because it required a steady amount of strength and concentration. Elena didn't want to step on anyone's face or hair, but it was very hard to find footing on the different shoulders because she had to be watchful of someone's feet as well. She could feel herself sweating and her heart pounded ungraciously as she finally made the last few steps over the top of the boat.

At long last, the Firebirds were standing on the deck of the ship and Declan accessed an Optivision screen with his Trademark.

"Firebirds," Declan read aloud from the Optivision screen for all to hear. "There are twelve tasks on board this vessel. One member is required to complete one of the twelve tasks. The selected member will scan his or her Trademark into the Optivision screen at one of the twelve stations, and so on, until each Trademark has been scanned."

Declan paused for a moment to look around.

"Let's work together, counterclockwise around the ship. If we're not sure how to complete a task or answer a question, we'll move on and go back to handle it at the end. Agreed?"

As a general murmur of agreement sounded and the Firebirds moved around to their first task.

Olivia Nelson stepped over to the Optivision screen at the first station and read, "One team member is required to climb up and over the mast of the ship."

"So, what are we, like, pirates now or something?" Abria said as a smile spread across Elena's face.

Elena watched Olivia scan her Trademark into the Optivision screen and then begin the ascent over the mast. And so it went, station after station, with the Firebirds being required to inventory cargo, present a manifest, and secure rigging.

When Melly volunteered to complete a rowing simulation, Elena thought seriously about pushing her off the side of the boat. From another Optivision, Fergie had to deduce the language that was being used by the foreign traders, which were simulated figures of humans in period clothing.

Then, Austin was chosen to negotiate the trading of goods on their vessel. Pigg found their location in the world based on astronomical readings and Declan scanned his Trademark at the rope-making station. Finally, they came to an Optivision station that had no supplies or simulated people.

Declan read aloud, "One member from your Unit must solve a riddle under the water."

Elena looked at Crosby Gamble because, beside her, he was the only other person who hadn't completed a task yet.

"I'll do it," Crosby said. "I'm the stronger swimmer."

"My swimming has improved a lot," Elena argued. "Plus, you may be the stronger swimmer, but I can hold my breath a minute longer than you can. And, let's face it, you're not great with riddles. Remember that last class with Booker when we were supposed to decode…"

"Yeah, yeah, I'm such a dimwit," Crosby interrupted her.

Declan surveyed the side of the boat and the water below quietly for a moment. Elena couldn't understand his hesitation about giving her this task, but she remained silent.

"Ransom can do it," Declan finally said. "Be safe, okay? It's a long way down."

Austin handed Elena a diving mask, which she secured tightly to her face. She took a deep breath and jumped off the side of the ship, but the fall was farther than she estimated. She hit the water so hard that it forced the air right out of her. When she resurfaced, she gasped for breath and immediately rolled into a floating position.

"You okay, Ransom?" Elena heard Declan call.

She couldn't speak, but she gave the thumbs up sign. Then, she rolled again. After taking another deep breath, she dove headfirst into the water.

As Elena looked through the clear water, she noticed that the ship had no hull, but instead there was a long, flat platform.

"*Figures that Grimsby wouldn't have actual boats in the lake*," Elena thought. "*Everything is always so fake around here.*"

Then, Elena noticed that the water was very shallow. If she had to guess she would have said it wasn't deeper than twenty feet. She looked for directions but couldn't see anything.

She resurfaced, gasping for air again.

"I can't see anything down there!" She shouted up to Declan. "I don't know what to do. What are the directions again?"

"It says to solve a riddle," Declan hollered back.

Elena rolled her eyes. "This whole dimwit exercise has been a riddle."

She took another deep breath and dove again, determined to be more focused. Elena saw the flat platform that the ship was built on and she saw the other three platforms for the other Unit ships. Then, she saw a diver from one of the other boats enter the water. This student looked as confused about the orders as she felt.

Elena swam a little farther down until she saw a strange formation of rocks near the bottom of the lake. She noticed some type of opening and a light shining on the other side.

Elena decided to swim to the light, but the moment she crossed through the opening the water instantly became so cloudy she could barely see. In addition, the temperature of the water dropped to bitterly cold. She tried to go back the way she came, but there was nothing behind her.

Elena scanned the cloudy water hoping to get bearings. Running low on breath, she spotted the light again, shining towards her left. She kicked as fast as she could, scooping her hands through the water in a frantic way.

When her head broke water, she gulped the air gratefully. She pushed the swim mask off her face and realized that she'd surfaced inside a domed cave with no shoreline. The light she saw before was shining through some sort of glass ceiling above her head.

"This literally makes no sense," Elena said in a frustrated tone.

Elena shoved the mask back onto her face. She tried several times to swim away to find an exit, but the water was so filled with debris that she couldn't see anything beyond the tips of her fingers. The only place she was able to get back to was the cave with the lighted ceiling.

The last time she returned, she noticed a pair of boots treading water.

"What are you doing here?" she exclaimed when she surfaced.

"When you didn't come back up, we worried you'd drowned. Though, now that I'm down here I kinda wish I hadn't come after you," Austin teased. "You always find trouble."

He winked at her playfully. She smiled sarcastically.

"Where's everyone else?" asked Elena.

"A raging thunderstorm started, so Bowen ordered the Firebirds back to shore. But, as always, they can't end this exercise unless we scan our Trademarks on the timer. So, how are we gonna get out of here?"

"Don't ask me," Elena said, the edges of her words filled with discouragement. "I've tried swimming in every direction around this little air pocket, but there's nothing to see out there."

Elena leaned her head back and peered into the ceiling of light above, it was the first time she'd stopped long enough to look at it. She imagined Marshall standing above her, smirking at their ignorance.

"Come on," Austin pleaded. "We can do this. It must be something so easy that it's right in front of our face."

As Elena watched the light move around the ceiling, forming different patterns, she had a sudden idea.

"What if we're not supposed to *swim* out of here?" Elena said. "Leave it to Marshall to design something that could be easily overlooked."

Austin looked up into the ceiling as well.

"An algorithm!" he exclaimed.

"Yes, but there's something strange about this light pattern," Elena said slowly. "It reminds me of something I've seen in my dad's dossier. But how is that even possible?"

"That doesn't matter now," Austin said. "Let's get outta here."

"How? I'm no good with those things. How would you solve it?"

Austin went to work right away, uttering nonsense under his breath. Elena examined the ceiling wishing that she could somehow help him, but this kind of code work had never been her strength.

For a short while, Austin seemed to be wrestling with how to solve the algorithm. But then, his fingers suddenly stretched out along the lines of the light. Whatever he'd touch must have worked because water rushed into Elena's face from the ceiling above.

Suddenly, she was swimming again. She kicked desperately after Austin's feet, hoping that he knew where he was going because she could tell neither up nor down.

The moment before she was sure her breath would run out, Elena's head broke water. She gasped for breath and spit water from her mouth. She saw the top of the Firebirds' ship in front of her, but waves were lapping dangerously against its side. A roll of thunder and a crash of lightning lit the sky.

"We've got to swim to shore," Austin hollered over the sound of the storm.

Elena tried to find the shoreline. She could barely make out the shapes of the other Firebirds waiting for them, but it was nearly impossible to see.

"I don't know if I can swim that far now," Elena replied. "I'm so tired."

"We'll go together," Austin encouraged.

As Austin started for the shoreline, the waves tumbled, crashing around Elena's head, forcing her under the water at times. For a few moments, she lost track of her direction, but then she could always see Austin in front of her.

Slowly, slowly, Elena could tell that she was getting near the shore. Declan, Abria, and Frankie Smiley rushed into the water to support Austin and Elena as they climbed out of the water.

"Next time, Ransom, I think I'll dive from the boat," Declan said with a toothy grin.

"Next time, Bowen, I'll let you," Elena grumbled.

The moment after she scanned her Trademark to stop the timer, Elena sank to the ground in exhaustion.

"If this is what class is like, I can't even imagine what Marshall will do to us during our exam."

¤ 15 ¤

Melly's Presentation

On the fourth day of the third week of the sixth month, Elena entered Hopper's classroom for second quarter exams. She pulled a seat down from the wall between Fergie and Austin. Every one of her Instructors were standing at the front of the stadium style room and waiting in silence for the students to be seated.

"While the exam is in progress," Booker began, "we ask that you remain seated. First, we'll watch," he turned toward an Optivision screen that flashed a set of words with Pigg, Kidd, and Frankie Smiley's faces. "The *Cyrus the Great* simulation."

Elena watched Instructor Booker select a few entries from the Optivision screen. Then, Pigg's voice echoed around the room, explaining the multi-state empire that Cyrus the Great created during the Persian Empire. The room filled from floor to ceiling with an exceptionally detailed map of Persia.

Pigg outlined the forty different provinces within the Persian Empire, he gave details about the system of government that was in place, and used words like *satrap* and *ethnocultural*. He spoke of the fact that the Persian Empire created the world's first mail system and that letters delivered contained official government matters. He explained how the mail carriers were able to cover over two thousand kilometers in seven days.

"One hundred and eleven rest stops were available on the route and all of them belonged to the king," Pigg's voiceover said excitedly.

Then, Elena felt a rush of wind in her face. Suddenly, a Persian warrior with a hide-covered shield and a seven-foot-long thrusting spear appeared beside her pupil station. She looked around and realized she was sitting in the midst of a professional army. She was thoroughly impressed by the attention to detail.

"The enormous geographic size of Persia and the constant struggle for power by the regional competitors warranted the creation of a professional army," Kidd's voiceover began.

When Kidd's presentation ended, the simulation morphed again into a family home, where Frankie's voice described the common attire and the life of the common resident.

"Persian children from their fifth year until their twentieth year were instructed to do three things well. Ride a horse, draw a bow, and speak the truth," said Frankie's voiceover. "Also, the entire culture considered the act of lying to be a cardinal sin and that it was even punishable by death."

Finally, the group portion of the exam began with boys' voices speaking at different intervals, describing the local customs, how the Persians offered sacrifices to elements like the sun and wind, and how Cyrus the Great allowed the Jews to return to Israel after decades of being held captive by the Assyrian and Babylonian empires.

Elena watched the construction of spectacular cities that were utilized for governance and inhabitation, temples that were made for worship and social gatherings, and mausoleums that were erected in honor of fallen kings.

"This is the city of Daskileion," said Pigg's voice. "It was an important province and a holy site. The structures included a provincial palace, government buildings, religious structures, and a Zoroastrian worship center, which included carvings depicting the Zoroastrian priests, known as Magi."

Elena could tell that Pigg had been instrumental in helping with every aspect of the simulations. She was proud of Pigg; he truly had a unique gift.

She felt that his group would get the top mark in the class even though she hadn't seen the other simulations yet. When their simulation ended Pigg's group received a loud round of applause and a standing ovation.

Booker said, "Very well done. Now, let's have," he turned toward the Optivision and the words "Pax Romana" appeared along with Elena, Fergie, and Melly's faces.

Elena felt a rush of excitement mixed with pride as the simulation began with a map of the Roman Empire during 27 BC and Fergie's voice giving the definition for Pax Romana. Her simulation was beautifully designed and intricately detailed, including a module where Elena could hear the workers tools as they added to a famous monument.

A few minutes later, Elena's part of the simulation began with a detailed timeline of the rulers in ancient Rome. Her exam included a section where the students were sitting inside a replica of the Senate building while someone was writing a new law for the government. She didn't hear as many gasps of excitement as she'd heard when Pigg's exam was playing, but there were a few claps and bursts of laughter in the right spots.

"Great job!" Austin nudged her in the shoulder.

As Elena's simulation was coming to an end, she began to feel very nervous about Melly's portion of the exam. She was expecting a white screen where Melly's simulation should have been, but instead she was sitting inside a traditional Roman house that contained every detail a person could think of including the paintings on the walls. Melly's voiceover described clothes and hair fashions, the common daily life of a typical family, and a smorgasbord of Roman cuisine.

"A common meal included dishes such as soft-boiled eggs in pine nut sauce, roast wild boar, ostrich ragout, veal escalope with raisins, Lucanian sausages, garum fish sauce, and seasoned mussels," said Melly's voiceover as Elena watched a table fill with food.

The simulation was so good that Elena could actually smell the columella salad, which was a mix of salted fresh cheese, mint, sliced leek, coriander, and parsley. Elena was stunned at the pure genius of the simulation. But, as

Melly's portion was coming to an end, Elena began to feel that her presentation was looking a little too familiar. And then, she could see it, in the tiniest details. Pigg's unique programming technique, including his personal signature, were in the edges of the simulation.

Elena had a hard time enjoying any of the other simulations, even the one that Abria had written about the wonderful traditions in ancient China, because she was completely consumed with Melly's part of their exam. She was certain that Pigg wrote the entire module, and she was extremely curious as to why.

As soon as the class was over, Elena followed Melly stealthily down the hall and into the nearest washroom with Fergie hard on her heels.

The moment the door shut behind them Elena grabbed Melly's arm and exclaimed, "Did you have Pigg write your simulation for you?"

Melly looked a little taken aback at first as she looked from her arm to Elena's stubborn face, but then she replied, "No, he just helped me a little."

"Really?" Elena scoffed. "Because it looked like he wrote the whole thing. I don't want you taking advantage of my friend."

"I am sure that Gribbin doesn't feel taken advantage of," said Melly. "But I'll be sure to ask him."

"You know, I think you always have a different guy around because you don't care about the feelings of others. You're so manipulative, controlling, and full of...what's the word?" — Elena put a finger on her temple and tapped it for effect — "Oh yeah, rubbish."

Melly laughed at her remark, but it was a manic laugh, like Melly was thinking of a way to cook Elena in a stew without anyone noticing.

"Oh, Ransom," Melly said lightly, though her eyes were aflame with anger. "You're always so..."

"Honest," Elena offered.

"I was going to say *coarse*," Melly replied.

"Leave Pigg alone," Elena threatened.

"Or what? You'll tell someone he wrote my simulation? Nice try, but that would put Fergie and your grade in jeopardy."

"Oh, I won't tell anyone what you did, Linus," said Elena. "But I will do everything in my power to make your life miserable."

"Hum, I don't think you will," Melly said simply and then she turned to walk toward the exit. "But you're welcome to try."

After the door slid shut silently, Elena turned to Fergie and said, "Do you think she believes what she says? I mean about Pigg not writing her exam for her?"

"I am not certain," Fergie admitted. "But that is the most disconcerting part, is it not?"

"What?" Elena asked as they walked back into the hall.

"If she is lying, she seems to feel no guilt in doing so," said Fergie. "But if she believes she is telling the truth, when in fact she is lying, then her lying is pathological. Either way, it presents a very risky situation for the Firebirds."

Before Elena had a chance to consider the long-term effects of what that would mean, her friends came running up, talking excitedly about the different simulations and congratulating one another on a great exam. She only felt relieved that second quarter break had officially begun.

However, her excitement for a break from classwork was fleeting. The next day she arrived for her scheduled time to work on the Independence with Kidd. He led her back to the engine room where Elena saw piles of machine parts and other items that she didn't recognize.

"I need you to sit here and affix these rotors on the turbine," Kidd said as he showed her exactly how he needed it done.

Elena tried to watch attentively, but his hand movements made no sense to her. Then, he started talking about compressor blades, exhaust assembly, liner assembly, and the proper placement of discs.

"So, I'm going to interrupt you now," Elena said shortly. "You said a whole bunch of stuff that makes absolutely no sense."

Kidd sighed loudly.

"I don't want you to do anything about those other things. I only need you to do the rotors, okay? Or else I can't finish working. Get it?"

Elena crossed her arms over her chest. "You really need to work on your people skills."

"I don't think that *you* are the right person to teach me about that," Kidd replied spitefully before turning to walk away.

Elena sat down in a huff in front of the first turbine. The impulsive side of her wanted to call Kidd a nasty name and scream at him that she didn't care if he ever finished the upgrade. But the logical side of her knew that they needed the aero-upgrade if they wanted to cross the ocean.

She sighed and picked up the first rotor. As she worked, she thought about her parents and about how much she wanted to know why they'd been murdered. Elena wished she already knew where all the artifacts were located so she didn't have to go through the hard work of learning.

After three hours of working, Kidd circled back around to Elena's workstation. She noticed that he started at the far end of the room and then moved down the line inspecting the turbines and rotors. When he finally got to her, Kidd had lines of disappointment etched on his face.

"You know, it's possible that you get worse the longer you work on this," he said dolefully.

Elena's feelings of resentment toward Kidd were unfathomable. She threw one of the gadgets she'd been using at his head and then stalked out of the hangar. She returned to her dorm room without speaking to anyone that tried to approach her along the way.

Even though Elena refused to return to the Station to help Kidd, Austin somehow convinced her to go back under the condition that she could be supervised by another person. So, she spent a lot of time with Declan, working with wires and bolts in the engine room.

"So, you want to tell me what's going on?" Declan asked one afternoon while they were cleaning up an extraordinary mess they'd made while trying to bring food to the Independence from the Firebird Station galley.

"What do you mean?" Elena replied as she pushed together a pile of aluminum containers that had fallen out of the box she'd been carrying.

"Do you want to tell me why you've been all stormy lately?" Declan clarified.

Elena rolled her eyes. "I'm always stormy."

"But lately it has been a bit more," Declan pointed out.

Elena put the last aluminum container in the box and said, "Do you realize that if Melly hadn't come to school that Pigg would be the one stocking the galley on the Independence instead of us?"

Declan nodded his head. "I know that you miss Pigg, but you shouldn't worry about it so much. It is Linus that he's spending time with after all."

Elena knew what Declan meant without him having to explain. She knew that soon enough Melly would get tired of Pigg's company and that he'd be back in their circle. However, she knew that Pigg would also feel hurt by the rejection and Elena wished she could spare him from the pain.

Despite Pigg not being present at the Firebird Station, Elena and her friends worked hard on the Independence until second quarter break was over.

○

The seventh month of school began with particularly warm weather. Even the late afternoon air was thick with humidity, making Elena's shirt cling to her everytime she walked outside.

"I'm sure that Instructor Niva has already informed you that by 100 AD, paper was used by the general populace in China," Booker said on their first day of class. "We also see the first appearance of the wheelbarrow, the development of religious practices in the American Indians, the classic age of the Maya civilization, and in 400 AD one of the first women scientists became the head of the Neo-Platonist school at Alexandria.

"So, for the next few classes I am going to facilitate a discussion about social class in some of these different societies. We'll discuss heredity, property, wealth, citizenship, mythology, religious practices, and trade in different cultures of the world that existed between 1AD and 500 AD."

For the rest of class, the Harrier Unit had a lively debate with some of the Firebirds about the Mayan civilization. Elena could tell which students from Harrier had researched the Mayan peoples for their second quarter exam simulation by the way they forcefully argued specific details of the evolution of their culture, language, and trade.

Elena could barely concentrate on the words that were flying around the room. Her mind was fixated on the Firebird Station, the Ransom Dossier, and trying to understand what the connection was between the Amulet, Cryptext, Catalan Atlas, and the other artifacts they still needed to find.

After dinner that evening, Elena gathered with Austin, Abria, and Declan in the Media Room to begin their homework.

"I know we're supposed to be studying, but Oscar Hunter from Raptor challenged Harper Gable from Falcon to a duel in the Simulab. I have to see it so I really need to get through this quickly," said Abria.

"I still have to finish Booker's essay on the difference between Confucianism and Taoism," Elena grumbled. "So, I'll pretty much be here until tomorrow. Also, Emerald has us in labs with the Harrier Unit to learn how the Chinese made paper in 100 AD. We'll have to meet up with them before next class. I really hate group work."

"At least the Harriers are nice. When we work with the Raptor Unit in Physics I want to run screaming from the room," Abria said.

"I can't believe we're still raising sheep and goats for Emerald. He's teaching us how to use goat milk to make cheese and sheep wool to make clothes. It's disgusting," Elena complained.

"I keep getting the Chinese Dynasties confused," Declan said absentmindedly, like he hadn't been listening to their conversation.

"I don't know how much more I can learn about the Kingdom of Kush. I had to watch Booker's tutorial three more times and I still didn't understand everything he said," Austin said. "And in Phonology, I had to rewrite the Hebrew symbols twice because I kept confusing them with Akkadian."

"Yeah, I'm supposed to be able to understand the Greeks' system of Physics and Astronomy," said Declan. "But the only thing that has made sense are the dimwit rope working modules with Hopper, which makes me confident that I could be a pirate if school doesn't work out."

"Oscar Hunter and Harper Gable have made it impossible for anyone else in their Units to advance in Basic Training because anytime someone is chosen as Lieutenant they take over," said Abria, her mind still clearly on watching their Simulab.

"It's a good thing that the Harrier Unit has Social Science to fall back on because their performance during Marshall's class is always so pathetic, though I'd never say it to their face," said Declan.

"Oh, I like Stella Grooms so much," said Abria. "She's just the sweetest. And her hair is a-maz-ing! I have to admit that I'm the teensiest bit jealous."

"Where's Pigg?" Elena asked after she pulled up yet another Optivision screen with homework. "He could use some help with Social Science. He was telling me after class that the people in lab group make him nervous."

"He's helping Melly with her homework," Declan replied.

"Again?" Elena said. "Oh, I want to punch that girl in the face. Did you hear that she talked Frankie Smiley into helping her with Niva's homework assignment and then she stole his original work and submitted it as her own before he could? Poor guy had to start completely over. And after what she did during our exam…"

Abria watched Elena with a strange smile on her face. "You're turning into quite a little gossip. I'm so proud of you!"

"I don't get why you're so upset about Melly cheating off Pigg when you did that for years," Austin said.

"First of all," Elena said snottily. "My cheating with Pigg was mutually beneficial. Melly just uses him. And second, I'm a reformed cheater so you can't throw that in my face anymore."

As Austin smiled, Elena noticed the door to the Media Room open and Melly walk in with a couple boys standing on either side of her.

Elena scowled. "How much you want to bet that Pigg's off somewhere finishing Melly's homework while she's here flirting with these dimwits? You know, if this was Rome, I think I'd throw her to the lions."

▭ 16 ▭

The Wilderness

On top of the rigorous classwork, Elena had to suffer Melly's constant presence every single time she tried to speak to Pigg because they were together whenever she saw him over the next few days.

During Phonology, Elena asked Pigg if he would join her in a group with Austin and Fergie, but he shook his head and walked off with Melly to a pupil station at the far end of the room. At lunchtime, she noticed that they continued to be alone at the farthest table from the Firebirds. Finally, during Physics, Melly answered for Pigg in an infuriatingly superior tone.

"We have a lot of work to catch up on, Ransom. Maybe you should be concerned about finishing your own work instead of what we're doing."

"Don't worry about him," Austin said as Elena sat down in a huff at their workstation. "He has a crush. He knows that we're his real friends."

Austin's words didn't make Elena feel any better. She was hoping that Melly would have given up on Pigg by now, especially since Melly was constantly hanging all over Harper Gable from Falcon when Pigg wasn't around. She wanted to plan some type of sabotage on Melly and Pigg, but she was sure that Austin wouldn't help so she tried to put it out of her mind.

However, as the Firebirds gathered for another horrendous swim lesson with Marshall the following day, she was frustrated once again that Pigg and Melly were standing off to one side of the room chatting.

Marshall finished explaining that each Unit would be required to wear a custom tactical vest that was designed for swimming. As the Firebirds began to gather around an equipment station to choose swim masks and tactical vests, Elena noticed that Pigg hadn't attempted to collect his gear because he and Melly were huddled in conversation. With a growing amount of irritation, she grabbed a tactical vest, swim mask, and swim fins, and started toward Pigg and Melly.

"Here," Elena said coldly as she tossed the equipment at Pigg who fumbled and dropped everything on the floor. "So you don't drown."

"Where's my stuff?" Melly asked in a sickeningly sweet voice.

"I don't care if you drown," Elena said over her shoulder as she walked back toward Austin.

"Why do you have to be so mean to her?" Austin whispered to Elena after she'd joined him poolside.

"I don't consider myself *mean*," Elena said. "I actually think that Melly brings out my best qualities."

"What do you think this is, like, for?" Abria asked, holding up a small whistle.

"You use the whistle if you find yourself in an emergent situation," Fergie replied in a formal tone. "Of course, you will need to be above the water to use it."

"Look at this breathing apparatus!" Declan said excitedly. He shoved the thing in his mouth and made a goofy face.

Elena smiled until she noticed Melly take the items she'd thrown at Pigg from his arms. As she watched Pigg go collect new swim gear, Elena decided that she was going to try to make Pigg spend time with her during their next group lesson. However, she never got her chance.

In Hopper's class, when Elena walked around the room to stand beside Pigg, she didn't have a chance to speak to him before Melly walked in and he hurried to be near her. Elena felt a strange mixture of rage and failure so extreme that she decided to give up on Pigg completely.

◻

As the eighth month was coming to an end, Elena felt overwhelmed from everything she'd learned during third quarter classes. Her brain was a blur of dates, cultures, religious practices, and maniacal rulers vying for their sense of purpose or power. She wondered how it was possible for her Instructors to include everything they'd learned on the third quarter exam, but she knew they would try.

As she and Austin sat in the Media Room reviewing their Smartslates and watching a miniature hologram of Instructor Copernicus' latest class, Elena dropped her head into her hands.

"I can't believe third quarter exams start in three days. At least we have tomorrow for one last review. Then, I assume we'll study constantly over the weekend. But I'm so tired." Elena rubbed her eyes forcefully. "When we're done with exams, I'm going to sleep our entire break."

"You can't sleep that much," said Austin practically. "Besides, I need you to help us work more on the Independence. Fergie said her parents are sending the last of the supplies for the aero-upgrade at the end of the week."

"Ugh…working with Wheeler on that hovercraft is completely miserable. He's so moody and he complains that I'm not doing things right. So, I think I'll skip out on that *fun* during our break." Elena looked around and frowned at Pigg and Melly who were sitting alone at a pupil station across the room. "Marshall was awful today, too. I wonder what he'll do to us in the next exam."

"If I had to guess, I'd say something terrifying and demoralizing."

Elena smirked. "Whatever it is, I hope we get to choose our own leader. The Firebirds always do best when you're in charge. You're such a great leader."

"I don't want to be a great leader," said Austin. "Just a wise one."

"What's the difference?" Elena asked.

"Great leaders are recognized in history whether or not they cared well for the lives of the people. Wise leaders may not get as much fame or glory, but they make a positive impact on the people who follow them."

Elena rolled her eyes; sometimes Austin could be a little too adult-like. "Okay, Confucius, that's enough thought for the day."

As it turned out, Elena soon learned that Austin was right about the way history remembered leaders because the next morning Booker made a point to explain the differences between the Roman Caesars and how the way they chose men to rule had a lasting effect on the entire Empire.

"The Emperor Nero ruled the Roman Empire from 54 to 68 AD. He focused much of his attention on diplomacy, trade, and enhancing the cultural life. But he was also a cruel tyrant who started the Great Fire of Rome, which destroyed three of the fourteen districts and severely damaged seven others. He also persecuted religious people. He was known for sacrificing these people during gladiatorial games and he also set their bodies on pikes and lit them on fire to light his gardens at night."

Elena heard Pigg let out a small gasp.

"No matter how much they tried, the Romans could not sustain their Empire forever," continued Booker. "In 285 AD, political division split the Empire into two separate governing sections, one in the East and one in the West. By 476 AD, the Eastern Roman Empire lost its last emperor."

Elena watched a simulation of the last Roman Caesar of the Western Roman Empire, Romulus Augustus, being overthrown by a Germanic chieftain on Booker's Optivision screen.

"For many centuries there was a common belief that the Roman Empire fell to barbarians. However, it is more accurate to say that Rome was a constantly emerging culture," Instructor Booker said as the Optivision filled with new images of landowners and plantations.

"After the Western Caesar was overthrown, the wealthier citizens of Rome fled to their property outside the city where they employed the serfs to work their land. This, in turn, created small villages. This kind of lifestyle led to a loss of technology and trade.

"The people on these plantations would not have received any formal education. Therefore, many never learned to read. Most people were born, lived, and died on the same plantation.

"In contrast, the Western Roman Empire transitioned into the Byzantine Empire, which continued for another thousand years. I've asked Instructor Niva to join us so she can show us the evolution of language in the Byzantine Empire."

As Instructor Niva stepped forward, Elena watched an Optivision fill with symbols. Elena had grown accustomed to this style of team teaching by now. The Instructors were trying to fill their brains with as much relevant information before the exam that they hardly ever switched classrooms anymore.

So, it was no surprise to Elena that Instructor Copernicus and Instructor Emerald were standing together in the AstroPhysics classroom later. For four hours, they took turns describing and detailing a civilization called the Hopewell Tradition, which started in New York and eventually included area from the Canadian territory all the way down to the southeastern parts of North America.

After a full day of review for their third quarter exam, Elena couldn't wait for dinner. She'd noticed that their meals had become more extravagant lately. In the past few days, she'd filled up on smoked ham hock and confit, chicken terrine, salmon and crab cannelloni, lemongrass velouté, and slow poached chicken breast stuffed with wild mushrooms and broad beans.

Tonight, she enjoyed a braised collar of pork with sweet potato puree and roast plum, lemon and mint crushed potatoes, and buttered spinach. It was a particularly extraordinary meal.

"I know our meals have been larger lately, but after a busy week like this I want to hold up my bowl and say 'Please, sir, can I have some more,'" Elena said, after she'd licked her plate clean.

"You could have told us you were, like, coming to dinner," Abria said, dropping in a seat at the table with Declan sitting beside her.

"Sorry, we were starving," Elena said. "And didn't feel like hunting the school for you. Besides, it looks like you found us okay."

Abria made a face at her, and they laughed.

Then, Pigg arrived looking sadder than Elena had ever seen him and sat down with a small thud.

"You were right about Melly," said Pigg dolefully. "She doesn't like me."

Elena knew that was true, but she felt bad for him anyway. "Why do you say that?"

"Well, last night I told her I didn't have time to help her with her homework, so she gave me a weird look and walked away without saying anything. Then, this morning, Harper Gable from Falcon was walking her to class and when I tried to say *hello* she completely ignored me."

"Well, that was the weirdest, non-relationship I've ever heard of. I tried to tell you she is a wolf in sheep's clothing, but you didn't listen," Elena said.

"Don't make him feel worse," Abria scolded her. She turned to Pigg, took his hand in hers, and very sympathetically said, "It's her loss. You're a great guy."

Pigg blushed but looked slightly cheered up by the compliment.

"Here, you can have my hazelnut and tonka bean cheesecake with roasted strawberries," Abria said, pushing her dessert toward him.

"You know what we should do," Elena said. "We should cut off all her hair while she's sleeping. Or we could paint a mustache on her face with some of Abria's nail polish."

Everyone at the table laughed and Pigg looked like he was starting to feel better. But then, Elena suddenly felt sick. Her vision blurred in and out and she felt as though she might topple sideways out of her chair. She looked at Austin.

"Elena...Elena?" His voice sounded distant and echoed. She reached for his hand, but she couldn't quite hang on to it.

The last thing she heard before she blacked out was the sound of Pigg's voice asking, "Does anyone else feel strange?"

Elena was off, soaring high in the sky amongst the clouds. She felt warm and exhilarated. She came to a castle crafted of puffy white. Her parents greeted her at the door. They walked together happily for a long time.

Suddenly, Elena could hear screaming. She watched the sky turn angry black. Her skin felt as though it was being pricked by hundreds of nettles. Then, there was a rustle of dead leaves and a faint scent of frost. Elena felt that her eyes were open, but it was so dark that she couldn't see her hands.

Far above her, clouds broke apart and the moon shown down giving enough light for her to see branches and leaves. She turned her head left and right, noticing tree trunks and pine needles covering a forest floor. The desperately cold temperature caused Elena to shake.

Slowly, she pushed herself into a sitting position. She was wearing a storm jacket that was lined with fleece and an aviator hat with flaps that covered her ears, yet she was still freezing.

Fear crept into every fiber of her being. She had no clue where she was or how she got there. She tried to think back to the last thing she remembered and eventually she recalled feeling dizzy during lunch. Something had gone wrong. Her lunch had been drugged or poisoned; she was sure of that. Now, she was alone in the unbridled dark.

Coming to terms with her situation didn't help Elena feel better until she remembered that at least Pigg had been drugged, too. Did that mean he was somewhere close by?

"Austin?" Elena called hoarsely.

Her cry was returned by a throng of howling animals coming from far away. A shudder of panic surged through her again.

"Think, think," she demanded. "I've had survival training. I know how to do this."

Elena reached out and felt along the ground until her fingers caught on something familiar. She knew without seeing that it was a tactical pack. Feeling relieved, she fumbled around, found the zipper, and unhooked the hololight from the zipper clip.

Elena flipped on the hololight, which was so bright that she was able to see far around her. She saw nothing except forest and no clear way to go.

"I need to find shelter so I don't freeze to death," Elena whispered as she stood up shakily.

She lifted the tactical pack over her shoulder and set off between the trees with the hololight above her head.

Before long, she came to the base of a rocky precipice. She followed along the rock face until she found a crevice that was large enough to hold her and the pack.

Elena opened her pack and was relieved to see a blanket right on top. She took the blanket, settled the pack in the crevice and climbed inside. Between the rocks, her storm jacket and hat, and the blanket, Elena began to feel warm. She also felt extremely tired, so she leaned her head against the pack and fell into a deep sleep.

The sky was bright and clear when Elena finally came to her senses. She pulled off the blanket and eased slowly out of the rock crevice. Her bones and muscles resisted, throbbing from being curled in the same position for so long. All around her, the forest was thick with green pines and trees with purple, red, and orange leaves. The colorful foliage had also collected along the ground, creating a soft stretch of earth through the forest.

The Grimsby campus was currently simulating the warm weather of the eighth month of the year, so Elena wondered why it was so cold outside. Then, she had the unnerving feeling that maybe she wasn't at Grimsby at all, that maybe she'd been taken somewhere else entirely.

Elena walked a little way into the forest. At first, it looked strange with its wide trunked trees and massive, exposed roots. Boulders covered with lichen grew up out of the ground like giants and tree branches hung low to the ground like creeping plants. Once or twice she flinched, thinking that she'd seen an animal or a predator, but really it was the colors moving along the horizon.

Finally, far in the distance, Elena saw a hanging tree that looked very familiar. As she came close enough to examine it, she realized that it was similar to the tree that grew in front of the Firebird Station concealing the door from view.

"At least I'm still at school," said Elena aloud. "I mean, I'm pretty sure I'm still at school."

Elena had spent so much time tromping the Grimsby grounds that she was certain of two things. One, the resident buildings, simulated lake and mountain, and the Gauntlet were located to the west of the Firebird Station, which gave her hope that she was not too far away. Also, she'd have to walk in the direction of the setting sun to find the campus.

Fortunately, it was already the middle of the afternoon, so Elena wouldn't have to wait long to get started on her journey. But first, a picnic seemed appropriate since she was not only miserable but also extremely hungry.

Elena spread her blanket across the ground and dumped the contents of her tactical pack on top of it. She separated out the flax seed protein bars, dried fruit packets, powdered soup mixes, and a canteen full of water. Then, she picked through two pairs of snow socks, one armorwear shirt, and a pair of insulated gloves that she promptly pulled on her hands. She found a billycan, a whistle, a medical kit, a pocketknife, and a firestarter.

From the very bottom of the bag, she pulled out a mysterious zipper pouch. She opened it and pulled out a large piece of canvas that she quickly determined was some type of tent, but she didn't have any poles in her bag. She crumpled it in frustration.

"Fantastic," said Elena. "I have half a survival kit."

As she shoved half a protein bar in her mouth, Elena wondered where Austin could be. Then, she began to get angry that the school thought it was perfectly normal to drop a fourteen-year-old girl out in the middle of nowhere without a compass or adequate supplies.

At long last, Elena could tell that the sun was beginning its westward journey. She packed her bag, carefully arranged it in the most comfortable position across her shoulders and fastened the chest straps tightly. Then, she set off through the wilderness thinking that she would like to see Marshall dangling by his ankles from any of the beautiful trees.

After walking a while, Elena began to feel warm, so she removed her outer coat and strung it through the straps on her back. It was bitterly cold even with the sun blaring down on her, but she wanted to avoid overheating. Hopper had taught them that it wasn't good to get sweaty in the cold because dampness decreased the quality of the insulation in clothing.

Fortunately, the forest was filled with arctic raspberry bushes, bearberry trees, reindeer moss, and rock tripe, so she stopped often to pick from the edible plants. Gathering berries and fungus along the trail reminded her of a time in her childhood when her parents had taken her to a small farm on the outskirts of Atlanson.

The farm was inside the Atlanson dome, but now that Elena thought about it, she had the distinct feeling that no one visited it much. An older man lived there. She couldn't remember the particulars, but it seemed like her dad was there on business. Elena and her mom walked through the property, picking berries and talking about the springtime carnival that opened every year in Atlanson square.

Elena found that she was smiling until she thought further about the farm. The secluded nature and the near absolute silence of the property had made everything feel dead. In fact, she might have even been afraid had she not been with her mom.

She remembered finding a room filled with books, scrolls, and strange artifacts similar to her dad's library. But there'd been something else. Elena had found a black and white photograph of a massive ship that was partly covered in snow. She'd never seen a photograph before and was mesmerized by the simple, static nature of it.

"That ship was from the Great Flood!" the old man shouted in her ear after he'd crept up behind her. Elena had jumped a mile out of her skin, but the old man didn't even notice. "I was there to see it in all its frozen glory, I tell ya."

At the time, it had been such a bizarre encounter that Elena had forgotten about it entirely. But now, in the quiet of the forest, it was all she could think about. What had her family been doing at that farm? Who was that strange, old man? How did her dad know him? And what possible business could her dad have there?

Quite suddenly, the ground began to slant upwards, and Elena started to ascend a rather steep hill. The climb was slow at first and the dense trees made it hard for her to see far in the distance. After a while, the foliage began to thin, and the sunlight and sky were becoming clearer. Elena realized that she was almost out of the lower parts of the forest. She was hopeful that once she reached the top of the hill, she'd be able to see the peaks of the resident towers in the distance.

With her last few steps, she smiled and reached the peak of the hill. Then, Elena let out a gasp and fell to her knees in despair. As far as her eyes could see, there was nothing except the tops of pine trees and rainbow-colored leaves in the valleys below.

"No!" she yelled out across the mountain peaks. "This can't be right. It doesn't make any sense!"

She thought she would know what to do when she reached the top of the hill. Where was the school? Where were her friends? Was she going in the right direction? Slowly, she realized that she had no hope of knowing how far she had left to go.

▢ 17 ▢

The Fall

Coming to terms with her surroundings was difficult, but eventually Elena realized that sleep was an absolute necessity if she was going to hike the never-ending miles of forest.

The sun was getting very low, but she had no desire to sleep on top of the cold mountainside, so she began to make her way down into the valley below. After an hour, Elena found a good spot to camp between a grouping of exposed, twisted tree roots that created a tangled web of fingers.

Elena hadn't noticed any dangerous animals on her trek, so she felt confident that lighting a fire would be safe. Plus, she was absolutely starving, and a warm dinner seemed appropriate since she felt so hopeless. She searched around for branches and soon had enough kindling to start a decent fire.

Elena dug a small pit with her hands and filled it with tiny sticks and dried moss. She used the firestarter to ignite the base and then added brittle wood and elderberry sticks. Warm relief began to set in when the fire began to grow, the flames rising ever higher.

She took the billycan from her pack and opened a pouch of tomato powder soup mix. Then, Elena took a risk and used most of the water from her canteen to hydrate the soup in the billycan. She hadn't seen any water along the way but hoped to find some soon. Fortunately, she'd found a log with a sturdy hook-like knot to hold the billycan over the fire. As the soup warmed, she tossed some reindeer moss and rock tripe in the pot.

Then, Elena pulled the tent pouch from her pack, unfolded the canvas, and tossed it over some of the tree roots. She tugged and pulled until it was secure enough to give her some shelter. She arranged some pine needles like a mat underneath the canvas, adding leaves in the hopes that it would provide additional warmth and comfort, and spread her blanket over the top.

"Not exactly a vision of luxury, but I guess it will suffice for one night," Elena said.

Elena was thankful that Hopper's survival classes had been detail oriented and comprehensive because it was making her movements feel more natural. Soon, she removed the soup from the fire so it would cool a bit and arranged some of the fruit she'd picked along the trail across a flat tree root.

"It's not the feast I was hoping for tonight, but a fine meal given my abysmal circumstances," Elena grumbled.

Dinner was lonely. She couldn't remember eating in complete solitude before. She wanted to know where Austin was and if he was safe. She wondered if Abria had awoken in the forest and what kind of situation her blonde friend was enduring with each passing minute. She was curious how Fergie's robotic structure would do in the wild.

As soon as she was finished eating, Elena made sure the fire was secure and settled into her blanket. She fell asleep rather quickly but was soon startled awake.

By the sound of the leaves crunching steadily, it seemed that someone was running wildly in her direction. She jumped up, scrambling to collect her things. However, there wasn't time to get everything, so she left it and dove into the nearest clump of tree roots. She crouched down, waiting quietly as the footsteps came ever closer.

At length, Pigg burst through an overgrowth of foliage and fell hard on the ground, his tactical pack knocking him hard in the head.

"Ouch!" Pigg cried. As he looked up, Elena stepped out of her hiding spot and his mouth fell open. "Elena!"

At first, Elena only stared at him in disbelief. But then, she felt so relieved to see him that she rushed over, dropped to the ground, and threw her arms around his neck, squeezing him hard.

"Elena!" Pigg said, sounding rather startled. "I'm shocked by this emotional outburst...unless...are you real?"

"Of course I'm real, Dimwit," she responded, pushing him slightly as she let him go.

"Ah, but the real Elena would have never hugged me. So, it's possible you are a robot or a simulation."

"I see your point," Elena said. "So, how do we determine if we're real?"

"We need to think of a clever question to ask one another. Something no one else would know the answer to," said Pigg. "We may have to consider several questions before we decide which is the best one because I'm sure Grimsby did extensive background checks on us."

Elena rolled her eyes and blurted, "What's the code to get through the door to Sector 7?"

"Good question," Pigg said admiringly. After he'd answered correctly, she nodded and he asked, "What's your favorite thing to do in Sector 7?"

"Skateboarding."

Elena could see Pigg physically relax.

"How did you find me?"

"I followed my nose," said Pigg. "Your supper smelled delicious. You got any left?"

"Sure." Elena pulled the billycan away from the dying embers.

"I'm freezing. Do you think we could stoke the fire back up?" Pigg asked as he sat beside the pit.

"Of course."

Elena poked around the fire pit until she noticed some orange embers and then tossed dried moss and twigs at it.

Pigg sipped loudly at the billycan. "What happened to us?"

"We were drugged, I'm sure of that much, while we were eating lunch," Elena replied.

"Humph, I guess I'll need to design an application for my PocketUnit that will scan all future meals for poisons. That is, if we ever get back to school." Pigg looked around uncertainly.

"We need to find Austin," Elena said. "He'll know what to do. At first light we'll start the search."

Pigg nodded. "I really struggled last night. It was so cold, and I didn't have much to cover myself with. I had no light, but I was beside a stream and the moon was shining down."

"Is the stream far from here? I need to refill my canteen."

"Not too far, just back there." Pigg took another large sip from the billycan.

"What did you do all day?" asked Elena.

"I sat by the stream and ate from my pack, trying to stay warm."

"You just sat there? All day!" Elena blurted in disbelief. "I had to hike miles to get here."

Pigg only shrugged. "I didn't know where I was. Hopper said it's best to stay put if you don't know where you are, right?" He waited for Elena to reply, but she only smiled sarcastically.

"So, what do you have in your pack?" Elena asked.

"Some protein bars, socks, an extra shirt, a medical kit, and a sleeping bag. What about you?"

"Pretty much the same stuff. Plus, I got a tent with no poles. That was exceptionally useful," Elena said sarcastically. "I wish we had a compass so we could figure out if we're even going in the right direction."

"Oh! I can help with that." Pigg reached into his shirt and pulled out his PocketUnit. "I always keep this hidden in my body bubble now."

An Optivision screen materialized in midair and Pigg used his fingers to scroll through several screens until he found what he was looking for.

"There's the school, right there."

"It can't be there. I was up on that hill," Elena said, turning to point toward where she'd hiked. "There are only hills and trees for miles in every direction."

"Unless we're inside a simulation of sorts," Pigg pointed out. "Or they've simulated the horizon."

"If you had your PocketUnit, why didn't you start hiking toward the school earlier?"

"I honestly never thought about looking for the school. I didn't want to freeze to death. Or starve! Starving to death would be much worse than freezing to death, don't you think?"

"I guess it's a good thing one of us has some sort of survival instincts." Elena yawned loudly. "I can't believe they did this to us."

"What?"

"Dropped us in the middle of nowhere in the freezing cold with practically no supplies."

"I bet it was Marshall's idea," said Pigg gloomily.

"At least now I know why we never see the upperclassmen," Elena said bitterly.

"What do you mean?"

"I'm sure they keep us away from them so we don't hear the stories about this awful training we're going through right now." Elena yawned again. "Let's not worry about it now, though. I'm so tired. You said you have a sleeping bag?"

Pigg grabbed his tactical pack and dumped everything out of it onto the ground.

"Oh, you have a tent too," Elena said, grabbing for the zipper pouch from the pile. "Did you get poles?"

"I don't think so, but I didn't realize that was a tent anyway."

Elena unzipped the pouch, unfolded the canvas tent, and strung it up with hers. Then, she gathered some extra pine needles beside her bed and Pigg laid his sleeping bag on top of it so they could lay close under Elena's blanket. After she'd secured the fire again, she climbed onto the mat under the blanket feeling grateful to get back to sleep.

Pigg was quiet for a minute and then said, "Elena?"

"Hmm?"

"In the survival guide it said something about huddling together unclothed to conserve body heat, so…"

"Easy there, Dimwit!" Elena said crossly, though she was smiling because she knew he couldn't see her face. "I'd rather freeze to death."

When the sun came up, Elena and Pigg each ate a protein bar and the rest of the fresh berries that Elena had picked the day before. Then, they readied their supplies to leave.

Elena followed Pigg through the forest toward the place where he had been left by the stream. She felt they'd walked a long time before she finally saw the water trickling in the distance.

"Pigg, this stream is over a mile away from where you found me. There's no way you could have smelled my dinner cooking last night."

Pigg shrugged. "You should never underestimate the ability of my nose to find food when my stomach is grumbling."

Elena drank an entire canteen full and forced Pigg to do the same. Then, they filled their canteens again. Pigg used his Touchdot to recheck the position of the school. At length, they set off at a steady pace through the frigid forest.

Elena wasn't sure why, but she felt peaceful and happy. Pigg had been talking non-stop since they woke up that morning and he'd gone on for twenty minutes about the proper way to make trail mix, yet she never felt annoyed.

Finally, Elena realized that she was happy because it almost felt like they were at home. Pigg had always been like the little brother you don't want to look after, but she was glad to have him there so she didn't have to pursue the wilderness alone.

About midday, Elena was looking up into the trees as she walked along, when she heard a small thud behind her. She turned to see that Pigg had dropped his bag and was removing a canteen from it.

"I need a minute," Pigg panted. "We've been walking a hundred years."

"I see some berries up ahead," Elena said indicating a grouping of trees with her finger. "I'll be there."

As she reached the berry bush, she dropped her pack to the ground, took out an extra sock, and began to fill it with fruit. Elena's fingers felt cold, but the sky was clear, and the sun was bright.

Then, Elena heard an odd sound and turned to see that Pigg was sprinting toward her with a panicked look on his face.

"What's going on?" she called.

"I heard a noise, back there."

As Pigg turned to look back, he tripped on a tree root and fell into Elena. The force of Pigg's body slamming against her knocked them both off their feet. Then, Elena felt herself falling. But it was more than falling to the ground. She and Pigg were tumbling over one another, gathering speed as they went.

Finally, Elena landed hard on her shoulder. She had shut her eyes tightly as they were falling and she felt happy to remain blinded, but Pigg's groans of pain forced her to look up. He was lying beside her in a tangled mess of brush and vines.

"Pigg, are you alright?" asked Elena in a strangled voice.

She tried to reach for him but felt pain immediately course through her left arm. She'd never dislocated a shoulder before, but she was in enough pain to accept that it was out of place. With a tremendous effort, she managed to get herself into a sitting position. Pigg was still groaning and didn't exactly seem conscious.

"Pigg! Pigg!" Elena half screamed. "Tell me what hurts."

"Everything," Pigg moaned. "But mostly, my legs."

Elena managed to army crawl with her one good arm toward his legs. She pulled at the torn sections of his pants with her right hand. Both his legs had sustained deep gashes and were heavily bleeding. She reached out for her pack, but sadly realized it wasn't there. She looked around and then up.

If she had guessed, she would have said they slid down a fifty-foot embankment and she felt quite certain that her pack was sitting at the top of it. Fortunately, Pigg had his bag. Unfortunately, it was still strapped to him.

"Pigg, I need to get your pack to get the medical kit."

Holding her left hand tightly to her chest, Elena used her right arm and shoulder to roll Pigg off his bag. He let out a terrible groan of pain. His eyes were rolled in his head, so she wasn't entirely sure he was fully conscious.

"Sorry, sorry."

Elena unzipped the bag and removed the medical kit. She opened the antiseptic wipes with her teeth and used them to clean the outside of Pigg's wounds. Then, she tore open the quick clot powder and sprinkled it along the gashes. Immediately, the amount of blood flowing from his legs slowed. She unrolled some white, mesh bandages.

"Pigg," Elena said forcefully, trying to rouse him. "I need you to hold this bandage with your finger."

Elena wasn't sure how, but between the two of them they were able to get the bandages tied securely to each of his legs. She removed the canteen from his pack and held it carefully to his mouth.

"You've got to drink a little, Pigg!" Elena said loudly. "Come on, Pigg! You've got to start waking up now."

Going was slow, but Elena finally managed to get some food and water into Pigg. Then, he seemed to get a little better. At least, he was a little more alert.

"Why are you holding your arm like that?" Pigg asked.

He'd been glancing at her arm for quite a while, but she was trying to ignore him.

"I'm pretty sure that I dislocated the shoulder," Elena said dully.

"Doesn't that hurt?"

"Nah, it kinda tickles." Elena gave Pigg a look of sarcasm and he smiled sheepishly. "Yes, I'm in a lot of pain. My shoulder needs to be set soon or else..."

Elena suddenly realized what needed to happen. If only Austin was there he'd be able to fix her shoulder in a second. As it was, Pigg was going to be Elena's doctor. The thought of this was so ludicrous to her that it made her laugh, and she felt a sudden rush of insane frivolity.

"Why are you laughing?" Pigg sounded alarmed. "We're in serious trouble. And I don't see that laughing..."

"You're going to have to set my shoulder." Elena grinned at him.

"What?" Pigg yelped. "I c-c-can't. I would pass out entirely, I'm sure of that."

"You can't pass out because my one good arm won't be enough to catch you," Elena said flippantly. "Look, it's really easy and I'll talk you through it, but you have to do this for me or else my arm will swell, then it'll get stiff and eventually" — Elena made her best serious face — "my arm will fall off."

"That's not true, is it?" Pigg asked in a frightened whisper.

"No, it won't fall off," she laughed. "But you've got to fix it, okay?"

Elena managed to get Pigg into a sitting position. Then, she took a knee beside him.

"I need you to pull hard like this," she made the motion with her other arm, "Everything's going to be alright."

Elena tried to brace herself, but the pain of feeling her shoulder forced back into place caused an unnatural cry to come out of her mouth. Pigg made a sound between a baby crying and a gasp for breath and slumped sideways onto the ground.

While Pigg was passed out, she used the time to change into the clean shirt from her bag. Then, she tied the sleeves from her dirty shirt together and made a sling for her arm.

Feeling a little refreshed by the scent of clean and the feel of dry garments, Elena moved out of the shadow of the embankment. She saw a wide meadow leading away from the school and a deep cavern to one side.

When she turned back toward the embankment, she noticed that it rose high along the horizon in every direction. She knew they'd have to somehow get back up the ridge if they wanted to get back to school, or that they would have to somehow walk around it, which seemed entirely unlikely because the mountainside continued in both directions.

However, Elena decided that she couldn't worry about school for the moment. Darkness was beginning to fill the forest and she needed to make a safe place for Pigg and her to sleep.

If they had to fall, they couldn't have picked a better spot. The hill gave them protection from the bitter wind that was beginning to swirl. Elena tossed Pigg's sleeping bag over him, tucked him in tightly, and then set to work building a proper campsite.

She dug a small pit with her right hand and filled it with sticks and dried moss. Then, she pulled the bark off an elderberry stick and bent a v-notch in it. She pressed down on the wood with her left shin and rubbed two pieces of elderberry together until an ember was produced. She placed the ember in the middle of a pile of dead moss and blew a steady stream of air to ignite a single flame. Then, she tossed the burning moss into the pit and gradually added more kindling sticks until a strong fire was crackling.

Elena arranged the tent canvas across some tree roots, making a fine lean-to and then gathered brush together for their beds. She was even able to scrape together a decent meal with the food left in Pigg's pack.

By the time Elena was finished, her left arm was aching and her hands were raw with cold, but she stood back to admire her work. Feeling certain that Hopper would have been proud, she took comfort that they had a decent place to sleep and a warm fire.

"How long have I been out?" Pigg asked.

Elena looked over, wondering how long he'd been watching her.

"It's hard to say," she replied. "Maybe a couple hours."

"I'm starving," Pigg said.

"Of course you are," Elena said. "You ate almost all your food, but here's a bar. Eat it slowly."

Pigg looked around at the campsite. "Did you put this together?"

"Actually, these little elves showed up. They strung up the tent on those tree roots, then they made beds for us, and finally they built this nice fire," Elena said playfully. "I'm impressed, aren't you?"

"Yes," Pigg said, looking at her seriously. "And extremely grateful."

Elena shrugged. "Whatever. You need to get up to stretch. Then, we've got to move you under the tent canvas and keep you warm."

Elena used her good arm to help Pigg to his feet. He let out a growl of pain, but he still managed to walk a bit and stand to relieve himself. Then, she tossed the sleeping bag on top of the brush mats she'd created under the tent canvas, helped him lie down, and covered him with her blanket.

"Elena, what are we going to do now?" Pigg asked.

"I'm not sure," Elena answered honestly. "But whatever we do can't be done tonight, in the freezing cold, while we're both injured. Let's rest now. We'll figure out what to do tomorrow."

Elena was nervous and scared, but she needed to put on a brave face for Pigg because having him nervous and scared wouldn't help anything.

"I'm going to stoke the fire again," said Elena. "Be right back."

She walked around the fire, poking it with a stick, while her teeth chattered uncontrollably.

"At least, it's not snowing," she called to Pigg.

But the moment after she'd said this aloud, it was as if someone was listening because white flurries began to sprinkle around her.

"Oh now, come on! Seriously?" Elena shouted at the sky. Then, she started kicking things around and stubbed her toe on a boulder.

"Grrr...Ahhhh...Rrrrroarrrr!" she screamed furiously. "I stubbed my dimwit toe!"

"You really have some anger management issues," called a voice that did not belong to Pigg.

◻ 18 ◻

Snow and Ice

Elena looked up to the top of the embankment to find the source of the voice. Kidd Wheeler's smug face was looking back at her, and she felt another burst of anger.

"Come down here and I'll show you some anger management issues," Elena barked at him.

Kidd held Elena's tactical pack up like he'd found buried treasure. "You know, you're supposed to keep the pack with you. It's supposed to help with sur-vi-val."

Then, he eased over some exposed tree roots and made his way slowly down the embankment. When he finally reached them, he said, "Out of all the Firebirds, I meet up with you dimwits first."

"Well, it's not like we're excited to see you either. We were hoping to meet up with a Firebird who acts a little less, you know, constipated," Elena said unkindly. "So, how about you turn around and walk the other direction? That way we can pretend that you didn't make this day any worse than it already is."

Kidd stood there silently, his eyes moving from Elena's face to her arm, and then around their campsite to Pigg under the tarp. He looked as irritable as ever, so it was impossible for Elena to guess what he was thinking.

Elena snapped her fingers in his face loudly.

"What's the matter? Did you have a stroke or something?"

"I need food and shelter," Kidd said impassively. "I only got a small supply of food in my pack and poles for a tent, but no canvas."

"What a relief!" Pigg blurted. "We both got tents, but no poles."

Elena made a face at Pigg. He shrunk down into his coat until she could barely see his eyeballs. She heard him squeak out the word "Sorry" before she rounded on Kidd.

"Look, I really don't think..."

"Freckles, you and Pigg are injured. I can't leave you here," Kidd said. "Even though I really want to," he added quickly. But the way he shifted his eyes away made Elena think that he really did want to be with them. "So, I'm going to set up a tent, build up your fire, and then I'm going to make some dinner."

"That's very helpful of you," Elena said as she attempted to cross her arms angrily over her chest, though it was awkward because she was in so much pain. "You going to poison dinner so we'll die and you can take our supplies?"

"I've got to be honest, it's tempting," said Kidd dryly as he removed the poles from his pack.

In silence, Elena watched Kidd untangle one of the tent canvases from the tree roots and string his poles through it to make a fine, weather safe tent. She filled the tent with pine needles while Kidd stoked the fire and filled his billycan with two packets of dried soup and water.

When Elena was finished prepping, she sat by the fire and was jealous to discover that Kidd had been given a tactical knife and sheath. The sheath was equipped with a rope, security whistle, and hololight. The knife had a sharpener, a signaling mirror, and a pop out storage bin for waterproof matches. Plus, the handle also served as a hammer.

"You know, this reminds me of a Simulab I tried once called Survivorman Wild," Pigg said suddenly. "The point of the simulation was to try and do everything in the wilderness without having any modern technology. I only lasted about three minutes before a spider bit me. Next thing I knew, my leg swelled to twice its size and then my body went into cardiac arrest."

Pigg smiled fondly at the memory. He then looked expectantly at Elena and Kidd, but they both simply stared at him without a reply.

"I never tried that Simulab again."

Silence fell again between them until the soup was heated through. Kidd poured a little into Elena's and Pigg's billycans. Then, they sat for a long time watching the fire and sipping soup while the snow flurries rained down ever thicker. Elena was freezing, but she refused to move closer to the fire because she didn't want to admit a weakness to Kidd.

"So," Kidd finally said. "What's the situation here?"

"We only have enough prepackaged food to last us about a day," Elena said, her voice revealing the nervousness she felt. "But there are berries and nuts in the woods, so at least we'll have some kind of nourishment."

"If worse comes to worst, we can just eat Pigg," Kidd said plainly.

Pigg made a pitiful yelp of terror.

"If we're going to eat anyone we'd start with you because you're bigger than the two of us combined. Although, I doubt we'd be able to make it a quarter of a day on those brains of yours," Elena said. "I'm willing to try though."

Kidd rolled his eyes. "You're always so pleasant to be around, Freckles. I can't understand why we're not better friends."

Kidd stood and ripped some vines from a nearby tree root. Then, he began to string them in a motion that was very familiar to Elena. He was making rope from the vines, similar to the kind they'd made during survival training with Hopper.

"Tomorrow, I'll set some snares and hunt for small animals, like rabbit or squirrel," said Kidd.

Elena doubted that he would find an animal. She hadn't seen one in the couple days she'd hiked. Her face must have registered the doubt she felt because Kidd looked at her and said, "What? You think I'm crazy?"

"I've thought you were crazy since I first met you." Elena couldn't help but think that he was trying to trick her with stories about the snares. "You do realize that it's snowing, and it will probably continue to snow through the night. So, I'm trying to figure out how exactly you plan to find rabbit out in the snow-covered woods."

"Tomorrow, I'll show you," Kidd said confidently.

Elena wasn't convinced, but she was too tired to argue. Pigg looked tired as well, so Kidd helped him into the tent and then Elena helped him into the sleeping bag. As she turned to leave, Pigg grabbed her arm.

"Are you going to leave me in here alone?"

"I've got to go use the outdoor facilities. But I'll be right back," said Elena assuredly.

Elena stepped out of the tent and zipped it up. Kidd was already back by the fire stripping bits of wood off the end of a stick with his knife. She momentarily felt a surge of thankfulness that he was there because, at least, they would have a warm place to sleep while it snowed, but she pushed those feelings aside.

"I thought I'd make us some spears," Kidd said.

Elena sat beside the fire across from him. "Why did you stay and help us?"

Kidd looked at her intently for a moment. Then, he sighed loudly and rolled his eyes.

"Marshall will know if I didn't stay to help. I have to maintain my personal scores if I'm to be considered for a leadership type position in our Unit."

Elena nodded her head. "Make my spear extra sharp. I think hunting is going to be therapeutic."

She rose from the fire and went back inside the tent, but Pigg was already asleep. She laid down beside him and snuggled into her blanket, feeling truly warm for the first time all day.

After listening to Pigg's faint snores for a while, she finally drifted off to a place where she was walking along a beach, her parents holding tightly to each of her hands.

She felt warm and relaxed and loved. Then, she suddenly broke off from them and ran toward the water. She jumped in frivolously, feeling complete contentment. Soon, the water turned dreadfully cold. She tried to get back to the beach, to her parents, but she couldn't move.

Then, Elena felt as though something were dragging her under the water. She tried frantically to reach the surface. She needed air, but she was pulled farther and farther to the depths. Suddenly, a series of lights popped across her eyes and she saw a cement structure very clearly in the water below her.

The thought of being pulled to a watery grave terrified Elena, so she began to scream for her parents even though she was far below the water now. She called their names again and again, yet she knew they couldn't hear her. She kept pleading, but nothing happened, and no one came to save her. Then, a black colored octopus swam toward her.

"Elena!" the octopus said sharply. Then, it wrapped its slimy tentacles around her and squeezed, speaking ever so softly, "Elena. Wake up. Everything is going to be okay."

Elena was slowly becoming aware of her surroundings. Her arms were heavy and there was a faint smell of burnt elderberry. Eventually, she realized that Kidd was keeping her arms pinned tightly to the sides of her body. His cheek was pressed up against her face and he kept whispering, "Elena, everything is going to be okay. Wake up, Elena."

Elena swallowed hard, her throat scratchy, and she noticed how hoarse her voice sounded as she said, "I'm awake."

Kidd moved away from her at once.

"What happened?" Elena asked him.

"Your screaming woke me up. I thought we were being attacked. But then I saw you struggling." Kidd sat back but watched her with empathy in his eyes. "I used to have nightmares like that when I was younger. My caregiver would hold me until I woke up. She said it was best to hold my arms down and coax me awake with a steady voice."

Elena began to tremble, so Kidd reached forward and covered her with his coat.

"Where was your mom?" Elena asked.

"Huh?"

"You said your caregiver would hold you," said Elena. "But where was your mom?"

"Oh," Kidd said softly. "She died when I was real young."

Elena, who was recently an orphan herself, felt the pain of this statement straight to her core. "I'm sorry."

"Yeah, well," Kidd said, suddenly sounding gruff. "It was a long time ago so it doesn't matter."

Elena wanted to tell him that it did matter. She wanted to say that no matter how much time goes by, losing a parent is always devastating; Austin was proof of that. She wanted to say that it was normal to still miss his mom, but she turned over, feeling that it would be some kind of intrusion to give her opinion to a person she didn't even like.

When Elena finally noticed that the sun was up, she was alone in the tent. She stretched and adjusted her arms, feeling stiffness in her left shoulder. She stepped outside the tent and saw a blanket of gleaming snow covering everything as far as her eyes could see, except for the space directly around their campsite.

"Morning!" Pigg said brightly. "Would you look at this? Wheeler was able to find bird eggs, mushroom, and some berries. It's almost a decent breakfast."

Elena smiled slightly and sat beside Pigg. Kidd reached over and handed her a billycan of eggs scrambled with wild mushrooms.

"It's a little gamey and it needs salt, but it's all we have," Kidd said.

Elena accepted the meal gratefully.

"How's your arm feeling this morning, Elena?" asked Pigg.

"It's a little stiff, but on the whole it's a lot better," Elena replied. "How are your legs?"

"I'm afraid to look at them because they hurt so much. When you take the bandages off later I'll have to close my eyes," Pigg replied.

Elena nodded and dug into her breakfast. It didn't taste entirely awful, and she was certainly hungry enough to eat it without complaining. They sat in silence, except for the little humming sounds that Pigg made as he ate.

At long last, Kidd stood and said, "I should probably go set snares."

"I'll come with you," said Elena. "Let me check Pigg's legs first."

As Elena bent over to roll up Pigg's pants, he said, "You're going to leave me alone?"

"Only for a bit," Elena said as she carefully unrolled Pigg's bandages.

He'd already closed his eyes, so she didn't feel ashamed for gaping at his legs with revulsion. They were screaming red and oozing with puss. Elena used some of the antiseptic wipes to clean off his wounds and then hurried to wrap his legs with clean bandages.

"We really need water and food. Wheeler will set some snares and I'll find more berries and nuts. We'll be back before you know it."

Elena picked up Pigg's canteen and one of the spears Kidd had made as he slung some of the rope across his back. Together, they moved across the snowy meadow and into the forest on the other side.

Before long, Elena's feet became so cold that it felt like her boots were made from blocks of ice and they began to tingle and hurt. Her shoulder was also tense. Any time she moved it too far away from her body, pain shot through her arm, but she didn't dare complain to Kidd about it.

After a short time, Kidd stopped at a narrow ditch between rocks and fallen tree limbs. She watched him take a rope he'd made and string it up between a narrow chasm. Then, he placed some berries and moss several feet away.

"Where did you learn that?" Elena asked.

"I grew up on a farm," Kidd replied, but he did not elaborate, and Elena decided not to question him further.

"I'll go this way a bit to see if I can find water," Elena said.

Kidd simply grunted and handed over his canteen, so she headed off alone into the wilderness.

The icy forest was remarkably silent, so quiet that Elena could hear absolutely every single crunch of the snow beneath her boots.

Soon, there was a small trickling sound that made her smile. She filled three canteens with water from a small brook, drank until she was full, and refilled her canteen.

As she circled back to Kidd, she found dozens of berry bushes and a palette of fallen pecans, so she filled her extra pair of socks until they were swollen. Feeling proud with her findings, she finally arrived at the place she'd left Kidd, but instead of gloating Elena's face fell. Kidd was holding up a fantastically white jackrabbit.

"At least we won't have to eat Pigg," Kidd said.

Elena wanted to laugh, but she couldn't make herself happy around him. They walked back to the campsite in silence.

When they arrived, Elena couldn't see Pigg anywhere.

"Pigg!" Elena called frantically as she ran toward the camp. "Pigg!"

"I'm in the tent," came Pigg's voice.

Elena sighed and opened the tent flap. "Come and see what we've brought." She helped Pigg out of the tent and back to the fire where he sat with a heavy thud. "How are you feeling?"

"A little tired still," Pigg said. "Did you get anything good?"

"Yes," Elena said. "Berries and pecans. And Wheeler caught a jackrabbit. So, at least we won't starve to death."

Moments later, Elena watched Kidd slice open the jackrabbit's belly feeling a little envious that he knew how to clean an animal. However, she didn't dare ask him to teach her because that would have been too humiliating.

"Oh, that is just..." Pigg said, gagging a bit before closing his eyes. "Very, very unpleasant. Did you really have to do that in front of me?"

"It's just a little blood," Kidd said. "It will only take a moment to clean and then we can get to the cooking part. That's what you're interested in anyway, right? The eating?"

Pigg opened his eyes. "Of course I'm interested in eating!"

"Why are you so squeamish about this?" Kidd asked as he hung the carcass over the fire and squeezed some berries over it, hydrating the meat. "I thought you were all about cooking?"

"I am," Pigg said. "It's just that everything I've cooked has already been prepped for the cooking part."

Pigg continued, peppering him with questions about cooking over a fire. Elena could tell that the talking annoyed Kidd, but he answered in a polite way.

They spent the rest of the day cooking, eating, resting, collecting firewood, and checking on the other traps that Kidd set in the forest. And finally, as the daylight began to fade, Elena and Kidd took turns tossing small sticks on the fire while Pigg told silly stories about the different Simulabs he'd tried in Atlanson.

The daylight faded slowly, casting deep shadows everywhere. The air was icy, but the sounds of the forest began to come alive. Suddenly, there was a strange noise bouncing through the trees. Elena and Kidd jumped to their feet quickly and moved to the edge of their campsite, looking out into the meadow. Kidd pulled his knife. Since Elena didn't have a weapon, she moved back and pulled a log from the fire. Then, they waited.

▭ 19 ▭

Melly's Stories

"What's that noise?" Elena whispered after a couple moments of silence.

Kidd walked out past the edge of their campsite toward the meadow. The noise continued echoing, eerily.

Finally, Kidd looked at Elena and said, "Someone's calling your name."

Elena felt a rush of hope that Austin had finally found them, so she began to scream, "We're over here! We're over here!"

Elena could hear a distant echo of snow crunching beneath running footsteps and finally she recognized her name being called again and again.

"Over here!" Elena shouted, as she began to walk toward the pasture in the direction of the voice.

Then, from the wall of trees a mop of blond hair appeared. Declan stood there grinning at Elena. He rushed toward her, picking her up in one motion, and spun her around. She wanted to laugh, but a sharp twinge in her shoulder caused her to cry out in pain.

Declan set Elena down gently and surveyed her quickly. "What's wrong?"

"Pigg and I had an accident. We fell down that hill," Elena said, pointing back toward their campsite. "And I dislocated my shoulder. Pigg set it for me."

"Pigg set your shoulder?"

Elena smiled at Declan sarcastically and he laughed.

"We've been walking for days," Declan said, and he turned around as Melly tromped through the trees.

Elena didn't even try to pretend that she was happy to see Melly.

"How did you find us?" Elena asked him.

"A little while ago, I began to smell your shampoo."

"My shampoo?" Elena said quizzically. "I haven't taken a shower in days."

"Awe, and that must be the other smell I'm now detecting."

Elena shoved Declan in the shoulder and then they moved together back toward the campsite.

He sat beside Pigg and said, "How are you feeling?"

Before Pigg could answer, Kidd said bluntly, "Could you hold off on the pleasantries and tell us what supplies you have?"

"No," Declan said flatly. "Pigg, how are you feeling?"

"Well, we had a nasty fall and I hurt my legs. And it's been freezing, but finally we got enough to eat today so I'm much better," said Pigg. "Elena has taken good care of me."

"And Bowen has taken good care of me," chimed Melly, after taking a seat around the fire. She looked longingly at Declan and laid a hand on his forearm.

Elena could tell that Declan was somewhat repulsed, but he was trying hard to be polite.

"When I woke up, I was up in a tree," Declan began. "I figured we must still be at school, so I began walking toward the setting sun. But it was so cold that I thought I must have been doing something wrong. That's when I found Melly and woke her up."

"It's fortunate he found you, Linus," Elena said. "Because we all know you couldn't make it for a second without a guy doing *something* for you."

"At least I ask for help when I need it," Melly replied, pleasantly enough. "I'm not proud like *some people*."

"There's a difference between asking for help and using people to get want you want," said Elena. "It concerns me that you don't see the difference."

"You know, I've noticed, you remind me of that girl from the Harrier Unit...what's her name? Anyway, she's the one who complains and complains yet no one seems to listen to her," Melly replied.

"And I've noticed that almost every time you open your mouth you're always talking about someone else," Elena quipped. "Do you have any thoughts or opinions that are uniquely your own or do you limit yourself to gossip because that doesn't require as much brain power?"

"Ransom!" Declan said abruptly. "We passed a stream on our way. How about you help me fill up our canteens before it gets so dark we can't see?"

Elena forced a smile and said, "Sure. Let me check Pigg's legs before we go."

As Elena squatted over Pigg, he whispered, "Don't leave me alone with them."

"We'll be right back," Elena assured him.

Then, she and Declan started off across the meadow with the snow falling around them and their hololights lighting the way.

"How is Pigg really doing?" Declan asked.

"His legs are bad," Elena admitted. "They're swollen so I can't tell if there're any breaks. He won't be able to walk. Plus, he has some deep cuts that are getting infected. Somehow, we've got to get out of here and start heading back to school or we're going to die out here."

"Do you know what direction we should start?" Declan asked.

"Yes, but the only way is back up that embankment that we fell from. Wheeler and I wouldn't have been able to get Pigg back up there ourselves, but now that you're here it shouldn't be a problem."

"Even if we get to the top, how can we get him back to school?" Declan asked as he dipped his canteen into the freezing brook.

"I have no idea," Elena admitted. "It's not like we can carry him the entire way."

"What we need is a sled."

Elena laughed loudly. But when Declan looked serious, she said, "Yeah, right! Where are we gonna get a sled out here?"

"I'll build one," Declan said so simply that Elena couldn't help but scoff. "Really! I can build one. There's a lot of thin, workable wood around and we have the tools we need. All we need is to make some rope to tie it together and we'll have a fine sled."

"Okay, you take care of that sled," Elena said doubtfully. "Now, come on. We've got to get back because I promised Pigg."

When they got back to camp, another tent had been assembled. Kidd was shearing another spear, Melly was poking at the fire, and Pigg was eating a protein bar, but they were doing this in complete silence.

"So, girls in one tent and boys in the other?" Declan asked as he sat beside the fire.

Elena and Melly looked at each other. She could sense that Melly was thinking the same thing that she was, that she would rather sleep in the snow than snuggle up with Melly.

"But you boys sustain more body heat than we do," Melly said sweetly. "So, it would be good if we girls split up. It will keep us warmer."

"I'm sharing a tent with Pigg just like last night," Elena said with finality in her tone that she hoped would not be challenged. "You three are welcome to figure out your own sleeping arrangements. Pigg, time to get you in bed anyway."

Pigg looked relieved when Elena suggested this and allowed her to help him into the tent. She settled him on the sleeping bag and then checked his legs, which appeared worse.

"How am I doing, Doc?" Pigg asked.

"You're going to be fine," Elena lied, because she honestly didn't know. "Sorry, I can't give you anything for the pain."

"That's okay. I'll get some sleep now. Everything will be better tomorrow."

Pigg fell to sleep instantly.

As Elena listened to his deep breathing she began to worry about Austin. Knowing that Declan had been up in a tree when he woke up made her wonder if Austin was hurt and all alone. She had no hope of finding him in the icy wilderness. Then, she thought of Fergie. She knew Fergie's parents had made her skin water resistant, but was her mainframe adaptable to snow? Elena was suddenly frightened by images of finding Fergie's frozen body.

Elena wondered if someone from Grimsby was watching all this unfold. Would anyone save them if they were in mortal danger? Elena already felt like she was in mortal danger. In the last three days, she and Pigg were injured, they were running out of food, and they hadn't even found half the Firebird Unit yet.

In a little while, the flap to the tent opened and Declan crawled inside, carrying his blanket in one hand.

"How are you doing?"

"Okay, you?" asked Elena.

"I'm splendid," Declan said. "You know, without Marshall and classes and homework it's almost like being on vacation out here."

Elena smiled and watched him settle onto his blanket.

"I'm thankful to be in this tent tonight," Declan continued. "The first night with Melly was the hardest. She kept trying to snuggle up next to me, even though we had the tent, and she had a sleeping bag. Then, yesterday I think she tried to fake a sprained ankle so I would carry her."

Elena rolled her eyes.

Declan was quiet for a moment, just smiling, and then asked, "Are you worried about the others?"

"Just about Abria. She hasn't had any makeup for three days," Elena teased.

Declan smiled widely, but then silence fell between them.

Elena stared up at the tent canvas and blinked away some unexpected tears.

"My parents have been dead a whole year now."

"One year tomorrow," Declan replied in such a strange way that Elena turned sharply to look at him.

She couldn't believe that he'd remembered the anniversary of their death. His eyes were filled with such intensity that she blushed and looked away.

"I'm really sorry. Is there something we can do to remember them?"

Elena shook her head, wishing away the lump in her throat.

"You could tell me a favorite memory you have," Declan prompted.

Elena couldn't even speak.

"Well, hey, do you only have that one blanket?" Declan asked, changing the subject.

Elena nodded.

"Here, take mine," he offered.

"Nah, I'm warmer than I have been on this entire trip. I'm fine, you keep the blanket."

Elena rolled over, feeling tired and miserable and wishing that Austin was there to hold her hand because he was the only one that had really known her parents.

"Good night."

She heard Declan sigh sadly and then he said, "Night."

The next morning during their pathetic breakfast, Declan pulled out the sawback machete that had been in his tactical pack. The machete had a finished wood handle grip and jagged teeth on the back of the blade, yet it was no longer than his forearm.

"Why did the guys get weapons?" Elena grumbled.

"I didn't get a weapon," Pigg said.

"They gave you more food than anyone else," Elena pointed out. "That was enough."

"This machete will be great for sawing down the trees we need for the sled," Declan said excitedly. "I'm going to climb that embankment and look around for the wood I need. Then, I'll get started, but I need each of you to make some rope while I'm gone so we can secure the sled."

"I won't be making rope," Kidd said dully.

"Excuse me?"

"I won't be making rope," Kidd said again.

"What will you be doing to contribute to getting us back to school?" Declan demanded.

Kidd looked at him steadily. "I thought I'd come up there and help build it."

Elena suddenly had a vision of Kidd tossing Declan back down the embankment once they were at the top, but she shook it out of her head and said, "That might be a good idea, Bowen. You know, just to get the wood together quicker. Pigg, Melly, and I can make rope."

Declan looked at her carefully and then nodded. "That's fine. I appreciate the help, Wheeler."

Minutes later, Elena watched Declan and Kidd scale the embankment with some of the rope that Kidd had already made slung over their shoulders. After they disappeared on the other side, Elena busied herself pulling vines from the nearby tree roots and handing them to Pigg and Melly.

After she was satisfied with the haul, she sat beside the fire and began to weave a rope. Even though it was extremely difficult with her sore shoulder, she pushed through the pain and made sure that her rope was extra strong and thick.

At long last, Declan called down, "We're done gathering wood. We need some rope now."

Elena looked at the rope lying against the cliff and then at Melly, who simply shrugged and said, "I'd rather not climb yet. My ankle is still sore from twisting it yesterday."

Elena rolled her eyes and threw some of the rope they'd made over her shoulder. She circled the end of the rope around her good arm and climbed slowly as Declan pulled her up the embankment. When she got near the top, he grabbed her gently under her arms and pulled her toward him.

"How's your arm?" he asked.

"Fine," Elena said, stepping away from him. She noticed several piles of wood that were divided by length. "Wow! Look at all this."

"You were right," Declan said. "It went faster with both of us working."

Elena watched Declan and Kidd lay two trunks flat on the ground a few feet apart. Using the newly made rope, they connected solid cross beams to each of the ends. Then, five logs in varying lengths were placed on each plank of wood and secured with rope. The final planks were fashioned to the tops of the logs and to the front bumper. A flat bed of short logs were tied together like a mat and then secured to the inside of the sled, making a fine bed for Pigg to sit upright.

"That's brilliant!" Elena praised. "Okay, let's see if it works."

"After you," Declan said, pointing her toward the sled.

Elena sat down on it and Declan gave it a little shove. The sled glided easily through the snow, pushing the white powder to either side. She smiled at Declan and Kidd, but Kidd didn't look pleased at all.

"We've spent almost the whole day doing this and I'm starving," he grumbled. "Can we get back to camp and eat something?"

Elena eyed Declan but didn't say anything. They took turns easing back down the rope to the campsite.

"Well, the sled is finished and it's going to work great," Elena said, trying to encourage Pigg when she arrived back at the fire. "I'll take a look at your legs."

"I'll go check the traps I set yesterday," Kidd said gruffly.

"I'll go with you and get some water," Melly said, hopping up.

Elena smirked, feeling annoyed that it was the first time Melly had offered to do anything for the others without complaining about it first.

While Kidd and Melly were gone, Elena began to feel relaxed. She and Declan checked Pigg's legs and cleaned them. Then, they built the fire back up and went off to pick berries together.

Declan mocked Melly quite a bit about the maneuvers she'd tried and the excuses she made to try to get Declan to carry her through the forest. Elena laughed freely.

Later that evening, Kidd cooked another jackrabbit over the fire, and they ate. Elena was beginning to feel quite peaceful. Though it was still incredibly cold, she was grateful for a warm place to sleep and having people around while she ate dinner, even if it would have been nicer for Austin, Abria, and Fergie to be there.

"This reminds me of snow skiing when I was young," Melly said, suddenly reminiscent.

"Snow skiing?" Elena asked curiously. "Where did you go snow skiing?"

"I was born in Turkey and was skiing by the time I could walk," Melly replied.

Elena was completely transfixed. "I'm sorry, just to clarify. You have memories from before you came to live in Crowfield Plantation?"

Melly nodded.

Elena looked at Pigg and Kidd. "Do either of you have memories before you lived in Atlanson?"

"Why do you care so much, Freckles?" Kidd asked defensively.

"It's just hard for me to believe," Elena said. "I don't have a single memory from when I was that young."

"Are you feeling a little jealous?" Melly asked sweetly.

Elena laughed, a little too loudly and said, "Melly, I could never be jealous of you."

The next morning, while Elena and Melly cleaned up the campsite, Declan and Kidd used the tent canvas to make a rescue basket and strapped Pigg into it.

Then, Elena watched as Declan and Kidd scaled back up the embankment, dragging the ropes behind them. When they were at the top, the two of them stood a few feet apart and yanked and pulled, lifting Pigg up.

After Pigg was safely at the top, they tossed the ropes back down. Elena watched Melly tie the carrier bags onto the ropes so the boys could haul up their supplies.

Finally, it was the girls' turn to go. Melly insisted on going first, so Elena tried to wait patiently, but her foot tapped incessantly the entire time Melly climbed.

When it was Elena's turn, she was feeling rather tired and anxious from having watched everyone go up the hill. She grabbed the rope the best she could with her good arm and Declan pulled her up the hill slowly. When she reached the top, she collapsed on the ground.

"I need a minute to catch my breath," Elena said.

She took some sips from her canteen while Pigg eased into the sled. After he was situated, Declan began to stack the tactical packs around Pigg so that the others wouldn't have to carry them. At last, they were ready and set off between the trees with Declan pushing the sled.

They hiked and hiked all day, stopping only briefly to eat lunch. Elena's feet hurt every second and her shoulder throbbed with every step. She tried hard to listen as Pigg and Declan shared stories back and forth and she made an effort to laugh at the right times but, in reality, she could feel that her body was beginning to rebel against every move she made. She honestly wasn't sure how much farther she would be able to go.

At long last, the sun had set enough that it was time to make camp for the evening.

"This looks like a fine spot," Elena said, feeling thankful that the hiking was finished for the day, though she didn't dare complain about her pain. "We'll set Pigg down there and he can take stuff out of the packs for dinner. Wheeler, if you and Linus could set up tents, then I can . . ."

"Ransom, for a girl," Melly interrupted. "You're entirely too bossy."

Elena suddenly felt anger flare up in her face.

"Not everyone can be a useless princess like you, Linus. Some girls actually like to use their brains."

"There you go again with that temper," Melly responded. "Listen, we've been walking for hours, so I'm not going to set up tents. I'm taking a break."

"Geez, Melly!" Elena shouted. "Why do you have to make everything difficult?"

"Oh, that's a silly question coming from someone who is ordering us around," Melly said.

"You know what? I don't care what you do. I'm going to get kindling for a fire."

Elena grabbed Declan's machete out of his hand and one of the spears from the sled and stomped off through the trees.

Eventually, Elena made her way into a clearing and noticed a small grouping of trees that would provide fine wood for a fire. She tossed the spear fiercely into the snow where it stuck with a thud.

Then, using her right arm, she swung the machete down against a tree and began stripping away the bark, each strike coming down harder and harder.

"You're not some kind of superhuman, so try not to hurt yourself." Declan had appeared from behind the trees.

"I made a perfectly fine lean-to for me and Pigg without help from anyone," she said indignantly.

Declan gave her a toothy grin.

"Ransom, you've been taking care of everyone for days. Why don't you let me take care of you for a while?"

"I don't need your help." Elena turned back to the tree and started chopping it again.

A moment later, Elena felt a firm grip on her shoulder and Declan said, "Ransom, if you don't let me take a turn I'll start to cry. And you don't want to see me cry. It's embarrassing."

Elena gave him a half-hearted smile and handed the machete over.

"Now, how about you go rest back at camp and think about something pleasant, like how fun it would be to tie Marshall to one of these trees and leave him out here in the snow for a week," Declan suggested.

"I can't rest with everyone else sitting there."

Declan took a swing at the tree. Then, he turned back to look at her.

"You mean with Wheeler and Linus there."

"As if things weren't bad enough, Linus has to have an attitude."

"She's just jealous of you," Declan said plainly.

"Nah," Elena said. "She's a bully, a liar, and a cheat. There's no room for jealousy given that repertoire of charming characteristics."

"I know that you're nervous because we still haven't found Austin," Declan said.

Elena was shocked to hear him say it and even more shocked when she realized that he was right.

"But don't worry about him. He's a survivor."

"Thanks, Bowen." Elena was beginning to feel better. "I should do a little hunting to see if I can get dinner for tonight."

"Okay, don't go too far. It's getting dark and I wouldn't want you to get carried away by any local woodland creatures."

Elena smiled slightly, grabbed the wooden spear, and eased off into the forest. She wanted to hide somewhere so she could take off her boots and socks because she wouldn't dare show her feet to the others. The feeling of bitter cold and painful tingling never ended, so she was almost afraid to look at them herself. However, she knew she needed medical attention and soon.

In a short while, Elena found a thick grouping of trees. She slid to the ground and was beginning to unlace her boot when she heard twigs crackling and snow crunching. Hopping for a rabbit or squirrel, Elena raised the wooden spear over her head. Then, quite suddenly, Austin appeared in the clearing.

"Lena!"

Emotions swelled in Elena's chest. They were saved! She jumped up and took off running straight into Austin's arms.

⌑ 20 ⌑

Saving the Firebirds

"I'm so glad you're here!" Elena cried with relief into Austin's ear. Tears leaked uncontrollably from her eyes. "It's been hard...confusing...it's been awful."

"Don't worry," Austin said in a comforting tone. "I'm with you. We're together now." He set her down and pulled a Broadcaster from his pocket. "Fergie and I have been tracing your Trademarks for several days now. Are Declan and Pigg okay?"

"Yes, everyone is fine."

"Everyone?"

"Oh, Wheeler and Linus are with us, too," Elena explained.

"Great! That accounts for everyone in the Firebird Unit."

"What do you mean?"

"When I woke up, I obviously didn't know where I was or what had happened. I found Fergie within the first few hours. She activated the Touchdot and we began tracking you, Abria, Pigg, and Declan. We decided to set up a base camp to wait for everyone. We saw you and Pigg come together. And eventually, Bowen. Abria joined us about two days in and we've been collecting the other members of the Firebird Unit as they've come along."

"How did they know where you were?"

"We built a large signal fire and kept it burning day and night. Then, eventually, Fergie discovered that the trees and rocks were sending out auditory signals and smelling sensory indicators to try and draw everyone closer together."

Elena suddenly remembered how Pigg said he'd smelled her dinner cooking and how Declan said that he found their campsite because he'd smelled her shampoo. In reality, it was part of the simulation that had been leading Declan straight for her.

"If you knew where I was, why didn't you come for me sooner?" Elena asked.

"I wanted to, especially after I figured you were injured. But you were so far away, farther than anyone else," Austin said, squeezing her shoulder affectionately.

"How could you tell I was hurt?"

"Well, you and Pigg just stopped moving. I assumed it was because one or both of you were injured. But we could see that Bowen was close by so I knew you'd get help."

"But you didn't answer my question," Elena said. "Why didn't *you* come?"

"First, because you were in the opposite direction of school. I knew that you'd need to come toward our camp. It would have taken an enormous amount of skill to hike out in the snow to get you and then have enough energy to hike back. Also, I was still looking for everyone else in our Unit. And I knew that you could do it. I knew that you could lead Bowen and Pigg to safety."

"We haven't been safe at all!" Elena said. "Pigg and I fell…and he banged up both legs…and I dislocated my shoulder, which *Pigg* had to set for me…and Wheeler and Linus are driving me completely insane!"

"I was watching you every second," Austin said assuredly. "If you'd stopped moving after Declan found you, I would have come. I was waiting for you to get close enough. Finally, when Fergie checked this afternoon, you were only a couple miles away. Everyone at our camp seemed well enough, so I started walking out to you."

Elena hugged Austin again.

"I was so worried. You know how I get when I'm anxious."

"I know, I know. I'm really sorry."

"Austin," Elena said in a hushed whisper even though they were alone. "I think I have frostbite on my feet. It's getting so hard to walk."

Austin looked at her compassionately and then lifted her into his arms. "Which way to the others?"

Elena directed him back through the forest toward their campsite, but just before they arrived, she said, "Wait. Put me down. I don't want anyone to know about my feet."

"Lena, you shouldn't walk anymore, especially if you have frostbite," said Austin.

"I can't bear to have Wheeler and Linus see me this way."

Austin gave her a troubled look, but said, "Alright, we'll figure something out, but you can't hike the mile back to our camp."

As Elena and Austin cleared the trees, she heard a huge gasp and saw Melly run forward.

"Haddock, what a relief to see you!" Melly said sweetly and she threw her arms around his neck.

"I've heard you had quite an ordeal," Austin said, smiling at the others as he pulled away from Melly. "But everything is going to be okay now. We have set up a camp not far from here."

Declan reached forward, shook Austin's hand and said, "Good to see you, Dude."

Austin and Kidd merely nodded at one another before he dropped to his knees beside Pigg and asked, "How are you doing?"

"Fine," said Pigg, who was still propped up on the sled. "Elena has been taking good care of me. Except, we're awfully hungry, tired, cold, and...I said hungry, right?"

Austin smiled. "I'm going to look at your legs and then we'll be off to the Firebird camp where there is plenty of food and shelter."

"I'm going to lay back so I don't have to look," Pigg said.

Elena watched as Austin unwrapped Pigg's bandages. She winced. Pigg's legs were red with poison and the lacerations were white with puss. Austin removed his Suturand from his pocket and Elena saw the laser tip active.

"Pigg, do you feel warm at all?" Austin asked as he placed his free hand on Pigg's forehead.

"Just a bit, you know," Pigg said. "But I mostly feel cold because it's freezing out here."

The Suturand burned away some of the angry flesh on Pigg's legs as Austin said, "Elena, you've done a great job on this leg" — though she could see in his eyes that Pigg was not doing well — "Thankfully, your legs aren't broken, but they are severely sprained. You shouldn't walk on them."

As he began to wrap Pigg's legs again he said, "Lena, I want you to stand on the back of the sled to brace Pigg and hold the packs so we don't have to carry them. Then, I'll push so we can get going."

"I can push," Declan offered.

"We'll take turns, okay?" Austin said, smiling.

Once everyone was situated, Austin pushed the sled into the wilderness and the others followed behind him. Then, Austin began to tell stories of how they had found some of the other Firebirds in the forest, but Elena could tell that he was only trying to keep everyone calm in the pressing darkness. They took turns holding the hololights out toward the forest. Elena's feet were still throbbing, but she was very thankful to ride on the sled.

After a short distance, little dots of orange appeared on the horizon and Austin said, "Those are the campfires. We're almost there."

As Declan offered to push the sled the rest of the way to the camp, Elena saw Abria running toward them.

She leapt into Declan's arms and squealed, "I was so worried!"

Elena smiled and stepped off the sled as Abria flung arms around her neck.

"I was, like, totally unprepared for this cold weather." She wiped a few tears from her cheeks and hiccupped a laugh. "After the training we did in the water it would have been more reasonable if we'd woken up on a beach. Then, at least I could have worked on a tan."

When they arrived at the campsite, Elena was impressed with how much Austin and the other Firebirds had completely transformed the icy wilderness. Four tents were set up between a dense area of trees. A dozen fires were burning at various places around the campsite. Some fires roasted rabbits and rodents and a clothesline of wet clothing was strung near another.

Elena noticed Fergie right away and they embraced briefly before Austin said, "Foreman, could you please bring some warm water to the medical tent?"

"Of course you have a medical tent," Elena quipped.

"We had to," Austin said. "Nelson got injured."

Austin led them to a tent that was set a little farther away from the others. Elena waited as Declan lifted Pigg off the sled and brought him inside behind Austin. Then, she peeked in and saw three beds of pine needles and three sleeping bags with Olivia Nelson propped up on one of the palettes.

"Nelson took a bad fall and slipped into the fire," Austin said as Declan settled Pigg down on one of the other sleeping bags. "Her arm was burned, but not too badly. Thankfully we have snow."

"And Haddock," said Olivia, sounding grateful.

"And the Suturand," Austin said. "I was able to laser away the dead skin immediately. But we had to keep her away from everyone so she wouldn't get infected. I don't have the supplies I need out here."

Declan exited the tent and stood beside Elena, who was peering in as Austin unrolled the bandages on Pigg's legs again.

"Ouch!" said Olivia. "What happened to you?"

"I fell down a hill," Pigg said glumly.

"Actually, it was more like the side of a steep mountain," Elena offered. "But at least we didn't break our necks."

Fergie arrived with a steaming billycan of water as Austin reached for a pile of green stems that had yellow strips of tassel hanging at the tips.

"This is called *witch hazel* and it will help with the swelling," Austin explained. "I'm going to make a poultice to put on your legs, so you'll need to lie very still for a while."

Austin wet the witch hazel with warm water, creating a soft moist mass that he packed against Pigg's skin. Pigg let out a sigh of relief.

"I have some herbs I can give you for the pain," Austin told him. Then, he turned to Fergie and said, "Would you brew some tea?" Then, he turned toward the tent door and said, "Okay, it's your turn, Lena."

Elena blushed as everyone looked at her. She reluctantly entered the tent and sat down on one of the sleeping bags. As Austin removed her boots she winced in pain.

When her socks came off, Abria gasped, Fergie moved a little closer, Pigg looked like he might faint, and Declan looked angry as he gazed at Elena's grayish, waxy looking feet.

"The good news is that you have frostnip, which is a beginning stage of frostbite. It's not severe yet, but we need to treat it right away," Austin said.

"Why didn't you tell me your feet were so bad?" Declan asked sternly.

"I wasn't trying to keep it a secret from you. Just from Wheeler, Linus, and Pigg."

"Why me?" Pigg asked defensively, but then he looked at her feet again and gagged like he might vomit.

"Because I've seen how well you handle injury," Elena replied.

Austin smoothed some green paste on her feet. Then, he wrapped them in a blanket that had been warmed by the fire.

"Listen," Austin said seriously. "You have to stay off your feet."

"But we've got to get back to school," Elena protested.

"If you don't stay off your feet you could lose your toes," said Austin.

Declan made a sucking noise through his teeth. "Personally, it would gross me out to see you without toes. So, you should really think about the rest of us who have to live with you."

"Yeah, Elena," added Abria. "How would you ever be able to enjoy some of the perks of being a woman if you didn't have toes? Like pedicures, high-heeled shoes, and proper foot massages."

"Practically, I think it would bother her more if she had to be bound to a chair her entire life," Fergie said. "Perhaps, she could learn to walk without toes, but it is improbable."

"Nah, in Atlanson they'd give her artificial toes," Pigg said. "She'd have physical therapy and have to learn to walk again, but at least she could still wear high heeled shoes."

Elena raised her eyebrows at Austin.

"This is the most ridiculous conversation I've ever heard," she said, but he only folded his arms over his chest and gave her a quirky little smile. "I can't believe I let you talk me into being friends with these dimwits."

Everyone laughed except Elena, who got straight to the point.

"So, Austin, what's the plan?"

"You, Pigg, and Nelson need to rest for another day," Austin said. "Tomorrow we'll build a couple more sleds so we can get you three back to school. Then, I'll assess your various conditions during the day to see when we might be able to leave."

"How far is it back to school?" Elena asked.

"We're not entirely sure," Austin said. "Fergie thinks maybe a half day's walk at least. But for now, rest. We'll bring you some dinner. Then, you should sleep."

Elena spent the following day in the medical tent with Olivia and Pigg. She tried to enjoy herself, but she couldn't help feeling a little uncomfortable when Abria and Declan visited to bring news about building sleds. She wanted to be out there helping in some way instead of inside feeling useless and helpless.

Pigg made up stories to pass the time. Olivia helped him invent games so they could take their minds off the boredom they felt. Fergie and Abria took turns bringing food and water throughout the day. Elena could tell that Kidd had taken to hunting or cooking or both, but she didn't dare ask anyone questions about where he'd been trapping.

Austin checked their wounds often and gave them the appropriate medical attention, but it was impossible for him to stay inside the tent all day. Sometimes hours would pass before Elena was able to see him again.

By the evening, she was feeling lonely and scared again, like she'd felt the first night she'd awoken on her own in the wilderness.

"I know this is a small tent and it's easier for you to sleep somewhere else," Elena whispered when Austin came to check on her. "But I was wondering if you could stay in here tonight. I feel..." But words failed her.

Austin squeezed her hand. "No problem."

As Elena settled down, Austin pulled a blanket beside her.

"Remember that bedtime story your mom would tell us when we were younger? The one about the two kids that left home for an adventure and met all kinds of struggles before they finally solved the mystery at the museum and returned home?" Austin asked quietly. "I know it was a story to help us conquer our fears, but I really think it was the sound of her voice that was most calming. Your dad would always make us special breakfast the morning of our birthdays. Remember? He was a great chef, though he'd never admit it."

Elena smiled. It was the first time she'd felt completely safe since the whole ordeal in the forest began.

"I miss them every day," Austin said.

Elena closed her eyes peacefully and slept so soundly that it only seemed minutes later that Austin was shaking her awake.

"Sorry to wake you, Lena."

As Elena's eyes came into focus she could see that he was smiling.

"But we're getting ready to leave now."

Declan helped Elena into one of the sleds, then handed her a protein bar and canteen of water for breakfast. She watched helplessly as he and some of the other boys packed up the medical tent.

At long last, the campsite had been completely broken down and the fires extinguished. Austin led the way through the snow-covered forest with Fergie at his side. The others followed behind, with Declan pushing Elena's sled.

The Firebirds talked and chattered a lot, taking turns to explain what had happened to each of them when they awoke in the forest and the events that transpired in order for them find one another. After seven or so stories, Elena realized that she was smiling and feeling relatively carefree.

Then, quite suddenly, she had an odd sensation that she was being pushed through a wall of electricity. She looked around feeling peculiar and then found they had reached the sunny, warm Grimsby training field. She turned and looked at where she'd come from, but she could only see blue sky and distant mountains that were not covered in snow.

"What happened?" Elena asked.

"I believe we passed through the wall of the simulation," said Fergie.

Elena stared at the resident towers, feeling very thankful that they were finally at school. Less than a minute passed before a team of medical robots converged on the Firebirds. Some of the students, including Elena, were packed onto a shuttle headed straight to the Medical Station.

"Where are you going?" Elena called to Austin as he climbed onto another transport vehicle.

"Debrief," Austin said. "You rest up. I'll see you when I'm done."

▭ 21 ▭

Sleepy Wolf

Beep. Beep. Beep. The sound echoed faster and faster through Elena's subconscious until her eyes finally opened. Her vision was blurry and obscured by bright lights and blaring white.

Eventually, she recognized several Optivision screens hovering around her body. She could see her blood pressure, heart rate, urine output, and blood sugar measurements. She sat forward slowly and noticed that someone was sitting beside her bed.

"You are in the Medical Station being treated for exhaustion and mild frostbite. The good news is that you will get to keep your toes and there is no permanent damage," said Hannibal.

Elena got the impression that he'd been waiting for her to wake for quite some time.

"Haddock excels at medical application. We would hire him today to work here and treat students if it were not for the rule requiring students to be in Level 4 studies before beginning a work study program at Grimsby."

When Elena didn't respond, Hannibal pressed on. "I am glad to see that you survived your third quarter exam."

Elena couldn't fully grasp this statement for several moments. But then she choked out, *"That was an exam?* You made us suffer like that *on purpose.* What was the objective? To see how many of us would die?"

"You were never in mortal danger." Hannibal looked serious. "And if the Firebirds had proved to be unfit for the challenge, we would have rescued you right away, as we had to do for several of the other Units, including the Harriers."

"We were hurt and needed help," Elena said firmly.

"We were monitoring the entire time," Hannibal assured her. "If you would have needed, I would have sent a team to get you."

"You know, we're only fourteen-years-old," Elena said angrily.

"Yet, look how much you learned and accomplished in seven short days."

Elena wanted to argue that they hadn't been short days at all, but she was beginning to feel fuzzy and sleepy.

"You rest now. You only have a few days left until the fourth quarter begins," Hannibal said. "I am very proud of you."

As he stepped out of the room, Elena looked around. Her vision was still blurred, but she noticed that Pigg was asleep in a bed near her and that Olivia was asleep across the room.

She was beginning to contemplate whether or not she could get out of bed when a Humanoid arrived with a tray of food.

"Your vitals have improved significantly," the Humanoid said in a robotic tone. It set the tray on a rolling table and wheeled it toward Elena's bed. "You are required to eat every single bite of this food."

"I would like to see my friends," Elena said, dismissing its comment. "Can you get them for me?"

"What are their names?" the Humanoid replied impassively.

"Austin Haddock, Declan and Abria Bowen, and Fergie Foreman."

"You can expect them shortly," the robot said before exiting the room.

Elena stared down at a plate of gray mush. She had a dull ache behind her eyes that made her stomach feel queasy. She had forgotten to ask how long she'd been asleep, so she decided it was probably best to eat something.

As she was finishing a cup of purple colored gelatin, the door to the room slid open and Elena's friends filed in looking happy to see her.

"Thank, goodness," Abria said in a singsong voice. "We were so worried when they, like, took you away. I was afraid you might never wake up again."

"Abria," said Declan through gritted teeth. "I thought we agreed that we weren't going to use the 'd' word during the first visit."

"I didn't say *dead*, Declan," Abria said assertively. "I said *never wake up*."

"What's the difference?" asked Declan.

Elena couldn't help but smile and be thankful that everything felt normal again.

Austin leaned forward, brushed his fingers across Elena's forehead and asked, "How are you feeling?"

"Better now that you four are here," Elena confessed. "So, what's been happening outside of the crazy ward?"

"Marshall made us go into debrief about our experience in the wild, like, first thing," Abria said bitterly. "He didn't even let us get cleaned up first and I was like, *Sir, I haven't taken a shower in a million years and I totally need to run a brush through this hair*, but he was like, *Get in formation and shut your mouth*. What a total, like, dimwit!"

"Did anyone say *why* we were put out there to begin with," Elena asked in a small voice. "Hannibal said it was part of our exam, but I'm not the only one who thought it was extreme, am I?"

"You're not the only one," Austin said in a comforting tone.

"We cannot expect the school to tell us the logic behind any part of our training," Fergie said in a tone of formality.

Elena rolled her eyes.

"Well, at least we know the frostbite didn't travel to your brain," Declan said. "You still have the classic eye roll mastered."

"There are my Firebirds!"

Elena looked at the door and saw Hopper's mess of rainbow hair bounce through it.

"You dudes look awesome! Aw, but I see that Pigg and Nelson are still out. Those tranqs are super strong."

"You know, a little heads up about the trek through the terrorizing icy wilderness would have been nice, Hopper," Declan said.

He grinned at them and the ring through his nose shifted in a way that made Elena's stomach jolt.

"You dudes did a great job without any warning. Not like the Harrier Unit. We had to pull them out before the first forty-eight hours had ended."

"Ransom was asking if any of the Instructors had explained why we were put out there in the first place," Austin said and then he crossed his arms firmly over his chest. "Maybe you would like to tell us?"

The grin on Hopper's face faded. "No one has ever asked me that before."

"Ever?!" Elena blurted. "Everyone is always just *fine* going out there?"

"Nah, plenty of students have complained." Hopper shrugged. "But I've never been asked why you rugrats go out. It's part of your infantry training. Sort of a review of what you've learned."

"What does *infantry training* mean?" Austin asked.

"You know," Hopper said, looking flummoxed. "Last year, your training was primarily focused on infantry development. This year is primarily maritime training and next year will be airborne training. Come on," he added after noticing their confused faces. "You know this. It was in a module of the Grimsby Initiation Memorandum."

Elena looked at Fergie in disbelief, but she replied, "He is accurate."

"I guess I need to start watching the *Manual of Manipulation*," said Elena.

"Anyway, dudes, I dropped in to see how you were gettin' along," Hopper said. "And to let you know that I'll be working on a little project for you in the next couple days. So, keep a look out for me on the weekends."

With that, he winked and slouched out the door.

A few days later, Elena was released from the Medical Station and the fourth quarter officially began. She heard gossip around the school that Oscar Hunter and the rest of the Raptors were rescued shortly after they'd arrived in the frozen forest because no one exhibited proper leadership skills. This made Elena feel much better about the simulation she'd been inside. However, her feet were still tender; a bitter reminder that their exam had been extremely difficult.

Instructor Booker started the quarter with a flurry of simulated exercises. During class, the entire room would morph into different time periods. He spent time explaining timelines, historical facts, trade routes, developments in technology, and local customs of the Early Middle Age.

He also had the Aves Company studying kings in different cultures during Medieval England, France, and Germany. Finally, the Optivision screen transformed into a complex system of battles as Booker lectured about how Arab forces conquered most of the Byzantine territories around 650 AD under the pretext of a holy crusade for Allah.

After being isolated in the frozen wilderness for so long, the fact that she had to tolerate a classroom full of students seemed overwhelming. She tried hard to focus solely on her work. She made notes on her Smartslate, wondering how many of the different civilizations would appear on her final exam.

Elena felt confident that she'd be able to remember dates and explain the different cultures, but she was beginning to doubt that she'd ever fully be able to interpret and understand the deluge of ancient symbols, pictograms, hieroglyphics, and pictographs that Instructor Niva had the Firebirds learn during Phonology.

Currently, they were studying the ancient Mayans, who had created an elaborate hieroglyphic writing system. When Niva introduced them to the writings from the Gupta Empire in India and Elena felt more confused than ever. The caricatures were explicit and comprehensive, and it made Elena's brain hurt as she tried to decipher each one.

Instructor Copernicus and Instructor Emerald combined their classes to bring the Iron Age in China to life. They also described the people of the Norse culture with north Germanic descent to help prepare the Aves Company for their classes with Hopper, who taught them the evolution of the Viking long ship and the trading, exploring, and raiding that the Vikings had done in areas of Europe, Asia, and the North Atlantic islands.

———

Elena kept up well with the homework she'd been assigned during the first week of the fourth quarter until the sixth day of the week when she finally refused to think about her classes for another minute. She hurried down to the Firebird Station and reclined in a lounge chair to rehash some of the details from the third quarter exam with Fergie, who chronicled her words into the Touchdot.

"Why are we doing this again?" Elena asked after stopping in the middle of her sentence about how Declan and Kidd made the rescue basket so they could pull Pigg up the embankment.

"In the woods, you utilized survival skills that none of the rest of us needed," Fergie said. "If we can capture everything that you learned whether it was how Wheeler cleaned the dead jack rabbit or how Bowen was able to build a sled from pliable wood and homemade rope, then we will have the information available to us if we ever need to use it in the future."

Elena leaned forward and put her chin in her hand.

"Linus was hanging all over Bowen and he was so annoyed. It was actually quite funny." She laughed, remembering Declan's face as he told her about Melly faking a sprained ankle so that he would carry her. It was so annoying when she was talking about the skiing Simulab and how good she is at it because her family lived in Turkey and they would go skiing all the time. What a liar! Like she'd be able to remember living outside the dome when no one else does."

Elena started to laugh again, but noticed a thoughtful look on Fergie's face and asked, "What is it?"

Without speaking, Fergie stood up and walked out of the room. Elena followed her to Research & Development and watched her friend access a map of the earth that she'd only seen once before. Then, Fergie opened the Catalan Atlas and somehow the maps synced together. As little red dots began to spread out across the hologram, Fergie grabbed the Ransom Dossier and began flipping its pages.

"What's wrong?" Elena asked, desperate to know. "What is it?"

Fergie used her fingers to zoom in on a portion of the map where one lone dot stood out against a range of mountains.

"Your dad's dossier lists a specific coordinate." Fergie pointed to the map. "This one is in Turkey."

"What is it?" Elena asked, feeling confused.

"A mountainous region called Ararat."

"Are you saying you think there's an artifact on the mountain?"

At that moment, Elena heard the Station door open and a few seconds later Austin and Declan arrived, pushing one another playfully through the door.

Then, Pigg entered with Abria behind him saying, "I told you already, someone will notice if we try to take that much food at, like, one time. I think we need to be a little more strategic in the way we take stuff out of the kitchen."

"What's going on?" Austin asked Elena and Fergie as his eyes settled on the map.

Elena explained what Melly had said in the forest. Then, Fergie showed the Firebirds the map with the red dot indicating a possible artifact had been located.

"So, you think there's an artifact on that mountain in Turkey?" Austin asked.

"The Dossier does not specify," Fergie said. "However, we know that Melly was specifically selected for the Firebird Unit because Hopper told us that the Firebirds weren't randomly selected. If Melly's family once lived in Turkey, it is safe to presume that her parents' artifact was left there and, more specifically, hidden in the mountain where we observe this red dot."

Elena paced the room. "Maybe we can ask her about it. And when I say 'we' I mean either Austin or Bowen because there's no way she's going to tell me anything about her childhood."

"It is possible that, like me, her parents told her about the artifact they possessed," Fergie said. "However, based on the statistics we have of our parents not sharing information with us about the Renegades' work, it is safe to assume that she knows nothing about the artifact. To involve her unnecessarily may put her in danger."

"Oh, we don't want that, do we?" Elena said sarcastically as she paced the room again.

"Look, so far each of our parents have left us some kind of clue or whatever to help us understand the work they were doing with the Renegades," Declan said.

"Except me," Pigg said. "And I'm perfectly happy to not contribute anything to this."

"Maybe Linus has something and doesn't know it," Declan continued as if he hadn't been interrupted. "Or she knows she has something and isn't supposed to tell anyone."

Elena heard the door to the Station open again and Hopper bounded into the room.

"I thought I'd find you rugrats in here," Hopper said while Fergie hurried to minimize the Optivision screen of Mount Ararat so that he couldn't see it. "You dudes really need to get outside and have a life."

"Spoken from the guy who's here checking up on us," Declan remarked.

"I'm not checking up on you. I'm here to make a delivery." Hopper held up a book similar in nature to the Ransom Dossier and said, "Here's what I promised you. The fake Alpha Manuscript is in the Vault. So, let's hope the Headmaster never inspects it too closely or else he might banish me forever."

Austin took the book from Hopper, handling it gently as though it may break. Without a word, he set the manuscript on the table in front of Fergie and opened it to the first blank page he found.

Fergie got up from her pupil station, retrieved the ampoule of fluid from the Amulet, and selected a dropper from the utensil pouch. She squeezed three drops of the fluid onto the page and then used the tip of a brush to spread it.

A few breathless seconds occurred. After nothing happened, Fergie moistened another portion of the page. And still, nothing happened.

"So, the pages really are blank," Pigg said.

"It is possible," Fergie said. "Although, it is also safe to assume that this is simply the incorrect substance for the page."

"What does that, like, mean?" Abria asked.

Austin sat down heavily in the nearest chair and rubbed the scar on his chin in an irritable way.

"She means that it's possible that the correct fluid exists, but we don't have it."

"It's a good thing you dudes can't leave the domes again," Hopper said with finality in his tone. "So, you don't have to worry about finding it. Keep the book, though, okay? Haddock, it's your father's work so hopefully it will give you some comfort or something. Well, I've got to be getting back. See you dudes later."

Austin picked up the Alpha Manuscript and held it close to his chest.

"It doesn't matter that we can't read it. We need to get across the ocean. And to do that, we need Wheeler to finish the Independence. I'll talk to him to see how much longer he thinks it will take."

○

The days stretched on with Elena back in the pool for Basic Training wishing that she could be anywhere else in the world; including the mountains in Turkey or back in the icy wilderness simulation because, at least, Marshall hadn't been there.

The Firebirds had been treading water for one minute with their arms only, their legs locked straight and still. When the timer sounded, she pulled herself out of the pool and completed fifty squats. Then, she jumped back into the pool with the other Firebirds and swam one hundred meters.

On the opposite side, she got out again and started fifty push-ups. Then, it was back in the pool for another one-hundred-meter swim, but this time with a free weight held over her head.

As Elena came out of the pool on the last set of exercises, she felt sure that class would certainly be over, but Marshall barked, "You will swim ten lengths of the pool and then one underwater. After that, do nine lengths and then one under water. After that, do eight lengths and one underwater and so on until you get down to one length and one underwater. When you've finished these laps you are free to go. Everybody ready? Go!"

Marshall's whistle sounded, but Elena was not ready and stood watching as her other classmates, except Pigg, jumped into the pool. She thought seriously about running for the door, but Marshall's voice reverberated around the pool area, "Ransom! Pigg! Get started. I don't want to be here all night."

By the time class was over, Elena felt weak and irritable. She had new patches of skin that were raw from being wet too long. She couldn't quite take a full breath of air and she was certain that the frostnip on her feet was going to reoccur.

As she grabbed a towel from the rack, Austin came up and said, "That was brutal."

"You mean, Marshall was brutal."

"I'm going down to the Station tonight with Wheeler to work on the Independence," Austin said. "Do you want to come?"

"Austin, I'm so tired," Elena grumbled. "I need to keep my level of stress at a minimum tonight. Being around Wheeler will not keep me at a minimum."

"Oh, come on," Austin said. "We'll get dinner and then you'll feel better."

"What's the hurry?" Elena complained. "Can't we wait until the weekend?"

Before Austin could answer, Pigg arrived by his side looking flustered.

"Oh no," Elena said to him. "Wheeler didn't steal your clothes again, did he? Because I'm in a bad mood and I really..."

"No, it's not that, although I'm still traumatized at the thought," Pigg said promptly. "It's just, while we were swimming, I had an idea about how we could search through Melly's stuff. So, will you meet me down at the Station later?"

Elena looked at Austin and shrugged her shoulders. "I guess I'm going down to the Station with you after all."

Hours later, Elena gathered with her friends in the Research & Development room. As they waited for Pigg, Declan, and Abria took turns telling silly stories about growing up in the Galilee Province. Elena soon realized that she was feeling a lot better.

At length, Pigg stumbled through the door and said, "Sorry I'm late. I stopped by the hydroponic farm and stole some valerian, skullcap, and wild lettuce. Then, I used the lab to create this serum." Pigg held up a vial of gray liquid. "I call it *Sleepy Wolf.*"

"Okay..." Austin said carefully. "What does the serum do?"

"Hypothetically, if we put it on Melly she would fall into a deep sleep. Then, we could search through her stuff to see if we can find anything about Turkey."

"That's brilliant, Pigg!" Elena said.

"I just made it and haven't tested it yet," Pigg admitted. "So, I'm not sure about the duration of effectiveness."

Before anyone had a chance to speak again, Pigg put a single drop of the gray liquid on his hand. He fell so quickly that no one had time to react. He smacked the floor with a heavy thud.

"Dimwit!" Elena exclaimed as everyone rushed toward him. "I can't believe he would do that without even warning us."

"Yeah," Declan said. "Also, you think he might have waited until he was sitting in a chair or something."

"Is he, like, breathing?" Abria asked nervously.

Austin leaned over him. "Yes, he's breathing. Bowen, help me get him to one of the bunks."

Austin and Declan lifted Pigg's lifeless body and carried him to one of the bunks in the front room. Then, Austin used his Suturand to scan Pigg's body for several moments.

"Well, he didn't break anything. But that serum acted so quickly that I won't be able to assess any other damage until he wakes up."

Elena and her friends walked back to the Research & Development room but stopped before passing through the doorway. The vial of Sleepy Wolf was lying on the floor in the center of the room.

"Okay, so who's brave enough to pick up the magic bottle of potion that Pigg made?" Declan asked.

"Not me. Did you, like, see what happened to Pigg when he touched that stuff? Wham!" Abria slapped her hands together. "He hit the floor before any of us could catch him."

"I will pick it up," Fergie said. "As the serum will have absolutely no effect on me."

She crossed the room, picked up the vial, and laid it carefully on the countertop.

"Pigg passed out before he even finished explaining if he had a plan for how we should use it," Elena said.

"How about we rub some of it on the handle of her hairbrush that way the next time she picks it up she'll pass out," Abria said thoughtfully.

"What if we are not in the room when that happens?" Fergie said. "We will have missed our opportunity."

"We could wait until she's asleep, but all the other girls would be there, and we would risk waking them up," Elena said.

"Unless you use the serum on all the girls," Declan suggested.

"We should not use it on every girl," Fergie said. "That will increase our probability of being caught."

"I know," Austin said. "We'll send her a message from Abria asking her to meet in the room before she goes down for dinner. Then, Fergie and Elena can be standing at the door. When she walks through, they can rub the vial on the back of her arm or neck or something like that."

Elena felt nervous about the plan, but no one else had a better idea.

An hour later, Pigg finally woke up. They waited around until he was conscious enough to disrupt the school surveillance and then the girls headed to their room.

Elena and Fergie stood on either side of the bedroom door waiting patiently for Melly to arrive.

"I'm, like, nervous." Abria was sitting on her own bed, twiddling her thumbs. "What if she doesn't come, or what if she does come but she has someone with her?"

"If she has someone with her, we'll abort the mission," Elena said plainly.

"You're very good at this, like, whole spying thing," Abria laughed.

The door suddenly slid open silently. Elena watched Melly's blonde head sweep by her. Then, she noticed Fergie lunge forward, but she lost her balance and fell forward, spilling the entire bottle of Sleepy Wolf on the back of Melly's neck. Instantly, Melly crashed face first to the floor. Elena heard a loud crack.

"That was entirely unforeseeable," Fergie said dully.

"That. Was. Awesome!" Elena said, grinning from ear to ear.

▢ 22 ▢

The Photograph

"Make sure she's breathing."

Elena and Abria worked together to turn Melly on her back. Her face was covered in blood and her nose was still bleeding.

"She's breathing, but her nose is broken. And she's going to have two black eyes," Elena said. "We should throw a party for Pigg later."

"Yeah," Abria laughed, pulling up the cuff of her sleve. The Touchdot shot out of the Broadcaster on her wrist and scanned an image of Melly's face. "This is going to make a fine keepsake."

"Ladies, can we be serious for a second?" Fergie said. "We have a lot of work to do before dinner is over."

Elena and Abria heaved Melly off the floor. They scanned her Trademark into the wardrobe, laid her on her bed, and turned her face toward the pillow so the blood would drain sideways down her face.

"I wonder how long she'll be asleep?" said Elena, leaning into Melly's closet with Fergie. "Wouldn't it be great if she slept for a month? I would love that."

"I guess I'll go get some tissue and clean her face up a bit," Abria said. "Be right back."

Elena and Fergie began to shift clothes on hangers, shoes on the rack, and makeup on the shelf. They went through drawers of jewelry, knickers and socks, and a thin storage compartment that was filled with square, translucent disks that Elena assumed were probably digital recordings of family adventures.

At length, Elena sat back on her heels and said, "There's nothing here."

She looked up in frustration and noticed a familiar photograph stuck to the underneath part of one of the shelves.

She reached up and said, "Look at this photograph! I've seen it before."

Fergie and Abria gathered on either side of her. Together, they looked at the black and white photograph of a massive ship that was partly covered in snow.

"Elena, where did you see this image before?" Fergie asked.

"It was at a farm near Atlanson," said Elena. "There was a crazy, old man living there. Maybe he was Melly's dad?"

"Her parents are officials in Crowfield Plantation," Fergie reminded her.

"Oh yeah," Elena said. "Maybe it was her granddad? I don't know. Why would she have this exact same picture that I saw on that farm? And why would it be hiding in her closet?"

The Touchdot flew from Fergie's Broadcaster and scanned the front of the photograph. Then, she turned the photograph over and said, "Look at these symbols!"

Elena saw some strange writing and asked, "Fergie, can you translate it?"

"Yes," Fergie said slowly, as her Touchdot scanned a copy of the writing. "This is some form of Hebrew. Translated loosely, it says *Tablets of Destiny*."

"What does that mean?" Elena said. "Do you think that's the name of the boat?"

"I am unsure, but I am more concerned about these series of numbers." Fergie pointed to another line of text on the photograph that Elena couldn't read. "Perhaps this is the longitude and latitude. However, we should get down to dinner to support the alibi that we were, in fact, eating instead of here searching through Melly's closet."

Elena slid the photograph back where she found it. Then, she checked to make sure that they'd put everything back in Melly's closet.

"What should we, like, do with Melly?" Abria asked.

"What do you mean?" Elena said. "We leave her here and go down to dinner like we planned. With any luck she'll sleep through the night and then we won't have to tolerate her talking about boys all evening."

"I know that was the plan," said Abria. "But that was when we thought we were going to give her a small dose of the potion. And that was also before she smacked her face on the floor. Don't you think we should take her to the Medical Station?"

"And say what exactly?" Elena asked. "*Oh, hi there! We drugged our classmate.* Somehow, I don't think that will go over well."

"Abria has a valid point," said Fergie. "We should make sure that she did not obtain any serious damage from falling. However, I do not believe that we should tell anyone what happened. I would suggest that we simply leave her there. After all, it is dinner time and plausible that no one will be there to witness us leaving her."

"Oh, good plan there," Elena said sarcastically. "There's just one problem, the whole school has surveillance. Someone will definitely see us."

Fergie raised her Broadcaster and said, "Pigg, are you there?"

Pigg's face appeared holographically on her wrist. "Reporting for duty."

"We are going to require an interruption in surveillance from our room to Medical for the next fifteen minutes," Fergie said.

Pigg was quiet for a moment, his eyes staring off as he worked. Then, he said, "All set to use Grimvator three."

"You're both brilliant!" Elena said as she grabbed Melly's ankles.

Abria and Fergie each grabbed an arm, and they lifted Melly off the bed.

"Geez," Elena groaned. "She's a lot heavier than she looks."

"Well, she's totally, like, passed out," Abria said. "Dead weight."

The three girls carried Melly awkwardly across the room. Elena opened their bedroom door and peered into the hallway, hoping that it was empty. Then, they moved down the hall to Grimvator three, but had trouble trying to navigate Melly through the doors. When they were finally inside, Fergie selected the Medical Station from the list on the Optivision screen as Elena dropped Melly's feet.

"Easy!" Abria said as she and Fergie stumbled forward.

"Sorry," Elena said, trying to pick up Melly's legs again. "It's just that she's so heavy."

"Pigg?" Fergie said into her Broadcaster. "Have you prepared the room for our arrival?"

Pigg's head appeared again on Fergie's wrist. "Yes, I can confirm that the Humanoids are currently occupied. Also, there are no other patients in the room."

Finally, the Grimvator opened at Medical. The three friends carried Melly into the large room and heaved her body onto the bed nearest to the door. Fergie opened several Optivisions and Elena watched Melly's vital signs come to life.

"What are you doing?" Elena asked.

"I am attempting to give the robot doctors as much information as I can about Melly's condition so they will know how to treat her quickly."

Moments later, over a plate of tomato salad with fennel croutons, stone bass with cream leeks, and cheddar bacon skinny chips, Elena began to describe the events that had unfolded in their room to Austin, Declan, and Pigg, who had a lump on his forehead from falling on the floor.

"She had a photograph in her wardrobe," Elena said. "An actual photo. Besides the one we stole from Bowen's apartment in New York, I've only ever seen one other photograph in my life and it was the exact same one that she had in her wardrobe."

"What was in the photograph?" Austin asked.

"It was of a ship that had been frozen in a block of ice and snow," Elena said. "I was a little girl the first time I saw that photo. It was at a farm near Atlanson and there was a crazy, old man living there. He told me that it was a ship from the Great Flood and that he'd been there to see it."

She noticed a grave look on Fergie's face and asked, "What's wrong?"

Fergie set her fork down and said, "During first quarter Advanced Historical Analysis, Instructor Booker spoke to us about a worldwide flood.

Many different civilizations recorded similar accounts of this flood. Remember?

He read the Epic of Gilgamesh, the story of Noah from the Hebrew Bible, and the Akkadian version of the flood. But there were also accounts in the Quran Islamic text, in the Quiche writings in Native America, in the Mayans records, in the Hindu puranic, and in Greek mythology."

"I'm not really, like, following..." Abria started.

"What if the stories are true? What if there really was some type of flood?" Austin asked before Fergie could speak again. "What if that photograph is of the ship from the stories?"

"If we assemble the facts, the photograph of the ship, the Hebrew writing on the back of the photograph, the fact that Melly's family lived in Turkey before moving to Crowfield Plantation, then it is plausible to conclude that the ship from the photograph exists," Fergie said in a formal tone.

"You said the writing on the back of the photograph translated to *Tablets of Destiny*. What if the Tablets are the next artifact? And what if it's on that ship?"

"Or it could be nothing," Pigg said irritably, thumbing the lump on his forehead. "Is it realistic that a boat from a story that was written thousands and thousands of years ago actually exists? Probably not. That was just a story that some old dead dudes made up."

"Not just *some old dead dudes*," Austin said. "The same story was written about by men from completely different civilizations."

"We have already confirmed that there is a red dot on the Catalan Atlas in Turkey," Fergie said. "Assuming the numbers from Melly's photograph represent the longitude and latitude of the location to where the photograph was taken, we can assume that there is an artifact located there."

"The truth is," Pigg said, sounding impatient. "I am tired of this, treasure hunting, whatever you call it. I was sorta hoping that we wouldn't have to do it anymore. We have our Decoys, after all. Can't we just send the robots for us?"

Austin looked at Elena with raised eyebrows. Then, he looked at Pigg sympathetically.

"You don't have to come with us, Pigg. I'm serious. You can stay here. No hard feelings from any of us."

Elena felt herself getting red in the face. She didn't understand how Austin could give Pigg an easy out like that and she wasn't sure how she was going to feel about Pigg if he declined to go with them.

As she was beginning to blurt out the word "Coward!" for the whole Mess Hall to hear, Pigg hung his head and said, "I'll come. I'm scared, okay. We almost died twice. I'd like to live to see my fifteenth birthday."

"We're all scared but we're going to get through it together," Austin said. "You're *not* going to die out there. I promise."

Elena thought it was a little much for Austin to promise that he could somehow control life and death, especially given how many people had died in the past couple years, but she bit her tongue.

"We'll go to the Station, confirm our theories, and make preparations for our trip to Turkey," Austin said, but he said it so simply that Elena immediately had doubts arise in her own mind.

Perhaps Pigg was right. The two artifacts they'd acquired had also required them to confront an ambush, which should have resulted in their death. She did feel an eager, desperate need to find artifacts, but at the same time she felt uneasy about the possibility that she could lose one of her friends. Elena still had serious reservations about the trip. In the end, Austin was going to make the journey to find the Tablets so she would go, too.

Finally, after the last few weeks of studying, the morning of their fourth quarter exam dawned. Elena sat at breakfast with her friends picking over a plate of banana ricotta hot cakes, apple compote porridge, and an open omelet with wild mushroom and cheese.

She was so tired that she was barely listening as Abria chattered on about Melly having to be quarantined to the Medical Station because they couldn't figure out why she'd fainted hard enough to break her nose in two places, and how Frankie Smiley had gone to visit her a couple times (which made Abria very jealous), and about how the entire Raptor Unit was going to visit Oscar Hunter's house for fourth quarter break because his parents live in an expensive palace on a lake.

After breakfast, Elena followed Austin and the others out of the Mess Hall and took a quick Grimvator ride to the exam room. She found the Optivision screen, where her face appeared in midair, without any trouble. A second after she stepped into place, Instructor Booker's holographic face appeared.

"During the exam, you will be given a certain point of time in history," said Booker. "This will be different from the other students in this exam. You will need to ascertain the time period, answer the historical analysis questions, and use the appropriate social science, whether that is agriculture, husbandry, or manufacturing. You will be required to give your answers in the native language of the time. The test is not time sensitive so make sure to move at your own pace through the simulation."

Then, the lights around her pupil station suddenly dimmed and the sound of the other students in the room faded away. Several Optivision screens lit up, creating a cocoon of Greek-lettered exam questions around her.

The first portion of the exam covered a wide range of details from the Byzantine Empire and required her to fill in a detailed map of when and where the Emperor Constantine moved the seat of the Roman Empire to Constantinople. She also had to complete a timeline of the four different cultural elements in Byzantine literature and arrange them into the five groups of prose that they were classified into.

She reviewed the architectural plans for Hagia Sophia, which was a building designed to replace an older church that was destroyed during the Nika Revolt. Then, there was a long section on government and bureaucracy, and how, unlike in Rome, the Senate ceased to have real legislative authority because the emperor in the Byzantine state had become the sole and absolute ruler.

Next, the test questions moved through the codification of law, regulating the behavior of the various trade guilds in Constantinople, and the administrative reforms that essentially created paths to aristocratic status.

Eventually, Elena had to assess the languages that existed in the multi-ethnic Byzantine Empire including Syriac, Aramaic, Armenian, and Georgian. And she had to translate a psalter in the Coptic language. Then, using the Greek text, she had to decipher a list of advancements in astronomy and mathematical sciences that were made during that period.

Following that assignment, she read a lengthy section of Byzantine cuisine to identify, a list of recreational activities to classify, and a section of ecclesiastical forms of music that were composed in Greek text to categorize as ceremonial, festival, or church music.

Questions about warfare technology followed, including the invention of Greek fire, the constant fortification of the walls of Constantinople, the many alliances made for trading, and the wartime tributes that were paid to keep neighboring nations from raiding the empire.

The exam was long and tiresome, but Elena felt confident about each Optivision screen of questions that she submitted for grading.

When her test was finally complete, it was already time for dinner. Elena ate with her friends in the Mess Hall feeling relieved. Yet, she also had an irksome knot in the pit of her stomach. She was happy to be leaving school a few days early, but the thought of flying across the ocean in a hovercraft that had been converted to an aerodynamic vessel sent her nerves on edge. At this point, she wanted to get the whole trip over with.

After dinner, Elena walked back to her room with Abria and Fergie. When she scanned her Trademark to open the bedroom door, she saw Melly standing on the other side, blocking the entrance. Melly was smiling, but Elena could tell that something was not quite right by the look in her eyes.

"Hello…" Elena said uneasily.

"You were going through my stuff," Melly said in a steady tone. She didn't break her smile, but her face was still unnerving.

"I don't know what you're talking about," Elena replied.

"I found your fingerprints on my photograph," Melly said. "The one inside my wardrobe. You drugged me and used my Trademark to gain access to my closet."

Elena eased around her into the room toward her bed and said, "I have no idea what you're talking about."

Melly approached her again, coming close enough to violate Elena's personal space. "If you ever go through my things again..."

"You'll what," Elena said mockingly. "Kill me?"

"Don't tempt me," Melly said and then she giggled in a sickly-sweet way and left the room.

Elena's mouth fell open in disbelief. "How can she smile so implicitly when she's so livid? I usually just punch things."

"Or people," Fergie added.

"Maybe she's a, like, cyborg or something," Abria giggled.

Elena snorted a laugh until she caught the look on Fergie's face. "Sorry, that was totally not nice."

"No offense taken," Fergie replied. "However, I am concerned about something that Melly mentioned. If Melly took your fingerprints off that photograph, then she has access to highly sophisticated equipment."

"Or she knows someone who does," said Elena. "Remember, her parents are government officials. I wonder what they're trying to hide?"

Fergie and Abria both shrugged, while Elena felt as confused as ever about what Melly may or may not know about the Renegades and the plans to remove Imperator from power.

23

Mount Ararat

"Do you think they're asleep now?"

Abria's face appeared right beside Elena's ear as she was lying in bed. Only a few hours had passed since Melly had confronted Elena about the photograph in her wardrobe, so she was more than ready to get away from her classmate as quickly as possible.

"I think they're all asleep," Abria whispered. "At least, I can hear a couple of them snoring and Melly had to go back to the Medical Station to have one last set of tests done before break starts. Anyway, I think we're clear to go now."

Elena got out of bed and pulled on her combat boots. Then, she followed Abria and Fergie to the narrow hallway alongside the washroom that led out to a veranda that overlooked the courtyard seven floors below.

Abria peered over the edge and gulped. "Okay, what's the plan again?"

"The building has crevices," Elena whispered. "It's actually easier than climbing up and down those dimwit rope ladders in Basic, so mind your footing and follow me."

Elena swung her leg over the wall and started down the building. She remembered how nervous she felt the first time she'd attempted this descent, but now it was second-nature. Soon, she and her friends were standing in the courtyard.

Elena led Abria and Fergie into the shadow of the farthest wall so they wouldn't be seen by surveillance. Then, they ran across the grounds, through the orchard to the edge of the school boundaries and pursued the dark forest.

When the girls arrived in the Research & Development room the boys were already waiting for them, including Kidd. Elena couldn't explain it, but she was always surprised when he followed through with a plan of any kind. Then she looked over at Pigg and gaped at his disheveled and partially torn clothing. He even had smudges of dirt on one cheek.

"What happened to you?" Elena asked.

"Oh, nothing," Pigg replied nervously. "I just fell the last few feet from the building. And I scraped my knee. Plus, I'm pretty sure that I've bruised my tailbone, but all in all I think getting me down the building as far as I did was a miracle."

Elena rolled her eyes as Fergie said, "We will wake the Decoys first and send them to our beds."

Elena moved to the opposite side of the room and opened a cabinet door. She looked at her Humanoid Decoy, still marveling that the robot looked exactly like her.

"Step forward and scan your Trademarks," Fergie instructed. "Each of you will need to give your Decoy a set of commands. Simply tell them that you wish them to go back to your bed in the resident tower and that they are to go to your home on Departure Day and assume your identity."

Elena stepped forward timidly and scanned her Trademark against the Decoy's Trademark. The robot's eyes fluttered open. Immediately, it looked annoyed.

"Why am I awake?" Decoy Elena demanded. "It's the middle of the night."

"I need you to...er..." Elena started.

"Get on with it," Decoy Elena said irritably. "I'm tired."

Elena felt instantly frustrated with her Decoy's attitude.

"Go back to school, scale the wall to my room, and get in my bed!" she said forcefully. "You'll need to go back to Atlanson on Departure Day and pretend to be me. You can stay with Austin's grandparents and..."

"Stop, stop, stop," Decoy Elena said sharply. "I've already been uploaded with your daily routine, so please don't bore me with it now." Then, Decoy Elena looked at the other Decoys and said, "Are the rest of you ready to go?"

With that, the robots followed Decoy Elena out of the room, down the hall, and out the Firebird Station front door.

Feeling slightly scandalized, Elena turned toward her friends and asked, "Am I really that moody and bossy?"

Everyone replied at the same time, so it was hard to tell exactly who said what. She was certain she heard a couple people say "yes" and someone said "an exaggeration" and someone else said "sort of" but Kidd said loudly, "You're actually worse."

Elena pursed her lips together, determined not to speak again unless spoken to. She and the Firebirds climbed onto the Independence and quickly prepared for departure, stowing their items, and getting strapped into their seats.

Kidd and Fergie settled into their captains' chairs and accessed dozens of Optivision screens. Soon, Elena noticed that the walls out the front windshield were slowly rotating around, but then she realized that it was the Independence that was revolving slowly and descending underground.

"The platform opens to an underground tunnel, which is essentially our exit route for Turkey. I have activated the Masquerade," Fergie informed them as the platform stopped revolving and the hololights lit a tunnel in front of them. "Although, I doubt that anyone will notice us where we are going."

After Fergie said the word "Masquerade" Elena had a distinct flashback to the first time they'd discussed the object. She knew now that the device projected the landscape around the Independence back onto the hovercraft, essentially making them invisible. Of all the reasons that Elena was thankful for her friends, their ability to understand and manipulate technology for illegal purposes was at the top of the list.

"From some of the machine parts your mom sent, I was able to build a power thruster," Kidd told Fergie as the Independence eased down a darkened corridor. "So, instead of this trip taking fourteen hours, it's only going to take seven."

"That's awesome. How did you know to do that?" Austin asked.

"Well, I *am* a genius at building things," Kidd said proudly.

"You're using the term *genius* very liberally, don't you think?" Elena asked.

"You know," Kidd replied. "I think your Decoy is actually a little nicer than you, Freckles."

Elena unbuckled her belt and left the command bridge without saying another word. She made her way through the hovercraft and into the cabin that she used as her room. She flung herself down on the lower bunk bed and closed her eyes, feeling tired and frustrated.

"It's going to be a long trip if you're at each other's throats the whole time." Austin had arrived at the door.

"I can't help it," Elena said. "He brings out the worst in me."

"Do you want me to bunk in your room tonight?"

"Nah, I'm really tired," Elena said gruffly. "Plus, you'll sleep better if you don't have to share with me. Apparently, I tend to scream when I have nightmares."

Austin smiled knowingly and walked away.

Elena turned over, hoping for sleep. However, as she lay there, it was like her brain decided it was going to ignore her tired body and she began to obsess over the past year and the changes that had come to define her life.

At this time last year, she was coming to terms with the fact that her mere existence was completely contrary to what she thought her whole life. The journey she'd been on to discover the truth behind the death of her parents had been a mystery of confusing elements.

She'd discovered that one of her friends was a robot and that Fergie's parents were helping the Firebirds fight against Imperator by enabling them on their journey. She also learned that Hannibal and Hopper were secretly fighting Imperator and that she'd have to be satisfied with not knowing everything about her circumstances because it was infuriatingly vague.

Elena had to resist the urge to go ask Austin for a sedative, like the one he'd given her after her parents died. Instead, she headed to the galley because she was sure Pigg would be there cooking. However, when she arrived, she found Kidd sitting on one of the bar stools finishing a canister of soup.

"What are you doing?" Elena noticed her tone was almost accusatory.

"Well, I'm in the galley, so obviously I'm eating," Kidd said.

Elena sighed. "I meant to say, who's operating the Independence? And I didn't mean to sound so grumpy when I said it."

"Foreman," Kidd replied coolly. "It's really a no-brainer when it's on autopilot."

Elena eased around the room to the refrigerator and began digging through it, looking for something, but she wasn't sure what. She was impressed by the amount of food that Pigg had been able to steal.

"You doing okay?" Kidd asked quietly.

"Of course," Elena said brusquely. "Why?"

"Well, after your little breakdown during third quarter exams I figured that heading off to the enchanted mountain might be a little much for you."

"Why would you care even if it was?" Elena said curiously and then she observed his back stiffen.

"I don't, I guess." Kidd stood rigidly and walked to the door, but then paused and said, "Don't have any of the mango. The whole batch has gone bad."

Feeling perplexed by her conversation with Kidd, Elena walked back to her cabin and found Austin on the top bunk.

"I thought I'd come check on you," he said.

Elena smiled slightly and flopped down on the bottom bunk.

"I couldn't sleep."

"I figured as much."

Elena pulled the Kairos out and fiddled with it between her fingers. She was starting to wonder why Kidd was always so mean to her when she noticed a strange reflection from her necklace. Elena turned toward the hololight on the washstand and twisted the Kairos from side to side. In the different corners and crevices of the necklace she noticed some strange symbols that looked very familiar to her.

She sucked in a gasp and said, "Austin, it's my name again in Akkadian lettering. It's on the Kairos."

Austin jumped down from the top bunk as Elena stripped the necklace from her collar. With their heads together, they turned the Kairos over and over in the light from the washstand until the symbols had been clearly determined.

"They're not in order," Elena remarked.

"I know what to do," Austin said breathlessly.

He took the Kairos into his hands. Using the tips of his fingers, he slid the crevices of the necklace in and out of the corners until all the Akkadian symbols aligned to spell the name "Elena."

Suddenly, the Kairos rose from Austin's hand and hovered in midair as it folded open to reveal a round face, similar to a clock, with two hands: one with a globe at the tip and the other with the shape of a sun at the tip. It had numbers, but it also had multiple round faces different sizes, each with a unique set of symbols.

Everything on the clock began to spin clockwise and counterclockwise at the same time. The clock hands revolved, and elevated circles rotated around the face of the clock while various symbols lit up. She had only seen it open once before and it had been so brief that she hadn't noticed the intricate work. She could now see every single line, number, symbol, and color.

A grin stretched across Austin's entire face. "Your dad was a genius!"

Elena and Austin hurried down the hall and to the command bridge where they found that Fergie was still manning her post at one of the captain's chairs.

"Fergie, look what we found!" Austin said.

Fergie looked down at the open Kairos, observing it earnestly.

"This is truly amazing!" She looked into Elena's face and asked, "Can you go ask Wheeler to come take the controls? I would like to take the Kairos to the lab to see if we can make any sense of it before we land."

Elena nodded and hurried out of the room, looking desperately for Kidd.

"Where could he be?" she wondered, feeling frustrated after she didn't find him in the seventh room she'd looked in.

"Wheeler!" She hollered loudly. "Wheeler!"

"What's going on?" Kidd asked gruffly. He was standing in the doorway of his cabin looking as if he'd just woken up.

"Fergie asked me to find you to fly the ship," Elena said.

Kidd gave her an exasperated expression and then pushed past her into the hallway, tromping toward the command bridge.

Not wanting to be around Kidd, Elena set off in the other direction toward the lab to wait for Fergie and Austin to arrive.

Minutes later, Fergie placed the Kairos on one of the tables in the lab and watched it spin for a moment. Then, she accessed several Optivisions from her Touchdot and Elena inspected some beams from the Touchdot scan the Kairos.

Finally, Fergie pulled the Ransom Dossier and the Alpha Manuscript from their protective casings and set the Cryptext on the table.

"We know that these items are connected in some way," Fergie said. "If we can discover the key to make them work together we could improve our efficiency at finding artifacts."

Fergie scanned the Ransom Dossier with her eyes and then reached forward to touch the Kairos. She attempted to pause one of the already revolving clock hands, but it simply shuddered in her fingers, so she released it at once.

She glanced at the Alpha Manuscript and then tried to adjust one of the levers on the Kairos. When it didn't move, she didn't force it. She moved the Cryptext closer to the Kairos, but it didn't seem to accomplish anything one way or another.

"I am uncertain how the Kairos may work at this point. I will have to do extensive research before I will feel comfortable trying anything extreme on it. However, one thing is perfectly clear," Fergie said plainly. "Elena, your dad was a genius."

"That's what I always say," Austin said with pride.

With hours to go before they reached their destination, Elena began to wander in and out of the various rooms on the ship. She casually chewed her fingernails, imagining an ominous mountain range swarming with ravenous creatures ready to devour them. However, it wasn't until she noticed that the

Independence was flying over a vast body of water that her anxiety peaked to the point that she began to rip fingernails off with her teeth.

Elena collapsed in the seat of the nearest picture window and stared out at the miles upon miles of uncharted ocean. She envisioned slimy sea creatures and had the same feeling of suffocation that she'd experienced when the Independence had sunk under the sand in New York City harbor.

If that wasn't enough to terrify her, she also remembered the dream she'd had in the frozen wilderness about the building under the water and the octopus that grabbed her. Could there be a building somewhere in the deep unknown?

Elena suddenly had a sensation that she didn't want to die alone. She jumped up and hurried back to the command bridge where her friends were sitting. She eased into a chair beside Austin but sat in near silence as the miles of sea eventually changed to land.

At long last, a spec appeared on the horizon. As Kidd operated the hovercraft closer, the spec became a vast mountain range, growing out of a long, flat plain. The tiptop peaks were blanketed in white, as if they had been dusted with the powdered sugar that Elena had seen at the chocolatier in the Galilee Province. The terrain was dotted by buildings, which led out to a lonely road that eased its way to the mountain. As they got closer, thick clouds covered the hills making visibility scarce.

"Moment of truth," Fergie said as they neared the lower part of the mountain. "Time to see if a boat exists up there."

Elena watched one of the dozen Optivision screens begin to flash and blink, apparently scanning the mountain as the Independence began to circle the lower hills.

For a long time, Kidd flew the hovercraft around and around as Fergie directed him. Then, finally, the screen began to transmit the outline of a peculiar object that was shaped differently than the rest of the rock, Fergie read the coordinates aloud and Kidd changed course.

As the Independence came around a small hill, a gigantic ship sitting on a bed of rock appeared in the front windshield. Elena's mouth fell open as Kidd moved the hovercraft closer.

"Look at it," Elena breathed, feeling overwhelmed by its stature. "It's real! It's actually real. Gilgamesh, or whatever, actually happened."

"The terrain is unstable," Fergie said after reading a different Optivision screen. "It would be unwise to land the Independence here because we could risk the integrity of the mountain."

"Can you find a safer spot that is not far from here?" Austin asked her.

Fergie began to flip through screens until she finally said, "Yes, we are not far from a more suitable location."

Once the new coordinates were put into the navigation system, Kidd circled around the area and landed the hovercraft a mile south of the boat so they could see it from the front window.

Austin pulled his carrier bag over his head and said, "Bowen, Wheeler, and I will take three of the Speedsters from the cargo bay and head up to the ship to see if we can find anything. The rest of you can stay here with the Independence."

Elena opened her mouth to protest, but Kidd said, "See this thermograph here?" He pointed at one of the blue screens hovering in midair. "It basically says it's freezing out there. Plus, I've been flying for hours. I'm tired. So, I'll be sitting this one out."

"I'll go in his place," offered Elena.

"But you had frostnip a few weeks ago," Austin said. "It's not a good idea for you to go hiking in the cold again."

"Yeah, Ransom," Declan said. "Remember the thing about your toes falling off. Ew!" He made a face that Elena would have laughed at if she weren't so angry.

"But you're going on Speedsters," Elena protested. "I can ride one of those. No walking involved."

Austin was already shaking his head.

"We still have to hike a bit and we'll have to climb around a frozen ship. You really need to stay off your feet."

"If you didn't want me to come, you should have told me in private," Elena spat at Austin.

"You're right," Austin said respectfully. "But you're still not going."

"You can't keep me here," Elena said. "I'll follow you."

"That's a good point," Declan said. "I think we should tie her up."

Elena's mouth fell open in disbelief. "You can't be serious?"

She looked at Fergie, Abria, and Pigg for support, but the three of them were staring at their jump boots.

She stamped her foot in a childlike way. "You can't be serious!"

"Lena, either choose to stay or we'll have to tie you up?" Austin said simply.

Elena crossed her arms over her chest and narrowed her eyes. "I dare you to try it."

Twelve minutes later, after a lot of kicking and screaming, Elena was tied to a chair in the galley and Austin headed out the door with Declan. She knew that Austin was only trying to keep her safe, but how could he tie her up and leave her? They had always been a team. No matter if she wanted to build a skate park or he wanted to break into the Grimsby school Vault, they had always done everything together.

Minutes after Austin and Declan left, Pigg arrived looking guilty.

"I thought I would make you something to eat."

"We just finished breakfast," Elena grumbled.

"Yeah, but I like to eat when I'm stressed." Pigg pulled out some crackers with cheese and shoved a bite in his mouth.

"Did Austin send you in here to watch me?"

"He said that if I sat with you it might help you calm down," Pigg said between bites. "But I don't see how I could possibly calm you down when you're mad that Austin wouldn't let you go, and that Declan had the idea to tie you up, and that Austin agreed to help him. *And* they actually *tied you to this chair and left you behind.* Yeah, I don't see how *he* expects *me* to calm *you* down after all that."

Elena pursed her lips together. This trip was not turning out like anything she'd imagined. As she tried to figure out a way to break the chair so she could get free, she suddenly realized that Pigg's mere presence gave her the perfect opportunity to be sneaky.

"Pigg?" Elena said imploringly and he simply grunted between bites of kiwi grapes. "In Austin's haste to tie me up, he and Declan did a little too good a job and now my hands are hurting. Could you come around here and loosen the rope?"

Pigg looked at her apprehensively.

"Pigg! I'm in pain," Elena said more directly. "If you could just loosen it a *little bit* so I'm not uncomfortable I'd really be grateful."

Pigg sighed loudly and moved toward her. He placed his hands on either side of the rope that was binding her hands and pulled. Elena felt her arms release.

A look of terror crossed Pigg's face as he pulled his hands forward and stared at the rope that was supposed to be attached to Elena.

"Oops!" Pigg said right before Elena shoved him hard in the chest and he fell backward across the floor.

"Elena, wait!" he called, but she was already sprinting down the hall toward the cargo bay.

When she arrived, Fergie and Abria were waiting for her. Fergie was packing the seat trunk of one of the Speedsters with a medical kit and some hololights while Abria pulled heavy coats out of one of the closets along with aviator hats and the tactical vests that Pigg had created for them that included a high glide compressed air parachute.

"If you knew I'd get free why didn't you come and get me?" Elena demanded from her friends.

"Plausible deniability," Fergie said plainly.

"I was hungry, so I thought I'd pack a, like, picnic," said Abria, holding up her carrier bag.

Elena hurried over to a wall of cabinets and started opening doors and drawers. Then, she began to shove ropes and hooks into a tactical pack. She also grabbed four crossbows and placed them carefully under the seat of one of the Speedsters.

"What are you doing?" Abria asked.

"Do you remember what Hopper taught us about climbing?" Elena said.

"I make it a point not to listen to everything he says because, honestly, it's a bit terrifying what can happen to a person that is lost in the wild," Abria said. "Most of the time I'm, like, thinking about my nails or wondering if I'm having a bad hair day or something."

"First, if we're with more than one person we should always be linked together with ropes and a harness," Elena said in a very teacher-like fashion.

"Second, if one person begins to fall, the others can support with their weight by anchor footing."

Elena filled a waist bag with pre-drilled rock bolts, the kind she knew that climbers used on mountains. "Third, if in immediate danger, use a grappling hook crossbow for support."

"Instructor Hopper never said that," Fergie corrected her.

"Okay, I made that last part up." Elena shrugged. "But I'm taking this because it looks so awesome and I've wanted to shoot one since the first time we found them out here. You each should take one, too, just in case."

Elena pulled a winter coat, gripping gloves, and a wool lined earflap cap from one of the cabinets. As she finished filling a tactical pack with necessary supplies, Pigg arrived in the doorway, out of breath and clutching his side as if he'd run a far distance.

"Cramp...cramp," Pigg exhaled. "Never run on a full stomach. What are you *doing?*"

"We're going after Austin and Declan," Elena said.

"You're going to leave me here *alone* with Wheeler?" Pigg asked, sounding scandalized.

"Look, you can either come or stay here and hide from Wheeler," Elena said bluntly. "But I'm leaving and nobody's gonna stop me."

"Oh, Elena," Pigg said in relief. "Hiding from Kidd is such a great idea. I can't believe I didn't think of it. Okay, so, happy trails girls." With that, he bounded happily out of the cargo bay.

"You've got to admire his determination to keep himself, like, out of harm's way," Abria said cheerfully.

Elena rolled her eyes and climbed onto one of the Speedsters. An Optivision screen appeared. She used it to access one of the modules, then she watched the cargo bay door open. Her Speedster eased out onto the terrain with Fergie and Abria following close behind her.

Once the cargo bay door was shut, the Speedster's Optivision screen lit up with a terrain sensor, tracking sensor, and automatic control system. Elena clutched the acceleration handgrip firmly and set off up the mountain toward the base of the Ark. The Speedster was thrilling to navigate over the rocks, but the temperature was dangerously cold. Every breath came with a sharp, icy edge. She parked beside Austin and Declan's Speedsters mere minutes after leaving the Independence.

Elena stared at the majestic ship, sitting heavily upon a bed of rock. The boat looked as if it had been ripped right in half because she could see straight into the middle of the ship. The crumbling sides were torn jaggedly, and the outer, splintered fragments drooped toward the ground. The multiple decks within its hull were caving.

"Where's the rest of the boat?" Elena asked.

"Given the altitude, the size of the ship, and the changing weather patterns we can logically deduce that it split apart at some point. As to the other piece, it could be higher up," Fergie said. The Touchdot from her Broadcaster flew out and a blue Optivision screen appeared to be scanning the wood of the ship. "Fascinating. Carbon dating puts this at around 14000 BC."

Suddenly, Austin appeared at an opening from one of the upper floors.

Elena expected him to scold them, but instead he blurted out, "I need help! Bowen fell and I can't see or hear him."

¤ 24 ¤

Avalanche

Elena felt a surge of panic and called to Austin, "How do we get up to you?"

"I don't know," Austin shouted back. "Most of the floors collapsed as we came inside. That's why he fell. I don't think we can get back out the way we came in and I don't think you'll be able to get through that way."

Elena turned on her heels. She threw open the trunk seat on her Speedster and grabbed one of the grappling hook crossbows. As she turned, she noticed that Abria and Fergie were also holding crossbows.

"Ladies, let's do this!"

Elena aimed the crossbow at the opening where Austin stood and shouted, "Step back!"

The grappling hook shot from the bow. She heard a loud thud after it disappeared through the opening. Abria's grappling hook bounced off the edge of the frozen wood and Fergie's hook lodged into the boat below the place where Austin stood.

"I'll activate the pulley system so I can get into the boat faster," Elena told Abria and Fergie as she grabbed another crossbow and slung it over her shoulder. "I can release the line back down to you, but you should each bring the other crossbows up in case we need them to help Bowen."

Elena secured a climbing harness to her waist. After she inserted the end of the grappling hook rope into the mounting clip, the line began to automatically retract, pulling her up toward the top of the ship where Austin was waiting.

After Austin helped her into the ship, she looked around. Wooden cages and enclosures varying in size and shape lined the walls, perfectly preserved by the frigid temperature.

"Where's Bowen?" she asked.

"I'll have to take you there," Austin said. "But first, help me get Abria and Fergie into the boat."

When they were finally able to get Fergie into the ark, she pulled a medical kit from her coat and Abria pulled an extra grappling hook from her shoulder.

"This way," said Austin.

As he stepped into the ship, Elena heard a strange groaning noise. He led them down a corridor and into a side hallway where there was a large, gaping hole in the floor. Austin twisted the grappling hook Abria had given him through one of the wooden beams and then laced the rope through his fingers.

"I'm going down."

"No way!" Elena said, grabbing his hand. "You're the only medical person we have. Plus, I'm lighter than you, so it won't be as hard for you to pull me back up."

"I can go," Abria offered.

Austin removed the Suturand from his pocket and said, "But you don't know how to use the Suturand, Abria." He handed the instrument to Elena. "Be careful."

Elena pulled at her neck and removed the Kairos.

She handed it to Fergie and said, "See if it will show you how to find the Tablets of Destiny."

Then, Elena stuffed a medical kit and the Suturand into her coat. She secured the mounting clip to the grappling hook rope. After she'd adjusted the settings so that the rope would release her down slowly, Austin helped lower her through the hole.

She held a hololight in front of her, but it was nevertheless shockingly dark. The shadows played on the wall and the glacial air made her shake with fear. After a while, her light finally caught on something familiar.

"Bowen!" she called after recognizing his jacket.

Declan was lying face down, but Elena could hear him groaning.

When Elena finally landed beside him, she unclipped herself from the rope. With a great effort, she managed to turn Declan onto his back. Blood trickled from his mouth and a cut on his head. She tore open the medical kit and used some of the sanitizing wipes to clean his head. Then, she placed a bandage over it, which seemed to slow the bleeding. As she started to wipe the blood from his mouth, Declan began to rouse.

"My rescuer," he said faintly, but his eyes were barely open, and Elena could tell that he was slipping easily in and out of consciousness.

Elena smiled at him and unzipped his coat. "Everything's going to be okay now." She moved the Suturand scanner over his head, body, and legs. "His ribs are broken on the left side," she called to Austin.

She looked around, trying to think. How were they going to get him out of the hull of the ship?

"Austin!" Elena said excitedly. "I'm going to use the parachute from my pack and wrap him up. Throw down another line. He'll be dead weight, but I think between the two lines the grappling ropes will lift him."

"Don't use the word *dead* when referring to me," Declan croaked, hacking a cough.

Elena punched the button on her pack. Her parachute shot out of the back. She laid the parachute down as close to Declan as she could get it.

"Bowen! Bowen!" she called, and his eyes fluttered. "Do you think you could move onto the parachute if you use me as a support?"

"I think so," Declan replied.

As carefully as she could, she wrapped an arm around him. Declan pushed off the ground with his good arm. He let out a tremendous groan of pain but was still able to shimmy onto the parachute. Elena grabbed the extra rope that had been tossed down to them and tied it securely to the canvas.

Then, Elena leaned over Declan and said, "See you in a minute."

Elena watched helplessly as Declan's body was slowly lifted back up through the cavernous ship. She held her hololight up, but soon Declan's body disappeared from view. She ripped off the glove on her right hand and chewed a fingernail. While she waited, she began to hear creaking noises that reverberated from every crevice of the ship.

"We've got him!" Austin finally called down.

Elena heaved a sigh of relief and then waited impatiently until the end of the grappling hook line was sent back down to her.

Once she was attached to the rope, Elena was lifted off the ground in a slow, steady motion until she finally reached Austin again.

"We've got to get out of here as quickly as we can!" Abria said urgently.

"Declan needs medical attention," Austin said steadily. "I'm going to give him a shot of adrenaline. It's the only way I think he'll be able to tolerate getting back to the Speedster."

Elena watched as Austin pulled a needle from the medical kit and stuck it into one of Declan's veins.

Within seconds, his eyes popped open, and he declared, "Wow! I feel terrible!"

"Bowen, we've got to get you out of this ship," Austin said. "You can use me and Elena for support, but we've got to get you up, okay?"

With a great effort, the four friends managed to get Declan back to the mouth of the ship where they'd entered. They helped him back into the parachute stretcher and lowered Declan out of the ship onto the ground.

While Fergie and Abria rappelled out of the boat, Austin swung the extra grappling hook over his back. As Elena braced herself to rappel out of the ship, there was a hair-raising sensation of tilting back and forth as the ark began to sway dangerously.

Austin's eyes widened with terror as he shouted, "Get down there! Hurry!"

Elena let the rope slip through her fingers so fast that she felt the flesh tear open even with her gloves on. Ignoring her wounds, she looked down toward the Independence, which appeared as a little spec of rock. She wished she could somehow warn them about the ship being unstable, but then noticed that Fergie was already trying to contact Kidd from her Broadcaster. She turned sharply back to the ship and watched with bated breath as Austin began to make his way down to the ground.

"Abria, grab the extra crossbows from the trunk of my Speedster," Elena said as she grabbed the crossbow that was lying on the ground and began to clip herself to Declan. "You and Fergie link yourselves together."

As Austin finally reached Elena there came a horrific crushing and cracking sound from the Ark. Elena's mouth fell open as pieces of the boat began to break off the sides and spill onto the mountain right where they stood.

"Come on!" Austin yelled as he and Elena hoisted Declan on either side of them. "The Speedsters are right there."

Then, the ground shook so violently that it sent them crashing to the ground. Elena looked back as larger pieces of the massive ship began to rain down on them. In a matter of seconds, she realized there was no way they'd have time to get back to the Speedsters before the ship broke apart completely and came hurtling after them.

"The Ark is breaking apart!" Austin cried.

"Austin!" Elena screamed. "The grappling hooks!"

Austin didn't need explanation. He aimed a crossbow high above his head and shot the grappling hook into the side of the mountain away from the Ark. One second later, Elena was swinging through the air toward the face of the mountain with Declan beside her. They landed with a thud, and she watched Fergie and Abria hit the mountain not too far from them.

Then, a tremendous thunder caused Elena to look back down to the earth. Pieces of the ark crushed their Speedsters as it began to slide. Clipping lower boulders and leaving a trail of debris as it went, the ship gathered speed. Elena looked ahead and could see that the path of the great ship was headed straight for the Independence.

"Wheeler!" Elena screamed into her Broadcaster. "Take off! Take off!" But she didn't hear a reply. "Pigg! Wheeler!"

The Ark was now sliding in a full avalanche. In mere moments, Pigg and Kidd would certainly be crushed to death under a pile of rubble. But then, Elena saw the Independence begin to rise slowly from the ground. An earsplitting crash reverberated over the tumbling wreckage as a portion of the Ark clipped the bottom of the Independence causing it to spin wildly. Elena watched, horror-struck, as the hovercraft disappeared from sight.

"Austin!" Elena cried in desperation. "Do you think..." But she couldn't even finish speaking. She didn't want to know if he thought they'd been crushed to death.

After what seemed an eternity to Elena, the avalanche came to rest. She and her friends climbed down their ropes onto a pile of rubble.

"We need to try to get back to the Independence," Austin said.

Elena looked wildly over the damage spread out before them and blurted, "But, we don't even know where it is!"

"We have to let Declan rest," Abria said, her words laced with desperation.

Austin looked at Declan as if he'd forgotten about the injuries he'd suffered during the fall. His face relaxed into concern.

"How are you feeling?"

"I'm fine," Declan said, though there was a heavy strain in his voice. "Let's get going."

"How can we even be certain that the Independence is still out there?" Fergie asked in a tone of practicality.

"It doesn't matter if it's there or not," Austin said. "All our supplies were swept away and we'll freeze to death out here. Looking for it now is our best chance of survival."

Elena and her friends started down the mountain but going was slow as they picked over boulders and pieces of shattered wood. It wasn't long before Declan began to let out horrible groans as they took turns supporting his weight down the mountain. Soon, Elena felt tired and hungry. Her hands were sore and bruised and her feet began to hurt with cold.

They started over the next rise when Elena saw a light coming from the other side of the hill.

"Hey!" Elena said loudly. "There's a light! A light!"

Elena and her friends began to shout desperately, hoping against all hope that Kidd and Pigg were miraculously alive.

Then, two Speedsters appeared with Kidd on one and Pigg on the other.

"How did you find us?" Abria asked, sounding relieved, but Elena could see the Optivision screen from Pigg's Touchdot hovering in the air beside him.

"Let's just say it's a good thing that Fergie had us scan our Trademarks into these things," Pigg replied holding up his wrist with the Broadcaster strapped to it.

"Wheeler, help me with Bowen," Austin ordered.

Kidd moved off his Speedster and an exhausted Declan practically fell against him.

"Austin," Elena said confidently. "You go back to the ship with Wheeler, Bowen, and Pigg. Bowen needs your help right away. Abria, Fergie, and I will wait here for Wheeler and Pigg to get back."

Austin took a moment to squeeze Elena's hand and then she watched as the Speedsters turned around and sailed out of sight.

Once the Speedsters were gone, Elena wrapped her arms around Abria and Fergie and sighed. They slid to the ground, holding one another.

"The guys are safe," Elena said, as relief washed over her. "They're all safe and everything's going to be okay now."

But, as it turned out, everything was not okay. When they got back to the Independence, Elena and Abria sprinted to Declan's cabin, removing their heavy coats and gloves in the process.

Austin looked up as they entered. "He busted his ribs and has a small concussion. I gave him something to reverse the effects of the adrenaline, so he's pretty groggy right now."

"I was just telling Haddock that it was very un-dude-like to send you into the ark to be my hero," Declan said to Elena, slurring his words a bit. "Because that made me the damsel in distress."

"Well, you're such a handsome damsel that I wouldn't worry about it," Elena said, smiling.

Declan smiled, too, right before he closed his eyes in sleep.

"We should go see if Wheeler has a report about the crash," Austin said.

"You go," Abria said, looking teary-eyed. "I'm going to sit with him a while."

"Is he going to be okay?" Elena asked Austin as they left the room together and walked toward the command bridge.

"He'll heal fine, but he'll be sore for a while," Austin said.

Before they even got to the bridge, Elena could hear Kidd's voice raised in anger. When they arrived, she saw Fergie at the control panel with dozens of Optivisions open.

"Oh, goodie, you're here," Kidd said sourly. "I was explaining to Foreman and Pigg that I don't know if I can get the Independence in the air again, but Pigg has so many questions that I want to ring his neck."

"Why?" asked Austin. "What happened to it?"

"I'm not sure yet," said Kidd. "I haven't had time to look at the ship, but the control panel has alerted to the fact that the Independence is damaged."

Elena sighed heavily and dropped into one of the chairs. "I think that's because the ship clipped the bottom of the Independence during the avalanche. It got one of the engines."

Kidd's mouth fell open in disbelief.

After a minute of sitting in silence, she asked Fergie, "What about the Kairos? Did it show you if there was an artifact on the ship?"

Fergie shook her head, looking sad.

"We destroyed the entire Ark and didn't find an artifact or the next clue," Elena said slowly. "We have nothing?"

Fergie hurried to the control console and accessed several schematics of the mountain on the screens.

"It seems to me that we have a couple options before us. We can go out on foot to search the area using a program on our Touchdots that was designed for detecting objects. Or we can fly over the crash site and use the onboard scanners to survey the area."

"Again, the ship is *damaged*," Kidd said, sounding impatient. "We can't just go flying around until I have a chance to look it over."

"Whatever you do, we have to fly over the mountain one more time before we leave here. We're looking for something important."

Kidd sighed loudly and sat heavily in one of the captain's chairs. "What are you looking for?"

"You don't know?" Elena asked incredulously.

"I wasn't part of the debrief, Freckles," Kidd said. "Haddock promised the free aero-upgrade in exchange for bringing you here. I do what I'm told and then get paid."

"We were attempting to locate an artifact called the *Tablets of Destiny*," Austin said as Fergie accessed the file and an image of the tablets appeared. "Though we don't have an image of what it looks like."

Kidd stood up quickly, staring at the screen in a wildly, perplexed manner. "Are you sure this is what you're looking for?"

"Yes, why?" asked Austin.

Kidd paced the floor. "You won't find it here."

"How do you know that?" Austin asked.

"Because I know where the Tablets of Destiny are," Kidd said with a look of bitterness on his face that Elena hadn't seen before.

Disbelief registered on her face. "Where are they?"

"At my home, on the farm in Atlanson," Kidd started. "But we won't be able to get them."

"*You* live on that farm outside the city?" Elena questioned. "With that creepy, old guy?"

Kidd nodded.

"I've been there before. My dad took me when I was a little girl. Is that guy your dad?"

Kidd shook his head, a grim frown set on his face. "He's my Guardian. And he's also a vicious tomb raider."

"What's a tomb raider?" Austin asked.

"A person who steals artifacts, treasure, and historical relics and hoards them. Tavington will never give up the Tablets. Never."

Elena felt despair consume her. They'd come so far, risked their lives, and possibly ruined their chances for getting home and the artifact wasn't even there to begin with.

Perhaps able to feel Elena's desperation, Fergie said, "We have inherited a tremendous task from our parents. At this point, it does not seem that the pieces are falling into place, certainly not in the way we would prefer, but our destiny has not been fulfilled yet, which means that we still have time to recover everything that has been stolen and everything that we still need to find."

Elena considered the concept of destiny again. She hadn't thought about it much since returning from the Galilee Province. Fergie's mom had been extremely confident when talking about how Elena's Kairos was a symbol of a *supreme moment in time*. Was it really their destiny to continue this quest now that it seemed that everything was working against them? Or was the concept of destiny a fantasy that was invented to help people have hope when they were feeling discouraged?

Austin rubbed his thumb through the scar on his chin and sighed. "Listen, we can't do anything about this now. We need to fix the Independence so we can get home. We'll worry about the Tablets later. We should get cleaned up and get some rest."

"Rest! We can't rest," Elena blurted. "We've got to assess the damage to the hovercraft so we can get out of here."

"Lena, we need to sleep," Austin said practically. "Our problems will still be here in six hours."

Elena felt her blood boil. She didn't want to rest. She wanted to fix things. But she also knew that she needed to agree with Austin in front of the others, even if she decided to do something different later.

Elena said, "Of course, you're right. We do need to rest. Plus, I'm freezing. I'm going to take a warm shower and find some heavy blankets."

Elena walked slowly from the room. But after she entered the hall, she hurried quietly to the engine room. Once inside, she closed the door and began fumbling around, opening different Optivision screens and trying to make sense of the schematics of the Independence. Unfortunately, it was a labyrinth of information that she couldn't hope to understand. Elena secretly began to hope that Kidd would find her so that he could explain what they needed to do to fix the hovercraft.

"Lena, what are you doing in here?"

Elena's breath caught in her chest. She shut her eyes and sighed. Then, she stood up from behind one of the control boards she'd been searching. She looked into Austin's face feeling a mixture of anger and guilt.

"I thought you said you were going to rest," Austin said.

"Changed my mind," Elena said, trying to sound standoffish.

"You mean, you lied to me," Austin replied.

"You tied me up and left me!" Elena shouted. "Do you have any idea how humiliating that was?"

She watched Austin's eyes to see if he would have a reaction, but she couldn't tell what he was thinking.

"Why did you hold me back? We always do everything together."

"Lena," Austin said, quite seriously. "During our exam, when we were out in the snow, I was scared while you were alone in the wilderness. I knew how cold it was getting at night and that you and Pigg were injured. You've done enough hard work this year to last a lifetime and all while still grieving for your parents. I wanted you to be safe."

"Austin, this thing we're doing where we try to solve riddles in the dossiers and go looking for artifacts...well...it's not safe!" Elena said forcefully. "We've already talked about this. We're going to make mistakes, fight, feel desperate, and get hurt. But we're doing this for our parents. We're doing this for the people who Imperator has imprisoned."

Her eyes burned with angry tears.

"Don't you know that we're better together? That we need each other to get through this? I shouldn't even have to say that to you."

Elena felt suddenly exhausted. She pushed her back up against the wall and slid to the floor. Austin walked toward her slowly and sat next to her, running a thumb through his scar again.

"You're right! Of course, you're right. I guess I let Grandpa Haddock's lecture after we got back from New York get to me a little. I want to keep you safe," Austin sighed. "But you're right, we make decisions together. We work together on everything. It's what we do."

Elena smiled slightly and punched him in the shoulder. Then, she closed her eyes and let out an expressive sigh, dreaming of the day that they would all be free.

THE ADVENTURE HAS JUST BEGUN

What will happen next to Elena, Austin, and their friends?

Follow Elena's story at

www.elenaransom.com

www.ingramcontent.com/pod-product-compliance
Lightning Source LLC
Chambersburg PA
CBHW030028180626
46810CB00001B/261